D0265725

Daemons Are Forever

Also by Simon Green from Gollancz:

The Man with the Golden Torc

Daemons Are Forever

THE SECRET HISTORIES: BOOK 2

Simon Green

Copyright © Simon Green 2008
All rights reserved

The right of Simon Green to be identified as the author of this work has been asserted by him in accordance with the Copyright, Designs and Patents Act 1988.

First published in Great Britain in 2008 by Gollancz
An imprint of the Orion Publishing Group
Orion House, 5 Upper St Martin's Lane, London WC2H 9EA
An Hachette UK Company

This edition published in Great Britian in 2009 by Gollancz

A CIP catalogue record for this book
is available from the British Library

ISBN 978 0 575 08483 4

10 9 8 7 6 5 4 3 2

Printed in Great Britain by CPI Mackays, Chatham ME5 8TD

www.orionbooks.co.uk

The Orion Publishing Group's policy is to use papers that are natural, renewable and recyclable products and made from wood grown in sustainable forests. The logging and manufacturing processes are expected to conform to the environmental regulations of the country of origin.

Men are mortal; but demons are forever

The name's Bond. Shaman Bond. The very secret agent.

Once upon a time, all that stood between the world you know and the forces of darkness was my family. Made strong and powerful by our golden armour, we fought the monsters on your behalf, keeping you safe. Every member of my family was raised from childhood to fight the good fight, in strictest secrecy. So you would never have to know just how dangerous a world you really lived in.

I was a field agent, licensed to kick supernatural arse. Your knight in shining armour, keeping the wolves from your door.

And then I found out it was all a lie. My family didn't protect the world; we ruled it, from the shadows. And the marvellous golden armour, that made us so much more than human . . . came at a hidden price too terrible to bear. So I brought my family down. And for my sins, they put me in charge. To run the family, and redeem it.

My real name is Eddie Drood. I am the world's last hope.

The world . . . is in a lot of trouble.

CHAPTER ONE
A day in the life

The world isn't what you think it is. Hell; even London isn't what you think it is. There are monsters round every corner, creatures in every shadow, and more dark conspiracies and secret wars going on than you can shake a really big stick at. You never get to know about this because the Drood family has field agents everywhere, to keep the lid on things and make sure everyone plays nice. When they don't, we kill them. We don't believe in second chances; we believe in stamping out fires before they can spread.

My family has been keeping the world safe for almost two thousand years. We're very good at it.

And then I found out the truth behind the lies, and nothing made sense any more. The last time I visited my nice little flat in London, my home away from home, my life seemed to make some kind of sense. I was an experienced field agent, complete with use name and cover identity, and the marvellous golden armour that made me so much more than human. I went where the family told me to go, and did what I was told, and it never occurred to me to ask any questions. It was my job to protect the world from whatever dark and nasty forces needed slapping down that week, and I had a good reputation for getting the job done, whatever the complications. I knew who were the good guys, and who were the bad.

I knew nothing.

My flat was in Knightsbridge, a comfortable first-floor apartment in a really nice area where no one knew who I really was. I made enough money to live in style as well as comfort, and no one ever bothered me. That was my life, just a few months ago. Until one day, with no warning, my family declared me rogue for no reason, and I had to go on the run to save my life. Searching for answers, I discovered the terrible truth about my family and the world, and nothing has been the same since.

Now here I was back in London again, with the wild witch of the woods Molly Metcalf sitting at my side as I drove my new car through the mostly empty streets. It was the early hours of the morning, the sun only just up, the birds were singing their little hearts out, and the air had that expectant, anything-can-happen feel that all big cities have at the beginning of the day. Molly Metcalf, anarchist and terrorist and a whole bunch of other ists that involved making trouble for the powers that be, stretched happily and beat out a rhythm on the dashboard with both hands to accompany the Breed 77 album playing on the car's sound system. A short and delicate china doll of a woman, with bobbed black hair, huge dark eyes and big bosoms, she was wearing a black leather catsuit, with a witch knife hanging round her neck on a long silver chain. Molly used to be one of the bad guys; probably still was, depending on how you looked at it. We had a lot of history between us, even tried to kill each other several times when we ended up on opposite sides of a mission. Now we were an item; and I'd be hard pressed to tell which of us was more surprised.

Me: I'm just another face in the crowd, trained to blend in without being noticed. And I've never ordered a vodka martini shaken not stirred in my life.

I sent my new car roaring through the streets with a complete disregard for traffic lights, traffic laws, and any and all forms of road etiquette. Though strictly speaking, it wasn't a new car. I'd had to abandon and destroy my beloved Hirondel during my time on the run, so I prevailed on the family Armourer to provide me with a new set of wheels. I was now driving a lovingly restored 1930 open-topped four-and-a-half-litre Bentley, in racing green with red leather interiors and an Amherst Villiers supercharger under the long gleaming bonnet. The wind slapped at my hair as we roared along, and I changed gears more than was strictly necessary, just to show off. It was a great beast of a car, stylish as all hell, and calmly glamorous in that way that modern cars don't even aspire to any more. I slammed her into top gear and put my foot down, and the Bentley surged forward like a hunting dog let off the leash. Molly whooped with joy, exhilarating in the speed and acceleration.

'This is one hell of a car, Eddie! Where did you steal it?'

'It used to belong to my Uncle Jack,' I yelled back, over the roar of the engine. 'Back when he was charging around Eastern Europe in the fifties, at the height of the Cold War, stamping out bush fires with extreme prejudice. They say he personally prevented three world wars, and very nearly started one when he was caught in bed with a politician's wife. And his mistress. Uncle Jack moved on to faster and flashier cars, but he always had a fondness for this one, and kept it going for years. He customised the hell out of it, of course. As family Armourer, he always had to have the best toys.'

'Such as?'

I grinned. I couldn't help myself. 'Bullet-proof chassis and windows, silicon gel-filled tyres so they'll never go flat, machine guns fore and aft firing explosive fléchettes at two thousand rounds a minute . . . EMP proof, spell proof, curse proof, plus all the usual hidden extras. The operating manual is the size of a phonebook. All of us kids used to pore over it in the Library, dreaming of the day when we'd be field agents and drive cars like it. And by the way: don't try and use the cigarette lighter. Flame-throwers.'

'Groovy! Let's try them!'

'Let's not. We aren't supposed to draw attention to ourselves, remember? Wait till we see a traffic warden. Or a street mime.'

It felt strange to be back in London, driving down familiar streets, after so much had happened. The streets looked the same, and no doubt the people went about their everyday lives as though nothing had changed; but everything had. The whole world was up for grabs with the family out of the picture, even if no one knew it yet. My family didn't rule any more, and the only reason the world wasn't tearing itself apart trying to fill the new power vacuum was that the other powers that be were waiting for the shoe to drop.

'Why are we going to your old flat?' said Molly.

'I already told you. And if you ask "Are we there yet?" one more time, I'll hit the ejector button.'

'This car doesn't have an ejector seat.'

'It might have. You don't know.'

'Talk to me, Eddie. You never tell me what you're thinking.'

'Hey, I'm not used to this whole being in a relationship bit, okay?

When you work as a field agent, you learn pretty fast you can't trust anyone.'

Not even those close to you?' said Molly, studying me solemnly with her huge dark eyes.

'Especially those. You always know where you are with an enemy; it's only friends and loved ones who can betray you.' I took a deep breath, and stared out through the windscreen. 'If I'm going to lead the family, and it looks like I'm going to have to because no one else is up to the job, I have to live at The Hall. If only because there are still far too many members of the family I can't turn my back on safely. The truth might set you free, but there's nothing that says you have to be grateful . . . But if I do have to live in that draughty old pile again, I want some of my favourite things with me. Just a few that matter, to make the place at least feel like home.'

'Never get attached to possessions,' Molly said briskly. 'They're just things; and you can always get more things.'

'You don't have a sentimental bone in your body, do you?'

'If I did, I'd have it surgically removed. I'm always moving on, and I never look back.'

'Well, yes,' I said. 'But you live in a forest. What would you take back to The Hall? Your favourite tree?'

'You forget, Eddie, I'm a witch. I might decide to bring the whole forest with me.'

I decided to change the subject before she set her heart on the idea. You never can tell with witches.

'So,' I said, as casually as I could manage, 'how are you getting on with the family? Everyone treating you all right? What do you think of the mighty and mystical Droods, now that you've had a chance to see us up close and personal?'

'Hard to tell,' said Molly. The music had stopped, I'd slowed the car, and it suddenly seemed very quiet in the Bentley. Molly produced a small silver snuff box out of mid air, snorted a pinch of something green and glowing, sneezed messily, and made the box disappear again. 'Most of your family aren't talking to me. Either because they think I led you astray, or because I've thwarted so many of their plans in the past . . . It's not like I killed that many of your people . . . They need to get over it, and move on. That was then, this is now. All right, so I used to practise the black arts, spread insurrection, mutilate aliens and abduct cattle; I was young! I needed to get things out of my system! That's no reason to run screaming when I try to talk to people.'

'They don't know you like I do,' I said reassuringly. 'Haven't you made any friends?'

'Your Uncle Jack's okay,' Molly said reluctantly. 'But he's always busy in the Armoury. And Jacob's good company. For a ghost. And a dirty old man. But apart from them, it's all been cold shoulders and nasty pointed comments just in range of my hearing. A few were quite unpleasant.'

I took my eyes off the road long enough to give her a really serious stare. 'Please tell me you didn't kill them.'

'Of course not! I turned them into things.'

'What sort of things?'

Molly smiled sweetly. 'Remember those pheasants we had last week, that you noted were out of season?'

I gripped the steering wheel so hard my knuckles went white. 'Oh, my God. You didn't—'

'Of course I didn't! Lighten up, Eddie! You can be so gullible sometimes. I turned them into toads and dumped them in the rock gardens for a while, to let them think things over. They're fine now. Except for a slight tendency to snap at passing flies.'

I sighed heavily. It seemed to me that I'd been doing that a lot more since Molly came into my life.

'If it helps, most of the family haven't exactly warmed to me, either,' I admitted.

'They respect you,' said Molly.

'Only because they're afraid of me. I destroyed their precious Heart, source of their wonderful golden armour. The one thing that made them better than everyone else. I proved the Heart was evil and the armour was an abomination, but they hate me even more for making them face the truth: that we're not the good guys, and haven't been for centuries. On top of which, they're all feeling helpless and vulnerable without their armour, defenceless in the face of the family's many enemies.'

'You promised them new silver torcs, new armour. Everyone applauded and cheered you! They did. I was there.'

'The enthusiasm of the moment . . . No, if I'm going to lead the family, I have to do it from the front. I have to inspire them to be great again. Have to prove myself with action, not just words and good intentions. Prove myself worthy to lead the family.'

'Prove it to your family?' said Molly. 'Or to yourself?'

My nice little flat was located in a very calm and quiet and civilised area, where no one knew who I was or what I did. They only knew me as Shaman Bond, a man of independent means who kept himself to himself, was never any trouble, and always remembered to put his garbage out on the proper day. So as I drew nearer to my quiet and secluded residential area, it came as something of a surprise to me to see so many people out and about in the streets who didn't belong there. I spotted spies and agents from a dozen different countries and organisations, all busily pretending to be perfectly ordinary people going about their perfectly ordinary business. But you can't fool a Drood.

I slowed the car and took a closer look. The signs were not good. Every approach to my flat had been covered by people who shouldn't even have known where it was. Word does get around fast, in the intelligence community. So I couldn't just drive up to my flat and park. All kinds of unpleasantness might ensue. I needed to be able to slip into my old place, gather up a few belongings and get the hell out again without anyone knowing I'd ever been there.

I pulled the car into the side of the road, some distance short of my flat, and stopped. Molly looked at me inquiringly. I quietly pointed out several of the enemy, prevented her from launching an immediate pre-emptive strike, and persuaded her to sit quietly while I examined the scene more fully, using the Sight. Like my old collar, my new silver torc allowed me to See much more of the world as it really was, rather than through humanity's limited senses. The world is a much bigger place than most people realise, full of the strange and the terrible, walking unseen and unsuspected alongside us.

There were a couple of elves, tall and proud and haughty. They live somewhere else now, and only turn up in our world when there's a good chance to screw us over or kick us when we're down. It's all they've got left these days. There were aliens: greys and lizardoids and a few things whose shapes made no sense at all. They really do walk among us. Tourists, mostly. If they look like getting out of hand, the family usually just spanks them and sends them home. Ghosts drifted here and there, trapped in repeating loops of Time. And there were things walking through walls, or scrambling up them, or hovering in the skies overhead. Far too many of them for it all to be a coincidence.

I shut down my Sight. You can't See the world as it really is for too long; the human mind isn't equipped to cope. Luckily, none of them could See me, as long as I wore the torc. They had to wait for me to reveal myself . . . I grinned. It was time to use one of the Bentley's really special features.

'Eddie, what are you planning?' said Molly.

I smiled at her beatifically. 'Brace yourself, sweetie. I'm taking this car up to eleven!'

I pushed the pedal to the floor, let go the clutch, and the Bentley surged forward, its engine howling like a wolf on the hunt. We shot past the hundred mark in a few seconds as I slammed through the gears, and then I hit the hidden switch and threw her into overdrive. Molly and I were forced back into our seats by the terrible acceleration, and the world blurred around us as we left it behind. The Bentley punched through its walls, and just like that we were somewhere else.

Freed from the everyday restrictions of Time and Space, the Bentley tore through the dimensions, day and night flickering on and off like a stroboscope. Stars blazed in somewhere else's night skies, in constellations never seen from Earth. There were strange sounds and a city singing in a million inhuman voices. Visions and vistas flickered on and off as we shot through them like a bullet, intangible and insubstantial, though whether they were the ghosts or we were is probably only a matter of opinion. Molly shrieked and howled with delight, and only the need to concentrate on the steering kept me from joining in. Drunk on speed, crazed on velocity, we hammered through the dimensions until I saw the sign I was looking for and took a sharp right turn back into our reality.

Different worlds dopplered past us as I slammed on the brakes, and when the Bentley finally shuddered to a halt we were sitting inside the garage underneath my flat. I quickly shut down the engine, and took my hands off the steering wheel. They were shaking, and not only from the exhilaration. Taking sideways journeys through adjoining dimensions is always dangerous. You can never tell what might notice you and decide to follow you home. I got out of the car on only slightly unsteady legs, and checked the car over carefully, to make sure we hadn't picked up any unwanted hitch-hikers. Paying special attention to the undercarriage.

Molly was already out of the car and dancing around it, punching the air with her fist. 'That was fantastic! Let's do it again! What *was* that?'

'A short cut,' I said, peering suspiciously under a front bumper.

'You take me on the best rides, Eddie!'

I straightened up, and she threw her arms around me and hugged me. I let her.

'Welcome to my garage,' I said. 'It's small, but poky. Now come on up and see my flat. Try not to be too underwhelmed. We can't all live in a forest.'

I studied the door to my flat carefully. Everything seemed normal, nothing out of place, but the door wasn't locked. I could tell. And I always lock it behind me when I leave. Secret agents can't afford to forget things like that. So I stood a safe distance away from my door and gazed at it thoughtfully, while Molly gazed at me.

'What's wrong?'

'Someone's been here.'

'Your enemies?'

'More likely my family. As soon as I was declared rogue, the Matriarch would have sent a team here to turn my flat over, looking for evidence she could use against me. And my family are never subtle about such things.'

'You think they left a booby trap behind?'

'No. I'd See a trap. More likely they just wrecked the place to leave a message. It's what I would have done, when I was a field agent.'

I took a deep breath, pushed the door open and went in. They'd trashed my home, and been very thorough about it. The furniture had been overturned, where it hadn't been smashed. They'd torn up the carpeting to lever up the floorboards. My possessions had been tossed all over the place, the drawers pulled out and emptied, their contents scattered everywhere. My computer had been torn apart to get at the hard drive, and the monitor had been smashed.

They'd even ripped the posters off the wall and torn them up.

Every room was the same. Nothing had been spared. They'd dragged the covers off my bed and cut open the mattress to search inside it. And on the bedroom wall, above the headboard, someone had spray-painted the word TRAITOR. The word hit me like a punch in the gut. A cold fist closed around my heart, and it was all I could do to get my breath. Molly came in beside me and saw the word on the wall. She slipped an arm through mine and hugged it to her side.

'Oh, Eddie, I'm so sorry. I'm sure this was a lovely place before—'

'I was never a traitor,' I said. I didn't recognise my own voice. 'I was the only one who stayed true to what the family was supposed to be.'

'I know, Eddie. Come away.'

'It's all right,' I said. 'It's all right.'

It wasn't, but I let her lead me away.

Back in the living room, I looked around me, trying to make some sense of the mess. They hadn't actually broken much. Probably didn't have the time.

'They did a job on you,' said Molly. She was trying hard not to step on things, but it was impossible. I loved her for making the effort, though.

'It's what I expected,' I said. 'I did worse, in my time, when I was a field agent. Turning over some villain's lair in the search for clues, or evidence. Or just because I could. It was part of the game, then. But . . . cosmic payback's a bitch. Do you believe in karma, Molly?'

'My karma ran over my dogma,' Molly said briskly. 'Didn't you think to put any protections around your home?'

I snorted. 'Tons of the bloody things. You'd have a better chance of breaking into Bill Gates's private porn stash. But nothing my family couldn't get through. I never thought I'd need to protect myself against my own family.'

Molly frowned. 'Wouldn't the neighbours have heard something and called the police?'

'No one ever hears a Drood at work,' I said. 'Or if they do, we make them forget it.'

'For their own good, of course.'

'Mostly, yes. Oh I see; you were being ironic. Sorry. I'm not always very good at picking up on that.'

'You and your whole family,' muttered Molly.

'What?'

'Nothing . . . What do you suppose they were looking for here?'

'The usual,' I said. 'Objects of Power, unauthorised grimoires and forbidden texts, information I shouldn't have had access to. Maybe even records of payments from outside the family. Anything they could use to condemn, pressure or blackmail me. My family has always preferred to negotiate from a position of strength. Fools! As though I'd leave anything that important lying around here, for anyone to find . . .'

'Right,' said Molly, smiling mischievously. 'Where do you keep your really secret stuff, Eddie? Your embarrassing photos of yourself as a kid, your teenage crush love letters and your personal naughty films? Any particular favourites you might want to bring along with you? I can be very broad-minded.'

'I don't have any of those things,' I said, with some dignity.

Molly sighed, and shook her head. 'For a secret agent, you've led a very sheltered life. Not to worry, Eddie. I'll be your porn.'

I smiled. 'And they say romantic banter is dead.'

It didn't take me long to gather up the few things I wanted to take with me. Some battered old Bruin Bear and the Sea Goat books that were my favourites when I was a kid. A framed photo of my parents, taken just before they went off to die on one last mission for the family. Molly studied the photo curiously.

'They look so young,' she said finally. 'Not even as old as we are now. Much the same age as my parents, when they were murdered by the Droods.'

'We have so much in common,' I said, dropping the photo into a carrier bag along with the books. 'I promise you; I will find out the truth about what really happened to your parents, and mine.'

'If you like,' said Molly. 'I told you; I don't believe in looking back.'

I rescued a dozen or so of my favourite CDs from the mess on the floor. (Molly drew the line at any of my Enya albums, which I thought was a bit mean. I don't object to her playing her Iron Maiden in the car.) And that . . . was that. I looked around, but there wasn't anything else I wanted to take with me. I looked down at the carrier bag. Not much to show for ten years in one place. Not much to show for a life.

'I did have some good times here,' I said.

'Yeah, right,' said Molly. 'I'll bet you were a real party animal at weekends.'

'No,' I said. 'I hardly ever brought people back here. Because people only knew me as Shaman Bond, and this was the only place I could be Eddie Drood. The family discourages field agents from having close friends, or anything else. Close associations might distil our loyalty to the family. And you can't ever be really close to anyone, when the life you share is a lie. Agents in the field live solitary lives, because we have to. Because when you care for someone, you don't want to endanger them.'

'And your family encouraged this?' said Molly.

'Of course. They wanted the family to be the most important thing in our lives; so we might never be tempted to turn away from them. I had more freedom than most and I still toed the family line, right up to the point where they turned on me. I had friends but I could never tell them anything that mattered. I had lovers, but never loves. It wasn't allowed. All I had . . . was the work.'

'If you start getting maudlin on me,' Molly said firmly, 'I will slap you, and it will hurt. I told you: never look back. All you ever see are mistakes, failures and missed opportunities. Concentrate on the here and now! You're running your family, you have the best toys to play with; and you have me! What more could mortal man desire?'

'My Enya CDs.'

'One slap, on its way.'

We both laughed. I took her in my arms and held her close. She nuzzled her face into my shoulder, and rubbed my back with her hands. I bent my head over hers, and breathed deeply the perfume from her hair. I felt . . . I could have stayed there for ever. But I had things to do.

'My world used to be so simple,' I said. 'I knew who I was, and what I was, and what I was supposed to do with my life.'

'No,' said Molly, not raising her head from my shoulder. 'You only thought you did. Welcome to the real world, Eddie. Hateful place, isn't it?'

'No,' I said. 'It has you in it.'

We left the flat and made our way down into the enclosed courtyard below, and then stopped as we realised the wrought-iron gates were standing wide open. I looked out into the street, and a whole army of heavily armed and armoured men looked right back at me. Molly moved in close beside me. Two black attack helicopters filled the early morning with their clamour as they manoeuvred into position above. I lifted my head and squared my shoulders. First rule of a field agent: never show fear. I sauntered over to the open gates for a better look.

There had to be at least fifty armed men, anonymous in body armour and dark-visored helmets, every one of them pointing their oversized guns at me. Automatic weapons, too; top of the line. They weren't taking any chances. I looked up and down the street. They'd blocked off both ends with armoured vehicles. Frightened faces peered out from the closed windows of neighbouring house. You didn't expect scenes like this in civilised Knightsbridge.

One armoured figure moved forward to face me, still careful to maintain a safe distance. He pushed his visor up enough to get an electric bullhorn under it.

'Edwin Drood, Molly Metcalf: you are ordered to surrender yourselves. Failure to do so will be met with all necessary force.'

I looked at Molly. 'So; how do you want to play this?'

She smiled sweetly. 'Oh, the usual, I think. Extreme violence and unpleasantness visited upon one and all, suddenly and horribly and all over the place.'

'My kind of woman,' I said.

'*Surrender or die!*' said the spokesman through his bullhorn.

'Do you mind?' I said witheringly. 'We're talking. We'll get to you in a moment.' I turned back to Molly. 'I'm a bit reluctant to go head to head with them here. Right out in the open, surrounded by innocent bystanders.'

Molly shrugged. 'They chose the setting. We could make a run for the Bentley, I suppose, and short cut our way out of this . . . but I don't do the running thing.'

'Same here,' I said. 'It does so tend to give the wrong impression. These scumbags need to be reminded of what it means to challenge a Drood.'

'And the wild witch of the woods, darling.'

'Of course, my dear.'

'*If you don't surrender right this minute . . .*'

I had to laugh. 'He doesn't know us very well, does he? Who do you think they are?'

'Big display of force, even bigger guns and not a grain of common sense among the lot of them. Got to be Manifest Destiny. The I-Can't-Believe-They're-Not-Fascists brigade. Truman must have got his act back together again. Who knew he'd still be mad at us, just because we destroyed his underground base and scattered his whole repellent organisation to the winds?'

'All-powerful cult leaders with delusions of godhood are often funny that way,' I agreed.

The spokesmen threw his bullhorn on to the ground and stalked forward to confront us. Molly and I turned round and fixed him with a thoughtful gaze, and he slammed to a halt. He was carefully not pointing his automatic weapon at us, just yet.

'Look,' he said, in the strained tones of someone trying to be reasonable under very trying circumstances, 'we both know you don't have your golden armour any more, Eddie. None of the Droods do. If I have to order my men to open fire, you'll end up riddled with so many bullets your family will be able to use your corpse as a colander. You'll have so much lead in you, your coffin will have to be labelled toxic waste, and even your DNA will end up in pieces. So will you please do the sensible thing and surrender, and we can all get out of here!'

'I think you pushed those metaphors a bit too far,' I said.

'Definitely reaching there, at the end,' said Molly.

'Nobody does really good villainous threats any more,' I said. 'In the old days, a real villain could made your blood run cold with just a simile.'

'Hell, I could make someone wet themselves with a baleful glare,' said Molly.

'Sorry,' I said to the spokesman. 'We don't do sensible. Do we, dear?'

'Certainly not,' said Molly. 'Bad for the image. Hey, what do you want to bet I can turn this creep into some kind of dripping snot creature before he can give the order to open fire?'

'You can't take on a whole army!' said the spokesman. His voice was becoming a bit hysterical. 'Extreme measures have been authorised!'

'Well,' I said. 'That's always nice to know. Now we won't have to hold back. I count fifty-seven armed men, Molly.'

'Probably more in hiding, as reinforcements,' said Molly. 'He looks the sneaky type. Nice to know they're taking us seriously, at least.'

'Who are you?' I said bluntly to the spokesman, leaning forward to try and peer through his dark visor. 'Your voice is familiar . . .'

'Codename Alpha!' he snapped, actually shying back a little. 'Are you going to come quietly, or not?'

'Oh, definitely not,' said Molly. 'We have a reputation to live down to.'

I gestured at the two black attack helicopters hovering overhead, stirring our hair with their downdraft. 'I really don't approve of those, Alpha. We're supposed to fight *secret* wars, behind the scenes of the world. The general public is never supposed to know about us and the things we have to do.'

Alpha shrugged. 'It's a new world now. You saw to that. Come on, surrender. This is your last chance.'

I looked at Molly. 'I feel like a little light exercise,' I said. 'How about you?'

'I feel like kicking some heads in and stamping on some throats,' said Molly.

'Never knew a time when you didn't,' I said. 'Let's dance.'

I armoured up, all in a moment. I subvocalised the old activating Words, and the silver strange matter held in the collar round my neck flowed suddenly forth, encasing my whole body from top to toe. Alpha stared blankly for a moment, and then actually screamed before turning and retreating rapidly back to his men. He'd been told I didn't have my armour any more, and he was wrong. I'd upgraded. I knew what I looked like. A gleaming silver statue, the perfect protective armour, seamless without any joints or vulnerable points. Even my face was a featureless silver mask, through which I could see and hear and breathe perfectly naturally.

I flexed my arms, and the silver armour flowed smoothly with me. I felt stronger, faster, sharper, like coming suddenly awake after a long doze. This was the great secret of the Drood family: the marvellous armour that makes us so much more than human, that lets us do our job no matter what the bad guys throw at us. Once it was gold, now it was silver. The details change but the war goes on. I closed my hands into fists, and heavy spikes appeared on the silver knuckles as I concentrated. I was looking forward to seeing what the new armour could do under battle conditions.

Alpha finally screamed an order through his bullhorn, and his men opened fire at once, concentrating their aim on me. I'd already moved to cover Molly, and I stood firm as a storm of bullets slammed into me. Instead of ricocheting harmlessly from my armoured form, as they used to with the golden version, the silver strange matter absorbed both the impact of the bullets and the bullets themselves. Swallowed them right up, as fast as they came. Safer on innocent passers-by, I supposed, but I did wonder whether the armour would have to crap the bullets out again later. I made a mental note not to have Molly standing behind me, after the battle was over.

The soldiers realised their bullets were having no effect and the fusillade died raggedly away. Molly immediately stepped out from behind me, raised her arms in the stance of summoning, and called down the elements.

'Awake, awake, ye northern winds . . .'

A great stormwind came howling down the road. It picked the soldiers up and sent them tumbling head over heels the whole length of the street. Some hid in doorways or behind cars, and concentrated their fire on Molly. The bullets punched through the raging wind, only to turn into rose petals before they got anywhere near her. She was protected by all the magics of the wild wood, and nothing from the material world could touch her. She only let me protect her because she knew it made me feel better. She gestured sharply, and lightning stabbed down from the darkening skies, picking out men in their hiding places and incinerating them.

New men arrived from concealing positions, carrying heavier weapons. They forced their way forward against the howling winds, step by step. Molly stabbed a finger at them, and the street was suddenly full of a dozen or so very confused-looking llamas.

Molly was on a roll.

But that kind of magic took it out of her, so I decided it was time for me to get hands-on. I charged forward into the mass of the remaining soldiers, moving at superhuman speed, driven by the inhuman strength of my armoured legs. I was in and among the men faster than they could react, striking out at them with appalling augmented strength. My spiked silver knuckles stove in reinforced helmets and smashed through Kevlar as though it was paper. Blood flew on the air, and men fell screaming. Still alive. I prefer not to kill if I don't have to. I'm an agent, not an assassin.

They crowded in around me, hoping to overwhelm me and drag me down through sheer force of numbers. They beat at me with gun butts and shot me in the face at point blank range. I picked them up and threw them this way and that, sending them flying the length of the street with my more than human strength. Men crashed into walls that cracked under the impact. More and more armoured men came running to face me, and I had to admire their courage, if nothing else. I went to meet them with a smile on my lips and a song in my heart. The good thing about fighting real scumbags like Manifest Destiny is that you never have to feel bad about the awful things you do to them. And it felt good to have a solid enemy to strike back at; to take out the frustrations of the day on. I waded right into the thick of them, fists flying.

Poor bastards never stood a chance.

Armoured cars came rolling down the street, firing really big guns from embrasures. Molly turned their gunfire into pretty butterflies, and then melted the cars' wheels with a wave of one hand. They ground to a halt, steel rims digging into the road. Molly scowled with concentration, so intent on the mischief she was working she didn't see the man closing in on her. Somehow he'd fought his way forward through the blustering winds and approached her in her blind spot. He raised a gun to shoot her in the head at close range, and she didn't know he was there.

I grabbed the nearest man and threw him at the gunman sneaking up on Molly. The man flew screaming through the air with unnatural speed, driven by the awful strength of my arm. He actually caught fire from the friction of the air, and was a mass of flames when he slammed into the man threatening Molly. The gunman just had time to look round, and then the burning man hit him so hard I heard bones break under the impact. Molly looked at the two bodies lying on the ground some distance behind her, and then at me.

'I knew he was there.'

'Of course you did,' I said. 'Do you think you could lay off the winds a bit? Even I'm having trouble keeping my feet.'

Molly frowned. 'They're not my winds.'

We both looked up. The two black attack helicopters were descending upon us. They came roaring in from both ends of the street at once, raking us with machine-gun fire, explosive fléchettes and long sticks of incendiaries. I stood there and took it, untouched by the bullets or the explosions or flames. The soldiers around me didn't fare as well, and broke away screaming and slapping at their burning armour. Molly turned briefly sideways from the world, and it all went right through her, like a ghost. But while she held herself midway between dimensions like that, she was helpless to fight back. So it was down to me to do something about the helicopters.

Bullets chewed up the street and fires sprang up fiercely on all sides. A thousand rounds a minute slammed into my silver chest and just disappeared. I didn't even rock on my feet. The explosions didn't move me, and the fires couldn't reach me. A Drood in his armour is an unstoppable force, and a terror to his enemies. I grabbed the nearest injured man up off the street, and threw him at the nearest helicopter. He hurtled screaming through the air and slammed into the helicopter's rear rotor. His scream cut off abruptly as blood and offal flew across the sky. The helicopter swung back and forth drunkenly, its rotor smashed, and then it fell to earth like a crippled bird.

The pilot made a last desperate attempt to aim the crashing helicopter at me. I stood my ground, braced for the impact. The helicopter loomed up, trailing smoke and flames. I could see into the cockpit, see the pilots screaming hate and defiance. And then the machine smashed right into me, and exploded. For long moments there was only fire and sound and thick black smoke, but none of it touched me. I stood unscathed in the middle of the inferno, and then strode calmly out of it, kicking bits of wreckage aside.

The other helicopter was coming in for another strafing run.

They were firing wildly now, half out of their minds with shock and desperation. The bullets hit the street and the houses, and even some of their own men. And then the bastards fired a Hellfire missile at me. Right in the middle of civilian territory. I stood my ground, braced for the impact, and caught the missile in my arms. The armour absorbed the blow, and I bent over, hugging the missile to my chest. It exploded, and my armour absorbed most of the energy. A whole lot of windows shattered, but no one was hurt. I glared up at the helicopter. I'd had enough of those idiots. They were losing it, big time. I jumped into the air as the helicopter swept towards me and, driven by the strength in my armoured legs, I soared up and grabbed onto the front of their cockpit. The helicopter swayed and lurched wildly under the extra weight. I drew back a silver fist, and punched through the reinforced cockpit glass.

'*Get out*,' I said coldly to the two pilots.

They pushed open the cockpit doors and bailed out. I didn't blame them. All the training in the world can't prepare you to face a Drood field agent in his armour.

The helicopter slammed down on to the street and skidded along, throwing up sparks and smoke. I rode it the length of the street, waited till it finally screeched to a halt, and then stepped calmly down from the shattered cockpit. Some days, it's good to be an agent. Molly strolled over to join me.

'Show off.'

I looked around the street. Most of the men were down, hurt or terrorised or not moving. The few still on their feet had thrown away their guns and were standing with their hands clasped behind their helmets. I almost had it in me to feel sorry for them. They'd thought they were coming to arrest one unarmed field agent and his girlfriend. Probably thought the size of the operation was typical military overkill. The winds Molly had summoned up were slowly dying away, but still sending furious little gusts this way and that, as though resentful at being disturbed against their will. Fires burned here and there, up and down the street, and thick black smoke curled up from the wreckage of the two helicopters.

Alpha walked slowly forward, gun and bullhorn abandoned. He stopped in front of me, and to his credit he looked defeated, but not beaten. He took off his helmet, and a great many things suddenly became clear as I recognised the middle-aged face. I sent my armour back into my torc, so he could see mine.

'Philip MacAlpine,' I said. 'Thought I recognised the voice. You used to have more sense than to get involved in a clusterfuck like this.'

'You know this creep?' said Molly.

'He's with MI5,' I said. 'Or at least, he used to be. Worked with Uncle James on a lot of cases, back in the day. I saw him around The Hall a lot, when I was a kid.'

'Please,' said MacAlpine. 'You're making me feel old.'

'What are you doing out in the field, Phil?' I said. 'And when did you join up with Manifest Destiny?'

MacAlpine shook his head quickly. 'I'm nothing to do with Truman's private army. This is an MI5 operation – though strictly speaking, of course, it isn't, officially. This comes under DDT.'

Molly looked at me. 'Pest control?'

'Department of Dirty Tricks,' I said. 'Departments within departments that don't officially exist for maximum deniability. Who set this up, Phil?'

He smiled briefly, and shrugged. 'You know I can't answer that, Eddie.'

'Molly,' I said calmly, 'you want to turn him into something more cooperative?'

'It was the Prime Minister's idea,' MacAlpine said quickly. 'He wanted us to establish whether the Droods really were as vulnerable as our intelligence suggested. So we could take the advantage while you were still weak.' He looked at the wreckage and bodies around him. 'So many good men, dead and injured. You didn't use to be this vicious, Eddie.'

'I only kill when I have to,' I said. 'You know that.'

MacAlpine looked at me, his face unreadable. 'I don't know anything about you any more, Eddie.'

'The politicians are getting restless,' I said to Molly. 'I suppose something like this was inevitable, once word started to get around. The politicians would love a chance to get their hands on a Drood and sweat some real secrets out of him. We'd better get back to The Hall; see what else is happening.' I turned back to MacAlpine. 'I'm surprised to see you here, Phil. Last I heard, you'd been thrown out of Special Operations for excessive violence.'

'Don't be silly, Eddie,' he said. 'That's how most of us get in. You must know . . . this won't stop here. The Prime Minister's taken too much shit from the Droods down the years not to strike back, now he sees an opportunity. All our agents are being called in for a pre-emptive strike against your family. Even the old bastards like me. All sins forgiven, if not forgotten. And it won't just be us. The whole world will be at your throat from now on.'

I considered him thoughtfully. 'How did you find out that the Droods don't have their golden armour any more?'

'Don't be naïve, Eddie. We have a whole department dedicated to studying every move your family makes. Reports have been coming in from all over the world of Drood field agents suddenly abandoning their posts and running for home by the fastest routes possible. We know something drastic has happened inside the family, Eddie. You can't hope to keep it secret for long. We'll find out.'

'You wouldn't believe me if I told you,' I said.

MacAlpine shrugged, started to turn away, and then looked back. 'Is it true? About James?'

'Yes,' I said. 'He's dead.'

MacAlpine nodded slowly. 'The old Grey Fox is gone. I thought he'd outlive us all. How did it happen?'

'Sorry,' I said. 'Family business. Now tell the Prime Minister to back off. Tell him what happened here. Tell him about the silver armour. And tell him the family isn't weak. Just . . . reorganising.

'No doubt he can expect a call from the Matriarch?' said MacAlpine.

'Eventually,' I said. 'Molly and I are leaving now. You and your people can stay and clean this mess up before you go. We're supposed to fight secret wars, not endanger innocent civilians! What were you thinking of?'

'I told you,' said MacAlpine. 'It's a different world. The old rules have changed. Thanks to you.'

Molly and I headed back to The Hall in the Bentley. Molly sang happily along to her Ramones compilation while I did some thinking. No one in the wrecked street would talk about what they'd seen happen right in front of them. The usual mixture of bribes, threats and the magic words *terrorists* and *national security* would see to that. All camcorders and camera phones would be confiscated, and if anybody did get stubborn and try to talk to the media, the Government would slap on as many D notices as necessary to muzzle them. Any real troublemakers . . . would be *made* to forget. It's a secret war, in an invisible world, and people have to stay ignorant if we're to protect them.

I had a lot of unanswered questions. How had MacAlpine known exactly when to stake out my flat? That much armour and manpower takes a lot of advance organising. Somebody must have talked, and the only people who knew were family. I'd known there were still members of the Zero Tolerance faction who hoped to sabotage and undermine me so they could seize back control of the family . . . but to talk to outsiders? To politicians? That was crossing the line.

Enemies without, enemies within. As if I didn't have enough problems.

CHAPTER TWO

Families; can't live with them, can't take them down to the river and drown them all in sacks.

The Hall has been home to the Drood family for generations. Even though, officially, it doesn't exist. You won't find it on any map, and you can't get to it by any ordinary route. The Hall stands alone, apart from the world; and it likes it that way. Don't come looking for us or something really nasty will happen to you; we're protected by sciences and magic and nightmares worse than both. The family has always taken its privacy and its security very seriously.

Especially after the Chinese tried to nuke us, back in the sixties. Just because we protect the world, it doesn't mean the world is always grateful.

The Hall has raised, nurtured and indoctrinated Droods for centuries. Trained us relentlessly to fight the good fight, and taught us everything we needed to know about the world except how to live in it. Most Droods never leave The Hall all their lives. Only approved field agents get to go out into the world and walk up and down in it, fighting our endless secret invisible wars, and smiting the ungodly till they cry like babies. The Hall is mother and father to us all; The Hall is family. I ran away first chance I got, and never looked back. Now, for my many sins, I was home again. Ostensibly to run the family in its hour of need, and redeem its soul from the evil ways it had fallen into, down the long centuries. When we moved from protecting Humanity to running it.

The Hall stands alone in the middle of its extensive grounds, brooding jealously over its idyllic domain. I drove the Bentley down the long winding gravel path, and machine guns rose silently up out of hidden emplacements on either side of the road and followed us as we passed before sinking grudgingly back down beneath the grass again. Sprinklers spread their gentle haze across the sweeping lawns, and wandering peacocks called out their welcomes and warnings. Gryphons patrolled the grounds, their gaze fixed firmly on the near future, the perfect guardians and watchdogs. When they weren't looking for something really foul and smelly to roll around in. I could sense force shields and magical screens snapping on and off ahead and behind us, as The Hall security systems recognised me and Molly and let us pass. No one gets in uninvited.

I slowed the Bentley down so Molly could enjoy the hedge mazes and the flower gardens, and the swans floating serenely on the lake. I liked showing off my home to her, even though she always went out of her way to seem unimpressed. And, besides, I was in no hurry to get back to The Hall and all the work and responsibilities that awaited me there. Why do you think I ran away in the first place?

The Hall loomed up before us, dominating the horizon, the guardian at the gates of reality. The long-standing abode of the Drood family, and Humanity's last defence against the forces of darkness. It's a miserable old dump, truth be told, draughty as hell and entirely innocent of modern innovations like central heating. I grew up thinking wearing long underwear from September to April was normal. The Hall is a huge sprawling old pile of a Manor House, knocked up in Tudor times and much added to down the centuries. Currently home to some three thousand souls, all of them Droods. You can marry into the family, but not out of it. We're like the Mafia: once in, never out. Unless you want to wake up with a unicorn's head in bed next to you.

I slammed the Bentley to a halt in a spray of flying gravel, and parked outside The Hall's front door – mostly because I knew I wasn't supposed to. Start as you mean to go on, that's what I always say. Molly jumped out over the closed side door while I was still turning off the engine, and I scrambled out after her before she could start any trouble. If anyone was going to start trouble, I wanted it to be me. First impressions are so important. We'd hardly made it through the front door and into the vestibule before a mob of angry family members descended upon us. It appeared they'd been waiting for some time to have a determined word in my ear, and they weren't prepared to take *No, not now* or even *Go to hell* as an answer. They all started shouting questions and demands the moment they clapped eyes on me, constantly raising their voices to be heard, and actually pushing and shoving at each other in their eagerness to get to me first.

Which was almost unheard of, in the disciplined, tightly structured and almost feudal system that our family has followed for centuries. It seemed when I challenged authority and got away with it, I unleashed a floodtide of repressed resentments. The family wanted change, and it wanted it now, but unfortunately it couldn't agree on just what should be changed, and how. Molly and I stood close together with our backs pressed up against the closed front door, as everyone in the crowd did their best to out-shout each other. The din was appalling, and the faces before me were strained and ugly with anger, impatience and determination.

I did my best to concentrate, trying to sort out some of what they were going on about. Some had questions about the new family policy, others wanted to know when they were going to get the new silver torcs, and a lot of them wanted to denounce other people as being against progress, or in favour of the wrong kind of progress, or guilty of the sin of not agreeing with the speaker's ideas. Some of the questions and demands were flat-out impossible, no doubt designed to embarrass me and make me look indecisive in front of the family. Did I mention I have enemies inside the family? Hard-core traditionalists and surviving members of the Zero Tolerance faction, still mad as hell that their little putsch hadn't succeeded and determined to sabotage and undermine me.

Hell hath no fury like a Drood with a grudge.

I did try to be polite and answer the questions of those nearest me, but no one could hear me in the general bedlam of voices. And no one in the crowd was willing to quieten down in favour of someone else. It's times like this I wish my armour was equipped with pepper sprays, or water cannon. In the end I looked at Molly, and she grinned mischievously. She muttered a few Words and made a sharp gesture, and suddenly everyone in the angry mob was entirely naked and wondering where the cold breeze was coming from. The bedlam died quickly away to a shocked silence, followed by a few squeaks and squeals as a hundred or so naked Droods did their best to cover themselves with their hands or hide behind each other. Molly glared about her, her smile entirely unpleasant.

'Right, everyone pay attention and stay quiet, or I'll send you where I sent your clothes. And your clothes aren't coming back. Or, at least, not in any condition where you could hope to wear them again. Ye gods and little fishes, look at the state of you. Living proof that most people look better with their clothes on. Now be good little naked people and run away terribly quickly before I decide to do something really amusing to you. Probably involving Möbius strips and your lower intestines.'

I never saw so many people disappear so quickly, or so many entirely unattractive arses. I looked at Molly, and she smiled sweetly.

'You see, you just have to know how to talk to people.'

'You haven't even heard of diplomacy, have you?'

'No. And aren't you glad?'

'Well, yes.'

And that was when the Sarjeant-At-Arms finally deigned to make an appearance. He was supposed to be guarding the front door: that was his job, to be the first and last face any outsider ever sees if they come through the front door without an invitation. The Sarjeant is in charge of Hall security and family discipline, which means he gets to hit people a lot; and he's never happier than when he's found an excuse to really lay the law down. He made my life hell when I was a child, beating me till the blood flew for the smallest infringement of the rules; and when I finally came back to The Hall to put the family in order, one of the first things I did was to beat the crap out of him. And then he had the nerve to say he only did it to toughen me up and prepare me for the world outside. He actually said he was proud of me, before he lapsed into unconsciousness. I'll never forgive him for that.

The Sarjeant-At-Arms was tall and broad, with muscles in places where you and I don't even have places. And though he affected the stark black and white formal uniform of a Victorian butler, it never fooled anyone for a moment. The man was a thug and a bully and proud of it; and therefore perfectly suited to his job. He had that stiff-backed, steely-eyed military look that promises you blood, sweat and tears in the future, and every bit of it yours. His impassive face always seemed as though it had been carved out of stone, but now it looked like someone had been at it with a chisel. The last time we went head to head, Molly hit him with a plague of rats; and now one side of his face was a mass of scars, and his left ear was missing. I gave him a stern look.

'I thought I told you to get your face fixed. The cosmetic sorcerers could put you right in an afternoon, and you know it.'

'I like the scars,' the Sarjeant said. 'They add character. And they're very good for intimidating people.'

'What about the ear?'

'Pardon?'

I scowled at him. 'Where the hell were you, when we got ambushed by that mob?'

'Right,' said Molly. 'Taking it easy in your cubicle, were you, with the latest issue of *Big and Busty* and the door locked?'

The Sarjeant ignored her, his cold gaze fixed on mine. 'About time you got back, boy. Whole place has been going down the crapper since you left. Family discipline is falling apart without the old certainties to keep them in line. They need you here, setting an example. Not gallivanting about back in the world on personal business.'

'You know, just once it would be nice to hear "Welcome home" when I come through the door,' I said wistfully. 'So stop bugging me, Sarjeant, or I'll have Molly turn you into a small steaming pile of something. You're not telling me that angry mob just happened. They couldn't have got near the front door without your cooperation.'

'Wanted you to see how bad things had got,' the Sarjeant said calmly. 'I'd have stepped in, if things started getting ugly.'

'I only put up with you so you can keep the pests off my back,' I said flatly. 'It's bad enough I got attacked outside my old flat by a whole bunch of MI5 goons, without being ambushed by my own family the moment I walk through the door. You let this happen again, and I will slam you against the nearest wall until your eyes change colour. Do I make myself clear?'

Give the man his due, even though no one had dared to speak to him like that in decades, and even though he knew I meant every word of it, he didn't flinch one bit.

'I needed to see who would act, instead of just talk,' he said. 'Now they've identified themselves as troublemakers, I can go after them and there will be spankings. Don't try to teach me my job, boy. You might run the family now, but I run The Hall. Now what was that about you being attacked by MI5? No one attacks us and gets away with it.'

'Trust me,' I said. 'They didn't. But they knew exactly where and when to find me, which means someone in the family must have ratted me out to the Prime Minister. So make yourself useful and find out who.'

His cold eyes brightened at the thought of authorised violence. 'Any restrictions on my methods?'

'I want answers, not bodies,' I said. 'Otherwise anything goes. Make them cry, make them talk. The family can't afford to be divided right now.'

'Hardcore, Eddie,' said Molly. 'What's next? Loyalty oaths and public executions?'

The Sarjeant-At-Arms inclined his head slightly to me. 'Welcome home, sir. Welcome back to the family.'

'Get my Inner Circle together,' I said. 'And have them wait for me in the Sanctity. We have urgent new business to discuss. I'll be along as soon as I can. I have to talk to the Matriarch first. How is she?'

'Still in mourning,' said the Sarjeant.

'Alistair isn't dead,' I said.

'Might as well be.'

The Sarjeant bowed stiffly to me, ignored Molly, turned on his heel and strode off into the labyrinthine depths of The Hall. He was never going to warm to me, and I wouldn't have known what to do if he had.

'You're really getting into this leadership thing, aren't you?' said Molly. 'Barking orders and handing out beatings. I guess breeding will out. You're every inch a Drood, Eddie.'

I shrugged apologetically. 'I swear I used to be so much calmer and easy-going before I came back to The Hall. There's something about having to deal with my family that makes me want to spit and curse and throw things. Preferably explosives. But I have to be seen to be in charge, Molly; I have to be hard on the family and make them toe the new line, or they'll turn on each other and the family will devour itself. I've taken away everything they depended on; now it's up to me to give them something else to live for. A new cause to follow.' I sighed tiredly. 'I hate all this, Molly. Not least because I have a horrible suspicion I'm not up to the job. But I have to do it . . . because there's no one else.'

Molly put a comforting hand on my shoulder. 'I could always turn more people into things.'

'Could you turn them into reasonable people?'

'Be real, darling. I'm a witch, not a miracle worker.'

We both managed a small smile. 'I don't like what I have to do,' I said. 'I don't like what I'm becoming. But I have to fight for every inch of progress. It's not me; it's them. My family could have Mother Teresa drinking straight from the bottle and calling for the return of hanging in a week. Look, I've got to go and see the Matriarch, and you can't come with me. It's going to be difficult enough for me to get in to see her. So you pop along to the Sanctity and keep the others amused till I can get there.'

'I see,' Molly said sweetly, and very dangerously. 'I'm your court jester now, am I?'

'Sorry,' I said. 'I'm still getting the hang of this being in a relationship thing. I meant, of course, take charge of things till I can get there. We are, after all, equal partners.'

'Well,' said Molly. 'I might settle for that. But only because I'm so fond of you.'

I went striding through the long corridors and hallways, the great circular meeting places and wide airy chambers, heading for the Matriarch's private rooms in the West Wing. People stopped what they were doing to watch me pass, and I smiled at those who smiled at me, and glared at everyone else to make sure they kept their distance. I wasn't in the mood to answer any more questions, particularly since I didn't have a whole lot of answers. Centuries-old wood panelling gleamed on every side with a comfortable patina of age and beeswax, and paintings by famous names hung on every wall. Everywhere I looked there were statues and busts and ornaments of great worth and antiquity: the accumulated tribute of the Droods, presented to us by the governments of the world because they were so grateful to us; and not at all because they were scared of us.

The whole wing had that calm assurance that comes from seeing generation after generation pass through its rooms and corridors. That slightly smug calm that says *I will be here long after you are gone.* From earliest childhood it's drilled into every Drood that we are only here to serve the family in its fight against evil. Soldiers in a war that never ends. Our motto: *Anything, for the family.* And I believed it. We had a holy cause and a holy duty, and our foes were dark and terrible indeed. Even after the lies I uncovered in the dark and secret heart of the family, I still believe. The Droods have to go on, because Humanity couldn't survive without us. I had to get the family back to what it used to be; to what it was originally meant to be.

The shamans of our tribe, standing between the people and the forces that threaten them. Fighting for them, dying for them. The protectors, not rulers, of Humanity.

The Matriarch had the very best quarters in The Hall, of course. A whole suite of rooms just for herself and her husband on the top floor of the West Wing. A whole suite, even though most of us had to make do with one room, and the youngest members lived in communal rooms and dormitories. In a place as crowded and packed to the seams as The Hall, the only real luxury is space. The Hall is big, but the family is even bigger.

As the new leader of the family, I could have thrown the Matriarch out and taken the suite for myself and Molly; but I didn't have the heart. Not after what I'd done to the Matriarch's husband, Alistair.

I could feel my heart beating faster as I approached the Matriarch's door, and my breathing tightened in my chest. I'd only ever been here once before, back when I was only twelve years old. I'd been summoned by the Matriarch herself for a personal interview; an unheard-of thing. The Sarjeant-At-Arms took me there, a large hand ever ready to smack me round the head if I dawdled. I was half out of my mind with worry. What had I done wrong this time? All kinds of things ran round my head, but nothing bad enough to warrant the Matriarch's personal attention. The Sarjeant knocked on her door, opened it, and pushed me in. And there she was, Martha Drood, sitting bolt upright on a chair, fixing me with her unrelenting gaze.

She had my latest school report in her hand, and she was very disappointed in me. Apparently it was full of comments like *Must try harder, Could do better,* and, most damning of all, *Intelligent, but lacks discipline.* Even at twelve, my character was pretty much set. The Matriarch scolded me in her coldest voice, while I stood sulking and stubborn before her. It wasn't my fault if I asked questions the teachers couldn't, or wouldn't, answer. I wouldn't be told, you see. I'd do anything if I was asked, but I wouldn't do a damned thing I was told if I couldn't see a good reason for it. And a family built on duty and responsibility could never accept an attitude like that. They'd tried beating respect into me, and when that didn't work, they sent word to the Matriarch. Who now condemned me as lazy and uncooperative, and told me I'd come to a bad end.

I think she was mostly angry because we were so closely related, and my failures reflected badly on her. More was expected of me, because of that. Even at twelve I was old enough to feel that was distinctly unfair, but I didn't have the capacity to put it into words. So I just stood sullenly before her, and said nothing.

Even when she tried to question me. In the end she threw me out, back to the tender mercies of the teachers and the Sarjeant-At-Arms. I think she was resentful at having to take time away from more important business to deal with me. I never felt I was important to her; and then she wondered why she was never important to me.

I stopped before the suite's door, took a deep breath, pushed it open and walked in without knocking. Start as you mean to go on, or they'll walk all over you. The luxuriously furnished antechamber was full of people, all of them suddenly silent and staring at me with cold and unfriendly faces. It seemed I wasn't the only one who wanted to see the Matriarch, now that she'd retreated into seclusion to nurse her injured Alistair. No one in the antechamber looked pleased to see me, but I was getting used to that. I scowled back at them and strode forward like I intended to trample underfoot anyone who didn't get out of the way fast enough. Usually that works; but this time no-one budged an inch. They stood their ground, blocking the way between me and the door to the Matriarch's bedroom on the other side of the antechamber. Openly defying me to get past them. Some were her friends, some were her allies; most were simply determined to deny me anything they could. They'd been people of power and position before I overturned the applecart. I stopped. It was either that or resort to throwing punches and head-butting; and I wasn't quite ready to do that yet. Not yet.

'Well, look who's here,' I said. 'The paid-up members of the Let's Turn The Clock Back and Pretend Nothing's Happened Society. It's times like this that make me wonder if we haven't been getting a little too slack over the rules governing inbreeding. Hands in the air, anyone who can count to eleven on their toes.'

A woman of a certain age stepped forward to confront me. I didn't know her, but I recognised the type.

'How dare you?' she said loudly. 'After everything you've done to the family, and to Martha and Alistair . . . How dare you show your face here?'

'That's right, dear. You tell him,' said a man behind her. Had to be the husband. He had that well-trained look. 'Have you no shame, Edwin?'

'Sorry, no,' I said. 'I'm right out. I'll have to send down to the shops for some more. Now get the hell out of my way of—

'Or what?' snapped the woman, folding her arms across her impressive chest. 'You can't bully us.'

'Actually, I think you'll find I can,' I said. 'Remember, I have a torc and you don't. But what I was going to say was: "Get out of my way or I'll call the Sarjeant-At-Arms, to come and take names and kick heads in."'

It was a bluff, but they didn't know that. They looked at the door behind me, as though expecting the Sarjeant to come crashing through at any moment, and you could see the defiance leaking out of them.

'Well!' said the woman of a certain age, but her heart wasn't in it. Her husband was already hiding behind her. I strode forward and the crowd parted before me like the Red Sea. I kept my back straight, my head up and my gaze ahead. When you're walking through a pack of dangerous animals, you can't show weakness for a moment or they'll go for your throat. I opened the door to the bedroom, stepped through, and closed the door quietly but firmly behind me.

I sighed inwardly. It bothered me that they didn't respect me the way they respected the Sarjeant-At-Arms. I was going to have to work on that.

The Matriarch's bedroom was surprisingly intimate and cheerful, for all its size. Comfortable furnishings, lots of light from the big window, flowers everywhere. Cards and messages of support stood propped up on every surface. There was a handful of people in the bedroom, there to give comfort and pay their respects. They hadn't expected to see me, but none of them said anything. They looked to Martha for their lead, but she didn't acknowledge my presence.

Alistair was sitting propped up by pillows in the great four-poster bed. He didn't look good. Even now, weeks after what had happened, he was still swathed in bandages like a mummy. He had the blankets pulled up to his chest as though he was cold, though a blazing fire had the room hot as a sauna. The bandages I could see were spotted with blood and other fluids seeping through. His right arm was gone. The surgeons couldn't save it, so they amputated it to the shoulder. His whole face was wrapped in gauze, with dark holes left for his eyes and mouth.

That's what you get for messing about with Hellfire. He should never have tried to use the Salem Special. That weapon never did anyone any good. And I might have been more sympathetic to his condition if I hadn't known that this was what he'd intended to do to my Molly.

Martha sat on the edge of the bed, beside her husband, feeding Alistair soup from a bowl, one spoonful at a time. As though he was a child. I could remember her doing that for me, once, when I was very small and the doctors thought the fever was going to carry me off. She sat with me day and night and fed me soup, and I survived. Maybe Alistair would be lucky too. Martha was dressed all in black, as though in mourning. Normally she was tall, proud, aristocratic and intimidatingly composed. Now she seemed somehow . . . smaller, as though something important had broken inside her. I didn't like to see her look that way. Her long grey hair, that she usually wore piled on top of her head, fell where it would, hiding most of her face. But her hand was steady as she fed Alistair his soup, and the back she showed me so firmly was almost painfully straight.

I had to talk to her, but I wasn't ready yet. So I looked at the other people in the room. I recognised some of them as acknowledged or supposed supporters of the Zero Tolerance faction. Hardly surprising they'd be here. The only chance they had of regaining influence, if not control, over the family lay in persuading the Matriarch to endorse their cause. I nodded calmly to a few familiar faces, and then stopped abruptly at one very familiar face.

'Penny?' I said.

'Eddie,' she said, in a calm, cool and entirely neutral voice.

'Good to see you again, Penny.'

'Wish I could say the same, Eddie.'

Which was par for the course. Penny had been my official contact in the family while I was still an agent in the field. I reported back to her after every mission, and she passed on any instructions or information the family thought I might need. I always liked Penny. She never let me get away with anything. Penny Drood was a tall cool blonde in a tight white sweater over slim grey slacks. Cool blue eyes, pale pink lips, Penny was sweet and smart and sexy, and sophisticated as a very dry martini. She was about my age, but I didn't remember her from my school days. There were a lot of us.

Even after ten years as my contact, I couldn't tell you whether she liked me or not. Penny never shared that kind of information with anyone.

'All right, people!' I said loudly. 'Nice of you to look in, but gosh look at the time, you must be going. Visiting hours are over until I'm through here. Hopefully you're more intelligent than the crowd outside, so we can dispense with the usual threats and menaces . . . Good, good. Head for the door, single file, no pushing or shoving or there'll be tears before bedtime.'

They left with their heads erect and their noses in the air, ignoring me as thoroughly as they could. Penny went to follow them, but I stopped her with a gesture.

'Hang about for a minute, Penny. I need to talk to you.'

'What makes you think I want to talk to you?'

'Because, unlike most of that crowd, you've actually got a brain in your head. Because you've always had the good of the family at heart. And because what I have to say is linked directly to the continued survival of the Drood family. Interested?'

'Maybe. You always did like the sound of your own voice too much, Eddie.'

'You wound me deeply.'

'I notice you're not denying it.'

'How's the Matriarch?' I said quickly, deftly changing the subject.

'As well as can be expected.'

'And Alistair?'

She shrugged and indicated the bed.

It was clear she wasn't going to give me an inch, so I gestured for her to stay where she was while I went over to stand beside the Matriarch. I waited for her to at least glance at me, but she kept on spooning soup into the dark gap in Alistair's bandages. I couldn't see any sign of him swallowing it. If it hadn't been for the slight but definite rise and fall of his bandaged chest, I would have wondered if he might be dead and no one had had the heart to tell Martha.

'Hello, Grandmother,' I said finally. 'I would have come sooner, but I've been very busy. Working for the family. How is he?'

'How do you think?' Martha Drood said flatly, still not turning around. Her voice was tired, but cold as steel, sharp as a razor blade. 'Look at him. Maimed. Crippled. Disfigured. My lovely Alistair. All thanks to you, Edwin.'

'How did he ever get his hands on the Salem Special?' I said. 'Awful weapon. We should have destroyed it long ago. And Alistair never knew anything about guns. So someone must have given it to him. Did you give him the gun, Grandmother, to use against my Molly?'

She looked at me for the first time, her face cold and implacable as stone. 'Of course not! Alistair was never a fighter. He abhorred guns. It was one of the things I loved most about him. No . . . he wanted to protect me. So he showed some initiative, for the first time in his life. He had to know how dangerous the Salem Special was, but all he could think of . . . was that I was in danger.'

'Turned out you were right about him after all, Grandmother,' I said. 'He was a good man and true, when it mattered. That's why you never told him the secret of the golden torcs. Never told him about the generations of Drood babies sacrificed to the Heart so we could wear the golden armour. You never told him, because you knew a good man like that would never have stood for such an abomination.'

'He didn't need to know! It was my burden, not his! And I did what I had to, to keep the family strong. Stronger than the enemies who would have dragged us down in a moment, if we had ever stumbled!'

'Martha?'

Alistair's bandaged head turned slowly, blindly, back and forth, disturbed by her raised voice, or perhaps because the soup had stopped. His voice was light and breathy, like a child's. 'Is there someone here, Martha?'

'It's all right, darling,' Martha said quickly. She went to pat him on the shoulder, and then stopped for fear of hurting him. 'Hush now, dear. Nothing for you to worry about.'

'I'm cold. And my head hurts. Is there someone here?'

'It's just Edwin.'

'Is he back visiting us?'

'Yes, dear. You rest quietly, and you can have some more nice soup in a minute.' She looked at me. 'He doesn't remember any of it. Probably for the best. Except . . . he doesn't seem to remember much of anything any more. He knows who he is, and who I am; and that's about it. Maybe some day he'll have to forget even that, to forget what you did to him. Damn you, Edwin, what are you doing here? Haven't you done enough harm? You killed my son James. The very best of us, and a better man than you'll ever be! You've destroyed my husband. And you've neutered the family by taking away their torcs. Left us defenceless in the face of our enemies, and the whole of Humanity undefended. I should never have let my daughter marry that man. Should never have let you run away. I should have had you killed years ago, Edwin!'

'Can't say any of this comes as much of a surprise to me, Grandmother,' I said, after a while. 'I always knew you felt more duty toward me than love. Children can tell.'

'What do you want, Edwin?'

'I want your help, Grandmother. Yes, I thought that would get your attention. I need your help and cooperation to rebuild the family and make it strong again. Strong and united. A divided family cannot stand, and the vultures are already gathering. I'm doing what I can to provide leadership but everywhere I look there's a new faction springing up. Your endorsement would go a long way towards unifying the family behind me. So I'm asking you to put aside all hurts and grievances, old and new, and help me.'

'No,' said Martha, quite calmly, enjoying the disappointment in my face. 'I won't fight you, Edwin, but I won't help you either. I'm going to let you run this family, and when you've run it into the ground they'll come to me . . . and beg me to lead them again. And I will. And I'll undo everything you've done and put the family back the way it was. The way it's supposed to be.'

'People will die, Martha.'

'Let them. Let them pay the price for disloyalty.'

Penny stepped forward. She actually looked shocked. 'But . . . Matriarch? What about *Anything, for the family*?'

'Leave me,' said Martha Drood. 'I'm tired.'

Penny and I walked back through the antechamber, side by side. The people waiting looked startled at seeing the two of us together, but had the good sense to say nothing. The ones I'd booted out of the bedroom couldn't wait to rush past me, desperate to ask the Matriarch what had happened. I wondered how much she'd tell them. Out in the corridor, I shut the suite's door firmly behind me, started to speak to Penny, stopped, and then led her a little further down the corridor. Just in case someone had their ear pressed to the door. I wouldn't put it past them. It was what I would have done.

'Penny,' I said. 'You see how things are. I need your help. I'm asking you for the same reason I asked the Matriarch; because I can't do this alone. Help me run things. For the sake of the family.'

Penny looked at me thoughtfully, her cool regard as unreadable as always. 'What precisely did you have in mind? As a secretary?'

'Join my Inner Circle. Help set policy. Help make the decisions that matter.'

She looked genuinely shocked for a moment, and I had to smile. Whatever she'd been expecting to hear, that hadn't been it. Membership of the Inner Circle would give her real power, and a chance of influencing me. She took a deep breath, which did interesting things to her tight white sweater, and was immediately her old cool and composed self again.

'Why in hell would you want someone like me, a hardcore traditionalist?'

'To keep me honest,' I said. 'To tell me the things I need to know, whether I want to hear them or not. To rein me in when I go too far, try to make changes too quickly. Or to spur me on if I start dithering. You've always been the sensible one, Penny. A terrible thing to hear, I know, but facts are facts. If I can't convince you something is right or necessary, maybe it isn't. And . . . you know a hell of a lot more about running things and organising people than I do.'

'Pretty much anyone knows more about those things than you do,' said Penny. 'I had to spend hours cleaning up your mission reports before I could pass them on.'

'So what do you say? Are you game?'

'Would I have an official title? I've always wanted an official title.'

'How about "my conscience"?'

'Yes,' said Penny. 'I could do that.'

'But first,' I said carefully, 'I have to ask, Penny: were you a part of the Zero Tolerance faction?'

'No,' Penny said immediately. 'They had some good ideas, but I don't believe in factions within the family.'

'Another good reason why I want you on my side.'

'What makes you think I'm on your side?'

It was my turn to consider her thoughtfully. 'You were my contact for years,' I said finally. 'You know me better than most. You know the things I've done for the family, the missions they gave me because they were too dangerous or too dirty for anyone else. You know I've always believed in what this family is supposed to stand for. I want to rebuild it in its own image, not mine.'

'Against my better judgement, I think I believe you,' said Penny. 'I'm not sure I believe *in* you; we'll have to see what happens. But I'm . . . prepared to be persuaded. Someone has to pull this family together, and if the Matriarch won't . . . But let me make one thing very clear, Eddie. I never fancied you. Not ever.'

'Of course not,' I said.

We both managed a small smile. I looked at my watch, and winced.

'The Inner Circle are waiting for me in the Sanctity right now,' I said. 'Come along, and I'll introduce you.'

'There's somewhere else we need to go first,' Penny said firmly. 'Trust me, Eddie, you really need to see what's happening in the War Room.'

'Oh hell,' I said. 'It's going to be one of those days, isn't it?'

So we went to the War Room. Which meant going all the way over to the North Wing, and down underground past the security measures and the goblin watchdogs, and finally into the huge steel-lined stone chamber that holds the family War Room. It's always a sight to set you back on your heels: the nerve centre of our secret wars, and the invisible armies who clash by night and by day. Huge display screens cover the walls, showing every country and major city in the world, along with a whole bunch of places that only people like us know are important. Bright-coloured lights indicate people we are watching, and ongoing problems in which we have an interest.

Family members sat in long rows at their work stations, concentrating on their work so they wouldn't have to look at me. Farseers covered potential trouble spots with their thoughts, while technicians worked their more than state-of-the-art computers for up-to-the-moment intelligence. Most of our secret wars are won in this room before a shot is fired, due to our superior planning and knowledge. And yet: something was definitely wrong in the War Room. I walked slowly round the work stations, peering over people's shoulders and scowling at the display screens on the walls. Penny strolled along beside me, saying nothing, letting me work it out for myself.

Nothing's happening,' I said finally. 'The maps on the walls should be lit up like Christmas trees, and the operations planning table should be a hive of activity; but nothing's happening. This is . . . unprecedented.'

'Which is why I wanted you to see it,' said Penny. 'So you'd have some idea of how the world is coping without the family looking over its shoulder. The threat boards are quiet because everyone else is too confused and too scared to start anything. They don't know why we've gone so quiet, and why so many of our field agents have suddenly dropped off the board. Are we hurt, are we weak – or are we running one of our fiendishly complicated and intricate operations, designed to suck people in and then stamp on their heads once they've foolishly taken the bait? We've done it before, after all. But look around you, Eddie. See how tense everyone is?'

'I thought that was just my presence.'

'Oh, get over yourself. Everyone here is running on hot tea and adrenalin, waiting for the other shoe to drop. Waiting to see which country or organisation or individual will finally start something to see how much they can get away with.'

'None of the lights show agents in the field,' I said suddenly. 'No ongoing operations.'

'That's because there aren't any,' said Penny. 'After you took away the family's golden torcs, the agents in the field had no choice but to go to ground. They'd been left helpless, vulnerable, without their armour; and we can't afford for any of our enemies to know that. Not yet. No one's been killed so far. But it's only a matter of time.'

I realised people all around me had looked up from their work stations to stare at me accusingly. I glared back, and they quickly returned to their work. I stood still, scowling furiously, thinking hard. This was my fault. I hadn't thought it through. When I discovered the family's golden armour was powered by the trapped souls of sacrificed children, all I could think of was to put a stop to it. I hadn't considered that I was putting other lives at risk. I don't think it would have stopped me anyway, but I hadn't thought. And ever since, I'd been too caught up in running The Hall to think about the big picture. That the world depends on the agents in the field to keep it safe, and the agents depend on The Hall.

'All right,' I said to Penny. 'Put out the call. All field agents to come home.'

'That could be dangerous,' said Penny. 'Staying out of sight is what's keeping some of them alive.'

'Well, tell them to use their best judgement,' I said impatiently. 'But unless they come back to The Hall to be vetted, they won't be considered for one of the new silver torcs. Tell them they can use the old secret paths; I'll authorise the extra expense.'

I moved over to the main operations table, picked up a sheaf of the latest reports and thumbed quickly through them. People around the table looked scandalised. Such material was only for the eyes of the Matriarch. Everyone knew I'd replaced Martha as head of the family, but it clearly hadn't sunk in for a lot of people.

'Where's Truman?' I said finally. 'I don't see anything about him here. Don't we have any recent updates about Manifest Destiny? They must be regrouping by now, so why don't I see anything on their new base, their new centre of operations? Come on, people; I'll settle for a best guess. An organisation that big can't hope to start up again without leaving all kinds of tell-tale traces. Follow the leader, follow the money, follow the threads on the message boards, but find them! They can't just have vanished!'

'Intelligence is working on that,' Penny said calmly. 'We haven't forgotten how to do our jobs, just because you're not here to hold our hands. But Manifest Destiny give every indication of having climbed into a deep hole and then pulled it in after them. They may be weakened, after what you did to them, and well done you; but their security is still first rate. And Truman . . . was and is a genius. You should have killed him when you had the chance.'

'I never had the chance,' I growled.

'What do you think he'll do now?'

'Hard to tell. He's a genuine fanatic, dedicated to his cause, running the world the way he thinks it should be run and everyone else eliminated. He was held back in the past by the Zero Tolerance faction . . . Without them to rein him in, God alone knows what atrocities he's planning now.'

'His old base, down below the Underground train system, is completely deserted,' said Penny. 'We've got a few people there, looking around, hoping to turn up something useful.'

'Hold it,' I said. 'There were only two field agents in London: me, and Matthew. I'm here, and he's dead, so who have you got running around under London?'

'Volunteers,' Polly said sharply. 'The work has to go on, even if you're . . . distracted. Not everyone wants to hide here in The Hall until you get around to handing out new torcs. Some of us still understand about duty and responsibility.'

'Don't lecture me,' I said. 'Just . . . don't. Not after everything I've seen and done. But you're quite right, of course. The work does have to go on. The world won't stand still because we're having a crisis in the family. Volunteers, eh? It's good to know we've got a few brave souls left. Have they turned up anything useful?'

'Ask them yourself,' said Penny. 'We've got a direct video feed set up. Fully secured, of course.'

'Oh, of course,' I said. 'All right, patch me through.'

Penny nodded to the communications board, and remarkably quickly one of the great display screens cleared to show shifting views of a dark, gloomy chamber with details picked out by jumping flashlight beams. Silhouetted figures moved jerkily among banks of silent equipment. It took me a long moment to recognise the usually bright shining steel corridors of Manifest Destiny's high-tech headquarters. All the electric lights were out and all the equipment shut down. Loose papers fluttered here and there, left behind in the rush to leave. It was like looking at the excavation of some recently opened tomb in the Valley of the Kings. A shadowy figure approached the camera.

'Will you please stop bugging me?' said a harsh voice. 'We'll contact you when we've got anything worth reporting. Whole place is a mess. We're having to move carefully because the bastards found time to leave a whole bunch of booby traps behind before they scarpered – trip-wires and grenades, mostly. Wouldn't bother us if we had our torcs, but as it is . . . We're moving deeper into the heart of the bunker, but it looks like they took everything of value with them and trashed the rest. A localised EMP took out all their computers; we'll bring back the hard drives just in case, but I wouldn't get your hopes up. Oh, and we've found some bodies. Too far gone to identify, unless you want us to take DNA samples. Looks like they were setting one last trap when it went off in their faces.

'That's it; end of report. Except to say it's cold and damp, and I'm sure I'm coming down with something. Now go away and bother someone else; we're busy. I want us finished and out of here before some other organisation gets the bright idea to come down here and see if there's anything worth salvaging.'

'This is Eddie Drood,' I said.

'Well, whoop-de-doo. Colour me impressed. You don't know who I am, do you?'

'No,' I said.

'Let's keep it that way. We'll be home soon; put the kettle on.'

And he shut down the video feed from his end. Everyone was looking at me, so I was careful to smile. 'I don't know who he is, but I like his style. He reminds me of me. See to it I get a full report from him the moment he turns up here. In the meantime, keep working on tracking down Truman's new base of operations. He's got to be planning something nasty to re-establish himself, and I want to know all about it well in advance.'

'You see?' said Penny. 'You can act like you're in charge when you put your mind to it.'

All meetings of my Inner Circle took place in the Sanctity, the huge open chamber that once held the damned Heart before I destroyed it. The Circle met in the Sanctity because it was the only place in The Hall I could be sure of absolute privacy. The Sanctity had been designed to contain the dangerous other-dimensional emissions of the Heart, and nothing could penetrate its powerful shields. The other-dimensional strange matter that I had brought to The Hall occupied the Sanctity now. It manifested as a warm happy crimson glow radiating from a single silver pearl of strange matter. Just standing in the glow made you feel good: calm and relaxed and secure, in body and thought and soul. In fact, it felt so good that access to the Sanctity had to be strictly limited, for fear of people becoming addicted. The strange matter swore that couldn't happen, but I've learned not to believe everything I'm told.

The point is that thanks to the Sanctity's shielding, and the strange matter's unusual emissions, no one can listen in on the Inner Circle's meetings. And there's always someone trying to listen in, in The Hall. It's the only way you ever learn anything that matters.

Penny came to a halt just inside the Sanctity's door as she took in the full effect of the scarlet glow. Her face softened, and she smiled a real smile, quite unlike her usual cool effort. She looked calm, and happy, and at peace with herself. It didn't suit her. She made a deliberate effort to push the effect away and regained some of her usual composure.

'Remarkable,' she said. 'Reminds me of standing in front of one of Klein's famous Blue paintings in the Louvre.' She noted my surprise and raised a supercilious eyebrow. 'I do have some culture, you know.'

'Then you should put yoghurt on it,' said Molly.

Penny and I looked round and there were the rest of my Inner Circle, staring at us suspiciously. The good feeling I'd had from the crimson glow vanished immediately. I hadn't expected this to be easy, but the grim faces in the assembled Circle made it clear this was going to be an uphill battle all the way. I took Penny by the arm and led her forward, glaring right back at the Circle.

'Penny is one of us now,' I said firmly. 'She's a full member of the Inner Circle. And I don't want to hear any more insults. I trust her, and so should you.'

'Just like that?' said Molly, dangerously.

'Yes,' I said.

Molly looked at the rest of the Circle. 'I'll knock him down; you get the straightjacket on him.'

'I need advisors from all parts of the family,' I said patiently, 'including the traditionalists.'

'You mean the ones who wanted you and me dead?' said Molly. 'The ones who declared you rogue and secretly ran Manifest Destiny behind the cover of the Zero Tolerance faction?'

'That's the ones,' I said, 'except that Polly was never Zero Tolerance. She told me so.'

'And you believed her?' said Molly.

'Of course,' I said. 'She's family.'

'So,' said Penny, 'this is the infamous Inner Circle? This is what has replaced the Matriarch's Council, sanctified by centuries of tradition?'

'Yes,' I said, 'and eventually the Inner Circle will give way to a new Council, to be elected by the family. It's about time we had some democracy around here.'

'Democracy?' said Molly.

'Shut up, dear, I'm talking,' I said. 'The old Council had to go, Penny. They were all corrupt. They knew the truth about the torcs and they never did anything about it. They knew the truth about the family's true role in the world and they just went along with it.'

'Elected,' Penny said thoughtfully, 'by the whole family; or just the ones you end up giving new torcs to?'

I grinned at the Inner Circle. 'You see? That's why she's here; to ask the necessary awkward questions.'

I looked round the Circle but they didn't seem that impressed. My Inner Circle consisted of Molly Metcalf, my Uncle Jack – the family Armourer – the ghost Jacob Drood, the Sarjeant-At-Arms, and now Penny. I could have ruled the family on my own – declared myself Patriarch, or something – but I'd seen where that led. Power tends to corrupt, and the Droods are the most powerful family in the world. So I chose people to advise me that I could trust to tell me the truth, whether I wanted to hear it or not; and who together might just be a match for me if I looked like getting out of control. Penny nodded formally to the other family members of the Circle, though she couldn't bring herself to look Jacob in his ghostly eyes, but she had only a cold stare for Molly.

'I might have known you'd stick your girlfriend in a position of power,' she said sweetly. 'You always were a soppy romantic, Eddie. You must know that she can't be allowed authority over the family. She just can't. I mean, she's an outsider.'

'She's with me,' I said flatly. 'Accept it and move on. Or there'll be tears before bedtime.'

The Armourer made his usual impatient harrumphing sound, meaning he had something important to say and he was going to say it whatever anybody else felt. He was a stick-thin middle-aged man with far too much nervous energy and not nearly enough self-preservation instincts; he was wearing his usual chemical-stained and lightly charred lab coat. Aided by a fiercely questing intellect and a complete lack of scruples he designed and built weapons and gadgets for agents in the field. He wore a grubby T-shirt under his coat bearing the legend *Weapons of Mass Destruction: Ask Here.* He once created a nuclear grenade, but couldn't find anyone who could throw it far enough. Two great tufts of white hair jutted out over his ears, the only hair on his head apart from bushy white eyebrows. He had calm grey eyes, a brief but engaging smile, and a somewhat jumpy manner, plus a pronounced stoop, from far too many years spent hunching over the designing board working on really dangerous things.

He was my Uncle Jack, and I would have died rather than disappoint him.

'I can't stay long,' he said abruptly, scowling fiercely about him in his usual manner. 'I've had to leave my interns alone and unsupervised in the Armoury, and that's always dangerous. To them, as well as their surroundings. And of course they're so much more vulnerable these days without torcs to protect them. Though it doesn't seem to have slowed them down any. I had to take a superstring away from one of them the other day. How did the Overdrive work on the Bentley, Eddie? I'm rather proud of that . . . I'm pretty sure I've got all the bugs out now.'

'Only pretty sure?' said Molly. 'Now he tells us—'

'It worked fine,' I said. 'I've put the Bentley into the Armoury for some minor repairs.'

'What? What?' said the Armourer, bristling. 'What do you mean, minor repairs? What have you done, Eddie? What have you done to my lovely old Bentley? You crashed it, didn't you? You crashed the Bentley after I told you I was only loaning it to you!'

'No, I didn't crash it,' I said calmly. You learn to keep your cool in conversations with the Armourer, on the grounds that he'll be emotional enough for both of you, and one of you has to be calm and it certainly isn't going to be him. 'I just picked up a few *very minor* dents and scratches during a trip through the side dimensions.'

'I'm going back to the Armoury.'

'No, you're not!' I said quickly. 'We have important matters to discuss.'

'Important matters, eh?' the ghost of Jacob said brightly. 'That sounds important.'

Jacob tried hard, but he just wasn't as focused as he used to be. When he lived (or rather, *existed*) in exile in the old Chapel behind the back of The Hall, he used to sit around quite happily in his ghostly underwear, watching the memories of old television programmes on a set with no insides to it. Most of the family wouldn't talk to him, but he and I had been good friends since I first sought him out as a child (because I knew I wasn't supposed to).

Now that he was officially one of the family again and had moved back into The Hall, Jacob had made something of an effort to smarten himself up. He still looked older than death, his face full of wrinkles and his bald pate graced with only a few flyaway silver hairs, but he had refined his ectoplasm into a smart tuxedo, even if the material tended more to navy blue than black, and he kept forgetting about the collar. But as a ghost of long standing – or at least a stubborn refusal to lie down – only his concentration held him together. And of late his thoughts had shown a distinct tendency to wander, which was why every now and again he'd suddenly be wearing a Hawaiian T-shirt over baggy shorts and a heavy red sash bearing the legend *Mortally Challenged*. He also left long trails of pale blue ectoplasm trailing on the air behind him when he made sudden movements.

Jacob the ghost was falling apart, body and soul, and he knew it.

The Sarjeant-At-Arms glared at Jacob. He disapproved of the old ghost's very existence, and wasn't afraid to let it show.

'Why don't you find yourself a nice grave and settle down?' he said pointedly. 'You know you shouldn't be here. Family policy on ghosts is very clear. Any ghost that shows up here gets sent on its way sharpish. No exceptions. Otherwise we'd be hip-deep in the things by now.'

'I'm exempt,' Jacob said firmly.

'On what grounds?' said the Sarjeant.

'Because I say so, and don't you bloody forget it. I'm exempt from anything I damned well feel like, on the grounds that I'll kick anyone's arse who says otherwise. Being dead is very liberating. You should try it, Sarjeant. Preferably soon.'

'Behave yourself, Jacob,' I said. 'Remember: I've still got that exorcist on speed-dial.'

'We need to talk about the witch's presence here,' Penny said stubbornly.

'No, we don't,' I said.

'I've got a better idea,' said Molly. 'Let's talk about your presence here, Penny dear. Are you another of Eddie's old flames, like that appalling Alexandra person?'

Penny snorted loudly. 'He wishes—'

'Are you going to introduce just anyone you want into the Circle?' said the Sarjeant. 'Don't we get a say in the matter?'

'If you've got anyone else in mind, suggest them,' I said. 'I'll take all the help I can get. I'm only running things now because I can't find anyone else I can trust. I'm the only one in this family without an agenda. The whole point of this Inner Circle is to set things up for the formation of a new elected Council, so they can take over and I can go back to being a field agent again, where I belong. Where I was happy.'

'Are you saying you haven't been happy since you met me?' said Molly.

'You are the only good thing in my life and you know it,' I said. 'So stop fishing for compliments.'

'Blow me a kiss right now,' said Molly, 'or I'll tell everyone where you've got a funny-shaped mole.'

'We need to discuss Jacob's position in the family,' insisted the Sarjeant-At-Arms. 'He's moved back into his old room in The Hall; the one he used to live in back when he was alive. He frightened the proper occupant so much he ran out screaming and has refused to go back.'

'I know,' said the Armourer, 'we've got the poor lad down in the Infirmary. I don't know what you did to him, Jacob, but he still hasn't stopped twitching. And he can't go to sleep unless someone holds his hand.'

Jacob sniggered. 'He shouldn't have been playing with himself when I materialised. And I am here because I'm supposed to be here. I like being back in The Hall – if only because it annoys so many of the proper people. Been a lot of changes since I was last here . . . I can't believe how crowded The Hall is these days. Family's been breeding like rabbits . . . we need to get more of the youngsters out into the world. Kick them out of the nest! Fly, little birdies! Yes, I know, I'm rambling; you're allowed to when you've been dead as long as I have.'

'Don't take this the wrong way,' I said, 'but why are you still here, Jacob? I thought you only hung around as a ghost so you'd be here to help me save the family from the Heart?'

'That's what I thought,' said Jacob, scowling. His eyes disappeared, leaving only deep dark pits in his face. 'But something is still holding me here, some force like an undischarged promise. My job here isn't over yet, dammit. Something is coming, Eddie. Something good, something bad . . . *something*.'

We all waited, but he had nothing else left to say. I decided it was very definitely time to change the subject, and since I wanted to remind everyone that I was in charge, I went with something that had been bugging me for some time. I stared sternly at the Sarjeant-At-Arms.

'What is your name? I can't keep calling you Sarjeant, and I'm damned if I'll go back to calling you sir, like when I was a kid.'

'Call me Sarjeant. It's my title.'

'I could have Molly rip it out of your living brain,' I said. I was bluffing, but he didn't know that. If the Sarjeant was so determined not to tell me his name, I wanted to know even more. It had to be something good.

The Sarjeant sighed, just a little. 'My name is Cyril.'

Sometimes things really are just too good to be true. I think the only thing that kept the whole Circle from collapsing into gales of hysterical laughter was our extensive knowledge of the Sarjeant's natural brutality – and that he could summon weapons out of thin air when he felt like it.

'Cyril?' I said happily. 'Bloody Cyril? No wonder you grew up to be a thug and a bully with a name like that. You must have loved your parents.'

'They were fine, upstanding people,' the Sarjeant said firmly. 'Now, if I may continue my report on the transgressions of the ghost, Jacob?'

'Oh by all means,' I said, 'don't let me stop you, *Cyril*.'

'There have been numerous reports of Jacob haunting the ladies' showers and changing rooms.'

'I keep getting lost.'

'You're not fooling anyone, Jacob,' I said.

'And,' said the Sarjeant, 'there have even been reports of him chasing the ghost of the headless nun through the catacombs.'

Jacob grinned. 'Hey, she's the only other ghost in The Hall. Can you blame me if I just want to swap a little ectoplasm? Nice arse, for a nun. Damn, she's fast on her feet; especially considering she can't see where she's going.'

'You're a member of the Inner Circle!' snapped the Sarjeant. 'You're supposed to set an example!'

'Oh I am, I am . . .'

'Stop that,' I said quickly. 'Your ectoplasm's going all quivery. Let us move on. Are we any closer to establishing who was behind the recent attacks on The Hall, just before I was summoned home? Do we have any new information?'

'Nothing. Not a word,' said the Armourer.

'Perhaps we should ask the strange matter,' said the Sarjeant, pointedly, 'since it did turn out to be responsible for the destruction of the Heart in the end.'

'Wasn't me,' said a calm and reasonable voice from inside the warm crimson glow. 'I was still searching for the Heart at that stage. I didn't even know it was in this dimension. You must remember: the Heart had made many enemies, from all the worlds and races it enslaved before it came here. Some of those enemies have been looking for the Heart almost as long as me.'

That sounded reasonable enough, but though I had much to thank the strange matter for, and it always said the right things . . . the fact remained that it was still very much an unknown factor. All we knew about it was what it had chosen to tell us. If it had been behind the other attacks, would it admit that? We had no way to compel the truth from it. I rubbed at my forehead as a grinding headache began. Being paranoid is very tiring, but when you're a Drood it's the only way to stay one step ahead.

'Strange matter—' I started.

'Oh please, call me Ethel.'

'We are not going to call you Ethel,' I said, very firmly.

'Why not? What's wrong with Ethel? It's a perfectly good name. I like it. It's honest, it's charming, it's . . . *me*.'

'We are not calling you Ethel!'

'Nothing wrong with Ethel,' said the strange matter. 'Winston Churchill had a pet frog called Ethel.'

'No, he didn't!'

'He might have. You don't know.'

'I'm calling you Strange,' I said. 'It's the only name that fits.'

'You have no sense of fun,' said Strange.

'Actually—' said Molly.

'Hush,' I said quickly.

The Armourer started on another of his impressive throat-clearings. 'How did you get on with the Matriarch, Eddie?'

'Not good,' I admitted. 'She told me to go to hell. She'd rather see the whole family collapse than prosper with me in charge.'

The Armourer nodded reluctantly. 'Mother always could be very stubborn . . . But you have to keep trying with her, Eddie. You need her on your side if you're to get the whole family moving in the same direction. She represents the past and tradition, and all those things that make the family feel safe and secure.'

'It isn't going to be easy,' I said.

'Of course it isn't going to be easy, Eddie! You killed her favourite son – my brother James! I know you had to do it, and even I still have trouble forgiving you. The old Grey Fox . . . he was the best of us, for so many years. And don't forget he had a lot of admirers outside the family: old friends and old enemies who won't be at all happy to hear he died at your hands. They could turn up here at any time, ready and willing to express their extreme displeasure . . . and then you're going to need the whole family backing you up.'

'We could say James had gone rogue?' Penny suggested tentatively.

'Who'd believe that?' I said. 'The Grey Fox always was the best of us. You'd better beef up The Hall's defences, Uncle Jack, just in case.'

I finally got to the meat of the meeting, and told them about MI5's ambush outside my old flat. The Armourer and the Sarjeant insisted I tell it all, in as much detail as I could remember. Molly chimed in here and there, sometimes helping and sometimes not. The Armourer and the Sarjeant both reacted very strongly when I told them who was behind the attack.

'The Prime Minister?' said the Sarjeant, incredulously. 'Who does he think he is, to take on the Droods? Man's getting thoughts above his station. We can't allow this to go unpunished, Edwin. People might think we were getting soft.'

'I've already sent him a very definite message,' I said.

'Killing a few MI5 agents won't bother him,' said the Armourer. 'As far as he's concerned, they're all expendable. We need to hit him where he lives.'

'Right,' said the Sarjeant. 'Can't have the Prime Minister getting cheeky. We need to slap him down hard, Edwin. Make an example of him.'

I shook my head slowly. 'We can't afford to show our hand and risk revealing how weak we really are. And no one else in power seems to be feeling their oats. Penny took me down to the War Room; it was all very quiet.'

'Quiet before the storm,' said Penny. 'Our researchers are all over the world's media, official and unofficial, getting a feel for each government's mood. And all our telepaths, scryers and clairvoyants are working full-time.'

I had to smile. Politicians only *think* they can keep secrets from the Droods.

'So far, everyone's being very cautious, not wanting to rock the boat until they know whether or not there're sharks in the water,' said the Armourer. 'I don't think they believe their own reports about how weak and disorganised we are at present. But that can't last. They know all our field agents have gone to ground, and most of them know, or at least suspect, about the golden torcs' disappearance. So sooner or later somebody's going to do something . . . if only just to see what happens. To see how much they can get away with. There might even be a direct strike against The Hall itself. Remember when the Chinese tried to nuke us, back in the Sixties?'

'We have to do something about the Prime Minister,' the Sarjeant said firmly. 'Something sufficiently unpleasant, to send a clear message to all the world leaders.'

'All right,' I said, reluctantly. 'Come up with some options and I'll look at them.'

'I thought one of the reasons you took over running the Droods was to free the world from Drood control,' said Molly. 'I distinctly remember you saying something about letting politicians make their own decisions.'

'I did,' I said. 'Turns out things are more complicated than that.'

'Isn't that always the first response of every dictator?'

'Look: survival first, politics second, okay?' I said.

'Just wanted you to be sure of what you're getting into,' Molly said sweetly.

'Speaking of survival,' said Penny, 'we need to get as many of the family as possible into the new silver torcs, as quickly as possible. We're just too vulnerable to sudden attack as things stand.'

I nodded reluctantly. 'All right. You guys get together and draw up a list for me to consider: those who should get their torcs right away; those who should once they've proved themselves worthy; and those who won't ever be trusted with a torc again.'

'Such as?' said Penny, her cool eyes openly challenging me.

'Anyone who knew about the secret of the golden torcs and just went along with it,' I said sternly. 'Any unrepentant Zero Tolerance, and anyone who'd more than likely use a torc to start a civil war within the family. Use your own best judgement. We're only talking about a small percentage of scumbags, I hope. Strange, any problem with producing so much strange matter for the torcs and armour, so quickly?'

'Please; do call me Ethel.'

'Not if there was a gun to my head.'

'You can have as many silver torcs as you want, Eddie,' Strange said easily. 'It's just a matter of bringing more of me through from my home dimension. I am great and limitless, wise and wonderful . . . But you don't really need torcs, you know. I could teach you all to be superhuman. You have such potential within you, you humans, to be far greater than any torc could ever make you. You could all shine like stars.'

I looked at the Inner Circle, and they looked at me.

'How long would this take?' I said.

'Years,' said Strange, 'generations, maybe. This whole consecutive time thing is a new concept to me.'

'I think we'll stick with what we know for now,' I said. 'The family needs to be strong as quickly as possible. But by all means consider the alternative, Strange; and let me know when you've got something more specific to tell me.'

'Oh goody!' said Strange. 'This is going to be such fun!'

'Any other matters?' I said quickly.

'Just one,' said the Armourer. He produced a small object wrapped in white samite from under his lab coat and passed it to me. I accepted it, and then unwrapped it with great care and caution. Gifts from the Armourer have a tendency to be downright dangerous, if not actually explosive. The object turned out to be a simple hand mirror with a silver frame and handle. I hefted it cautiously a few times, just in case, but nothing happened. And the face in the mirror was quite definitely mine, so . . . I looked inquiringly at the Armourer.

'Jacob and I have been studying in the Old Library,' said the Armourer, 'when I can tear him away from his . . . other pursuits. And we've turned up some quite remarkable items. A number of books thought to be long lost or destroyed, a number of ancient maps of dubious provenance but with exciting possibilities . . . and a handful of lost and quite legendary treasures. That is Merlin's Glass. It disappeared from the Armageddon Codex in the late eighteenth century, under somewhat murky circumstances. Jacob discovered it inside a hollowed-out book about voles.'

'Don't even know what made me look there,' Jacob said cheerfully. 'I was just looking for something with dirty pictures.'

'Hold everything,' said Molly, 'though not literally in your case, Jacob. Merlin's Glass – are we talking about *the* Merlin?'

'Oh yes,' said Jacob.

'He was a Drood?' said Molly.

'Hardly,' said the Armourer. 'We do have our standards. No, he was Merlin Satanspawn, the Devil's only begotten son, born to be the Anti-Christ – but he refused the honour. He always had to go his own way . . . But according to some quite fascinating records in the Old Library, he did work with the family on occasion. When it suited him. And apparently he owed us a favour, which he repaid by gifting us that mirror.'

Molly reached out for it and I handed it over. She muttered some Words over the mirror, made a few quick gestures – even held it upside down and shook it in the hope something might fall out – but nothing happened. Molly sniffed, and handed the mirror back to me.

'All right,' she said. 'I'll bite. What's it supposed to do?'

'It can be used to make contact with other members of the Drood family, in the Past or the Future, to ask them for advice or information.'

There was a pause, and then Molly said, 'No offence, guys, but I think you got stiffed on the deal. I mean – it's not the most useless magic object I've ever seen, but it comes pretty damned close.'

'You're a witch,' the Armourer said kindly, 'and therefore used to thinking mainly in terms of the here and now. The Glass has many uses. Vital information lost in this time can be found in the Past, before it was lost, or in the Future, after it has been rediscovered.

The greatest family tacticians of the Past – or the Future – are now ours to consult. We can even take specific advice from the Future on which matters to pursue, and which are best left strictly alone—'

'If this Glass is so useful,' I said, 'how did it happen to go missing for so long?'

'Ah,' said the Armourer, reluctantly. 'There are many stories about that. The one I tend to believe the most, because I dislike it the most, is that someone asked the Glass a very specific question, and got a very specific answer that disturbed the shit out of him. So he took the Glass and hid it to prevent anyone else from asking the question, or learning the answer.'

'I can't see this family giving up anything that useful so easily,' said Molly.

'I can,' I said. 'The Droods have always been very cautious about anything involving time travel, ever since the Great Time Disaster of 1217, when the family almost wiped itself out after inadvertently setting up a Möbius strip Time Paradox. There're still some rooms in The Hall we can't find because of what we had to do to break free. And we don't even think about what might be happening even now to the poor bastards we had to abandon in those rooms. The human mind just isn't equipped to deal with all the possible complications and downright nasty ramifications of mucking about with Time.'

And then I stopped short as an idea came to me, hitting me hard enough to stop my breath and curl a cold hand around my heart. I looked into Merlin's Glass and my face stared back at me, so cold and harsh and determined I barely recognised it.

'Can I contact *anyone* in the Past?' I asked, and even I could tell that the voice didn't sound like mine. It sounded reckless, dangerous, even. Everyone looked at me sharply. I think Molly got it first, perhaps because her mind had already begun moving along similar lines. I looked at the Armourer, and I think anyone else would have flinched at what he saw in my eyes. 'I know it's dangerous,' I said, 'and I don't care. Tell me, Uncle Jack: can I use this Glass to talk to my parents in the Past, before they were murdered?'

'I'm sorry,' the Armourer said gruffly, kindly. 'I thought of that. There's always someone we'd like to speak to in the Past: friends and relatives and loved ones, gone too soon, before we could say all the things we meant to say to them. The things we put off saying, because we always thought there'd be time . . . until suddenly there wasn't. But the Glass doesn't allow anyone to ask questions for personal gain, only for the good of the family – and the Glass can *always* tell the difference. It's a built-in safety factor, perhaps, to prevent – well, abuse of Time.'

'Or perhaps the sorcerer Merlin Satanspawn just had a built-in nasty streak,' said Molly.

'There is that,' said the Armourer.

'I need to know what really happened to my father and my mother,' I said, 'and I will find out the truth, whatever it takes.'

'I spent years trying to find out,' said the Armourer. 'So did James. She was our sister, poor dear Emily, and we loved her dearly. We even approved of your father, or we'd never have let him marry her. But the truth is . . . no one seems to know. The odds are it was just a stupid mistake. Poor intelligence, insufficient briefing, too many things going wrong at once . . . It happens. Even on the best planned missions.'

'There's always the Time Train,' said Penny, unexpectedly.

'No there isn't,' the Armourer said quickly.

'What the hell is a Time Train?' said Molly. 'And why do I get the feeling I'm really not going to like the answer?'

'Must be your witchy senses working overtime,' I said. 'Damn, I haven't thought about the Time Train in years . . . It's a means of travelling through Time, though perhaps a little stranger than most. No one's used it for ages. I suppose it is still functional . . . isn't it, Armourer?'

'Well, yes, technically,' said the Armourer, 'but some things are just too dangerous to mess with.'

I had to raise an eyebrow. 'This from the man who wanted our best telepaths to try setting off all the atomic warheads in China – by having them *think really nasty thoughts at them*?'

'And it would have worked, if the Matriarch hadn't stopped me,' said the Armour sulkily. 'All my best ideas are ahead of their time.'

'I am changing the subject right now,' I said firmly. 'One thing must be clear to us all: the family has to Do Something, something Big and Important and Dramatic, to prove to the whole world that the Droods are still as strong and nasty as ever; that the family is still a force to be reckoned with. We need to pick a target, some seriously unpleasant enemy, and hit them with a really powerful pre-emptive strike force. We need to wipe them out, once and for all.'

'Now you're talking, boy!' said the Sarjeant-At-Arms.

'Sounds good to me,' said the Armourer. 'Under the Matriarch the family's been far too *re*active when we need to be *pro*active.'

'Who did you have in mind?' said Molly. 'Manifest Destiny?'

'No,' I said, 'they're still weak. Stamping on them wouldn't impress anyone. We need something . . . bigger.'

'There are two main threats to Humanity,' the Armourer said ponderously, slipping into Lecture Mode. 'Doesn't matter whether they're scientific or magical in origin, mythical or political or biblical; all of Humanity's enemies can be separated into two distinct kinds. There are those who do us harm because they hope to gain something from it; these we call demons. And there are those who are too big to care about us, but who might do us harm just because we're in the way; those we call gods, for want of a better word. The family is trained and equipped to deal with demons. The gods are best handled delicately, from a safe distance and through as many intermediaries as possible.'

'I've already killed one god,' I said, 'and the Heart screamed just like a human as it died.'

'I helped,' said Strange. 'You couldn't have done it without me.'

'Perhaps,' I said, 'but then, you would say that, wouldn't you?'

'Can we please put the delusions of grandeur to one side, just for the moment?' said Penny. 'And concentrate on planning a strategy.'

'Not attacking any gods sounds like a really good strategy to me,' said Molly.

'I'm voting for demons.'

'Demons sound good to me too,' said the Armourer. 'There's never any shortage of demons screwing over Humanity.'

'All right,' I said, 'demons it is. Anyone want to throw some names onto the table, just to get us started?'

'The Stalking Shrouds?' said the Sarjeant-At-Arms.

'They were pretty much wiped out last year,' said Penny, 'fighting a turf war with the Cold Eidolon in the back streets of Naples. Both sides are still recovering. Be ages before either of them can mount a decent threat again.'

'The Loathly Ones?' I said. 'I hate soul-eaters.'

Penny frowned. 'There has been some intelligence of late that they've been gathering together in big numbers, down in South America. No one seems to know what for, and that's never a good thing.'

'I'd really like to do something about the Mandrake Recorporation,' said Molly, 'if only because they creep me out big time.'

'Not really a good enough reason to go to war with someone though, is it?' said the Armourer.

'The Cult of the Crimson Altar?' said Jacob. 'They're old-school Satanists, offshoot of the original Hellfire Club. Never liked them. They turned me down for membership back when I was alive, the black-balling bastards.'

'Currently in major schism,' Penny said briskly, 'over some piece of dogma so complicated and so trivial that no one outside the Cult can make head or tail of it. The Cult's been killing itself off for the last six weeks, and at the rate they're going I doubt there'll be enough of them left at the end to form a social club.'

'The Dream Meme?' said the Sarjeant, hopefully.

'No!' said the Armourer. 'We still don't know for sure who or what they are, or even what they want. And yes, Cyril, I have heard all the latest conspiracy theories, and I'm not convinced by any of them. They're just a supernatural urban legend, like the Sceneshifters.'

'Vril Power Inc?' said Molly. 'Everyone's favourite nightmare from the Second World War?'

'Gone into politics since the reunification of Germany,' said Penny. 'No surprises there.'

'Enough names,' I said. 'We need to send a message. A strong message. So I say we take on the Loathly Ones. No one likes soul-eaters, so no one will ally with them, even against us. I say we track down this new gathering of theirs, send in an armoured force and either wipe them out for good or, at the very least, send them back to whatever hell they came from. It's only right, when you consider the family was responsible for bringing them into this world in the first place.'

The Armourer and the Sarjeant-At-Arms scowled. They already knew that. Penny and Jacob looked shocked; they didn't. Most of the family didn't; it was just another one of those nasty little secrets the old guard liked to keep to themselves.

'Think I'll contact my old friend Janissary Jane,' I said. 'She knows all there is to know about fighting demons . . . well, when she's sober, at least. Penny, since all our field agents are coming home, I want you to put out a call for all rogue Droods to come home too, all sins forgiven, if not forgotten. They've learnt the hard way how to survive in the world without family back-up, and they have skills we can use and profit from. Besides, I've been a rogue and I've met rogues, and I don't like to think of them being left out there in the cold.'

'*All* the rogues?' said Penny.

'Well, obviously not the real shits, like the late and very unlamented Bloody Man, Arnold Drood,' I said. 'But there aren't many of the real bad seeds left, are there?'

'Only a few, thank the Lord,' said the Armourer. 'We've been weeding them out down the years. Tiger Tim is still hiding out somewhere in the Amazon rainforest, because he knows anyone even half-way civilised will kill him the moment he shows his face . . . and Old Mother Shipton is finally running out of identities to hide behind. We're pretty sure she's running a baby cloning service in Vienna at the moment. Our agent there was actually closing in on her, before the present difficulties . . .'

'And they're the only monsters left?' I said.

'The only ones we know of,' Penny replied. 'But really, Eddie, calling back the rogues, the scum we threw out for being crooks or cowards or subversives? The family isn't going to like this.'

'We often don't like the things that are good for us,' I said calmly. 'And as with so many other things where the old Council was concerned, the rogues aren't necessarily what you were told they were. Some were just troublemakers who insisted on telling the truth. The family needs new advice, new tricks, new ways of looking at things, and I'm betting the rogues can supply that in abundance. I'm also bringing in a few friends from outside, to help out with guest tutorials: Janissary Jane, of course, as I've already mentioned. And I thought maybe the Blue Fairy.'

'*Him?*' said Penny. 'He's a drunk, a thief and a lecher; he has no principles, no scruples . . . and he's a *half-elf*! You can't trust him!'

'He'll fit in perfectly,' I said. 'Besides, I hear he's a new person since his near-death experience.'

'If you're bringing in your old friends, I want some of mine here too,' said Molly, 'if only so I won't feel so outnumbered.'

'Okay,' I said, 'who did you have in mind?'

'Subway Sue and Mr Stab,' said Molly, smiling sweetly.

'*Are you crazy*? A vampire who sucks the good fortune out of people, and the uncaught immortal serial killer of Old London Town? Over my dead body!'

There would probably have been heated words and raised voices at that moment if all the alarms hadn't gone off at once. The Hall was under attack.

CHAPTER THREE
Good and evil; it's all relatives

In the old days, when a general alarm sounded the whole family would run to defend The Hall; but we were warriors then. Now everyone ran to the designated shelters to hide till it was all over. My fault, of course, for taking away their golden torcs. The Droods weren't used to feeling human and vulnerable. So the Sanctity and its adjoining rooms had become the new Panic Room for the Droods; though of course no one would ever dream of using such a term. But as I came out of the Sanctity, followed by the rest of the Inner Circle, so many people were running down the corridor towards me with fear and desperation written clearly in their faces, it disturbed me to realise how easily the spirit of my family could be broken.

I was going to have to do something about that, and soon.

Strange protected the Sanctity and the other rooms, its other-dimensional shields guarding the family from any outside attack. The family would be safe there, while I investigated whatever it was that dared attack us. Strange was also responsible for powering our science and magic-based defences, and it worried me how quickly we'd become dependent on this replacement for the destroyed Heart. I hadn't freed us from one other-dimensional master just to hand us over to another. No matter how seemingly benevolent. One more thing for me to worry about . . .

Strange had said he could do even more for us, but that would mean bringing more of his substance through into this dimension, and even he had to admit he had no idea exactly what effect so much strange matter might have on the physical laws of our reality. Strange matter wasn't natural here, and our world didn't like having it around. Besides, Strange was powerful enough as he was. Trust has always been a difficult thing for me, even before I found out what the Heart really was. So, on behalf of the family, I politely declined Strange's offer.

Which was why it was now up to me to defend the whole damned family from attack.

The Droods came pouring through the corridors towards the Sanctity, their faces pale and strained. The alarm bells were maddeningly loud, but the Sarjeant-At-Arms still made himself heard over the din, haranguing and bullying the crowds into some kind of order as they filed quickly into the Sanctity. He didn't need to use much of his trademarked brutality; most of the family were glad to hear an authoritative voice telling them what to do. But then, that's always been their problem. The Sarjeant scowled at the nervous faces streaming past him, and seemed actually ashamed to see the family reduced to such a state. He didn't look at me, but then he didn't have to. I already knew who he blamed.

'I'm going to the War Room,' said Penny, shouting to be heard over the general din. 'Someone needs to keep an eye on the big picture. Always the chance this attack was designed to distract us from something really big happening somewhere else.'

'Right!' I said. 'Go! Report back when you get a chance.'

But she was already off and running, forcing her way through the tide of approaching Droods by sheer assurance. I'd done well in choosing her. I looked around for Jacob, but he'd disappeared. I turned to the Sarjeant.

'You stay here and keep a lid on things. Molly, Uncle Jack – we need to get to the Ops Room. Find out who or what we're up against before we have to go out and face them. Sarjeant, if they should get past us and get in here . . . improvise.'

I set off at a steady pace, ploughing through the increasingly packed corridors, and Molly and the Armourer stuck close behind me. There was a growing sense of panic on the air. My first instinct was to armour up, but I couldn't do that. It would have upset the other Droods who didn't have their armour any more, because of me.

I felt like shouting *Look! It seemed like a good idea at the time, okay?*

'Who do you think is behind this?' said Molly, squeezing in close beside me. 'Manifest Destiny, maybe? Could Truman have finally got his act together?'

'Unlikely,' I said. 'We'd have heard something.'

'Could be the Prime Minister,' said the Armourer. 'Expressing his displeasure at having his best secret agents sent back to him in boxes.'

'If they'd been able to capture me, then The Hall might have been next,' I said. 'But after what I did to his best bright-eyed boys, he's probably still hiding under his desk and whimpering. No. This could be any of the groups we were just discussing, keen to get their pre-emptive strikes in first. Look, save your breath for running, people. We need to know what we're getting into before we show our faces outside.'

The Operations Room was way over in the South Wing, so we were seriously short of breath by the time we got there. The halls and passageways were increasingly deserted and abandoned, eerily silent. It was a relief to get to Operations, and hear voices talking in a calm, professional way. The Ops Room is a high-tech centre designed to oversee all The Hall's defences, from sensors to shields to our various weapons systems. It took the three of us a few minutes to get through the strict security protocols, and then Molly and the Armourer and I hurried in and the great steel door hissed shut behind us, cutting off the clamour of the alarms. The quiet was a blessed relief, and I took a long deep breath to steady myself.

I'd never been to Operations before; it was mostly put together after I left home. Unlike the War Room, Operations is a much more modest affair: a reasonably sized room packed full of computers and other assorted baffling high tech, tended by a dozen or so technicians, under the Head of Operations. There was no hurry or bustle or sense of urgency here; men and women sat serenely at their work stations, doing their jobs efficiently and expertly. These people hadn't forgotten what it was to be a Drood. They kept their heads in an emergency because that was what had been drilled into them; because decisions made in this room could affect the safety of the whole family.

Holographic displays snapped on and off in mid air, showing rapidly shifting images of The Hall, inside and out, and sweeping views of the grounds and all possible approaches. I moved quickly from screen to screen, but I was damned if I could see any sign of an invading force anywhere. The skies were empty, the grounds were uninhabited, and all shields were intact and in place. Something must have set off the alarms, but what? I headed for the centre of Operations, and Molly and the Armourer fell naturally in on either side of me. I was glad to have them there. I was starting to feel well out of my depth. I listened carefully to the murmur of voices around me as the technicians spoke quietly to each other in calm, professional but utterly baffled voices.

I have rising power levels. All boards are green, all weapons systems on line.

Can anybody see anything? My sensors are clear, right across the board.

Hold it, I'm getting something. A definite Infernal presence.

Infernal? Are you sure?

Hey, it's not something you can easily confuse with anything else. There's something from the Pit, right here in our back yard.

Get ready to switch the lawn sprinklers to holy water. And somebody put in a call to our clerics.

Code Red. I repeat, we have Code Red. Shutting down unnecessary systems for the duration.

Why weren't we warned? What happened to those wonderful and very expensive new sensors I spent last week installing?

Silent as the grave, the lot of them. Whatever's out there, the sensors can't see it. Even the gryphons didn't see this coming.

Who's got my Jaffa Cakes? You know I can't function without Jaffa Cakes.

All weapons systems on line and available. Find me a target and I'll blow big meaty chunks out of it.

'Over there,' the Armourer said quietly in my ear. 'See that large, intense type in the button-down suit? That's Howard, the new Head of Operations. I used to have him down in the Armoury with me, but he didn't have the patience. But he was a hell of a lot smarter than the average Drood, so we put him here and within a year he was running the place. Oh look, he's finally deigned to notice us and he's coming over. This should be fun.'

'Didn't this use to be the old laundry?' I said.

'We contracted that out,' said the Armourer, 'to make room for this new up-to-date Operations centre. The old one was constantly having to be upgraded, and was only held together with spit and sealing wax anyway. We've spent the last ten years installing the most sophisticated weapon systems this family has ever seen, along with the computers to run them. We could hold off a whole army from here.'

'If we could see them,' I murmured.

The Armourer scowled. 'I don't understand it. The grounds are jam packed with all kinds of surveillance. A mole couldn't fart without us knowing about it. Ah, Howard! Good to see you.'

'Good?' he snapped, slamming to a halt in front of us. 'What's bloody good about it? I blame you for this, Edwin.'

'Somehow, I had a feeling you might,' I said. 'Hello, Howard.'

He sniffed loudly. He was large and blocky, with a red face and a prematurely receding hairline. His hands were clenched into frustrated fists at his sides.

'Hall security has been an utter shambles since you and your girlfriend walked straight through our best defences,' he said bitterly. 'They're very sensitive. You upset them. Took us weeks to get them calmed down and operating properly again, and now this! Are those more of your friends out there?'

'I very much doubt it,' I said. 'And Howard: keep it down to a roar when you speak to me, there's a good chap. Or I will have Molly turn you into something small and wet and squishy, which I shall then step on.'

'What am I?' said Molly. 'Your attack dog?'

'You know you love it,' I said.

'Grrr,' said Molly.

I looked back at Howard. 'Let us keep very cool and calm about this, while we figure out what the hell's going on.'

Howard sniffed loudly again. 'Yes. Well . . . We're doing the best with the equipment available to us. You try running a twenty-first century defence system on a nineteenth-century budget. I told the Matriarch to her face: you get what you pay for.'

I began to like him a little better. 'I'll bet that went down well,' I said.

He smiled slightly for the first time. 'I was escorted out of the War Room so fast my feet didn't touch the ground. All right, everybody. Let's try the sensors again. Boost the power and plug in all the options, see if we can scare up a useful image or two for our illustrious guests. As long as you understand this is all your fault, Edwin. Whatever happens.'

'Story of my life,' I said.

The Head of Operations moved quickly back and forth among his people, encouraging here, cajoling there, getting the best out of them with quiet efficiency. The Hall's defence systems sprang into life, searching for a target. There was enough firepower there to blow a hole through the moon or blast it right out of orbit. I watched, fascinated, as the holographic displays showed hundreds of guns rising up out of the wide lawns, their long barrels sweeping back and forth as the fire computers struggled to lock on. Sonic weapons, particle beams, nerve gases, stroboscopic lights and hallucinogenic mists . . . And no, we don't give a damn about the Geneva Conventions. If I'd known about this, I'd never have dared to break in . . . Of course, I'd had the Confusulum then to back me up. Hopefully, our mysterious new intruders didn't.

Howard came back to join us. His face looked even more flushed, and he'd actually unbuttoned his tie. 'We're still having problems getting a clear image of our intruders. We've narrowed down the location to somewhere near the lake, not far from the boating sheds, but something in their basic nature is confusing the hell out of the sensors.'

'I heard someone use the word "Infernal",' said Molly.

'Yes, well,' said Howard. 'That's always a worrying word to hear, isn't it? Most of our defences are scientific these days, rather than magical or mystical.'

'Then let me help,' said Molly. 'I know a lot about things Infernal.'

She moved over to the nearest work station, muttering certain unpleasant Words under her breath, and then leant past a startled technician and thrust her left hand and arm through his monitor screen. Her arm ghosted through the screen right up to the elbow, and suddenly the whole Operations Room was full of a bright otherworldly light as Molly's magic manifested in all the systems at once. Discharging energies sputtered around her like ethereal fireworks. A great surge of power swept through the work stations as her magic melded with and boosted the systems. And just like that an image appeared on the air before us, showing a crystal-clear view of two men standing together beside the lake, right in the middle of The Hall's extensive grounds. The image zoomed in to give us a close look at their faces.

'You're welcome,' said Molly.

Two ordinary-looking men. One my age, in his early thirties. Tall, pleasant enough, wire-rimmed glasses. The other was pale, dark-haired, disturbingly handsome. He appeared young enough, until you looked into his very dark eyes, and then he seemed a hell of a lot older. Just two men, standing together. No army. No obvious threat. Except they couldn't have got this far unless they were quite extraordinary people.

Howard leaned forward sharply. 'That's it! We're locked on! Stand by, people, we're going to hit them with everything we've got!'

'No, you're not,' said the Armourer. 'We need to talk to them. And besides, it wouldn't do any good.'

'What?' Howard looked at the Armourer, baffled.

'I know who they are,' said the Armourer. 'Or at least, I recognise who one of them is, and what the other one is. The one with the glasses is family.'

'Ah,' said Howard bitterly. 'I might have known. Only family could get past family defences.' He peered dubiously at the image. 'Can't say I recognise him.'

'You wouldn't,' said the Armourer. 'He hardly ever comes home. That's Harry Drood. James's only legitimate son.'

'And, unfortunately, I recognise the other guy,' I said. 'I met him once before, briefly, in the prison cells under Manifest Destiny's old headquarters. They'd imprisoned him inside a pentacle, and cut out his tongue, just in case. And he was still the most dangerous thing there. He's a half-breed demon, offspring of a succubus. I left him there to die when I brought Truman's operation crashing down around his head . . . I should have killed the unnatural thing when I had the chance.'

'You never had the chance,' said Molly. 'Half-breeds like that are very hard to kill. They may look like us, but they all have one foot in the Pit. But what's he doing here, side by side with a Drood?'

'I don't know,' I said. 'But it's not going to be anything good. Harry Drood . . . I've heard stories about him.'

'Most of them are true,' said the Armourer. 'Harry's always been one of our best field agents, if a little too independent. Not unlike you, Eddie, in many ways.'

'But why appear out of nowhere like this?' I said. 'In the company of a demon?'

'You killed his father,' said the Armourer.

'Yes,' I said. 'That's going to haunt me for the rest of my life, isn't it?'

'At least now we know how they got in,' said Howard, sounding a little more cheerful. 'No mystery any more. Our defence systems were never designed to recognise something as rare or unnatural as a half-breed hellspawn.'

'All right, Howard,' I said. 'Put the Ops Room on standby, but keep all weapons on line. Just in case Harry's invited some more friends to drop in later. But don't start anything without express instructions from me. Molly, Uncle Jack, let's go and welcome Harry home.'

'Is it okay if I take my arm out of the computer first?' said Molly.

Molly offered to teleport us to the lake, but I thought it better we take our time and walk. I didn't want Harry to think he could panic us into acting precipitously. No, let him wait. The three of us left The Hall and strolled unhurriedly across the wide expanse of open lawns towards the lake. It was a nice summer's day, warm sunshine and a pleasant breeze. Bright blue sky, with hardly any clouds. And it would have been a pleasant enough walk, if I hadn't had such a bad feeling about the coming encounter.

A Drood and a hellspawn: together? Not that long ago I would have said such a thing was impossible. But I'd learned a lot about what the family was capable of since then. Little of it good.

Molly linked her arm through mine as we walked along. She was always happier when she was out in the grounds. She was, after all, a witch of the wild woods, and the old grey stone of The Hall imposed on her free and easy nature. She chattered happily as we walked, and I did my best to go along, but both of us could tell my heart wasn't in it. My mind was ahead of us, at the lake.

'Harry Drood,' I said finally to the Armourer. 'There was a scandal about him, wasn't there?'

'Oh, yes,' said the Armourer. 'Though it was never discussed outside the Matriarch's Council. You see James only married once, and then expressly against the Matriarch's wishes. Only he could have got away with something like that. He married the infamous adventurer and freelance spy, Melanie Blaze. A very successful operative, in her own sneaky, Machiavellian and underhanded way. She and James made a great team, important players back in the sixties. Whenever you heard of a secret base being blown up or an untouchable villain being assassinated, you knew it had to be James and Melanie. Everyone admired them, even their enemies, and every Drood wanted to be them.

'James only brought Melanie home a few times. The Matriarch was very cold.

'And then Melanie disappeared into the subtle realms, on some secret mission or other, and never resurfaced. That was . . . fifteen years ago now. James went in after her several times, with and without family approval, but he never found her. He was never the same after that.'

'James was like a second father to me,' I said. 'He brought me up after my parents were killed. But I don't think I ever even met Harry.'

'Harry . . . was always very much his mother's son,' said the Armourer. 'She raised him outside The Hall. Away from the Matriarch. James visited him as much as he could, but . . . I don't know, Eddie. James and I were close, but there were some things he just wouldn't talk about. There was something going on with Melanie, or Harry, but . . . Anyway, after Melanie disappeared, James insisted we find work for Harry as a field agent, and the Matriarch kept him busy with missions in foreign climes. And like you, Eddie, Harry lived for his work and never came home.'

'I was never allowed out of the country,' I said wistfully.

'But Harry was James's son,' said the Armourer. 'And James was always Mother's favourite. Still, Harry proved to be an excellent field agent; very resourceful, always got the job done.'

'But what kind of a man is he?' said Molly.

'I have no idea,' said the Armourer. 'Harry was always . . . distant.'

'Is he James's only son?' said Molly.

'Hell, no,' said the Armourer, chuckling. 'Harry was James's only *legitimate* son, but he has any number of stepbrothers and stepsisters scattered across every country in the world, from all the woman James had . . . relationships with, down the years.'

'He never could keep it in his trousers,' I said. 'Got him into trouble more often than I care to think about.'

'James was very romantic,' the Armourer said firmly. 'Always falling in love with a pretty face, and usually living to regret it. The family has never officially recognised any of these . . . offspring, but to keep James happy we usually made arrangements to keep them gainfully employed, doing useful work for the family. On occasions when we needed more than usual distance, or deniability.'

'I thought your family didn't approve of half-breeds?' said Molly.

'We don't,' I said. 'They're never invited home, and we never send them Christmas cards. The Droods are a very old-fashioned family in some ways; but that's what happens when you've been around for centuries.'

'But it's still okay to make use of them for dangerous jobs?' said Molly.

'The family can be very pragmatic when it wants,' said the Armourer. 'That's how we've survived for centuries.'

We finally got to the lake. The dark blue-green waters stretched away before us, serene and undisturbed, the far shore so distant we couldn't even see it from where we were. There's an undine in it somewhere, but she keeps herself to herself. The first thing I noticed was that the swans were gone, presumably fled to the other end of the lake. And when I saw the two men standing on the lake shore before us, I understood why.

Harry Drood smiled briefly at the Armourer, gazed coolly at me, and nodded briskly to Molly. He looked tall and well-built in his sharply cut grey suit, and behind his wire-rimmed glasses his face had that unremarkable look that made the Droods such natural secret agents. No one looks twice at us in the street, and we like it that way. Harry was holding a dead swan by its broken neck, as though it was something he'd just happened to pick up. For an intruder and a swan-killer, he looked remarkably casual and at ease.

The half-breed demon beside him had all the calm and poise of a predator crouched and ready to launch an attack. He looked human enough, until you took in the details. He was a good six feet six tall, slender but powerfully built, with an unnaturally pale face, night-black hair and eyes, and a mouth so thin he hardly had any lips at all. He wore an Armani suit and wore it well, along with an old school tie I couldn't believe he'd come by honestly. Both his hands were thrust deep in his pockets, and he grinned at us all impartially. There was no humour in the smile; just a predator showing its teeth.

Up close, he reeked of the Pit: a sour and sickening stench of sulphur and blood. The grass beneath his feet was blackened and smouldering.

'Hello, Uncle Jack,' said Harry, in a light pleasant voice. 'I've come home. No need to prepare a fattened calf for the prodigal son; I think I'll have swan. I was always very fond of swan.'

'You might have asked first,' said the Armourer.

'But then you might have said no,' said Harry reasonably. 'And I really think I'm entitled to something special for my homecoming feast, after so long away.'

'Aren't you going to introduce your unnerving companion?' I said.

Harry smiled briefly at me. 'Oh, yes. How very rude of me. This is my good friend and companion, Roger Morningstar.'

'I know who you are, you son of a bitch,' said Molly, and her voice was very cold. 'I told you what I'd do to you if I ever saw you again.'

She threw up her arms in the stance of summoning. Dark clouds boiled in the sky overhead. Lightning bolts stabbed down, blasting the ground around Roger; but they couldn't touch him. He just stood there, smiling easily at Molly, while the rest of us dived for cover. Molly howled with fury and unleashed all the elements at once against the hellspawn.

Harry and the Armourer crouched down and scurried hurriedly out of range, while I armoured up. Hail hammered down, thick shards of ice with razor-sharp edges. I stood between Harry and the Armourer and the worst of it, protecting them as best I could. Roger wasn't harmed at all. Gale winds blew, lightning struck, hail slammed down, and Roger Morningstar stood his ground, untouched and unmoved, smiling his maddening smile.

Molly quickly exhausted herself, and was soon reduced to throwing sputtering fireballs at Roger, none of which came close to hitting him. The dark clouds drifted away, and the elements settled themselves. I moved quickly over to Molly before she could move on to more dangerous methods, armoured down and murmured calming, soothing words into her ear from a safe distance until she stopped glaring at Roger and turned sharply away, hugging herself tightly. I knew better than to bother her while she was in such a mood.

Harry and the Armourer came to join us. 'Would anyone care to explain to me what that was about?' said the Armourer a bit testily.

'We used to date,' said Roger, in a surprisingly pleasant voice.

'It was a long time ago!' said Molly, still deliberately not looking at him.

'You never thought to mention this before?' I said.

She glared at me. 'Do I quiz you about your old girlfriends?'

'Yes.'

She sniffed. 'It's different for a girl.'

'But he's a hellspawn!' I said. 'A half-breed demon!'

She shrugged. 'It's always the bad boy who makes a girl's heart beat that little bit faster.'

Some conversations you just know aren't going to go anywhere good, so I turned my attention back to Roger. 'The last time I saw you, Truman had you trapped inside one of his holding pens. With your tongue cut out.'

'And you left me there to die,' Roger said easily. 'How very Drood of you. But I escaped, amid the general chaos. No one tried to stop me. No one dared. And I grew back my tongue. We hellspawn are very hard to kill.'

'Then how was Truman able to capture and mutilate you in the first place?' I said, perhaps a little pointedly.

Roger showed his teeth again, in the smile that wasn't a smile. 'Oh please! Like I'd be foolish enough to tell you.'

'All right,' I said. 'Why are you here?'

'Revenge,' said Roger, and for a moment bright crimson flames flared in his dark eyes. 'Truman must pay for what he did to me . . . but even I can't hope to take down an organisation the size of Manifest Destiny on my own. Which means I need allies, and your family seems the best bet. You want them destroyed almost as much as I do; and the enemy of my enemy can be my ally, if not my friend.'

'You expect us to trust you?' said the Armourer.

'Of course not. But as long as we have a cause in common, it's in my best interests to be useful to you.'

'And he's with me,' said Harry, very firmly. He was standing beside Roger again, as though he belonged there. 'Roger and I go way back; old friends, old allies.'

'Dear Jesus,' said the Armourer. He sounded honestly shocked. 'What have you been doing, Harry, what depths have you sunk to, that you could even consider befriending a thing of the Pit?'

'When your family turns its back on you, you have to find your friends where you can,' said Harry. 'Right, Eddie? Now; no *welcome home* for me, Uncle Jack? After these long years away, serving the family faithfully and well in foreign climes, with never even a *thank you* in return?'

'You could have come home any time,' said the Armourer. 'The Matriarch might not have been too happy about it, but your father and I would have stood by you. We told you, we both told you often enough. But you always had some excuse or another.'

'I'm here now, Uncle Jack. Because of my father.'

'You heard,' I said.

'Of course I heard. The whole world knows you murdered my father, dear cousin Eddie. So here I am, representing the Grey Fox's old friends, allies, lovers and enemies, all of us very upset that the legendary James Drood is dead. We want to know why. We demand answers.'

'It was a duel,' I said simply. 'Armour to armour. He fought well, and died honourably.'

I didn't even glance at Molly. Her part in James's death was no one's business but our own.

Harry looked at me, his head cocked slightly on one side. 'That's it? That's all you have to say?'

'That's all there is,' I said. 'I was at war with my family, and he got in the way.'

'Then . . . you didn't murder my father and take away everyone's torcs so you could take over the family and run it unopposed?'

'No,' I said calmly. 'It wasn't like that.'

'It really wasn't,' said the Armourer. 'He's telling the truth, Harry. Don't you think I would have avenged my brother by now, if I thought he needed avenging?'

'Well, well,' said Harry. 'How very intriguing. I can see I shall have to investigate further. Either way, I have come home at last, with my good friend Roger, to serve the family in its hour of need. Tell me how grateful you all are.'

'We can always use another experienced field agent,' I said. 'But the hellspawn . . .'

'Please, call me Roger.'

'Don't trust him, Eddie,' said Molly, at my side again. 'You can't trust anything he says. Hell always lies; except when a truth can hurt you more.'

'I'll say it again, for the benefit of the hard of thinking at the back,' said Harry. 'Roger is with me. I vouch for him, and guarantee his behaviour while he's here at The Hall. And he does have a right to be here. He's family, like me.'

'What?' said the Armourer. 'Have you lost your mind, Harry? How can a thing of the Pit be family?'

'Because we share the same father,' said Harry.

Roger smiled widely. 'Mother was a succubus, my father the illustrious James Drood. How about a big family hug?'

The Armourer shook his head slowly, dully, as though he'd been slapped hard. He looked suddenly older and frailer. I have to say, it took my breath away. I glanced at Molly, but she shrugged to show it was news to her too.

'That's right,' Harry said brightly. 'Roger is my stepbrother. And your nephew, Uncle Jack.'

'The old Grey Fox really did put it about,' said Molly. 'But even so, a succubus? That's . . . tacky.'

'Lust demons are aristocrats in Hell,' said Roger. 'Gathered souls are currency, in the Pit.'

'Shut up,' said the Armourer. 'Just shut up.'

'Yes, Uncle,' said Roger.

'It's funny how Roger and I first met,' said Harry. 'That was down to the family. Father and I were working together on a mission, as we often did when we ended up in the same part of the world at the same time. We were in Paris, tracking down that legendary thief and assassin, the Fantom, and Father took me to a certain little out-of-the-way nightclub on the West Bank, where information of all sorts could be found with a little effort. Grimy little place, called the Plus

Ça Change . . . And that's where I met Roger. We got to chatting, while Father beat the necessary information out of a bunch of biker *loups garous,* and the two of us got on famously. Father and I never did catch up with the Fantom, but Roger and I kept in touch.'

'Then welcome home, Harry,' I said. 'And you too, Roger. Come back to The Hall with us, and we'll see you settled in. But get out of hand even once, either of you, and I will knock you down and riverdance on your head.'

'It's only tough love,' Harry said to Roger. 'You'll get used to it. It's the Drood way. How is the dear old Sarjeant-At-Arms, Eddie?'

'Still running things with an iron fist in an iron glove,' I said, not rising to the bait. 'Come along, and bring your swan with you, Harry. Waste not, want not.'

'Good to be home, Eddie,' said Harry. 'Can't say I've ever felt this welcome before. I suppose you and I have that in common, at least. We never were our family's favourite sons.'

There were snorting, coughing sounds, and we both looked round. The gryphons had tracked us down at last, and ambled over to check out the newcomers with a good sniffing. Harry tolerated it in a resigned sort of way, and then the gryphons turned to Roger. They didn't like his smell at all, and growled at him in deep rumbling voices. One actually snapped at him, and Roger kicked it in the ribs, sending it flying a dozen feet away. I moved quickly to stand between him and the gryphons.

'Don't,' I said.

'Or?' he said.

It was a blatant challenge, and one I had to meet if I was to have any authority at The Hall. I subvocalised the Words, and armoured up in a moment, the silver strange matter flowing over me like a second skin. I made a silver fist and held it up before Roger's face. And as he watched, I grew thick silver spikes out of the knuckles. Roger surged forward inhumanly quickly, his fingers like claws, his impossibly wide smile full of teeth like a shark's. I stood my ground and punched him in the face with all my armoured strength. The blow stopped him dead in his tracks, the sheer force of the impact slamming his head back so hard it would have broken an ordinary man's neck. Roger staggered backwards, and then quickly recovered his balance. He shook his head slowly, and put a hand to his face.

His nose was broken, though no blood flowed. Roger gripped the broken nose with his left hand and snapped it into place with a painful-sounding click. I winced at the sound, and I'm sure I wasn't the only one.

'Show off,' Harry said easily to Roger. 'Now behave yourself. I guaranteed your behaviour, remember? You want to make me look bad?'

'Of course. I'm sorry, Harry.' Roger smiled briefly at me. 'It won't happen again. No hard feelings, I trust?'

I armoured down, and looked at him, and then at Harry. It occurred to me that the two of them might have set this up in advance, just to see what the new armour could do . . . Tricky, underhanded, and just a little paranoid. They were Droods, after all.

'Let's go back to The Hall,' said the Armourer. 'It's getting cold out here.'

CHAPTER FOUR
Sons and lovers

'It's good to have you home again, Harry,' said the Armourer. And your . . . friend. Come with me, and I'll find you a place to stay. Don't quite know where I'm going to put you, though. The Hall is so crowded these days you couldn't swing a cat without taking someone's eye out.'

'We could always put them in the dungeons,' I said.

The Armourer looked at me coldly. 'You know very well we don't have dungeons any more, Eddie. They were converted into billiards rooms long ago.'

'You have billiards here?' said Molly, brightening up.

'Oh, yes,' I said. 'They're very popular. In fact, you have to queue to get in.'

'One more joke like that, and I'll rack your balls,' said Molly.

'What's wrong with putting me in my father's old room?' said Harry. 'The Matriarch hasn't got around to reassigning it yet, has she? Thought not. Dear Grandmother always was very sentimental . . . where her son was concerned. And who has a better right to the Grey Fox's room, than his only legitimate son?'

'Well, yes . . . I suppose so,' said the Armourer. 'Yes, James would approve. Come along with me, Harry, and . . . Roger, and I'll get you settled in.'

'See you later, cousin Eddie,' said Harry.

'Yes,' I said. 'You will.'

The Armourer led the two of them away across the lawns and towards The Hall. Molly and I watched them go, while the gryphons wandered back to crouch beside us, snorting and growling unhappily. I patted a few heads and tugged a few ears, and they wandered off again, content enough. It bothered me that they hadn't been able to predict Harry and Roger's arrival in advance. Made me wonder what else the hellspawn might be able to hide from us.

'And this was starting out to be such a good day,' I said finally. 'Now Harry's back itching for a chance to stick a knife in my back, and if that weren't enough he's brought a half-breed demon with him. I mean, I'm not prejudiced, but . . . dammit, he's a thing from Hell!' I looked at Molly. 'Did you really go out with him?'

'Not one more word out of you, Eddie,' she said coldly. 'Or you will never see me naked again.'

We went to my room in The Hall. I felt an urgent need for a little down time. When I decided I was going to have to move back into The Hall, so I could keep a proper eye on things, I had to decide where I was going to stay. My old room was long gone, give over to someone else in the family when I left to be a field agent. (Crying *Free! Free at last!* all the way.) And it wasn't like I had any fond memories of the poky little garret room. Too hot in the summer, too cold in the winter, and every time the wind blew in the night I had to get out of bed and jam a handkerchief into the gap between the window and the frame to stop it from rattling. (The family has never believed in central heating; makes you soft.)

Since I was running the family now, I could have taken any room I fancied. I could have thrown the Matriarch out of her special suite, and no one would have stopped me. But I didn't have the heart. It would have been cruel . . . to Alistair. *You big softy*, Molly said later, when I told her, but she was only partly right. Even then I knew I didn't want to make an enemy of Martha Drood, because I might need her help . . .

In the end, I chose one of the better situated rooms in the West Wing, and booted out the poor beggar who was living there. He in turn picked someone lower down on the food chain and evicted them, and moved into their room. And so it went, for several days, until you couldn't move in the corridors for people hauling their belongings from one room to another. Presumably the poor bastard at the bottom of the pile ended up moving into the communal dormitory with the children.

(There are no guest rooms in The Hall. Only family gets to live in The Hall.)

Even so, Molly wasn't especially impressed when she saw where she'd be staying with me. She couldn't get her head round the fact that members of the most powerful family in the world only got one room to live in. But that's what happens when a family's numbers expand faster than we can build on new wings. Another generation or two, and we'll have to find or build a new home; but no one was ready to talk about that yet.

I let us into our room, and Molly immediately ran over to the bed and threw herself on to it. She sank half out of sight into the deep goosefeather mattress, and sighed blissfully.

'Still don't care much for the room, but I do love this bed. I feel like I could sink all the way down to China.'

'What's wrong with the room?' I said patiently.

'Far too much like an hotel room,' Molly said. 'Very luxurious, I'm sure, but it has no character. It's . . . cold, impersonal.'

I smiled at her. 'When did you ever stay in hotels, O wicked witch of the woods?'

She wriggled cosily on the bed. 'Oh, I get around. You'd be surprised, some of the places I've been. And it's not like I can take my forest everywhere with me . . . Still, I'll say this for hotels. I love room service. You pick up the phone and they bring you food, every hour of the day and night. I always pig out at hotels. Particularly because I never stick around to pay the bills . . .'

'There's no room service to be had here,' I said sternly. 'And you're expected to clean up your own mess. There are no servants among the Droods; or at least, not as such. We're encouraged from an early age to look after ourselves. Builds character, and self-reliance.'

'How very worthy,' said Molly. 'Let it be clearly understood between us that I do not do worthy. Was this really the best room you could have chosen, out of all those available?'

'I chose this room because it used to be my parents',' I said. 'Back when I was a child. I can just about remember visiting them here. It's hard to be sure. Memories from that age are never reliable. My mother and father weren't often here, you see; as field agents they lived outside The Hall.'

'And you weren't allowed to live with them?' said Molly, sitting up and propping her back against the wooden headboard.

'No. All Drood children are raised in the dormitories so they can be properly trained and indoctrinated. Loyalty is to the family, not our parents.'

'Harry wasn't raised here,' Molly said.

'No. Which gives you some idea of how much the Matriarch disapproved of Uncle James marrying an unsuitable without permission woman. Anyone else would have been declared rogue.'

'I like the furnishings and fittings,' said Molly, tactfully changing the subject. 'Everything in here's an antique, but in splendid condition. Hey, if there aren't any servants here, who polishes the wood and brass?'

'We take turns, when we're young,' I said. 'Character building, remember? I hated it. I can still remember my hands going numb from the cold as I cleaned the outside windows in the depths of winter, because the water in the bucket always went cold before you were finished. And don't even get me started about trying to scrub brass with Duraglit when you can't feel your fingers . . . Bugger character building. All it taught me was never to own anything made of brass, and be sure to tip my window cleaners very generously.'

'Feel free to vent, Eddie,' said Molly. 'Don't hold anything back.'

'At least I talk about my past,' I said pointedly.

'Oh look,' said Molly. 'I'm changing the subject again. I like the television. That is one seriously big fuckoff widescreen television. And five speakers for surround sound . . . Cool.'

'Only the best for the family,' I said. 'But I wouldn't have thought you watched much television in the woods.'

'I'm a witch, not a barbarian. I like the cooking shows. Love *Masterchef*. I suppose you watch the sci-fi channels?'

'No,' I said. 'I like to leave my work behind when I relax. I prefer the comedy channels.'

Molly hugged her knees to her chest and looked at me thoughtfully.

'What are we doing here, Eddie? Why are we hiding out in your room?'

'Not hiding,' I said. 'It's just . . . sometimes it gets a bit too much for me, and then I need to get away from it all. I took on running this family because I had to. But . . . I don't know what I'm doing. I lived alone for ten years, and never had to worry about anyone else. Now I have all these people depending on me, and looking to me for answers and decisions that will shape the rest of their lives. I don't want to let them down.'

'They let you down,' said Molly.

'They're still keeping secrets from me,' I said. 'Harry's only the latest. And he's all I need: a rival pretender for the throne.'

'He hates you because he believes you killed his father,' said Molly. 'He doesn't know I killed James Drood.'

'No one can ever know that! It's one thing for me to kill him in a duel; I'm family. But you're an outsider. They'd kill you on the spot if they even suspected. And me too, for hiding the truth and daring to care more about you than the family.'

Molly smiled at me. 'Every now and again, you remind me of why I fell for you so hard. Come over here and sit down beside me.'

I sat down on the bed, by her side, and we put our arms around each other and snuggled close, and for a long time we didn't want to say anything.

'You are allowed to hold me, when you're feeling down, you know,' said Molly. 'It's allowed, when you're in a relationship.'

'So we are definitely in one of those relationship things, are we?' I said.

'Yeah. It sneaked up on me when I wasn't looking. You can squeeze my boobies, if you like.'

'Good to know.'

'Roger and I were never close,' she said, not looking at me. 'And we weren't together long. It was at the time in a girl's life when she really feels like being mistreated by someone big and rough. Even though you know it's bound to end in tears.'

'And did it?'

'Oh, yes. I caught him in bed with my best friend. And her brother. Something of an eye-opener . . . I set the bed on fire while they were still in it, and walked out on him. I'm pretty sure I never really loved him. It was . . . one of those things, you know?'

'I once had a brief relationship with a sex android from the twenty-third century,' I said. 'Damn, but we've known some interesting times, haven't we?'

We laughed together quietly. Our bodies moved easily against each other. I never really felt at home, the way I did in Molly's arms. Like I'd finally found out where I was supposed to be.

'Never leave me,' I said suddenly.

'Where did that come from?' said Molly.

'I don't know. I just need to hear you say it. Say it for me, Molly.'

'I will never leave you, Eddie. I'll always be with you, for ever and ever and ever. Now you say it.'

'I will love you every day of my life, Molly Metcalf, and after I die, if you're not there in Heaven with me, I will go down to Hell to join you. Because Heaven wouldn't be Heaven without you.'

'You smooth-talking devil, Eddie Drood.'

Some time later, when I'd got my second wind, I dressed again and opened the bag I'd brought from my London flat. I set about distributing my few possessions around the room. It didn't take long. A row of CDs on one shelf, my favourite books lined up on another. In alphabetical order, of course. I'm very strict about things like that. And some favourite clothes that didn't even come close to filling the massive mahogany wardrobe. I looked at Molly, who was attacking her tousled hair in the mirror.

'Don't you have any clothes you want to hang up? Women always have clothes. And shoes . . . and things.'

She shrugged easily. 'Whenever I get bored I magic up a new outfit. I only have to see something I like, and I can duplicate it with a thought. I've never paid for a new outfit in my life, and they always fit perfectly. I've been recycling the same material for years.'

I hope you take time out to wash it now and again, I thought, but had enough sense not to say out loud.

I stepped back and looked at my possessions scattered around the room. They looked . . . sort of lost. They were present-day, transitory things in a room that had been here before I was born and would still be here after I was gone. There weren't any of my parents' old possessions still here. They would have been thrown out or redistributed long ago, when the next occupant moved in. The family has never encouraged sentiment. We aren't supposed to care about possessions, because only the family is important. Look forward, never back. And never get too attached to anything or anyone; because the enemy will use that against you.

They don't tell you the enemy sometimes includes the family.

'Don't you want to bring anything here from your old place?' I said to Molly.

She shrugged lazily. 'I have my magical iPod, full of my favourite music. Endless capacity, no batteries to run down, and it can pick up any tune from any period. It can even sing harmonies with me on karaoke nights. But that's it, really. I've never cared much about *things*. You can always get more things . . . With my magic I've raised beg, borrow and steal to an art form.'

'So,' I said. 'What do you think of the infamous Drood family home, now you've been here for a while? Is it everything you thought it would be?'

'All that and more,' said Molly. 'It's certainly . . . impressive.'

'You don't like it,' I said, and was surprised at how disappointed I sounded.

'Don't be upset, sweetie,' said Molly. She came over and slipped an arm round my waist. 'It just isn't me, that's all. I feel . . . shut in, oppressed, all the time I'm inside. I'm the spirit of the wild woods, remember? I need nature, and open space, and room to breathe! Not this dead wood and cold stone.'

'You don't mind hotels.'

'Only because I know I can walk out of them whenever I feel like it. I'm stuck here, with you. Not that I don't want to be with you, I do, I do, but—'

'We have extensive grounds,' I said. 'You could walk in them all day and night, and still not see everything there is to see. And you know I wouldn't want to keep you here if you were unhappy.'

'Of course I know that, Eddie!' She kissed me quickly. 'This is coming out all wrong. I want to be with you, and you have to be here. I know that.'

'We won't always have to be here. As soon as the new Council's ready to take over running things, I will demote myself to field agent and be out of here so fast that anyone watching will end up with whiplash.'

'But how long will that take, Eddie?'

'I don't know. It'll take . . . as long as it takes. Molly—'

'Hush. It's all right. We'll work something out.'

'Yes,' I said. 'We will.'

And all the time I was thinking, *If she couldn't stay here . . . If she left, would I go with her? And leave my family to tear itself apart? Risk the whole future of Humanity, because I left my job unfinished? Would I damn the world, to be with her? Would I do that? Could I do that?*

In the end she let go first, and went to check the state of her make-up in the bedside hand mirror.

'So,' she said brightly. 'What's the story with the Time Train?'

'I was hoping you'd forgotten about that,' I said.

'Is it really a time machine?'

'Oh, yes. Well, sort of. It started out as someone's pet project. Sooner or later every Armourer gets a bee in his bonnet about something . . . some favourite theory, some great idea they're convinced will make their name immortal within the family. If they can just convince the Matriarch to fund it. One guy was convinced he could build a bomb powerful enough to blow up the whole world.'

'What happened?' said Molly, fascinated.

'When the Matriarch couldn't make him see what a really bad idea that was, she had him put in suspended animation.'

'Why not kill him?'

'Because someday we might need a bomb powerful enough to destroy the whole world.'

Molly shuddered. 'Your family can be downright scary sometimes, Eddie. So the Time Train is one of these obsessions, is it?'

'Pretty much. I don't think we've used the thing a dozen times in the two centuries since it was constructed.'

'Why not?' said Molly. 'I mean, I can think of a dozen really good uses for a time machine, any one of which could make us impossibly rich.'

'Thought you didn't care about things?'

'It's the principle of it.'

'It's not that simple,' I said. 'The possibilities for really appalling cock-ups, disasters, tragedies and paradoxes are enough to give anyone nightmares. Don't even ask me how the Time Train works, or I'll start to whimper. Time travel, theory and practice, make my head hurt. Do me a favour, Molly, and change the subject again.'

'All right . . . Let's talk about the people we suggested bringing in as tutors. And don't pull a face like that, Eddie Drood. The wind might change and then you'd be stuck that way. You know we have to discuss this.'

'Only because my choices were sane and practical, and you chose two monsters!'

'They are not monsters! Or at least, not all the time. And really, Eddie. Sane and practical? Yeah, right. Janissary Jane has a good reputation as a fighter, especially when she's got a few drinks in her, but let's be real about this: she is way past her prime.'

'She's a veteran demon fighter,' I said. 'Do you have any idea how rare that is? She's been killing demons for longer than most demon fighters live. There's a lot she could teach us, if we can persuade her to come here.'

'All right. What about the Blue Fairy?' Molly pulled a sour face. 'He's weak, Eddie, and always will be. And he's a risk. He's a half-elf, and you can never trust an elf. They always have a hidden agenda. Believe me, I know.'

I raised an eyebrow. 'Are you about to tell me of another old boyfriend?'

'An elf? Please!' Molly shuddered theatrically. 'I'd sew it up first.'

'Pushing that unexpected mental image firmly to one side,' I said, 'my choices are defendable. Yours are completely unacceptable. I mean, come on . . . a psycho killer and a luck vampire?'

'They've been good friends to me,' Molly said firmly. 'And they can tell your family about a world they know nothing of. Weren't you the one who said that there was more to this world than just good guys and bad guys? Subway Sue and Mr Stab can open your family's eyes to a whole new way of looking at things. That is what you wanted, isn't it? To break wide open the Droods' narrow world view and teach them new ways of thinking? Like I did with you?'

'Well, yes, but—'

'No buts. They'll make excellent tutors. As long as they're watched carefully. And maybe even excellent warriors in our upcoming war against the demons.'

'If Mr Stab even looks at a girl in a way I don't like, I will kill him,' I said.

'You can try,' said Molly. 'And trust me, I'll kill that Roger bloody Morningstar first chance I get. You should never have allowed him inside your home. I don't care what he says, or who vouches for him; his first allegiance will always be to Hell.'

'Don't worry,' I said. 'He won't be here long. The family doesn't allow outsiders to move into The Hall.'

'I'm an outsider,' said Molly.

'But you're with me. We're a couple, sharing a room. Such things are . . . accepted, if officially frowned upon. Provided you're senior enough to get away with it.'

'The more I learn about your family, the less I like it,' said Molly.

'You see?' I said. 'We have so much in common. Come on, let's get out of The Hall for a while and away from the bloody family and its demands.'

'Right,' said Molly. 'We'll pick up the tutors. They're going to take some persuading to come here, and who can be more persuasive than us?'

'Exactly,' I said. 'I need to look in on Harry first, before we leave. I want to make it very clear what will happen to him if he tries to stir up trouble for me with the family while I'm away.'

'You really think a few harsh words are going to stop him?' said Molly.

'No, but hopefully it will make him think twice, and by then we should be back again. Especially if I remind him that I have a torc, and he doesn't.'

Molly considered me. 'Are you planning on giving him one of the new torcs?'

'Of course,' I said. 'He's James's son, and an excellent field agent in his own right. The family needs experienced men like him. But I don't think I'll tell him that, just yet.'

'And what if, after he gets his torc, he challenges you to a duel for the leadership of the family? What if he doesn't even bother with a challenge, and just ambushes you?'

'Oh, I don't think he'd do that.'

'Why not? He hangs around with a hellspawn!'

'Yes, but he's a Drood. The family would never accept a back-stabber as leader and he knows it.'

Molly sighed. 'You have such faith in your family, Eddie. Even after all the things they've done to you.'

'The Droods are good people at heart. We're trained from childhood to fight the good fight. We . . . lost our way, that's all. And Harry does have an excellent reputation. If he can do a better job than me as leader, let him. I'd be quite happy to stand down and go back to my old job as field agent, with no responsibilities to anyone save myself.'

'You really think he'd let you go?'

I grinned. 'He will if he knows what's good for him.'

Molly laughed, and hugged me hard. 'That's my Eddie! You could be the most powerful man in the world running the most powerful organisation in the world – and you really would give it all up, wouldn't you?'

'First chance I got,' I said. 'I never wanted any of this. I've always had issues with authority figures. I certainly never wanted to be one. All I want is you, and a life for us together.'

She kissed me, and then pushed me away. 'Go and talk to Harry. I'll have a wander round the grounds. Where shall we meet?'

'At the Armoury, in an hour,' I said. 'If we're going after Janissary Jane, the Blue Fairy, Subway Sue and Mr Stab . . . I want to be really well armed.'

I checked with the Sarjeant-At-Arms to make sure Harry had ended up where he was supposed to be, in Uncle James's old room. The Sarjeant always knows where everyone is. That's part of his job. The Sarjeant allowed that the new arrival was indeed in the Grey Fox's old room. He seemed to find that appropriate, but I could tell something was on his mind.

'Something's bothering you, Sarjeant,' I said. 'Don't you approve of Harry returning home at last?'

'He seems a pleasant enough gentleman,' the Sarjeant said slowly. 'But his . . . companion, that's something else. Never thought I'd live to see the day when we allowed a hellspawn under our roof.'

'Harry vouches for him,' I said. 'As is his right. But feel free to keep a very watchful eye on anything Roger Morningstar gets up to while he's here.'

The Sarjeant nodded. 'Like I needed you to tell me that, boy.'

'Don't push your luck, Cyril. What can you tell me about Harry?'

'Nothing you don't already know.'

'My Uncle James never spoke about him to you?'

'No. He never did. The Grey Fox never discussed his relationships outside the family.'

'Did you ever know James's wife, Melanie Blaze?'

The Sarjeant's mouth twitched briefly in something that might almost have been a smile. 'I had the honour of meeting that lady on a few occasions. A most remarkable personage.'

I waited, but that was all he had to say. I nodded to the Sarjeant, and he turned and walked briskly away. I shrugged, and made my way through the winding corridors of the West Wing to what used to be Uncle James's room. I spent a lot of time there when I was younger, enjoying his company when he was resting at home in between assignments. In many ways, he was the father I never had. I was like a son to him; so why did he never talk to me about his real son, Harry?

I was so preoccupied with my thoughts that I didn't think to knock; just opened the door and barged right in, like I used to when it was Uncle James's room. And then I crashed to a halt as I saw Harry Drood and Roger Morningstar. They were together, in each other's arms. They were kissing. They broke apart immediately, and stared coldly at me, standing shoulder to shoulder. I turned unhurriedly, and closed the door carefully behind me.

'You really should learn to lock your door around here,' I said.

'You saw,' said Harry.

'Yes,' I said. 'I saw.'

'Are you going to tell everyone?'

'Why should I?' I said. It's no one's business but your own.'

'If you were to inform the Matriarch,' Harry said slowly, 'and the family . . . You know they'd never accept me as their leader. The family is very old-fashioned about some things.'

'That's their problem,' I said. 'I don't give a damn. Is this why you never came home?'

Harry and Roger looked at each other and relaxed slightly. Harry took Roger's hand and squeezed it reassuringly.

'This . . . is why my father never spoke to you about me,' said Harry. 'Though he often spoke to me about you. He had great faith in you, Eddie. Said you had it in you to be as great a field agent as him. He never said that about me, even though I tried so hard to impress him. He was everything I ever wanted to be . . . But he could never come to terms with the fact that his only legitimate son was gay. It meant so much to him, you see, to continue his line within the family. And for that he needed a legitimate child . . . The Droods have always been very big on bloodlines. The Matriarch gave him hell for marrying my mother. You can imagine what she would have said if she'd ever found out about me.

'To be fair, he could have disowned me, but he didn't. But it meant we were never as close as we might have been. And it meant he could never allow me to come home. No one from the family could ever know that the famous womaniser James Drood had sired a bum boy. He had his reputation to think of.'

'He protected you,' I said.

'Yes,' said Harry. 'But he never accepted me.'

'Look,' I said. 'I don't give a wet slap whether you're gay or not. But I have to ask: how can Roger be your . . . partner when he's also your stepbrother?'

Harry smiled crookedly. 'If his being a hellspawn doesn't bother me, why should anything else? We knew we were meant for each other the moment we met in that awful little nightclub in Paris.'

'Even hellspawn have hearts,' said Roger.

'You stink of the Pit,' I said bluntly. 'He's a demon, Harry. You can't trust him or anything he says. Demons don't love anyone. They can't.'

'I'm only half demon,' said Roger. 'I'm half human. And very bothersome that can be, at times. I have all the usual run of human emotions, though I never let them get in the way before. I was there in that nightclub on purpose, sent to seduce Harry, as a way of getting at James and through him the Droods . . . but instead our eyes met, and that was that. I was in love, much to my alarm. We fell for each other right then and there, and we've never been apart since.'

'Are you complaining?' Harry said fondly.

'No,' said Roger. 'Never. But it does mean I can never go home again. They'd never understand.'

'I know the feeling,' said Harry, and squeezed Roger's hand.

'You can't trust him, Harry,' I said, trying my best to get through to him. 'He's a hellspawn! They lie like they breathe. It's natural to them!'

'I don't trust anyone,' Harry said flatly. 'Not this family, and least of all the man who murdered my father.'

'It wasn't murder,' I said. 'It was a fair fight. Neither of us wanted it, but—'

'Yes,' said Harry. 'It always comes down to the family, doesn't it, and the awful things we do because of it. Tell me this much at least: tell me my father died well.'

'Of course he did,' I said. 'He went down fighting to the last.'

Harry looked at me, his head cocked slightly to one side. 'There's something you're not telling me, Cousin Eddie.'

'There's a lot of things I'm not telling you,' I said. 'I keep my secrets to myself. So should you. I won't tell the family you're gay . . .'

'How very noble of you,' said Roger.

'But the longer you two stick around together, the sooner someone will realise. And the holding hands is a dead give-away.'

Harry glanced down at the hand holding Roger's, but didn't let go.

'Thank you for the kind advice, Cousin Eddie. And your reticence on our behalf. More than I had any right to expect from you, I'm sure. But don't make the mistake of thinking that we're ever going to be friends.'

'I'll settle for allies,' I said. 'We're going to have to find a way to work together, in the bad times that are coming. For the good of the family, and the world.'

'Oh, of course,' said Harry. 'Anything, for the family.'

CHAPTER FIVE

These two baby seals walk into a club . . .

Visiting the family Armourer is always an interesting experience, and often an excellent chance to test how good your reflexes are. There's always something loud and noisy going on, usually of an explosive nature, and how productive a visit you have can depend on your ability to duck and cover at speed. So when I went to visit the Armoury, set deep in the bedrock under The Hall (so that when things inevitably go wrong at least the rest of the family will be protected from the awful consequences), my first surprise was how quiet and peaceful everything seemed. The Armoury is basically a long series of connected stone chambers, packed to bursting with equipment, work benches and testing areas. And its own adjoining Infirmary, just in case.

The place seemed busy enough. Interns in stained lab coats clustered around computers and chalked pentacles, chattering animatedly with each other as they designed new terrible things to unleash on the enemies of Humanity. One young man with recent scorch marks on his coat was working industriously on a portable lightning generator, while another was cautiously testing an aerosol that could spray plague in any chosen direction. Judging by the look of him, he was having problems with blowbacks. Giving him plenty of room, I moved on, and then looked up to see an intern walking upside down across the high stone ceiling, using boots that stuck to the stone. He waved cheerfully to those watching from below, and then one foot slipped right out of the boot and he was left dangling precariously from the one still stuck to the ceiling. He called piteously for help, and another intern, with what I fervently hoped were only temporary bat wings sprouting from her back, fluttered up to assist him.

Meanwhile, half a dozen interns with the same face stood together in a tight circle, arguing fiercely over who was the original, and who were the clones. And one guy sat giggling inside a glass pyramid while an endless stream of butterflies flew out of his nose. Just another day in the Armoury, basically.

So why did the whole place seem so . . . subdued? No sudden bangs or fires or clouds of poisonous gas drifting on the air . . . I strode through the Armoury, stepping carefully over clumps of colour-coded wires and the occasional exploded test animal, and finally spotted the Armourer himself, sitting hunched over a work bench, as usual. He was tinkering with some new gadget, trying to make it do what it was supposed to do through a combination of craft, genius, bullying and bad language. He looked round as I sat down beside him.

'This is your fault, you know. This unnatural peace and quiet. It's the lack of torcs; makes my interns far too cautious. I haven't had any real work out of them since they started worrying about consequences. We need those new torcs down here, Eddie.'

'Then make sure the list is ready for me when I get back,' I said patiently. 'I'll see that everyone who needs one gets one.'

The Armourer looked at me sharply. 'Get back? What do you mean, get back? You're not off again, are you? You haven't been home ten minutes!'

'I find my family is best appreciated in small doses,' I said solemnly.

'Yes, well, there is that,' said the Armourer. 'But while the cat's away, you may find the rats getting damned uppity. It's only your presence and example that's holding this family together in these troubled times. And now that Harry's back . . .'

'Don't worry about Harry,' I said. 'I can handle him, if I have to.'

'Oh, good,' said Molly, strolling over to join us and kicking a wandering dodo out of the way. 'Does that mean we don't need to be nice to Roger any more, and I'm free to kill him in slow, horrible and innovative ways?'

'You really do nurse a grudge, don't you?' I said.

'You have no idea,' said Molly.

'I was telling Uncle Jack that we're off to look up a few old friends,' I said. 'You ready to go?'

'Of course. Are you?'

'Not quite.' I turned back to the Armourer. 'We could use some of your latest gadgets and dirty tricks on this one. What have you got?'

'Ah,' said the Armourer, brightening up. He was always happiest when discussing new methods of murder and mayhem. 'I might have a few new things that will chill and thrill you, only waiting for some brave soul to test them in the field.'

'Hold it,' said Molly, peering over the Armourer's shoulder. 'What is that you're working on there?'

He scowled. 'It's supposed to go bang. And it doesn't.' He picked up a large lump hammer and hit the black box before him. Molly and I both flinched, and I wrestled the lump hammer away from the Armourer and put it down safely out of reach. His scowl deepened. 'You have to teach technology to respect you! It needs to know who's in charge!'

'You can try again later,' I said. 'When we're both safely out of range. Now, tell me about your new gadgets.'

'Yes, well . . . To start with, you'd better have this.' He took a heavy sheaf of handwritten papers out of his desk drawer and gave them to me. 'This is your instruction manual for Merlin's Glass. Don't let anyone else see it. I wrote it out in longhand so there'd be no record in the computers. Something this powerful needs to be kept strictly confidential.'

'There's over forty pages here,' I said feebly.

And more to come,' said the Armourer. 'The damned thing's full of extra options, many of which I don't fully understand. Yet. Typical Merlin; couldn't just make the Glass he was asked for, had to show off . . . These are just the options I've identified so far, along with the activating Words. And don't go experimenting, Eddie; the thing's probably full of booby traps for the unwary. It's what I would have done. And Merlin Satanspawn was apparently renowned for his strange and unpleasant sense of humour.'

'You sure he wasn't a Drood?' I said, thumbing quickly through the pages.

'Pay attention, Eddie. The two most useful options are these: the Glass can see everywhere in the Present, as well as the Past and the Future, and it can also be used as a door, for immediate transport to anywhere in the world. Just tell it where you want to go, tug at the frame till it's big enough and then step through.'

I gave up on the pages, folded them neatly and stuffed them into an inside pocket of my jacket. 'Thank you, Uncle Jack. I'm sure it'll be very helpful. But I was hoping for something a bit more . . . aggressive.'

'Hold everything,' said Molly. 'If the Glass can show us scenes from absolutely everywhere in the Present, we can use it to spy on people in the shower, or on the toilet! Maybe even take incriminating photographs! The possibilities for blackmail are endless!'

'You can take the witch out of the wood . . .' murmured the Armourer.

'Let's test it!' said Molly. 'Go on, you know you want to.'

I took the silver-framed hand mirror out of my pocket, and hefted it thoughtfully. 'I suppose we should try it out, in the spirit of scientific enquiry. Just to make sure it can do what it's supposed to do.'

'That's my boy!' the Armourer said cheerfully.

I sighed. 'You are both such a bad influence on me.'

I used the activating Words I'd memorised from the pages, and ordered the Glass to show me what the Matriarch was doing, right then. Molly and the Armourer crowded in on either side of me as we stared into the Glass. Our reflections became dim and uncertain, and then were suddenly replaced by a view of the Matriarch's bed-chamber. It was as though we were watching from some place by the door, unseen and unsuspected. Martha was sitting on a chair beside the bed, ignoring Alistair, who stared up at the ceiling, making low dreamy sounds. Presumably there had been a heavy dose of something in the soup. The Matriarch's bedroom was still full of friends and supporters, but now she had new guests: Harry and the Sarjeant-At-Arms. I wasn't really surprised to see either of them. Harry, because he needed support if he was to establish a new power base inside the family, and the Sarjeant because I'd always known which way his sympathies went, even before I invited him into my Inner Circle. Keep your friends close, and your enemies closer; especially when they're family.

No Roger, though. Presumably Harry was hoping out of sight would mean out of mind. The three of us stared into the hand mirror, watching and listening silently as the voices in the room came clearly to us from far away.

'Hello, Grandmother,' said Harry, leaning over to kiss her offered hand. 'It's been a while, hasn't it?'

'There were reasons,' said the Matriarch. 'As well you know. But you are here now, back where you belong, and that is all that matters. It is good to see you again, Harold. You have your father's looks . . .'

'And my mother's, so I'm told,' said Harry.

The Matriarch ignored that. 'Much has changed, but the family's needs must come first. You can serve the family now, more than you ever did in your self-imposed exile. James was always my favourite son, high in power and esteem. Be my favourite grandson, Harold. Take control of the family back from the traitor Edwin. Restore the proper way of things. And all old . . . arguments, shall be forgotten and forgiven.'

Harry smiled. 'That's what I'm here for, Grandmother.'

I shut down the Glass with a Word, and the scene was swept away by our returning reflections.

'Treacherous little scumbag,' said Molly. 'Didn't take him long to stick his knife in your back, did it?'

'Can't say I'm surprised by any of this,' I said, slipping the Glass into my pocket. 'Disappointed, but not surprised.'

'Want me to turn him into something small and icky?'

'I can stop Harry,' I said. 'If I have to. Grandmother believes in bloodlines; in children and grandchildren and great-grandchildren.'

'Am I supposed to understand that?' said Molly.

'No,' I said.

'You and your family's secrets,' said Molly. 'Like I care.'

'I'll keep an eye on the prodigal son till you return,' growled the Armourer. 'But don't rely on me to stop him from making mischief. I may be Inner Circle, but I don't have the power or influence I once had. Nobody does any more. The whole family's fragmented, arguing with itself over what we should do next, and what we're supposed to be. So don't stay away too long, Eddie. Or you might not have a family to come home to.' He sniffed loudly, and then ostentatiously changed the subject. 'And be careful with that Glass! I'm still trying to work out what the drawbacks might be. There are always drawbacks with something that powerful. What little I've been able to discover about past uses of the Glass comes from texts in the Old Library. Jacob was helping me research, but he's disappeared. Again. Don't suppose you know where he is?'

'I haven't seen him since the Circle meeting,' I said.

'He disappeared when Harry turned up,' Molly said thoughtfully. 'Could there be some connection?'

'I doubt it,' I said. 'Not everything that happens here is part of some conspiracy; it just seems that way. I should never have encouraged Jacob to leave his Chapel. I only wanted him here in The Hall because I needed his support. He was always so much more . . . together, in the Chapel. He knew who he was there. He only left the Chapel to save me . . .'

The Armourer put a large comforting hand on my shoulder. 'And not everything bad that happens here is your fault, Eddie. Jacob will turn up. He always does . . . unfortunately. You couldn't get rid of him with bell, book and candle. Now, the Glass . . . I've got some of my people working their way through the Old Library, looking for mentions of the Glass, or Merlin, but without an overall index it's a slow process. And the current Librarian isn't much use. He didn't even know the Old Library existed until you rediscovered it. Now all he does is roam the stacks going *Oooh!* and *Aaah!* and trying to keep my people from reading the older texts in case they damage them. Idiot. Those old books can look after themselves. You could probably pour boiling napalm on them and not even mark their covers. Some of them would probably fight back.'

'Then you'll be pleased to know that one of the rogues I'm planning to bring back is our long lost William Dominic Drood,' I said. 'He always was the best Librarian we ever had.'

'Damn right!' said the Armourer, brightening again. 'You found William? Well done, Eddie! I never did believe that nonsense about him going rogue when he disappeared. I knew him well, back in the day; a first-class mind. Where has he been, all these years?'

I shot a look at Molly before answering, but there was no easy way to say it. 'William . . . isn't the man he used to be, Uncle Jack. He had some kind of confrontation with the Heart before he left, and something bad happened to him. He held himself together long enough to go to ground, but then he had a breakdown. He's currently residing in a sanatorium.'

'A lunatic asylum?' the Armourer said incredulously. 'You mean he's crazy?'

'It's not such a bad place,' Molly said. 'They're looking after him properly there. Eddie and I visited him recently. He was . . . distracted, but he was also quite sharp, for a while. I think the Heart did something to his mind. Now that it's gone, perhaps the effects will disappear too.'

'I'm sure he'll feel a lot better, once he's back in The Hall,' I said, just a bit weakly.

'Hell,' the Armourer said gruffly. 'This whole place is a madhouse at the best of times. He'll fit right in.'

'New weapons?' I said, figuring that was the best way to take the Armourer's mind off things.

He sniffed loudly again. 'I don't know if I want to trust you with any of my good stuff. The Bentley came back covered in scratches, and I still haven't forgiven you for breaking my one and only reverse watch. And you lost that special directional compass I made for you!'

'Let us take it for granted that I am careless and ungrateful, and never appreciate anything you do for me, and move on, shall we?' I said patiently. 'I still have the Colt Repeater, but I could use something more . . . dramatic.'

'I've got that nuclear grenade.'

'No,' I said, very firmly.

'All right. How about a portable sonic generator that can make your enemies' testicles swell up and explode in slow motion?'

'Oh, please!' said Molly.

'Tempting, but no,' I said. 'I'd prefer something a little less . . . conspicuous.'

'You were always fussy with your food, too.'

'Moving on, please.'

'I've got a short-range teleporter I've been fiddling with,' said the Armourer, scrabbling through the junk piled up before him on the work bench. 'Jumps you instantaneously half a mile in any direction. Think of a place, say the Words, and go. Completely untraceable. And unlike Merlin's Glass, completely undetectable.'

'That's more like it,' I said. 'Why only half a mile?'

'Because any further than that and you tend to arrive in an

arbitrary number of separate pieces,' the Armourer admitted reluctantly.

'I don't like the sound of that,' said Molly.

'You are not alone,' I said.

'Oh, go on,' said the Armourer. 'Give it a try. Ah! Here it is.' He held up a simple copper bracelet, breathed on it, polished it on his grubby coat sleeve and handed it to me. It looked very much like one of those bracelets people wear to ward off rheumatism. The Armourer grinned. 'I've been trying to find someone to test it in the field for me. And given your current circumstances, being able to be suddenly somewhere else can only be an advantage.'

'He may be scary, but he has a point,' said Molly.

Reluctantly, I slipped the copper band round my wrist. 'With my luck, it'll probably turn my skin green. And you still haven't offered me a decent weapon.'

'You don't need a weapon,' said Molly. 'You've got me.'

'She's right, you know,' said the Armourer.

Molly and I used the Merlin Glass to transport us to our first destination: that notorious drinking dive, neutral ground and den of iniquity, the Wulfshead Club. All I had to do was tug at the Glass's silver frame while muttering the right Words, and the mirror stretched like a piece of silly putty until it was the size of a door. Our reflections vanished, replaced by a dim and gloomy view of our destination. Molly and I stepped through – and we were standing in a familiar deserted back alley, deep in the heart of London's Soho. The Glass snapped back to its usual size, and I put it away.

The Wulfshead Club is a well known watering hole for all the strange and unusual people in the world. And for those just passing through. No one's quite sure exactly where the club itself is located, and the very anonymous management like to keep it that way, but there are authorised access points at locations all around the world, if you know where to look. And if your name's on the approved list. This isn't the kind of club where you can get in by bribing the doorman. Either you're a member in good standing, or you're dead.

I took a quick look round to make sure we were unobserved. The alley was empty, apart from general assorted garbage and a handful of rats with very strong stomachs. The only sound was the distant roar of passing traffic. It was barely early evening, but already the alley was heavy with shadows, dark and impenetrable. The stained brick walls were covered with the usual graffiti: *Dagon shall rise again! Vampires suck!* and the somewhat more worrying *Superssexuals of the world unite.*

I moved over to the wall, said the right Words and a massive silver door appeared, as though the door was shouldering the lesser reality of the wall aside. The solid silver was deeply etched with threats and warnings, in angelic and demonic script. There was no door handle. I placed my left hand flat against the disturbingly warm and sweaty silver, and after a moment the door recognised me and swung slowly open. I always find the wait a tad worrying. Because if your name isn't on the approved list, the door will bite your hand right off.

I looked at Molly. 'Remember, my name here is Shaman Bond. Slip up, and you could get us both killed.'

She smiled sweetly at me. 'You know, it's almost charming this need you have to hold my hand and explain everything to me. But if you don't cut it out sharpish, I will slap you halfway into next week.'

'After you,' I said, and followed her into the Wulfshead.

We walked into a savage blaze of light and a righteous blare of noise. Music was playing, people were drinking and dancing and making deals in corners, and the whole damned joint was rocking. Harsh lighting bathed the packed crowd in constantly changing primal colours, and the music never stopped. Molly and I made our way through the surging mass of bodies with a combination of smiles, charm, and a complete willingness to use our elbows in violent and unprovoked ways. We were heading for the high-tech bar at the far end of the club, a nightmarish art deco structure of steel and glass, complete with computerised access to more kinds of booze than most people even know exist. You want a Strontium 90 mineral water with an iodine chaser? Or a wolfsbane cocktail with a silver umbrella in it? Or maybe angel's urine with extra holy water? Then no wonder you've come to the Wulfshead.

Rumour has it the management keep the bar stock in a different dimension. Because they're afraid of it.

The Walfshead Club prides itself on always being totally up to the minute, if not a little beyond. The great plasma screens on the walls show constantly shifting glimpses of the bedroom secrets of the rich and famous, interspersed with tomorrow's Stock Exchange figures, while go-go girls dance in golden cages suspended from the ceiling, wearing only wisps of feathers. For the more traditionally minded, lap dancers in black leather strips gyrate on raised stages and hump their steel poles into submission. Tonight, a group of Satan's Harlots out on a hen night were line dancing up and down the long steel bartop.

You can find all sorts at the Wulfshead, if they don't find you first, preparing for a caper or a war, or recovering afterwards. Janissary Jane drank here between her regular shifts as an inter-dimensional mercenary, because she found the place restful. Which tells you a lot about the kind of places she works in. I didn't see her anywhere yet, or hear the tell-tale sounds of screams and gunfire, so I bellied up to the bar with Molly at my side. The bartender wandered unhurriedly over to serve us. I've never bothered to remember his name. There's a dozen of them behind the bar, all of them clones. Or homunculi. Or probably something even more disturbing.

He nodded familiarly to both of us. 'Hello Molly, Shaman; been a while. The usual?'

I nodded, and he fussed over an impressive collection of nozzles and cables behind the bar before handing over a Beck's for me and a Buck's Fizz for Molly. (She believes the orange juice makes it healthy.) I felt a little relieved that my use name was still good here. As far as the Wulfshead crowd was concerned, I was Shaman Bond, a small-time operator and familiar face on the scene; nothing more. I'd put a lot of time and effort into establishing my cover identity, and not just because no one here had any love for the Droods. In the Wulfshead, I was no one important, no one special, and nothing was expected from me. Which was really very liberating. Especially now.

Back at The Hall, most of my family either worshipped me, feared me or hated me. Or any combination of the three. Edwin Drood had become the most important person in the most important organisation in the world. But here, Shaman Bond was just another face in the crowd. It was as though a great weight had been lifted from my shoulders. I put my back against the bar and looked out over the milling throng, nodding easily to a few familiar friends and faces.

Harry Fabulous was sliding unctuously through the mob, working the crowd with a wide smile and a hearty handshake, your special Go To man for everything that was bad for you. Last time I was in, he was offering pirate DVDs of Muppet films from another dimension: *Citizen Kermit* and *Miss Piggy Does Dallas*. Lined up along the great length of the bar I could see a ghost called Ash, a minor Norse godling, and the Indigo Spirit, complete with leather costume, cape and cowl, taking a brief break from his crime-fighting.

And finally, there was Janissary Jane her own bad self, shouldering her way through the packed crowd to the bar in search of a fresh whisky bottle. One of the bartenders was waiting for her, and she snatched the refill out of his hand and drank the cheap whisky straight from the bottle. She looked like the soldier she was: tall and blocky with muscular bare arms, a ramrod straight back and black hair cropped close to her head so an enemy couldn't grab hold of it in a fight. She might have been pretty once, but all that was left now was scars and character. Her army fatigues were scorched and torn and stained with dried blood, and I knew up close she would smell of blood and smoke and brimstone. The whisky was actually a good sign; gin made her maudlin, and then she tended to shoot people. Mostly people who needed shooting, but it did tend to put a damper on the party atmosphere.

The Wulfshead has never objected to her presence. Apparently, they feel she gives the place character.

I called her name, from a safe distance, and her head came round quickly, one hand dropping to the gun at her side. I stood very still until I was sure she'd recognised me, and then gestured for her to come over and join Molly and me. She took her hand away from her gun, nodded stiffly, and made her way down the bar, shouldering people aside when they didn't get out of her way fast enough. No one was dumb enough to object. This was Janissary Jane. Demon killer, seasoned warrior and complete bloody psychopath. She stopped before Molly and me, studied us a little owlishly, and then toasted us both with her whisky bottle.

'Hello, Jane,' I said easily.

'Hello *Shaman*,' Janissary Jane said pointedly. She was perhaps the only other person here who knew I was a Drood. 'What do you want with me?'

'I'm organising a major operation against some demons,' I said. 'I could use your advice and expertise. You'll get the going rate for the duration, plus a generous bonus if we pull the thing off successfully.'

'Hold it,' said Molly. 'We're paying her?'

'Of course,' I said. 'She wouldn't come otherwise. Would you, Jane?'

'I am a professional,' said Janissary Jane. 'But who exactly would I be fighting for?'

'Does it matter?' I said.

'Of course it matters!' Janissary Jane said sharply. 'There are worse things than demons. Like the Droods, for example . . .'

'Not this time,' I said. 'We're targeting the Loathly Ones, and we won't stop till they're either wiped out completely or banished for ever.'

Janissary Jane whistled soundlessly, and took another drink from her bottle. She gazed at me. 'The Loathly Ones. That's . . . ambitious. Hate demons. Bastards. But soul-eaters are the very worst . . . On the other hand, I've been hearing things. About the Droods. Word is something bad has happened to them. No one seems too sure what, but there are those going round saying they've lost their power.'

'There are always rumours,' I said easily. 'All you need to know is that the money's guaranteed. We're serious about the Loathly Ones, Jane. And we could use your help.'

'Damn right you could. The Loathly Ones are hardcore demons. Soul-eaters don't just kill you, they make you into them.' She smiled. 'There's no way I'm missing out on this. If the Loathly Ones are finally going down, I want to be there to kick the last few heads in. You want me, you got me.'

'Great,' I said. 'I've got to pick up a few more people, and then I'll take you back home to meet the folks.'

Janissary Jane raised an eyebrow. 'Home? As in . . . The Hall? Damn! Never thought I'd see the inside of that place.'

'So, what have you been up to, Jane?' said Molly, a bit put out at being excluded from the conversation for so long.

'Oh, keeping busy,' said Janissary Jane. 'Recently got back from another Demon War. Truth be told, I'm getting a bit long in the tooth for these runs, but the call went out and I signed up, like always. Ended up in this alternate timeline where technology had become so advanced they'd forgotten about magic. They thought they were opening a doorway into another dimension; turned out to be a Gate to Hell. The demons came pouring out, killing everything in sight, howling with joy at such easy prey . . . and all the technology in the world wasn't enough to stop them.

'The sun turned black, the rivers ran with blood, and demons covered the earth in all their endless varieties of horror. Nowhere was safe. There were no churches, or holy places. And weapons only designed to kill people had little effect on demons. Humanity in that place had forgotten the old protections. They learned fast, though. And somehow they got the call out to us. We opened up our own dimensional door, and off we went again to fight the good fight.

'And to kill demons. Hate demons.'

'How many wars have you fought in?' I said, honestly curious.

She shrugged. 'I don't know. Too many. Won some, lost more, and lost too many good friends along the way. I'm a lot older than I look; serial regenerations will do that to you. Though they don't stop you feeling old inside. Once I fought because I believed in my cause. Then because I hated demons. Now, just because . . . it's what I do.'

'Still,' I said. 'An actual Hell Gate, a direct link between a material plane and the Pit: that's rare, isn't it?'

'Very,' said Janissary Jane. 'Or Humanity would have been wiped out long ago. We had a whole army of seasoned demon fighters, heroes and warriors and soldiers, veterans of a hundred wars; and all we could do was die. We had the weapons and the tactics, but they had the numbers. I saw cities burning, mountains of severed heads, waded through blood and guts . . . The screaming never stopped. Eventually the very laws of reality started to change, warped by the presence of so many demons. We fought them for every inch, climbing over the bodies of our own fallen to throw ourselves at the enemy . . . and none of it did any good. We killed and killed, and still they came, laughing at us.'

She stopped speaking then. She started to raise the whisky bottle to her mouth, and then lowered it again, as though she knew it wouldn't help. Her cold grey eyes were far away, lost in memories she couldn't forget, no matter how hard she tried.

'So what happened?' Molly said finally.

'That dimension isn't there any more,' said Janissary Jane. 'The demons were winning, so we blew it up to prevent them from using it as a base to invade other dimensions.' She smiled sourly. 'To save the universe, we had to destroy it. Some things never change. And only I escaped to tell you the tale. Buy me another drink, Shaman. Something stronger.'

'You don't have to join up with us,' said Molly.

'Yes, I do,' said Janissary Jane. 'I need a battle I can win.'

'Oh, dear God, it's you,' said a familiar voice. We looked round, and there was the Blue Fairy. He was looking a lot better than the last time I'd seen him, but that wouldn't have been difficult. That Blue Fairy had been on his last legs, physically and spiritually, and the figure before us was leaner, fitter, and dressed in the very smartest style. His face was still utterly dissolute, the few handsome traces remaining almost buried under lines of hard experience, but you had to expect that with the Blue Fairy. He had lived not wisely but too well; and it showed. He scowled at all of us, but me in particular.

'My half-elf nature told me I'd be meeting someone important at the Wulfshead this evening, but if I'd known it was going to be you, I'd have stayed home and hidden under the covers until I stopped shaking.'

'You're looking good, Blue,' I said. 'Especially considering the last time I saw you, you were fighting for your life with some monstrosity you'd fished up from another dimension.'

The Blue Fairy shrugged. 'Turned out it was just what I needed. Some kind of psychic vampire that ate all my addictions. I suppose it's possible I subconsciously drew it to me.'

'Some people have all the luck,' said Molly.

'Hardly,' said the Blue Fairy. 'Or I wouldn't keep bumping into you people. Either way, I now have my health back, and my pride and, reluctant as I am to admit it, I am currently looking for some good works to get involved with, for the sake of my much abused karma. Since my nature brought me here, am I to take it you can help me out?'

'Got it in one,' I said. 'I'm putting together an operation to take down the Loathly Ones, once and for all. A family outing, you might say. We could use your help, Blue.'

'Is the money good?'

'Of course.'

'Yes, well, it would have to be.' The Blue Fairy shook his head dolefully. 'Never thought I'd see the day when I ended up aiding and abetting your notorious clan.'

'It's Shaman Bond here,' I reminded him quickly. The Blue Fairy was another of those I'd been forced to reveal my true identity to, when I was on the run. It seemed to me that there were far too many of them, but short of organising a cull, I didn't see what I could do about it.

'Yes, yes, I hadn't forgotten. I'm not entirely sure what I can contribute, apart from years of expertise in surviving appalling situations, but I'm in.'

Molly gave me a significant look over the rim of her glass, and I knew what she was thinking. *You can't trust him. He's half elf, and you can never trust an elf. They always have a secret agends, and another agenda hidden inside that.*

'Well, well, well, look what we have here,' said a loud and cheerful voice behind us, in a strong Russian accent. 'If it isn't our dear old friend and customer, the Blue Fairy. Looking very prosperous, I would have to say. Fancy meeting you here, in this very expensive and upmarket establishment, when you have so many debts to be paying.'

We turned to look, and there standing before us were two very large gentlemen in expensive long black leather coats, with shaven heads and nasty grins on their unpleasant faces. The Blue Fairy took one look at them and tried to hide behind me.

'Blue,' I said, 'am I to take it you know these people?'

'Unfortunately yes,' said the Blue Fairy. 'May I present to you the Vodyanoi Brothers, Russian mafiosi who relocated to London after making Moscow too hot for them. I borrowed a hell of a lot of money from them when I thought I was dying, and spent the lot on wine, drugs and two very pretty rent boys. I honestly thought I'd be dead long before the time came to pay any of it back. Unfortunately, while the money is gone, I am still here, and these gentlemen want their money back. Along with a quite extortionate amount of interest.'

'Indeed, yes. We are Vodyanoi Brothers!' said the thug on the left. 'I am Gregor Vodyanoi, and this is being my baby brother Sergei Vodyanoi! We are being very dangerous people.'

'Very dangerous people indeed!' said Sergei, glaring at us in turn. 'Oh my word yes.'

'Show them how dangerous we are, brother,' said Gregor.

Sergei produced an outsized handgun from his coat pocket, put it to his left temple, grinned at us with very large teeth, and then shot himself in the head. He rocked on his feet from the impact, but didn't fall. There was no spurt of blood from the wound in his head, and the hole quickly closed. Around us, people were quietly backing away. Sergei gargled a few times, and then spat the deformed bullet out into his hand. He showed it to us, while Gregor slapped his brother proudly on the back.

'Unusually dangerous, I think you'll agree,' said Gregor. 'Now, there is a question of moneys owed to us. Substantial moneys, with much in the way of interest. Due right now, oh my word yes.'

'Or very much else,' said Sergei. 'We are Vodyanoi Brothers, and no one is taking the advantage of us.'

The Blue Fairy looked at me. 'Help?'

'I should have known you'd be more trouble than you were worth,' I said.

'I suppose an advance is out of the question?'

I smiled at the Vodyanoi Brothers. 'Any chance we can work this out in a civilised manner?'

'We do not do civilised,' said Gregor.

'Bad for business,' said Sergei.

'Either he pays up, or we eat him,' said Gregor, smiling widely. 'Setting an example is being very important, in our line of work.'

I turned to Molly. 'Darling, could you take care of this?'

'Of course, darling,' said Molly. She snapped her fingers, and the Vodyanoi Brothers vanished, replaced by two small and warty and very surprised-looking toads sitting on the floor. I looked reproachfully at Molly.

'I meant, take care of the problem financially.'

'Then you should have said,' said Molly, sipping her drink.

I shook my head. 'Can't take you anywhere.'

'I hate to rain on your self-satisfied parade,' said Janissary Jane. 'But I have a feeling things are about to get really unpleasant.'

We looked back at the toads just in time to see them swell rapidly in size, throw off their toad shapes and burst out in all directions until abruptly the Vodyanoi Brothers were standing before us, still in their black leather coats, and looking distinctly peeved. The Blue Fairy tried to hide behind me again.

'That was really not very nice,' said Gregor.

'Not in the least friendly, or businesslike,' said Sergei.

'Time to become dangerous, brother.'

'Extremely dangerous, brother.'

And they changed shape again, shooting up to become taller and broader, their faces lengthening into muzzles, their black coats replaced by the silver grey fur of enormous wolves. Werewolves. They towered over us, all teeth and claws, with great muscles rippling under their thick pelts. They stank of blood and death and the joy of the kill. They snarled happily, showing huge teeth in their long jaws. I glared at the Blue Fairy.

'You couldn't have told us in advance that they were shape-shifters?'

'You never gave me a chance!'

'Next time, talk faster!'

I couldn't call up my armour without revealing my true identity to the whole damned club, so I drew my Colt Repeater and shot both werewolves repeatedly in the head. The impacts rocked them back on their wolf legs, but even as my bullets smashed their long skulls and ripped their wolf faces apart, the wounds were already healing. The Colt was incapable of missing, but it couldn't provide silver bullets. I made a mental note to have a quiet word with the Armourer about that when I got back. The Vodyanoi Brothers howled fiercely as they pressed forward, into the face of my bullets. I'd hurt them, but that was all.

The Blue Fairy had already disappeared under the nearest table. Janissary Jane produced two long punch daggers from the tops of her boots. The jagged edges of the long blades gleamed with silver. Janissary Jane grinned nastily and waded into the two werewolves, hacking and stabbing at them with her very nasty blades. Blood flew on the air as the knives cut deep, and she dodged and ducked every blow the two huge werewolves could throw at her; doing what she did best and doing it magnificently.

Until one of the Vodyanoi Brothers finally connected with a solid blow, and Janissary Jane went flying into the watching crowd. She hit the floor hard, and didn't rise again.

People were backing away in all directions now, but not so far they couldn't get a good view of what was happening. Many were already laying bets, and cheering or booing as the mood took them. The Wulfshead's security measures finally kicked in, spraying the Vodyanoi Brothers with holy water from the sprinklers and targeting them with lasers from the light fittings; neither of which bothered the two huge werewolves in the least. The club did have more stringent measures, but presumably the management were reluctant to use them unless the fight escalated into something that could threaten the whole bar. Which meant . . . my friends and I were strictly on our own.

Molly had been tossing spells at the Vodyanoi Brothers for some time now, but they slid off, unable to get a grip on the werewolves' slippery unnatural nature. The toad spell had only worked because it caught the brothers by surprise. Molly had been reduced to throwing fireballs at them, but though the silver grey fur burned fiercely and smelled appalling, it quickly repaired itself.

So I took out Merlin's Glass, shook it to its full size, said the proper activating Words and darted in between the two werewolves. Vicious claws slashed through the air, only just missing me, and then I reared up, clapped the Glass over the nearest werewolf, and transported it instantly to the Arctic Circle. The other brother stopped dead, astounded, and I clapped the Glass over him and sent him to the Antarctic. Good luck walking home from that one, boys . . .

The club's security systems immediately shut down, and relative calm returned to the Wulfshead as everyone paid off their bets and went back to what they were doing. I put Merlin's Glass away, and went to see how Janissary Jane was. She was already sitting up, and checking herself for injuries. Tough old broad. She slapped my proffered helping hand aside, and got to her feet unaided.

'I'm fine. Don't fuss, Shaman. Take more than a couple of imported werewolves to put me down. They'd never have tagged me at all if I hadn't already been a bit tired from the last Demon War.'

'Of course,' I said soothingly, but I had to wonder. There was a time when no one could have tagged her under any conditions. Maybe she was getting a little old. But then, I only really wanted her as a tutor, not a soldier. We went back to Molly, who was dragging the Blue Fairy out from under his table. One of the bartenders nodded his thanks to me.

'Nicely done, Shaman. Very handy little device you have there. Where did you find it?'

'EBay,' I said.

'Of course,' he said. 'Where else?'

CHAPTER SIX
Four tutors and a cemetery

Janissary Jane has fought armies of demons in indescribable Hell dimensions, and the Blue Fairy has battled countless demons within himself, but they both looked distinctly worried when I told them I was sending them to The Hall alone while Molly and I continued our search for more tutors. My family's home does have a certain reputation, mostly by our own choice. Guests are rare, and trespassers are eaten. So in the end I used the Merlin Glass to open a gateway between a quiet corner of the Wulfshead and the family Armoury, and sent Janissary Jane and the Blue Fairy through into the Armourer's somewhat surprised care. In fact, Uncle Jack looked distinctly startled as I pushed them through the gap, and then closed it quickly before he could object. I'm a great believer in letting people sort out their own problems.

Molly stared at the Glass as I shook it back down to normal size. 'That is a seriously useful item, Eddie. Many possible uses occur to me. What say, when we get back, we use it to transport a whole bunch of piranha into the Matriarch's bidet?'

I had to smile. 'You have the best ideas, Molly.'

'Is that yes or no?'

I turned back to the bar and summoned the nearest bartender. 'Subway Sue and Mr Stab: have they been in recently?'

The bartender considered, while conspicuously polishing a glass that didn't need it. 'No . . . Come to think of it, I haven't seen either of them in here for some time now. Some weeks, at least. Which is unusual.'

'Damn right it is,' said Molly, frowning. 'Sue must have gone to ground after that nasty business with Manifest Destiny. But Mr Stab? Nothing upsets him.'

'Any idea where we should look for them?' I said.

'Of course!' she said immediately. 'I always have ideas. I am Idea Woman! Give the Glass a shake, sweetie. We're going underground.'

To be exact, Molly had the Glass transport us to the Underground Tube station at Cheyne Walk, which was apparently one of Subway Sue's favourite haunts. We stepped out into the shadows at the end of a platform, and no one noticed because no one pays any attention to anyone but themselves when they're waiting for a train. Molly and I strolled through the various tunnels and platforms and finally discovered Subway Sue working her way down a crowded platform. I almost didn't recognise her at first. An aged, bent-over woman wrapped in the rags and tatters of charity clothes, she shuffled slowly along, and people drew back rather than make contact with her. She looked like just another homeless person, begging for spare change. Even Molly had to look twice before she recognised her old friend, and then hurried up to her, horrified. Subway Sue looked round sharply when Molly called her name, and then she flinched and turned away, as though she didn't want Molly to see what had become of her.

Molly grabbed her by the shoulder and turned her firmly round, and then pulled a face and rubbed her hand vigorously against her hip to clean it. I didn't blame her. Up close, Subway Sue smelled pretty ripe. Molly glared into Subway Sue's grimy face.

'Jesus, Sue, what the Hell happened to you?' she said, blunt as ever. 'You look like shit.'

'Why this is Hell, nor am I out of it,' said Subway Sue. 'Ah, the old jokes are still the best. Hello Molly, Edwin. What are you doing down here?'

'Looking for you,' I said.

'Well, you've seen me so you can go away again,' Subway Sue said firmly.

'Not until you tell us what happened,' said Molly, just as firmly.

Subway Sue sighed, and it was a very tired sound. 'My luck finally ran out. All of it.'

'But you're a luck vampire,' I said. 'Why not steal yourself some more?'

She gave me a long, martyred stare. 'If it were only that simple . . . Looking like this, it's hard to get close enough to anyone for long enough for me to drain off any serious luck. And besides – oh hell, you're not going to go away until you've heard the whole sad story, are you?'

'Absolutely not,' said Molly.

'Then come with me. We can't talk here. Not in front of civilians.'

She led us down to the end of the platform while everyone else politely looked away from her as though her poverty might be catching. Subway Sue stopped before an unobtrusive door marked 'Maintenance Staff Only', opened the heavy padlock with a frankly filthy brass key, and then led us into an empty cupboard. She pulled the door carefully shut behind us, and then pushed at the far cupboard wall. It slid back jerkily under her urging, revealing a large stone cavern beyond, lit by a single electric light that sprang to life as we entered. And this was where Subway Sue lived.

It was really just a hole, decorated with bits of junk she'd salvaged. There were empty cans and plastic bottles, to hold water. Plastic containers to store bits of food in. And a pile of blankets to sleep on. The place looked like somewhere animals lived. Molly looked around her, openly horrified.

'Sue, *what happened*? You're one of the most famous luck vampires in London. I thought you had this great place in the West End, where you lived in comfort and luxury?'

'Everyone thinks that,' said Subway Sue, sitting down heavily on her pile of blankets. 'And for a time it was true. I had the best of luck, stolen from the rich and the powerful, and what I didn't use myself I sold for enough money to bring me everything I ever wanted. But . . . I used it all up. And when luck turns against you, it really goes bad. As though there's some . . . balance that must be maintained. How do you think someone as lucky as me got captured by Manifest Destiny in the first place?'

'I did wonder about that,' I said.

'One of my own betrayed me,' said Subway Sue. 'Not actually a friend, at least, but someone I knew. He swallowed the lie of Manifest Destiny and believed everything Truman promised him, the fool. He sneaked up on me while I was distracted during rush hour, and drained off most of my luck before I knew what was happening. And Truman's thugs were ready and waiting to hustle me off.'

'What happened to the bastard?' said Molly. 'Want me to hunt him down for you?'

'No need,' said Subway Sue. 'His extra luck enabled him to escape Truman's goons when they came looking for him, but he's been on the run ever since. From them and his own kind. He's alone now, for as long as he lives.

'I used up every last bit of luck I had, helping us break free from Truman's concentration camp. And after I escaped, in my desperation, I made the mistake of trying to drain the luck from an inter-dimensional traveller passing as human. It felt my touch immediately, and knew me for what I was. It . . . did something to me, and now my luck is always bad.' She smiled humourlessly. 'After all these years of passing as a homeless person, so I could get closer to my prey, now I've become what I pretended. Payback's a bitch. What are you doing down here, Molly? I never wanted you to see me like this. What do you want from me?'

'I want to hire you as a tutor for the Drood family,' I said. 'Teach them about the real world, and the things they don't even know they don't know. You'll have to live at The Hall, and you'll have to curb your . . . inclinations, but the pay will be more than good enough to buy you a whole new life, once you leave us.'

'You see,' Molly said to Subway Sue, beaming widely, 'your luck has changed.'

'No,' said Subway Sue. She looked away from us, and seemed to shrink in on herself. 'Look at me. I'm no use to you like this.'

'Things will be better at The Hall,' I said. 'We can fix you up, no matter what's been done to you. We'll make a new person out of you.'

'That's what I'm afraid of,' said Subway Sue. 'I've heard stories of what happens to people who get taken to the Drood family home.'

'Only some of them are true,' I said.

'Trust me,' said Molly. 'I won't let anything bad happen to you.'

'But what can I offer to the high and mighty Droods?' said Subway Sue. 'What can I teach them that they don't already know?'

'The strategies of survival,' I said. 'How you survive, when you've lost everything you ever depended on.'

Subway Sue glanced at me, and then at Molly. I did my best to smile reassuringly.

'Eddie's running The Hall's affairs these days,' said Molly. 'Things are different there now.'

'I need to open my family's eyes to the kind of lives they don't know exist,' I said. 'Come and be a tutor. Share your experience. Help shape how the Droods see the world.'

Subway Sue smiled briefly, but didn't seem convinced. 'You and your family have been hunting me and my kind for centuries. Hunting us down like vermin, for the sin of being what we are. You have the blood of my family and my friends on your armoured hands, Drood. And you want me to work for you? I'm not that bad off.'

'Yes, you are, dear,' Molly said kindly. 'You must believe me when I tell you I'll see you safe at The Hall. I don't know if you can trust the whole family, but you can trust Eddie. He's taken his family by the scruff of the neck and seriously shaken up the way they do things. He wants to change the way they think, and how they see the world; and that's why I suggested you as one of his outside tutors. You won't be alone there. We're going after Mr Stab next.'

'Oh, wonderful,' said Subway Sue. 'That's supposed to make me feel safe? But anywhere has to be better than here. You have no idea how much you miss plumbing till you don't have it any more. And I do owe you, Edwin, for helping free me from Truman. You know he's reorganised at a new location?'

'Nothing specific,' I said. 'Any idea where we can find him?'

'I hear rumours, that's all. He's supposed to have a secret underground base, outside London, in a place of ancient power. You should have killed him when you had the chance, Drood.'

'I'll try harder next time,' I said. 'You ready to go?'

'Hell, yes. It's not like I've got anything to keep me here, is it? Or anything I want to take with me.'

I did the business with Merlin's Glass, and pushed her through the opening into the Armoury where Uncle Jack was waiting. He glared through the gateway at me.

'Eddie! Wait a damned minute!'

'Sorry, Uncle Jack! No time! Catch you later!'

And then I shut the Glass down, cutting him off before he could come up with lots of good reasons why I couldn't keep lumbering him with the job of looking after my new tutors. Molly looked at me.

'What do you suppose that was about?'

'Nothing that can't wait till we get back,' I said airily. 'Now for Mr Stab.'

'I wish you wouldn't pull faces like that, Eddie. I'm sure they're not good for you.'

'I am taking a hell of a risk on your say-so,' I said. 'If anything goes wrong when we get him back to The Hall—'

'It will be my fault; yes, we've established that. Look, Eddie, I know how dangerous he is. I know that better than anyone. But I'll be there to keep a very stern eye on him, and . . . well, how much damage can he do in a house full of Droods? Even his old magic is hardly a match for Drood armour. I need you to trust me on this, Eddie.'

'I do trust you,' I said. 'I just don't trust him. But if this is so important to you . . .'

'It is,' said Molly. 'I need to believe that people can change. Even the worst of us.'

'All right,' I said. 'Where do you think we should look first for the most notorious uncaught serial killer of Old London Town?'

'I've been thinking about that,' said Molly. 'And I think we should start with the Order of Beyond.'

'You have got to be kidding,' I said. 'You mean that place down Grafton Way, where possessed people sit around and spout gibberish at each other? What would Mr Stab be doing in a place like that?'

'Listening,' said Molly. 'He thinks if he listens long enough, he might learn some ancient secret or knowledge he could use to alter the conditions of his immortality.'

'To cure him?'

'Or make him a better killer.'

'You are not filling me with confidence about this, Molly.'

'Let's go.'

'Before or after we have a rush of sense to the head?'

'Oh, hush. Be a good boy and I'll buy you a nice dinner afterwards.'

'I am so easily bribed.'

Merlin's Glass took us straight to Grafton Way, in one of the older, more traditional parts of the West End. You can find all sorts in that area: embassies for the smaller countries, company houses, literary agencies. And the Order of Beyond, located in the middle of an ordinary, unassuming terraced row, with nothing to mark its presence but a simple brass plaque on the wall, giving the name of the place and the stern admonition 'No Revenants, Reincarnations or Repo Men'. I hit the buzzer, and when a cold voice from the intercom demanded my name and business, I said 'Shaman Bond', and after a pause the door clicked open. My cover identity has a long and carefully established reputation for turning up anywhere, and for being basically harmless. Just another face on the scene, with a keen interest in anything illegal, immoral or unnatural. Shaman Bond was a chancer, a small-time operator, and nothing at all like Eddie Drood. Which was what I liked most about him.

The reception area turned out to be deliberately blank and anonymous, with no clue as to what lay in wait below. Bare walls, bare floor, and a very professional receptionist sitting behind a very simple reception desk. The receptionist seemed typical enough, with the usual blankly attractive face, eyes of pure ice, and a smile that meant nothing at all. The kind who lived and died by her appointments book, and who wouldn't make an exception for anyone, even if you set her heavily laquered hair on fire. I knew we weren't going to get along. Molly and I strode over to the desk as though we were slumming it just by being there, and planted ourselves directly before her. She ignored us, of course, giving her attention to the papers spread out before her, to put us properly in our place. So I leaned over, grabbed her papers and threw them up into the air, smiling easily into her horrified face as the papers fluttered down around us.

'Hi,' I said. 'Shaman Bond, at your service. The very dangerous person standing beside me is Molly Metcalf, the rightly legendary wild witch of the woods. She has expressed an interest in seeing what goes on at the Order of Beyond, and since I'm far too scared of her to say no, I said I was sure you'd let her in.'

'Because if you don't, I will take names and kick arse,' Molly said cheerfully.

The receptionist struggled to regain her calm. 'Do you have a reservation?'

'No,' said Molly, 'I'm going to enjoy it thoroughly. Starting with you, if you don't get a move on.'

I saw the receptionist reach for an alarm button under the desk, and I wagged a warning finger in her face. 'Molly Metcalf? Turns people into things? Has a very nasty sense of humour . . . Is any of this ringing bells?'

'Go right down,' said the receptionist. 'Never wanted this job anyway.'

She moved her hand across to press another button under her desk, and a large trapdoor opened in the floor on the other side of the room, rising slowly and silently of its own accord. Molly and I wandered over to it, and looked down. A long stone stairway fell before us, leading deep into the earth. There was a strong smell of blood and brimstone, and a distant murmur of voices. I insisted on leading the way, and Molly made me pay for that by crowding my back all the way. The trapdoor slammed shut behind us with a loud, solid and very final-sounding thud. The bare stone walls beaded with water like sweat, and the air grew hot and close as we descended. I could feel presences below, like heavy weights pressing down on the world and making it cry out. We were going into a bad place, where bad things waited.

Finally, the steps curved suddenly round to one side and deposited us into a great natural stone cavern, deep beneath the street. The flagged floor stretched away in all directions, covered with blue-chalked pentacles, circles of salt, and rows of squat solid cages made of steel and silver and brass. All designed to hold safely and contain the poor possessed creatures who were the whole reason and purpose of the Order of Beyond. There were men and women, and even children, trapped like animals. Some sat and talked calmly, reasonably, arguing that they really didn't belong in a place like this. Others howled and raged and threw themselves at the cages that held them prisoner, beating at the solid bars with hands that felt no pain. And others just sat and watched sullenly, hatefully, with unblinking eyes, waiting for someone to make a mistake.

Before every possessed prisoner sat a member of the Order, coaxing and cajoling the possessor into speaking to them. It usually didn't take much. The possessors do love to talk, to tease and threaten and horrify the listener with lies, half-truths and terrible facts.

No one in the Order of Beyond was interested in helping any of these people. They didn't give a damn for the victims. They just wanted to listen and record everything they heard. There were microphones everywhere, and the most sophisticated recording equipment, and a whole bunch of scribes with pens and paper to set down what was said by those voices that couldn't be recorded, because technology wouldn't accept their existence. And sitting comfortably all around, listening intently, were the invited guests, the very well-paying clientele of the Order of Beyond. Who came hoping to hear bits of forbidden knowledge, or hints of the secrets of Heaven and Hell. The Order of Beyond sent full transcripts of everything heard to an extensive mailing list (for an extortionate fee, of course), but there was nothing like being there in person to hear it for yourself. And just maybe to get the jump on everyone else.

Molly and I stood cautiously at the bottom of the steps, letting our eyes adjust to the dim lighting, the rise and fall of harsh overlapping voices, and the stench of hate and fear and things that shouldn't be allowed in our supposedly sane and rational world. Not all the voices sounded human, though they came from human lips.

There is a river in Hell, made up of the tears of suicides. Tears are wine, among the damned.

Beware the Many-Angled Ones, the Hyperbreed! Beware the Black Sun and what incubates inside it! Beware the howling that never ends, and the teeth that rend men's souls! Even death is no escape from what lies waiting, in the worlds beyond the worlds!

They watch you from the other side of your mirrors, only pretending to be your reflection, waiting and biding their time. And then, in the dead of night, they come out while you're sleeping, grab you and force you back into the other side of the mirror, so they can take your place and do terrible things in your name. Just because they look like you, it doesn't mean they are you.

Blood shall rain down, and offal, and the great Beast that is Babalon shall come again, and all Hell shall rise up with her, and . . .

The Celestials are coming to judge us all, in their million-mile-long spaceships, and we shall be as ants before them . . .

Please, I don't want to be here, I shouldn't be here, there's something running up and down inside me, and it hurts it hurts it hurts . . .

You can hear broadcasts from Heaven and Hell every day, on certain designated frequencies. To hear a recording, phone any of these numbers . . .

'Okay,' said Molly. 'Most of this is bullshit, and I should know.'

'I wish you wouldn't say things like that,' I said. 'I find it very disturbing to be constantly reminded that I'm in love with the original girlfriend from Hell.'

Molly shrugged. 'You can't be a witch of any standing unless you're prepared to make deals with both sides. And I have to tell you, Eddie, that which side is which depends very much on where you're standing.' She studied the shadowy figures in their various cages and sniffed loudly. 'People pay good money to listen to this shit? I half expected one of them to start spouting pea soup yelling "Your mother knits socks in Hell!" Demons lie. It's what they do.'

'Except when a truth can hurt you more,' I said.

And then a grossly fat man with a purple birthmark covering half his face called me by name. My real name, not my cover identity. In the great babble of voices I was pretty sure it had gone unnoticed, for now, but I moved quickly over to the silver barred cage before he could use the name again. My torc would keep the recording devices from picking up anything concerning me, but I didn't want to draw anyone's attention. I needed to be just Shaman Bond here. The possessed man was entirely naked, with strange designs daubed over his dead-white skin in dried blood and shit and vomit. He giggled softly, and patted his fat hands against the bars of his cage, so I could see he'd bitten off all his fingers. His unblinking eyes were full of blood, and when he spoke his voice was like a child gargling with razor blades, like your best friend telling you he's slept with your wife, like a cancer growth if it had vocal chords.

'Edwin Drood, sweet prince of a ruined family, we meet again. Do you remember me? We spoke once before, in the cellars under Dr Dee's House Of Exorcism. I promised you the world and everything in it, and you turned me down. Too good to listen to the likes of me. But here you are now, searching for wisdom in the strangest of places. Shall I tell you what you need to know, sweet Drood?'

'You don't know anything I need to know,' I said.

'But I do, I do! Nothing is hidden, from Heaven or Hell. You seek the undying killer, the saint of slaughter, Mr Stab. And I know where he is.'

'And you'll tell us, for a price?' said Molly, standing close beside me, as though to protect me. 'What are we supposed to do, break you out of here? I don't think so.'

'No charge, no charge at all, little witch,' crooned the awful presence behind the fat man's unblinking eyes. 'Because getting what you want won't make you happy, or free, or wise. You humans make your own way to Hell, with every step you take. And so I give you Mr Stab. My very own poisoned chalice, a gift from Hell to clutch to your family's bosom.'

'You demons are so full of yourselves,' said Molly. 'If you're going to tell us, tell us.'

'As you wish, dear little indentured soul. Go you now to the Café Night, and someone there will tell you exactly where to find dear Mr Stab.'

He was still laughing loudly when we left, a horrible, dirty, disturbing sound, even though the attendants shocked him again and again with cattle prods to try and shut him up.

And so by Merlin's Glass we went straight to Café Night, a deliberately dark and gloomy establishment tucked away in a corner of Kensington you can't get to without trying really hard. From the outside, the café looked like just another coffee house, a place for suburban mums to sit down after a hard day's shopping and catch up on the latest gossip. But that was a simple glamour, with an attached *Move along, nothing to see here* spell to keep the uninformed from entering. Café Night has a strict entrance code, and non-members enter at their own risk. It started out as a meeting place for vampires and those foolish romantic types who longed to be their victims. It was called Renfields back then. These days the Café Night catered for the kind of immortals whose presence wouldn't be tolerated anywhere else.

I kicked the door open and strode in like I was there to condemn the place on moral health grounds. The café was distinctly gloomy, with artfully arranged track lighting to keep it that way while still allowing you to see who or what you were talking to. The background music drifted from the Cure to the Mission to Gregorian chants, and the air was perfumed with the sickly reek of rotting lilies. Café Night was big on atmosphere.

Shadowy faces glared at me from every table, but nobody moved and nobody said anything, because I'd taken the precaution of armouring up before I crashed my way in. No one here would say a word to a small-time operator like Shaman Bond, so it was time to be Eddie Drood again and command respect the hard way. My silver armour might not be as familiar yet as the golden, but it still marked me for who and what I was; and what I might do if I didn't get the answers I wanted. So the various immortals, dark and dangerous creatures in their own right, were quite happy to sit still, keep their heads down and hope I'd pick on someone else.

A few did get up to leave, heading for the rear door the moment I entered. But I'd already sent Molly round the back, and the fleeing immortals stopped dead in their tracks as they found her there, lounging threateningly. The immortals retired sullenly to their seats, and Molly came forward into the café to smile at me. Everywhere, cold eyes moved quickly from me to Molly and back again, but still no one had anything to say. They hadn't lived for so very long without learning to keep their mouths shut until they knew what was happening.

I studied the various faces unhurriedly from behind my featureless silver mask (there's something about the lack of eyeholes that really freaks people out), and finally settled on the few major players present. The only ones who might admit to knowing Mr Stab, and where he might currently be found. They weren't exactly top drawer, any of them. An elf lord in delicate filigreed brass armour, chased and etched with protective spells in old elvish. A monk in a tattered red robe, with a face so lined it was almost impossible to make out his features, marked as significant only by the Sumerian amulet around his neck. A couple of Baron Frankenstein's more successful creations, dressed in black leather from head to toe to hide their many scars. And a painfully thin presence in a grubby T-shirt and faded jeans who I only knew by reputation: the Hungry Heart. He had a plate full of steaming raw meat set out before him, and he was cramming it down as fast as he could shove it into his mouth. Blood dripped down his working chin, unnoticed.

Proof, if proof be needed, that immortality isn't everything.

The elf lord looked vaguely familiar, so I started with him. He sneered openly as I strolled over to his table, disdain written all over his arrogant, high-boned features. He made no move to get up or reach for a weapon but, even sitting still with both empty hands resting on the table top, he was still the most dangerous thing in the café, and both of us knew it.

'I know you,' I said. 'Where do I know you from, elf lord?'

'I was there,' he said, in his sweet, sick, magical voice. 'Leading the attack on you, in our ambush on the motorway. After your own family betrayed you to us. We came at you on our dragon mounts, singing our battle songs, with our brave new weapons. We had you outnumbered, we had our arrows of strange matter, and still you triumphed. Elf lords and ladies of ancient lineage, friends and family I had known for centuries, all fell beneath the thunder of your terrible gun. I am the only survivor of that day, but rest assured, foul and cursed Drood . . . the Unseeli Court does not forgive or forget.'

'Good,' I said. 'Neither do I.'

'We shall be at your throat all the days of your life!'

'Of course you will,' I said. 'You're an elf.'

And then I turned my back and ignored him. Knowing that would piss him off the most. There was no point in questioning an elf. He'd cut his own tongue out before taking the risk he might say anything that would help me. I looked thoughtfully at the monk in the scarlet robe and he straightened self-consciously under my silver gaze.

'Know, Oh mortal,' he said, in a surprisingly rich, deep and commanding voice, 'that I am Melmoth the Wanderer, that original lost soul upon whom the legend is based. Long have I wandered across the world, through lands and peoples whose very names are now forgotten.'

And then he stopped, because everyone else in the café was laughing at him. I couldn't really blame them. I'd already met a dozen Melmoths in my time, all claiming to be the original, along with as many Draculas, Fausts and Count St Germaines. Even immortals have their wannabes. I leaned in close for a better look at the Sumerian amulet and the monk flinched back in his chair. Up close, the thing was clearly a fake, so I turned my back on the monk too, and looked at the Frankenstein monsters.

They were both tall and on the large side, but they could still have just about passed as human, as long as they kept well wrapped up. Here at the Café Night, among their own kind, they didn't bother, and their black leather motorcycle jackets hung brazenly open, revealing long Y-shaped autopsy scars on their torsos. One had started out as male, and one as female, but such subtle distinctions had not survived their surgical rebirth. They were monsters, with nothing human in their faces or thoughts. Their complexions were grey, their lips black, their eyes yellow as urine, the eyelids drooping slackly away from dry eyeballs. Long rows of stitches showed on their foreheads, where the Baron had sawed open their skulls before dropping a new brain in. Unlike everyone else in the café, these two weren't scared of me, or even impressed. They had left such emotions behind them in the grave. Their thoughts and their hearts were cold, and they didn't care about anything I might threaten to do to them because the worst possible thing had already been done. No point in asking them anything.

That left the Hungry Heart, sitting alone at his table, set well aside from everyone else because some things are too disturbing, even for an immortal. A man so thin he was hardly there, but driven by a terrible energy. He looked up at Molly and me as we approached his table, but kept on stuffing his face with the raw meat, chewing desperately, even pushing pieces back into his mouth with his long bony fingers. He managed a sort of smile and blood trickled down his chin.

I knew his story. Everyone did. It's one of the great cautionary tales of our time, the gist of which is: never piss off a voodoo priest with a mean sense of humour. The Hungry Heart lives forever in the grip of an unrelenting hunger, never satisfied; and he can only survive by eating his own body weight in flesh every twenty-four hours. He has to dope himself heavily just to get a few hours of sleep every now and again. So never sleep with a voodoo priest's daughter, never get her pregnant and then abandon her, and never do a runner afterwards, thinking fleeing halfway across the world will put you out of the voodoo priest's reach.

Good thing he wasn't a vegetarian, I suppose. That would have been really terrible.

No one knows how old the Hungry Heart is. Or how long the poor bastard might live. Depends on his strength of will, I suppose. He finished the last scrap of raw meat on his plate, licked his bloody fingers, gazed sadly at the empty plate, and only then looked at me and Molly.

'Any meat will do,' he said, in a surprisingly soft and ordinary voice, 'as long as it's raw. Human flesh is the best. It's like a drug . . . Got a real kick to it. Wonder how much of a jolt I'd get from eating a Drood?'

'Sorry,' I said. 'Tinned meat isn't on the menu today.'

'What do you want?' said the Hungry Heart, all the tiredness of the world in his voice. 'No one here wants any trouble. We have enough of our own. All we want is to nurse our wounds in private, among our own kind.'

'Just looking for a little information,' Molly said breezily. 'We're trying to locate Mr Stab, and we've been given to understand that he frequents this place.'

'Now that really is an insult,' said the elf lord rising gracefully to his feet, a slender shimmering dagger in his hand. 'As if even we would tolerate such an abomination as Mr Stab in our select little circle. We do have our standards.'

'Yes,' said the monk, standing and, pulling back the sleeves of his crimson robe to reveal arms corded with muscle. 'You come in here and insult us to our faces? Associate us with the likes of Mr Stab? There's a limit to the abuse even we will take.'

The Frankenstein monsters were on their feet too, looking even larger and more imposing. And the Hungry Heart sighed, pushed his empty plate to one side and stood up also.

'I'm hungry,' he said. 'Anyone here got a can opener?'

'I might have,' said the monk. He produced a short knife from under his robe. 'This is the blade that cut Judas Iscariot down from the tree where he hanged himself, in Haceldama, the Field of Blood. Legend has it this blade can cut through anything. Maybe even Drood armour.'

He lunged forward incredibly quickly for one so old. The dagger slammed into my side, skidded across the silver armour in a flurry of sparks, and swept on, leaving my armour entirely undamaged. The monk staggered forward, caught off balance, and I hit him in the head. The whole left side of his face flattened, bone crunching and splintering, but he didn't fall. He raised the knife to cut at me again, so I grabbed his head with both silver hands and turned it all the way round so he was looking backwards. His neck broke loudly, but he still didn't fall. I pushed him away and he staggered off around the café, lost and bewildered.

By now everyone else in the café had run for the doors, not wanting to tangle with a Drood in full armour, and I was happy enough to see them go. They would only have got in the way. The two Frankenstein creatures had closed in on Molly, reaching out for her with their large, mismatched hands. Molly laughed in their ugly faces and hit them with a simple spell that made all their stitches come undone at once. The two monsters cried out in harsh, hopeless voices as ancient catgut exploded like rows of firecrackers in their skin, undoing them like zips. They fell apart, bit by bit, their separate pieces pattering to the floor, slowly at first and then in a rush. Hands fell from arms, arms from elbows and then from shoulders. Legs collapsed. Torsos hit the floor hard and opened up, spilling long-dead preserved organs on to the floor. The heads were the last to go, features slipping one by one from the face, until finally the skull cracked open and the dry grey brains fell out.

By then I had my own problems. The elf lord was closing in on me, smiling his nasty superior smile. He waved his long shimmering dagger meaningfully before me, and I knew what it was, what it had to be. The blade was made of strange matter, presumably put together from bits left over after the forging of the silver arrows that so nearly killed me in the motorway ambush. Could a blade of strange matter cut through armour made of strange matter? I decided I didn't want to find out. I concentrated and the armour around my hands extended into long silver killing blades. Just like my Uncle James taught me, when he was trying to kill me.

The elf lord and I circled each other slowly, taking our time, looking for weaknesses in stance and style, for hesitations and openings. Finally we darted in and out, cutting at each other with gleaming blades, come and gone in a moment. The armour made me supernaturally strong and fast, but he was an elf, so we were fairly matched. And for all my family's extensive training, he had centuries of experience; so he struck the first blow. His dagger came flying in out of nowhere, slipped gracefully past my defence, and slammed into my ribs. I cried out despite myself, but when the blade met my armour, the armour absorbed the blade into itself. The elf lord was left standing there with only a knife hilt in his hand.

I ran him through. You get a chance with an elf, you take it. You might not get another. My hand slammed against his chest, my extended blade splitting his heart in two. He grabbed my arm with both hands, as though that might hold him up. I twisted the blade, and he fell down, and died.

I retracted the silver blades into my hands, flexed my shining fingers, and looked round to see how Molly was doing. She was staring disgustedly at the Hungry Heart who was squatting over the disassembled Frankenstein creatures, feasting on their ancient flesh. He looked up and smiled apologetically.

'Tastes like dust, but flesh is flesh and beggars can't be choosers. If you really must find Mr Stab, and I can't think of any good reason why you'd want to, I suggest you try the old Woolwich Cemetery.'

'What would he be doing there?' said Molly.

'You ask him,' said the Hungry Heart. 'I wouldn't dare.'

The Merlin Glass transported us instantly to a gloomy, overgrown and deserted cemetery in Woolwich Arsenal, down in the dark heart of the East End on the far side of the Thames. The cemetery was mainly Victorian, dominated by over sized tombs and mausoleums and fancy graves. That whole period was fascinated with death and all its trappings, and the graveyard was positively littered with statues of weeping angels, mourning cherubs and enough morbid carvings and engravings to make even an undertaker shout, 'Jesus! Get a life dammit!' Long exposure to the elements had scoured away the angels' faces, giving the statues a sour surrealistic look. The cherubs still looked like dead babies, though. In fact, I think that was the name of a cartoon series I saw as a kid: *Casper, The Dead Baby.*

Molly and I set off down the single gravel path, heading deeper into the extensive cemetery grounds. The place looked abandoned. The grass had been left to grow and there were weeds everywhere, even pushing thick tufts up though the gravel path. There were no flowers on any of the graves, and the headstones were so weathered it was hard to make out the inscriptions. A cold wind was blowing, light was fading as evening descended, and shadows were creeping everywhere.

'I like this place,' said Molly.

'You would,' I said.

'No, really. It's . . . restful. Modern cemeteries are far too busy for my tastes. Once I'm gone, I don't want to be bothered with visitors or flowers. Bury me deep, set up perimeter mines to discourage the body-snatchers, and let me rest easy till Judgement Day. I'm going to need the peace and quiet to think up some good excuses.'

'All Droods get cremated,' I said. 'To make sure none of our enemies can play unpleasant tricks with our remains.'

'Maybe you could have your ashes shot into outer space, like Timothy Leary,' said Molly.

I had to smile. 'Anything to get away from my family.'

'I don't see Mr Stab anywhere,' said Molly. 'And I don't see what he would be doing in a place like this anyway.'

'We're not that far from his original killing grounds,' I said. 'Back when he first made a name for himself in 1888.'

'Maybe some of his victims are buried here.'

'Somehow I don't see Mr Stab as the sentimental kind,' I said. 'And anyway, from what I've been able to make out on these tombstones, most of them date from long before Jack the Ripper.'

We walked up and down and back and forth in the cemetery, and still no sign anywhere of Mr Stab. Given the sheer size and scale of the cemetery grounds, it would take hours to cover it all, and besides, I was getting impatient. And cold. I'd dropped my armour when I left Café Night, but now I subvocalised the Words and called up enough armour to cover my face. With a little concentration, I can see infra-red though the mask, and it didn't take me long to locate the only other human heat source in the darkening graveyard. I armoured down again, rather than risk putting Mr Stab on the defensive, and led the way over to where he was standing, doing my best to appear calm and unthreatening and not in any way worried. He doesn't like it when people he's trying to have a conversation with are clearly scared shitless of him. In fact, for an immortal serial killer, Mr Stab could be quite remarkably touchy.

He was dressed in the formal clothes of his original period: all stark black and white, with a top hat and even an opera cloak. When stalking his victims he could blend in like anyone else, but when he was off duty, so to speak, he preferred the clothes he was most comfortable with. He was a tall and powerful man, with broad shoulders and long arms. He had a wide paternal face, like a kindly old family doctor . . . until you looked into his eyes. And saw the horrors of Hell looking back at you.

He turned slowly to face us as we drew nearer. 'Molly,' he said. 'How nice. And Edwin Drood, again. An honour.'

'What are you doing in a place like this?' said Molly, blunt as ever.

'Just . . . visiting,' said Mr Stab. He smiled vaguely, showing large blocky teeth grown brown with age. He gestured at the graves around him. 'Once this was a fashionable place, with people simply dying to get in. Special trains brought the fortunate deceased here from all over the country. Long ago now, and no one remembers any more. Except me. I have friends and family here; people who knew me when I was just a man. The last people to remember me as I was, before I became a name to frighten people with.'

I found it hard to think of Mr Stab as ever being normal, with a normal life, and he must have sensed it, because he made a brief dismissive gesture and looked at me coldly.

'What do you want with me, Edwin Drood?'

I explained the situation, but he was shaking his head even before I finished. 'What makes you think I would be so foolish and trusting as to place myself into the hands of my long-time enemies? More importantly, even if you could manage to convince me of my safety, why should I go to the one place where I would never be allowed to kill? I must murder, Edwin. It is my nature.'

'After the tutoring is done,' I said, 'you can murder as many Loathly Ones as you like.'

'The Droods have opened up their Old Library,' said Molly. 'Packed full of forgotten and forbidden texts from centuries back. Somewhere in that Library there must be information on how to . . . if not reverse, at least moderate the conditions of your immortality. Give you some control over it. So you wouldn't have to kill all the time.'

Mr Stab considered her thoughtfully. 'And what makes you think I want that?'

'Because you've refrained from killing me and my friends,' said Molly. 'And I've never known you do that for anyone else.'

He nodded slowly. 'You want me to do this thing, Molly? Even though you must know it can only end in tears?'

'I want you to do this so it won't,' said Molly.

'Then so be it,' said Mr Stab.

I opened the Merlin Glass to the Armoury, and waved Mr Stab through. He was greeted by an exceedingly harried-looking Armourer, and I shut the mirror down quickly as Uncle Jack looked very much like he wanted to say something, but I was pretty sure it wasn't anything I wanted to hear. I put the Glass away, and turned to Molly.

'I think we've done enough for one day, don't you? I reckon we're owed a little down time before we have to report back. What shall we do?'

'Well,' said Molly, linking her arm through mine, 'I did promise you a good meal, and since we're in London for the evening . . . What say we take in a West End show and have dinner afterwards at the Ritz?'

'Sounds good to me,' I said. 'But we'll never get tickets for anything decent at such short notice.'

'I'm a witch, sweetie, remember? Trust me, tickets are not going to be a problem.'

I thought it best to give the family time to adjust to their new tutors before I showed my face at The Hall again, so the theatre and a nice meal it was. We went to see the new production at Shaftesbury Avenue, *Prince of Thieves: The Musical*. Starring Robbie Williams as Robin Hood, Paris Hilton as Maid Marion and Ricky Gervais as the Sheriff. Music, book and lyrics by no one you've ever heard of. Tickets were not a problem; Molly did a Jedi mind trick with the theatre staff, and we ended up in a private box. Afterwards we went to the Ritz, and ordered the very best of everything, secure in the knowledge that we had no intention of paying for any of it.

Hey, I keep the world safe and Humanity protected. I'm entitled to a few perks and privileges.

'An interesting production,' I said to Molly, over pieces of lightly browned toast piled high with Beluga caviar.

'Yes, but why is there such a preoccupation with translating successful films into stage shows? And why didn't they sing the Bryan Adams song? It's all most people remember about the film anyway.'

Several bottles of really good champagne later, we stiffed the waiter with an imaginary credit card, tangoed giggling down the Ritz steps, and used the Merlin Glass to take us home. We stepped through into the Armoury, where the Armourer was waiting for us. He did not look happy.

'What the hell did you think you were doing, landing me with those four psychopaths? I have enough trouble looking after the psychopaths who work under me! And I have more than enough work to do without baby-sitting your special needs friends!'

I looked around but there was no sign of any of my tutors. I fixed the Armourer with an only slightly owlish look.

'Uncle Jack, what have you done with them?'

He sniffed loudly. 'I handed them over to Penny and let her take care of them. You know she loves organising things. And people.'

I looked at him, shocked and suddenly stone cold sober. 'You did *what*? She'll never be able to handle a dangerous bunch like that! The Blue Fairy alone could walk all over her without even raising a sweat, never mind Mr Stab! Where are they now?'

'I'm sure I don't know. Ask Penny. Now get out of here. I've got a pocket universe that needs stabilising.'

I activated my mental link with Strange, in the Sanctity.

'Red alert, emergency, emergency!'

'Oh, hello, Eddie! Welcome back. Did you have a nice time in town? Did you bring me a present?'

'Never mind that—'

You didn't, did you? You forgot all about me.'

'Where's Penny and the four tutors she's supposed to be looking after?'

'At the lecture auditoriums, of course. She's already got the first tutorials up and running. It's terribly exciting!'

I cut contact with Strange, before I said something one of us would regret, and used the Merlin Glass to transport Molly and me straight to the lecture halls in the South Wing. I had this horrible mental picture of a room full of dead Droods, with blood running down the aisles, while Janissary Jane and Mr Stab played football with their severed heads. But when we arrived in the lobby outside the auditoriums, all seemed calm and quiet. Penny was walking unhurriedly back and forth, listening at first one door and then the next. She jumped a little as Molly and I appeared through the Glass, and then hurried over to us, making shushing gestures.

'Thanks a whole bunch for dropping those four on me!' she said, the effect somewhat limited by her hushed tone.

'Blame the Armourer,' I said automatically. 'Where are they, Penny? Has there been any trouble?'

'None,' said Penny. 'I thought the best thing to do was put them to work straight away. Let the family see what they could do. So I gave them an auditorium each, told them to talk about what the hell they liked, and much to my surprise they took to it like ducks to water. It's worked out rather well. It's standing room only for all four lecture halls, and when was the last time that happened?'

'And there haven't been any . . . incidents?' said Molly.

'Not yet,' said Penny. 'A part of me keeps waiting for the other bomb to drop.'

'Why are we whispering?' I said.

Penny raised an eyebrow. 'Well, we don't want to interrupt them, do we?'

I moved over to the nearest door and slipped quietly through to stand at the back of the lecture hall. Molly was quickly there at my side. Subway Sue was up on the stage, striding back and forth, hitting the fascinated packed audience with what it was like to live on the very edges of society. To be in the city, but not part of it, alone and unsupported, surviving entirely on your wits.

'You don't know how easy it is to fall off the edge,' she said. 'All it would take is one really bad day, and any one of you could end up like me. I had a home and job and a life, once. I had friends and family. And then I lost them, one by one. Lost them, or had them taken from me. And so I ended up a homeless person, living on the streets, because even after everything else is gone, the streets are always there. In time I became a luck vampire and made a new life for myself. I could have had my old life back, but I didn't want it any more. I'd become somebody else, and my old life wouldn't have fit. But, once again, I had one really bad day and I lost it all again. The one thing you have to learn is never to depend on anyone but yourself. Because there's nothing you can have that the world can't take away.'

The audience were transfixed, breathless. They'd never encountered anyone like Subway Sue before. I slipped back out the door, Molly behind me, and we went to look in on Mr Stab. He stood entirely at ease on the stage, glaring calmly out at his equally packed audience, as he lectured them on the skills of murder, the stalking of victims, the joys of slaughter . . . and how even the smallest seeds of evil can flower in a man and corrupt him. He talked of hunting prey, of tracking a target unsuspected for days or even weeks, if necessary.

'You need to know these things,' he said. 'You don't have your legendary armour any more. You cannot be invincible warriors, so you must learn to become hunters. You must acquire the techniques of ambush and fighting and killing. And no one knows more about that than me. Learn from me, and I guarantee that most of you will survive the great war that's coming.'

In the next auditorium, the Blue Fairy was sitting relaxed on a bar stool on the stage, drinking a cocktail with a little umbrella in it, while he lectured on elves and their often unsuspected interventions in the modern world.

'The elves are long gone,' he said. 'They walked sideways from the sun centuries ago, dropping out of our world for ever. Everyone knows that but, like most things everyone knows, it's a crock of shit. Most of the elves are gone, but some remain, intent on revenge. They hate Humanity, for ruling the world that was once theirs, and they live to do us harm and bring us down. They'll side with anyone, or anything, that will help them in their endless bitter cause.'

And finally we listened to Janissary Jane tell the family how to fight demons. She marched back and forth across the stage, her cold, practical voice making what she had to say even more disturbing and scary.

'Demons,' she said flatly, 'cannot be reasoned with, or bought off. You can't negotiate with them. They see us only as a commodity; something to be used. Some come from Hell, some from the Past or the Future, and some from other worlds or dimensions. It doesn't matter. All you have to remember is that they exist only to destroy everything you care about. They'll take your lives, your world, your souls, and use them for their own purposes. And never give a damn. They're locusts, sweeping through a field until nothing is left. Unless you fight them with everything you've got. And you're going to have to learn to fight as an army, because this is a war. You can't be warriors any more, fighting individual duels. You can't be heroes. You have to be soldiers, fighting in a great cause. You have to learn to be an army; because there are armies of them.'

Penny smiled as Molly and I wandered, a little dazed, back into the lobby.

'Well, Eddie,' she said. 'Looks like you finally did something right.'

'You're welcome,' I said.

'Bitch,' said Molly.

'You're welcome, bitch,' I said.

CHAPTER SEVEN
A thousand and one damnations

It was early afternoon on a bright and breezy summer day, and the grounds of The Hall rang with the merry sound of organised mayhem. Janissary Jane had half the family out doing military exercises again. Separated into groups with terse, efficient names like Alpha, Beta and Omega, men and women charged up and down the lawns yelling their battle cries and frightening the gryphons. Group attacked group with blank ammunition, wooden batons and even bare hands, and generally ran themselves ragged under Janissary Jane's barked orders. Watching happily from a comfortable deckchair in the shade of a broad parasol, I thought they looked pretty good. Even if they were making a hell of a mess of the carefully cultivated lawns. The team of gardeners had already thrown a major wobbly, and slouched off for a collective sulk and brew-up in their shed.

Janissary Jane had been putting the family through its paces for over two weeks now, and I had to say the family were taking to military training and discipline like ducks to water. We are trained to fight the good fight from an early age, but the torcs made it easy. It's not difficult to play at soldiers when you have the armour to make you fast and strong, and keep you from getting hurt. But not many actually have the aptitude for it. Which is one of the reasons why field agents have always been such a small part of the family.

Training without a torc was a whole different matter. You could get hurt, and so could your opponent. Surprisingly, that hadn't put off as many of the family as I'd expected. If anything, they embraced the new training. Because it felt more . . . real. So their achievements felt more real. And they practically worshipped Janissary Jane, who'd done everything the Droods had and more, without the aid of the family armour.

Penny came strolling across the lawns to join me, looking cool and collected in a blindingly white summer outfit, despite the heat of the afternoon. She stood over me, and I offered to pour her a glass of champagne from the bottle I had cooling in an ice bucket. She sniffed disdainfully.

'Are you sure you're comfortable enough there, Eddie? Got everything you need? Perhaps you'd like me to rush back and bring you out a footstool?'

'Oh, would you?' I said. 'I'd be ever so grateful.'

'Blow it out your ear.' Penny looked at the men and women dashing excitedly back and forth in their groups and throwing themselves upon each with much enthusiasm and violence. 'They do seem to be getting into it, don't they?'

'Damn right,' I said. 'I'm exhausted just sitting here watching them. More importantly, it's doing a hell of a lot for family morale. Everything they're accomplishing comes from themselves, not from their armour. It's doing wonders for their self-confidence.'

Penny looked at me. 'And that's why you brought Janissary Jane here?'

'To set an example, yes. I cut the family off at the knees when I took away their golden torcs. Took away their pride, their self-esteem and their confidence. Janissary Jane is beating it back into them the hard way, and they love it.'

'I take it you've noticed Harry is also watching from a safe distance, along with several of his traditionalist chums?'

'Of course,' I said. 'He never wants to be a part of anything I organise, but he never misses anything that's happening. He's probably making notes for his regular report to the Matriarch. She can't be seen to be taking an interest personally, but Harry's been her eyes and ears ever since he got here.'

'I told you we should have brought him into the Inner Circle,' said Penny. 'Keep your enemies close and all that.'

'No,' I said flatly. 'I don't trust him.'

'You keep saying that, but you won't say why.' Penny waited, but I had nothing more to say. She sighed heavily. 'All right, his best friend is a hellspawn, but you're shacked up with the infamous witch of the wild woods. And you let her into the Inner Circle.'

'I trust Molly,' I said. 'Hell, I even trust you, Penny dear. Harry, on the other hand . . . is perhaps a little too much like me. Crafty and devious and following his own flag.'

'You brought the Sarjeant-At-Arms into the Circle,' said Penny. 'And you hate his guts. And you know very well he reports everything we say back to the Matriarch.'

'Cyril's different,' I said. 'I can trust him to put the good of the family first. Even over the Matriarch.'

'Well, much as I hate to interrupt this important bit of loafing about you're so involved in, I have been sent to remind you very firmly, up to and including the use of violence if necessary, that it's time for the Inner Circle meeting in the Sanctity. We've finally got a list of prospective candidates for the new torcs.'

'About time,' I said, heaving myself gracelessly out of the deck-chair. Not that far away, two teams of warriors in training lost their temper and jumped each other, brawling across the lawn with much flailing of fists, kicking and occasional biting. Janissary Jane hurried over to break it up, and I decided it was time to leave them to it. They'd have to manage without my moral support.

We met in the Sanctity again, under the comforting crimson glow of the manifesting Strange. We'd settled on that for his name, even though he kept plaintively insisting he felt much more like an Ethel. You have to draw the line somewhere. The Armourer was already there, of course, along with the Sarjeant-At-Arms. Molly was waiting at the door when Penny and I arrived. She gave Penny a long, hard look, and made a point of taking my arm in hers as we joined the rest of the Inner Circle.

'Jacob is still missing,' said the Armourer, not bothering with the usual hellos and how-are-yous. 'It's been two weeks since anyone's seen him. He hasn't been back to the old Chapel, and even the headless nun has been asking rather plaintively what's happened to him. Though what she sees in him . . . I'm beginning to think something's happened to him.'

'How could anything have happened to him?' said Penny. 'I mean, he's dead. Has been for centuries.'

'More likely he's up to something,' growled the Sarjeant-At-

Arms. Ever since he'd been outed as a Cyril, his voice had taken on a distinctly lower tone. 'No doubt something foul and appalling, which he will find terribly amusing.'

'Jacob can look after himself,' I said firmly. 'I'm sure he'll turn up when he's needed. Whether we want him to or not. In the meantime, Penny tells me that you've finally agreed on a list of prospective candidates for the new torcs.'

'Yes, finally,' said the Armourer, glaring round impartially. 'Fifty names have been arrived at, decided by due process, and after much deliberation, shouting and hair-pulling—'

'Which means,' the Sarjeant said heavily, 'that it's time to talk about launching our first attack. We need to put on a massive show of strength as soon as possible. Prove to the world that we're strong and united and still a force to be reckoned with.'

'No,' Penny said immediately. 'We're not ready yet. We need more time, more training, and a hell of a lot more than fifty torcs before we can successfully put a force in the field.'

'They looked pretty good to me just now,' I said mildly. 'And for once, I am forced to agree with the Sarjeant. Quick, someone take a photo. We need to do something big and aggressive, and we need to do it now. Some politicians, and other enemies, are growing increasingly restless. Reports are coming in from all over the world of sabre-rattling between countries, of invasions and excursions into disputed territories,that would never have happened in the old days when we ruled with a golden fist and made everyone play nice. And then there are the usual suspects, stirring up trouble here and there to test the waters and see what they can get away with. Dr Delirium, the Cold Eidolon, and Truman in his new base, wherever that is, and I can't believe we haven't got a decent line on that yet. Remind me to kick someone's arse about that. No, people; we have to do something right now. Strike some shock and awe into our enemies; prove we're still in the game and that bad boys will be severely spanked.'

'Then pick a target,' said the Sarjeant. 'Anyone, as long as they're a danger. You're the one who kept going on about the Loathly Ones . . .'

'This is all going too quickly,' Penny said stubbornly. 'Move before we're ready and it could backfire. We can't afford for the world to learn how weak we really are.'

'How will you know when you're ready?' Molly said reasonably. 'Training can only do so much. Eventually you've got to kick the little birdies out of the nest and see whether they fly.'

'I don't know if this qualifies,' Strange said suddenly. 'But I'm picking up a new report coming in to the War Room. It seems to be saying we have a definite location for a large gathering of Loathly Ones.'

We sat up straighter and looked at each other. Reports had been coming in for some time now that the Loathly Ones had been gathering together in unusual numbers somewhere down in South America.

'Where?' I said.

'The Nazca Plain,' said Strange. 'You know, the place they have the big lines dug into the ground that make up shapes you can only see clearly from orbit, or something. In his *Chariots of the Gods* Von Daniken said they were really landing pads for spaceships.'

'Hold everything,' said Molly. 'You've read Von Daniken?'

'Oh, sure!' said Strange. 'I love a good laugh.'

We trooped straight down to the War Room, carefully not hurrying too much so as not to draw attention to ourselves. The family watched everything the Inner Circle did with great interest, and they did so love to gossip. If we were about to launch our first big attack, I didn't want the information getting out in advance. The staff in the War Room were more than a bit surprised to see us, as the report on the Loathly Ones was still coming in from our agent in the field, one Callan Drood. We had hardly any agents out in the world at the moment, as it was hard to get anyone to volunteer without the protection of a torc. The Droods have a lot of enemies. Luckily, some of the younger members of the family were keen to prove themselves, and hopefully fast-track themselves for one of the new torcs.

I knew Callan. I'd been impressed by his attitude, and his thoroughness, when I found out he led the team searching through Truman's old stamping ground under London. I suggested he might like to volunteer for field work, and he jumped at the chance. Though of course he had to be sarcastic and opinionated about it, so he could pretend he'd been talked into it against his better judgement. He didn't want anyone to think he was a push-over. So I smiled, and sent him to South America. And now he'd been the one to find the Loathly Ones for us.

South America! What the hell were they doing there?

Callan's face filled one of the main display screens. He didn't look too happy about things, but then he never did. His young broad face was sunburned, his thin blond hair was plastered to his skull, and the sweat was dripping off him. In the background was a tall bluff face of some dark sandstone and a sky so blue it was almost painful to the eye.

'About time you got here,' he snapped. 'It's a hundred and thirty in the shade and there isn't any shade. Soon as this briefing has finished, I'm going to find a swimming pool and drink it. I'm looking out over the Nazca Plains, and the Loathly Ones have been gathering down there for the last six months. They're building something out on the plain. I don't know what it is, but I really don't like the look of it. Local government have been well bribed to stay away, and the whole area is out of bounds for tourists. There are guards on all the main approaches to turn people back and discourage anyone from asking too many questions.'

'Can you describe this thing they're building?' said the Armourer.

'Not really. It's big, maybe a hundred feet tall, and half as wide, some of it's machinery and some of it isn't, and it makes my head hurt to look at it. There are hundreds of Loathly Ones here, swarming over the bloody thing and adding bits to it.'

'Could be a weapon of some kind,' said the Armourer.

'No, really! You think so?' said Callan. 'And here I was, thinking it was probably the centrepiece of a Loathly Ones theme park. Look, just get the hell down here, okay? This whole thing is creeping me out big time. Bring reinforcements. And cold drinks.'

'Could this new structure be in any way connected with the ancient lines on the plain?' said Penny.

'Damned if I know,' said Callan. 'Nothing obvious, anyway.'

'The lines are thousands of years old,' said Penny, frowning seriously. 'Laid out in their gigantic patterns so long ago that no one now remembers who did it, or why. They're even older than our family.'

'There may be something in the Old Library,' said the Armourer.

'The location can't be a coincidence,' said the Sarjeant-At-Arms. 'Callan, are you sure there isn't any connection?'

'Look, I'm telling you what I see. And I am not getting any closer for a better look. The Loathly Ones have been attacking anyone or anything that shows up on the plain, and I like my soul where it is, thank you very much. If you want to know more about the lines, read your Von Daniken.'

'Don't say you read him too,' said Molly.

'Of course. He has a lot of good insights. If I didn't know better, I'd swear he was one of us.'

'Thank you, Callan,' I said quickly. 'Keep an eye on things till we get there, and report any new activity.'

'Remember the cold drinks.'

I gestured for the communications people to shut down the display screen and then I looked round at the rest of my Inner Circle. 'This is it. The opportunity we've been waiting for. The Loathly Ones getting together in unprecedented numbers and maybe building a new super-weapon? We can't allow this to continue.'

'I don't know about unprecedented,' the Armourer said. 'I seem to recall something similar back in my grandfather's day. I'll have to look it up in the family records.'

'They don't normally take over anything bigger than a small town,' said Penny. 'And even then they go to great pains to hide it from the rest of the world. This kind of public display is out of character.'

'You mean it could be a trap?' said Molly.

'I don't see how,' I said. 'They're right out in the open. And that thing they're building worries me. No, we've found our first target. Taking out a major gathering of the Loathly Ones is the best way to announce to the world that we're still in business.'

'But we don't know enough about the situation,' Penny said stubbornly. 'We have no idea what it is they're building, or the dangers involved in destroying it. We don't even know for sure what defences the Loathly Ones have put in place around it. We need more information before we commit ourselves to a main assault.'

'The only way we'll get more information is to go down there and kick the Loathly Ones around till they tell us what they're doing,' said the Sarjeant.

'Exactly,' I said. 'We need to move now, before they finish whatever it is they're doing, and before they realise we know about it. So. We take in a strike force, led by our new torcs, destroy as many of the Loathly Ones as possible, and tear down whatever we find there. I said we were going to war against the Loathly Ones, and this will be a great beginning. Penny, tell the family that we're ready to hand out the first fifty torcs. We'll make a whole ceremony of it. The new knights in armour of the Drood family.'

'Don't you want to check the names?' said Penny.

'No,' I said. 'I trust your judgement. Why? Is there someone on the list you think I might object to?'

'Just the one,' said Molly. 'Harry.'

'I'd have been surprised if he wasn't on the list,' I said. 'He's an experienced field agent. And James's son.'

'But you don't trust him,' said Penny.

'Of course not,' I said. 'He's James's son.'

We held the torc-giving ceremony in the Sanctity, celebrating the bestowing of fifty new torcs on deserving members of the family. The Sanctity was packed from wall to wall with excited family, standing shoulder to shoulder. More filled the corridor outside. We had to set up vid screens all through The Hall so everyone in the family could see. This was the start of a new era for the Droods, and I wanted everyone to feel a part of it. Even the Matriarch and her supporters were looking in, from her suite. I checked. Strange shed his beneficent light over us, and even broadcast some suitable music, complete with trumpets and fanfares in all the right places.

One by one they came forward and knelt before the crimson glow: the fifty, the chosen few, the new knights of the family, and out of nowhere a silver torc appeared around their necks. A great cheer went up for each of the fifty names, and the family applauded them till their hands ached. There were smiles and tears everywhere, and much stamping of feet. There was a common feeling that these torcs were special, and these fifty men and women special because they had earned their torcs.

At the end, the Inner Circle pushed me forward to say a few words. I didn't particularly want to, but everyone there seemed to expect it of me. I got a pretty good cheer as I stepped forward, though perhaps not as good a cheer as the fifty chosen ones got, and it quickly died away as I raised my hands for quiet.

'This is the start of a new day,' I said. 'For the family, and for the world. No more sitting around waiting for threats and then reacting to them. We're going to take the fight to the enemy. And we're going to start by bringing down the Loathly Ones! I shall lead a strike force against their new base of operations: fifty torced men and women and two hundred volunteers, armed with the very best toys the Armoury can supply. Salute these warriors! The Droods are going to war, and the Loathly Ones are going down! Mark this day, my family, my friends. It's time to show the world that the Droods are back in town!'

Afterwards, Molly said to me, 'Whoever told you that you know how to make a speech?'

'It's a dirty job,' I said. 'But someone's got to do it.'

We flew down to South America in the family's private fleet of Blackhawke aircraft. Great big beasts of the sky, smooth and sleek and driven by powerful engines we reverse-engineered from an alien starship that crash-landed in a Wiltshire field in 1947. Five planes, carrying fifty men and women with their new torcs, two hundred heavily armed volunteers, myself and Molly, Janissary Jane and Mr Stab, and Harry and Roger Morningstar. I could have done without that last addition, but Harry wouldn't go without him. Molly and I were there because it was my plan, Janissary Jane because she'd trained these people and knew more about fighting demons than all the rest of us put together, and Mr Stab because . . . well, basically because I wanted a vicious supernatural serial killer on my side in case anything went wrong.

And I wanted to have him close, where I could keep a watchful eye on him.

Mr Stab hadn't joined the rest of us in the Sanctity for the bestowing of the torcs, but then I hadn't expected him to. He wasn't what you'd call a social animal. So afterwards I sent Penny to look for him, to tell him about the forthcoming attack on the Loathly Ones. When she didn't report back after a reasonable time, I got a little worried. I found a private place, locked the door, tuned the Merlin Glass to the Present, and ordered it to look in on Penny and Mr Stab, wherever they might be. My reflection vanished from the mirror, replaced by a view of the two of them walking together in the grounds. Just walking, and chatting. Penny seemed completely at ease in Mr Stab's company; even after I'd gone out of my way to warn her about what he was and what he'd done. Their voices came to me quite clearly.

'I wouldn't have thought you were the fresh-air and wide-open-spaces type,' said Penny. 'I had you marked down as a town mouse.'

'I prefer it out here,' said Mr Stab.

'Is the room we've given you not comfortable enough?'

'I've known many rooms, down the years,' said Mr Stab. He kept his gaze straight ahead, not looking at Penny. 'All pretty much the same, places to stay for a while before I'm forced to move on again. These days I carry a little notebook to remind me of where I'm staying and what name I'm currently using. No home for me; not any more. Just another of the many human things I had to give up, to be what I am. My room here is perfectly adequate. Even luxurious. But no, I'm not comfortable here in The Hall. I'm not allowed to murder, you see, and I find that very trying. It goes against my nature. It grinds against my soul until I can't see anything but blood. And that's why I spend as much time as possible in your extensive grounds, away from . . . temptation.'

'I don't think I've ever heard you say so much at one time,' said Penny. 'You're a very interesting man, Mr Stab.'

He looked at her for the first time. 'You're not scared of me?'

'I'm a Drood,' said Penny. 'It takes a lot to scare us. And anyway, you'll be off to South America soon, to fight the Loathly Ones. There'll be killing enough then to satisfy anyone – even you.'

'It's not the same,' said Mr Stab. 'I have to murder, to tear the flesh and spill the blood, to see the suffering in their eyes. It's what I do. It's all I have.'

'And you always kill women?'

'Yes. Because it's the only form of intimacy I can ever know now. My punishment and my reward.'

'Is it true . . . Have you really done all the things they say you have?'

'Oh, yes,' said Mr Stab. 'All that, and more. Make no mistake,

Penny, I have done terrible things, and gloried in them. I have thrust my arms deep into the guts of horror and brought them out dripping red up to the elbows. They called me Jack the Ripper, and I was. The things I did, to poor Marie Kelly, in that small shuttered room . . . I opened her up like a book and read her secrets. I sent the press a letter, once, and gave them my address. From Hell, it said. And that was just the beginning.'

'And you . . . *have* to kill? You're driven to murder?'

'Yes.'

'Then if you don't have any choice, it isn't really your fault, is it?'

'Yes, it is, Penny. I killed those six women of my own free will, savouring the agony and terror in their dying eyes, breathing in their last exhalations like the finest wines. And if this particular form of immortality isn't quite what I thought I was buying with my ceremony of slaughter, it's the hell I earned for the evil I did, back in that unseasonably warm autumn of 1888.'

'But you haven't killed anyone here,' said Penny.

'I gave my word,' said Mr Stab. 'But it won't last. It never does.'

'This is a new place. You've never known anywhere like Drood Hall. All kinds of things are possible here. Even redemption. Come back to The Hall with me, maybe I can show you that you're stronger than you think you are.'

He looked at her for a long moment. 'This can only end badly, Penny.'

'I don't believe that,' said Penny. 'I've never believed that.'

I watched through the mirror as she casually slipped an arm through his and led him back across the great grassy lawns to The Hall.

I must have been frowning in my seat on the plane, because Molly dug me in the ribs with her elbow. 'What's up, sweetie? Afraid of flying?'

'No, it's not that. I was . . . thinking.'

'Well stop frowning like that; you'll get lines. You know, this really is some plane, Eddie. I've flown first class on all the best airlines, on faked tickets of course, but never anything to match this. Really comfortable chairs, plenty of leg room, and it hardly seems like we're moving. I'll bet the US President doesn't have it this good on Air Force One.'

I had to smile at her enthusiasm. I was pretty excited myself. I'd never been allowed out of the country before. Never been on a plane before. I kept looking out the window to make sure it was real. And yet . . . there was something in the air in the long cabin, an atmosphere of tension and anticipation. Torced and untorced family members sat side by side, not talking much, trying to pretend they were reading the books or magazines they'd brought with them. The Blackhawke's augmented engines would get us to our destination in under two hours, but that was more than enough time for everyone to think of everything that could go wrong. I was no different. This was the family's first big military operation since I took control and changed everything. We had to win this one. For all kinds of reasons.

I wondered what I was going to do about Penny and Mr Stab. *It's always the bad boy that makes a girl's heart beat that little bit faster.*

As if I didn't have enough to worry about.

By the time we'd crossed the South American continent and descended over the Nazca Plain, we'd got over the novelty of flying and were more than ready for a little action. Molly had trouble getting her head round the fact that because the torcs made us invisible to all forms of detection, it meant the planes we travelled in were essentially invisible too. There wasn't a radar installation or spy satellite anywhere that could detect our presence, even for a moment.

'Look, trust me,' I said finally. 'No one knows we're here, no one knows we're coming. Compared to us, stealth bombers are painted bright pink with big neon signs on them saying "Hello, Sailor, come and get me!" Our only worry is avoiding other aircraft, because we won't show up on their radar. We're staying well above the usual commercial flight paths, but there's always the chance of bumping into some secret military job, or even the occasional UFO.'

'Hold everything,' said Molly. 'UFOs, as in flying saucers? Close encounters of the extremely unlikely kind, where they stick things up your bottom? Really?'

'Not as such,' I said. 'But there are a hundred and thirty-seven different alien species currently running around on Planet Earth that we know of. Most of them we keep in line through various long-established treaties and agreements; others we just step on hard now and again, to remind them not to make waves. But there are always a few unidentified objects zipping through the stratosphere on their own inscrutable business, and they can be a damned nuisance sometimes.'

'Real aliens!' said Molly. 'That is so cool!'

I had to smile. 'You don't have any trouble that we're on our way to slap down a bunch of soul-eating demons, but the thought of aliens get you all excited?'

'That's different,' Molly said stubbornly. 'I don't tend to bump into aliens in my line of work. All I know is magic. Vampires, werewolves, ghouls and necromancers, no problem. Deal with them every day. But most of what I know of aliens comes from Ridley Scott's *Alien* and John Carpenter's *The Thing.* Tell me that is not representative of most aliens, please. There must be some like ET?'

'Would you rather have the truth, or a comforting lie?' I said.

'Oh, shut up. Are we nearly there yet?'

We landed at a private airfield, far away from anywhere civilised that might ask awkward questions about things like passports and visas. The family owns or leases such places in countries all over the world for such occasions as this. (Through a series of concealing false names and cut-outs, of course.) We filed off the Blackhawkes and the heat hit us like a hammer. The sun was directly overhead in a cloudless sky and my skin actually smarted from the impact of the sudden heat. I armoured up immediately in the interests of self-preservation. The family didn't need a strike force leader with sunstroke. The other torced Droods immediately followed suit, leaving the rest of the strike force looking distinctly mutinous. Molly worked a quick but subtle magic, and after that it was always shade wherever they happened to be standing.

Mr Stab, Roger Morningstar and Janissary Jane didn't seem to notice the heat. They'd endured much worse in their time.

I had a quick chat with the guy running the airfield for us, an old rogue with a dark wrinkled face who'd served the family well and loyally for many years. And would continue to do so, as long as the money kept coming. My armour didn't throw him; he'd seen it before. Though he did compliment me on my new colour scheme. I asked him what he knew about the unusual business down on the Nazca Plain and he told me what he could, in excellent English.

It seemed foreigners had been coming to the plains in small groups for several months now. All nationalities, all types; but not the usual tourists. These were strange people, even for foreigners: talking and acting oddly, though he found it hard to be specific about what bothered him about them. *As though they were always thinking of something else,* was the best he could manage. They bought many things in the surrounding towns and always paid cash. The local merchants loved them and hoped they'd stay for ever. When I pressed him on what these strangers had been buying, he said mostly technology, off-the-shelf stuff and special orders, and an extraordinary amount of livestock. All kinds. Presumably for slaughtering, since none of the foreigners professed any interest in farming; and they bought far more than they could ever hope to eat.

I thanked him, and slipped him a little extra for his trouble to cement friendly relations. I didn't need to worry that he might talk about us; he knew better than to talk about Drood business. He'd helped bury the previous airfield owner after he got a bit too talkative. No one betrays the Droods and lives to boast of it.

Janissary Jane got the expeditionary force sorted out into squads and loaded onto the fleet of jeeps the owner had provided, and we set off on the long hard journey to the Nazca Plains. There was no scenery and no road, just an endless jolting ride across a sullen empty desert under a baking sun. The trip seemed to last for ever, but finally we came to a halt at the base of a cliff overlooking the plain. We disembarked from the jeeps, did a certain amount of stretching and stamping our feet, and then we climbed the steep rise to the top and looked out over the plains. Callan Drood was waiting for us there, very sunburned, and extremely pissed off that we hadn't brought any cold drinks with us. Molly conjured him up an iced bottle of Pepsi and he drank it so fast he gave himself a headache.

I looked down at what the Loathly Ones were doing on the Nazca Plains. From this height they looked like ants, swarming around and over the huge structure that rose up from the heavily lined and grooved stone plain like a single alien skyscraper. It had to be three hundred feet tall now, a strange and unearthly mixture of styles and materials. Its shape made no sense. My mind couldn't seem to cope with the unexpected dimensions and distortions. Just looking at it made my eyes hurt. Callan came forward to join me.

'It's better if you look at it for only a few moments at a time. I'm pretty sure we're looking at something that exists in more than three spatial dimensions, and what we see is only our minds trying to make sense of it. Don't ask me what the hell it is, or what it's for, but the Loathly Ones are all over it, day and night, inside and out. There's a single opening at the base, and a lot of what goes in never comes out again. I get the feeling it's almost finished. The pace of work has accelerated in the last twelve hours, like they're fighting a deadline. Where are my cold drinks? I was promised cold drinks. And I'd better get a torc out of this. I've spent weeks out here, dodging the bastards' patrols. Very heavily armed patrols, I might add. They kill anyone who gets too close, even clearly harmless tourists, whether they've seen anything or not.'

I gestured for him to shut up, and he did. My silver mask allowed me to zoom in on the towering edifice down on the plain, so I could study details as though I was right on top of them. The alien structure struck me as much a machine as a building, designed to do . . . something, but the more I looked the less sense it made. It didn't take me long to discover what they'd been doing with so much livestock. The Loathly Ones had incorporated bits of them into the structure. Parts of the tower were clearly technological, even if I couldn't identify it, but other parts were just as clearly organic. Living flesh, whole organs, bloody guts and connective tissues, even entire brains and heads – all alive, maintained as part of the functioning structure. I'd never seen anything like it before, and I've seen my share of alien and other-dimensional technology.

Janissary Jane came forward to stand on my other side and I described what I was seeing to her. She nodded slowly.

'I have seen something like this before. It's not a Hellgate. Not as such. But it's definitely a gateway of some kind.'

'So they're planning to open a door to somewhere else,' said Molly, joining us to show she wasn't going to be left out of things. 'Maybe they've heard you declared war on them, Eddie, and they're running for home while they've still got the chance.'

'A nice thought, but no,' I said. 'They were building this long before I took control of the family.'

'And I don't think it was designed to open a gateway to Outside,' Janissary Jane said slowly. 'It looks more like it's designed to summon . . . something, from Outside, and bring it through into our world.'

'Reinforcements?' said Molly. 'More Loathly Ones?'

'No,' said Janissary Jane. 'With the power this thing uses, it would have to be something more powerful . . . something far worse than the Loathly Ones.'

'Something worse?' said Callan. 'What could be worse than soul-eating demons?'

'Stick around,' I said. 'If we don't shut this thing down before they can open their gateway, you might just find out.'

'I want to go home,' said Callan. 'I hate it here.' Molly produced another iced bottle of Pepsi for him and he wandered off to kick moodily at the unyielding ground.

We took turns to peer over the edge of the cliff, and study the movements of the tiny figures scurrying around down below. There were hundreds of them, men and women and even some children, scrambling over the huge structure with no regard for their own safety. Heat haze muddied the air between us and them, even with the help of the silver masks, but the extreme temperatures didn't seem to bother the Loathly Ones at all.

No one was obviously in charge, no orders were given, but they seemed to know exactly what to do. When I zoomed in on any particular individual worker, the strangeness of them hit me hard. They didn't move like humans move, and their faces were blank. Sometimes they would all move at once, in prefect precision, like flocking birds. There was nothing human left in them but their shapes; everything else had been driven out by the Loathly Ones.

This was all new to Mr Stab and he insisted on having it explained to him. So I did my best to give him the short version.

The Loathly Ones come from somewhere else, outside Space and Time as we understand it. They have no physical presence in our world, so to survive here they have to invade a body, mentally as well as physically. Preferably human, but not always. When a Loathly Ones invades, or infects, a human body it eats or corrupts or drives out the soul (opinions differ), and inhabits the remaining husk.

Which soon burns out from the unbearable stresses and strains the new owner puts on it. But even after the body dies, and slowly decays, it still goes on, driven by the unearthly energies of the Loathly One. Until the body finally falls apart; and then the Loathly One goes looking for a new host. We call the infected humans drones. Basically, they're zombies driven by an alien will, for alien purposes.

They destroy lives, and eat souls. And the family brought them here, for their own purposes. We should have known they'd get out of control.

'Sometimes they take over whole towns,' said Harry, unexpectedly. 'They start with one family, then proceed to the entire community, house by house. When they've taken control of everyone they force the town out of our reality and into some kind of pocket dimension, hidden from human detection. Then they use this hidden base to launch attacks on adjoining towns. Luckily they always give themselves away by being too greedy. The family wipes these towns out as fast as we find them.

'I was involved in one such cleansing, a few years back. It was in France, down in the Bordeaux region. They call such towns ghoulvilles. The local authorities sent out a call for help after they stumbled across one during a routine missing persons investigation. I was the nearest field agent, so I took the call. Joined up with a French demon specialist; Mallorie, her name was. A bit bookish, but she knew her business. The Armourer whipped up a dimensional key and shipped it out to us by the usual unnatural express route. And Mallorie and I led a French Special Forces Unit into the ghoulville.'

He stopped for a moment, remembering. His face was calm, reflective; but his eyes were haunted.

'Terrible place. Every nightmare you've ever had. The light was fierce, almost too bright for human eyes to bear. The gravity fluctuated, and directions seemed to switch back and forth when you weren't looking. The air was barely breathable, and it stank of blood and offal and rot. We'd come in hoping to find someone to rescue, but it soon became clear we were too late. There were men and women and even children all over the ghoulville, but all of them were infected. The Loathly Ones had eaten their souls. The children were the worst. They tried to hide what they were, to trick us into getting too close, but they had no idea how to act like children.

'They attacked us. Not even trying to act like humans any more. They came running from every direction, flailing their arms like retarded children. Came at us with all kinds of weapons, with bare hands and even bared teeth. We killed them. Shot them down, cut them down, stamped their dying faces into the bloody ground. Something about them, human but not human, something that used to be human but was now hopelessly corrupted, drove us crazy. We killed and killed, up one street and down the next, kicking corpses out of the way, till the gutters ran thick with blood. Some tried to surrender, but it was a trick to let them get close to us.

'When we were finished, we burned the town down. Left nothing standing. It took us hours, to be sure we'd got all of them. We searched the houses, sometimes dragging people out of hiding places under stairs, or in the backs of wardrobes. By the end, as we tramped out of the burning ghoulville and returned to our own world, even hardened French ex-paratroopers were weeping openly. Sometimes . . . I dream I'm still back there, and always will be.'

He looked around. We were listening intently. He'd dropped his armour so we could see his face while he talked, but now he armoured up again, becoming a faceless silver statue. As though he could keep out the memories that still haunted him.

'So when we get down there,' he said. 'Remember: they may look like people, but they're not. They're demons. Kill them for what they've done. And for what they make us do to put things right again.'

The watching Droods nodded and murmured quietly to each other, hefting their weapons. Mr Stab was still looking down at the plain, apparently unmoved by what he'd heard. But I liked Harry rather better for hearing what he'd been through.

And I even liked Roger Morningstar a little more, when he put an arm round Harry's silver shoulders to comfort him.

'So,' said Mr Stab, still not looking round. 'The infected humans are drones. And that thing down there is . . .?'

'A Nest,' I said. 'And we're the exterminators.'

'Splendid,' said Mr Stab. 'When do we start?'

Janissary Jane split us up into the arranged squads, with designated team leaders. Every group had some torced Droods to lead the charge and hopefully soak up some of the initial punishment. She gave us a brief refresher talk on tactics, which basically boiled down to, *Don't bunch up. Don't get separated. Kill everything down there that isn't us* and *Destroy that thing they're building before they can get it working.* There were no last-minute questions, no discussions or drop-outs. We were ready for action. Molly called up the spell she'd been working on since we got there and a great wind arose, picked us up surprisingly gently, and carried us down the side of the cliff to deposit us safely on the Nazca Plain.

We started running the moment we hit the ground, heading for the towering structure before us. The drones saw us coming and dropped everything to run straight at us, blocking the way with their bodies. Noises came from their distorted mouths, but there was nothing human in the sound. Some had improvised weapons, most just had bare hands, with fingers curled like claws. There was no emotion in their faces, or no emotion we could read, and they bared their teeth like animals. They weren't even trying to pretend at being human any more. They saw the armoured forms leading the charge and knew we were Droods.

More of them came running, from every direction. Men, women, children, even some animals. The Loathly Ones aren't fussy about what they possess. It's all flesh to them. But as our first squads slammed into the first wave of drones, even more came swarming out of the single opening at the base of the towering structure. More and more and more of them, far more than the structure should have been able to contain. Instead of the hundreds of drones we'd been expecting, suddenly there were thousands of them. Maybe hundreds of thousands . . . and still more and more came running and howling out onto the plain from the single opening.

The fighting had barely begun and already we were hopelessly outnumbered. But I couldn't call for a retreat. I'd committed us to this assault. We had to go on, and we had to win, before the Loathly Ones could open their gateway. Our two forces tore into each other, silver fists beating down inhuman faces; but already a terrible sense of hopelessness was seeping through me.

There were so many of them . . .

The drones hit us hard, all of them supernaturally strong from the alien energies burning within their stolen, dead or dying bodies.

They threw themselves upon the first torced Droods, trying to bowl them over through sheer force of numbers. When that didn't work, they clung on to silver arms, clasped silver legs, trying to force them off balance and drag them down. The armoured Droods stood firm, striking about them with their silver fists. Human skulls smashed and splintered under the terrible force of these blows, necks snapped and heads were torn off bodies. The armoured Droods broke backs and arms and legs, smashed in chests and stamped on heads. Blood and guts flew on the air and ran in streams down gleaming silver armour. Dozens of drones died in the first few moments of the battle but the sheer mass of numbers soaked up the momentum of our charge and all too soon we were stopped dead in our tracks. Killing and killing, but making no progress.

The Droods without armour opened up with the weapons the Armourer had provided. Heavy-duty hand cannon, grenade launchers and even pointing bones and curse throwers. The drones fell in ranks as the guns raked back and forth, mowing them down, but there were always more drones, pressing forward, forcing their way past the beleaguered armoured Droods. We hit the drones with everything we had, and it wasn't enough. They didn't care about the damage they took, they felt no pain or fear or horror. A hundred could die, if it meant one would get through to kill.

Our plans and tactics disappeared, replaced by a brute struggle to survive. The squads were overrun or forced apart and it was everyone for themselves. Most of the unarmoured Droods were dragged down and slaughtered in the first few minutes, overwhelmed by the sheer numbers, by drones who ran uncaring into the face of their weapons. Droods died screaming under flailing fists, hands like claws, and stabbing, clubbing weapons. I could hear them all around me, their human screams mixed with the inhuman howling of the drones.

And then, impossibly, even the armoured Droods began to fall, as the drones brought strange and unnatural weapons out of the towering structure. Some armoured Droods disappeared, teleported God knew where whenever one drone pointed a shimmering piece of tech at them. Some Droods fell victim to howling energy blades that ghosted through the silver armour to cut up the flesh inside. And one corpse with radiation burns and glowing eyes stamped through the chaos, somehow unsaying the Words that activated the armour, so that it disappeared back into the collar, leaving the owner dazed and helpless and vulnerable.

Mr Stab appeared out of nowhere and cut that drone's throat with a long shining scalpel.

I ended up fighting side by side, and then back to back, with Molly Metcalf. Drones came at us from every direction, sometimes with weapons and sometimes without. I fired my Colt Repeater again and again, picking off drone after drone with my gun that never missed and never ran out of bullets, but soon they were too close, vaulting over the bodies of the fallen to get at me. I put the gun away, grew silver spikes on my gleaming fists, and waded into them with all the terrible strength and speed my armour gave me. I struck them down and they fell broken and bloody before me. I ripped the faces from their heads, smashed their skulls, broke their bones and stamped on them when they fell. I picked them up and used them as living flails with which to beat the enemy. Blood and gore streamed down my gleaming armour, unable to find a hold. I stamped and spun, striking out with impossible speed; I formed my silver hands into cutting blades and thrust and hacked, butchering everything that came within reach. And still there seemed no end to them.

They beat at me with their hands and their weapons and none of them could touch me. But the drones with the terrible weapons were drawing slowly, inexorably, closer.

Molly was hitting them with every offensive magic she knew, chanting and cursing at the top of her voice. Drones were transformed into helpless things and were trampled underfoot. Sometimes their shape collapsed, and ran away like muddy water. She called down lightning bolts from the sky, called up fire from sudden cracks in the hard ground, called stormwinds to blow them away. Strange forces crackled on the air before her, incinerating anything that came too close. But her voice was cracking from the strain and I knew she wouldn't be able to keep this up for long. Magic takes its toll, and even her hoarded energies wouldn't last long at this rate.

I looked around during a brief lull in the fighting. I could hear Molly coughing and hacking painfully behind me. My unarmoured Droods were down, dead. Slaughtered, for all their fine training.

About a dozen armoured Droods were still fighting, striding slowly through the chaos, striking down their enemies. Islands in a sea of death. Janissary Jane had been right. I didn't need warriors. I needed an army.

Mr Stab strode elegantly through the madness, no blood staining his fine clothes. He cut and slashed with almost inhuman grace and precision, killing everything that came within reach, and none of the drones could touch him. He was protected by forces far worse than theirs. He stalked the battlefield like a harsh Victorian god of war, smiling a terrible happy smile, completely at home in Hell.

Roger Morningstar fought side by side with an armoured form I could only assume was Harry. Fierce flames burned around them, consuming every drone they touched. Roger was smiling too. Harry fought well, with short, controlled, brutal movements, striking down the drones with almost clinical precision. As though it was a job he happened to be extremely good at.

And Janissary Jane cut a bloody path through the roiling crowds with her infamous old sword, unstoppable in her cold and terrible fury. The greatest demon killer that ever lived.

She fought her way over to join Molly and me. I was wringing with sweat inside my armour, exhausted and running on fumes. My arms ached from so much effort, and my back was killing me. The armour can perform wonders, but I have to work it. And yet still I fought on, determined not to fall for as long as Molly needed me. Reduced to that, and no more. Janissary Jane yelled into my silver mask.

'It's the tower!' she shouted over the roar of battle. 'Something's happening! I can feel it! I think the gateway's opening!'

I clubbed down the nearest drones and turned to look. She was right. I could feel it too. A great light was shining out of the single opening, and more sprang from a hundred openings in the jagged sides of the huge structure. The air distorted and rippled around it, and it was nothing to do with heat haze. I could sense if not see the gateway opening behind the tower, a vast and growing circle, like a black sun. And on the other side of that opening . . . something unbearably huge and awful and terribly aware. Pressing inexorably against the weakening barrier that was the only thing keeping it out of our small and terribly vulnerable world. Something so big I couldn't even grasp the shape or nature of it. Like God walking angry in the world . . .

Whatever the Loathly Ones had summoned, it was here, waiting for the gateway to fully open, and then it would come through and do horrible, unspeakable things to us. Just because it could.

Something far worse than the Loathly Ones could ever hope to be.

I looked quickly around me. I counted ten armoured Droods still standing. I called to them through the armour.

'Get to the base of the structure! Everyone grab a part of it, and bring the bloody thing down!'

I turned to Molly. She was swaying on her feet, blood running from her nose and mouth, and even leaving bloody tear tracks on her cheeks. Her body was breaking down under the strains she was putting on it, to channel her desperate magics. She looked at me, trying to work her mouth, but her eyes were vague. I yelled her name, grabbed her shoulder with my silver hand, and squeezed till she winced. Comprehension came back into her face.

'We have to get to the base of the structure, quickly! Molly! Can you clear us a path?'

'I'm tired, Eddie. So tired . . .'

'*Can you do it?*'

She glared at me. 'Yes! Yes, I can do it! I'm Molly Metcalf, dammit. But you'd better be right about this, Eddie.'

She thrust one arm in the direction of the towering structure – and every drone between us and it exploded into bloody gobbets. I made a mental note never to get Molly really mad at me, grabbed her arm, and we ran for the tower down the narrow aisle she'd opened. Aisles had opened up between the other armoured Droods and the tower, and they were running too. We raced across the cracked stone ground, while the drones recovered their senses and ran to fill the gaps. We smashed them out of the way, knocked them over and ran them down, racing for the tower. We got to the base of the huge structure and I yelled for the armoured Droods to grab on to anything that looked substantial or load-bearing. Molly and Janissary Jane, Mr Stab and Roger Morningstar worked hard to keep the drones back, as we took hold of the tower and ripped its underpinnings out.

For a long moment nothing happened. The tower was huge, and there were only eleven of us . . . but we were Droods, and we had the incredible strength of the armour on our side. We ripped the support right out from under the tower and brought the bloody thing down.

It roared and screamed like a living thing, and explosions ran through its shape like a string of firecrackers. Lights shone from a thousand new openings, while cracks ran up and down the exterior. Shudders ran through the whole height and width of it, and pieces started falling away. It swayed upon its crippled base, and then slowly the whole great length of it nodded forward and fell, stretching out across the stone plain. Slamming down like the hand of God.

The gateway closed. Gone, just like that, and with it all traces of the terrible thing on the other side. The tower almost leisurely measured its length along the plain, and shattered into a million pieces as it hit. Most of the drones were crushed underneath it, and the few who survived turned and ran in a hundred directions. I let them go. I was busy hanging on to Molly, who was protecting us all with a simple force field, using up the last of her strength.

When it was finally over, only fifteen of us were left standing. Molly clung to me, trembling in every limb, and I held her to me, only our shared strength keeping us on our feet. Roger Morningstar was holding Harry. Janissary Jane was on the radio to Callan and his people, left behind on the cliff, yelling for him to bring down transport for us. We had to gather up our fallen and get them out of here before the authorities arrived. Most of the Droods dropped their armour; they looked dazed and shell-shocked. Mr Stab stared around him at the massed heaps of the dead and smiled.

Harry let go of Roger and limped over to confront me. Behind the impassive silver mask, his voice was cold and harsh.

'We stopped the gateway opening. We brought down the tower, and killed most of the Loathly Ones. But was it worth it, Eddie? Look at how few of us are left! Everyone else is dead! This was a debacle, a disaster. We've never lost this many in a single operation, in the whole history of our family! All so you could play the hero one more time. When we get back, I'll make sure everyone knows this was your fault!'

'Of course you will, Harry,' I said tiredly. 'That's what you do. Go running to the Matriarch, like the clever little toady you are. See what good it does you.'

'If you hadn't taken away the torcs, most of those people would still be alive!'

'Yes. You're probably right there.'

'You should have given everyone new torcs. Not just the ones you trusted to support you.'

I didn't say anything. What could I say? He was right.

Harry turned his back on me and walked away. Molly finally let go of me and pulled something out of a hidden pocket.

'I found this in the wreckage of the tower. It's so full of potential magic it all but shouted at me. You recognise it?'

I turned it over and over slowly in my hands. It was an amulet of some kind, deeply etched with Kandarian symbols. I could only translate one word.

'Invaders,' I said.

'Wonderful,' said Molly. 'The Martians are coming.'

'No,' I said, too tired even to smile. 'I'm pretty sure this was part of the summoning spell. An invocation, to bring through whatever that was we stopped. Except . . . this is very definitely plural. Invaders . . . Not just one.'

'I may puke,' said Molly. 'All we went through, just to stop one . . . what?'

'Something from Outside,' I said. 'An invasion force of something far worse than soul-eaters. Move over. I think I want to puke too.'

'Invaders,' said Molly. 'Called by the Loathly Ones. Does that mean more nests, more towers, somewhere else in the world?'

'Almost certainly,' I said. 'Maybe in every country. This was only the beginning.'

'God, you can be a real pain in the arse sometimes,' said Molly.

'Comes with the job,' I said. 'Let's go home.'

CHAPTER EIGHT
Family matters

We came home in the Blackhawkes. Those wonderful sleek and silent planes. Nothing wrong with them. Completely untouched. But they seemed terribly empty, carrying so few of us home. With only eleven torced Droods left we had to spread ourselves out across the planes so we could fly undetected through foreign airspaces, above a world that didn't know what we'd saved it from. None of the other Droods would even look at me as we climbed aboard our separate planes. Molly sat beside me, holding my hand, talking softly to me; but I couldn't tell you a single thing she said. All I could think of was what we were carrying in the cargo holds of the planes. The dead Droods.

The news went ahead of us. Bad news always does. When the Blackhawkes touched down on the landing field behind The Hall, it seemed the whole family had come out to watch. And when I and the terribly few survivors of my first disastrous mission descended from the planes, we did so to utter silence. To ranks of shocked faces and condemning eyes. I could have fobbed them off, told them there'd be an official statement later. Could have walked right through them and gone inside. But I didn't. I stood and waited with everyone else, as the bodies were unloaded from the cargo holds.

We hadn't been able to recover them all. Most of the bodies on the plain were either crushed into pulp by the falling tower or so messed up from the fighting we couldn't tell who was who, or what was what. Some had been reduced to bits and pieces. We had spent hours under the hot sun, digging through the wreckage and sorting through the carnage, the blood and the offal and the stench; but in the end we brought less than half of the family home. The watching crowd made soft, shocked noises as the first bodies appeared. They'd never seen so many dead Droods before. No one had. Such a tragedy, such a loss of life in one operation, was unprecedented. Some people cried out at the sight of familiar faces, broken and disfigured and smeared with dried blood. Some people made to rush forward, but the Sarjeant-At-Arms was there with his people to keep order. Family dignity must be maintained at all times.

The family doctors and nurses soon ran out of stretchers, even though they were dropping the bodies off in the mortuary and returning as fast as they could. So when the stretchers ran out, they improvised with tables and trolleys and other flat surfaces. The doctors loaded the bits and parts of bodies into black plastic garbage bags to be sorted out later. The crowd didn't like that, but the decision had been made to get the bodies off the planes and out of sight as quickly as possible. It wasn't my decision. I was too numb to think of anything except how badly I'd screwed up. No; someone in the Inner Circle had thought ahead and made the decision for me. How very thoughtful of them. Though, of course, this wasn't to spare my feelings, but the family's.

I stood in the shadow of my plane, and made myself watch silently until every last body had been carried into The Hall. Brought home, at last. That was my duty, and my penance. Molly stood beside me the whole time. I held on to her like a drowning man, clutching her hand so hard I must have hurt her, but she never made a sound. I never said a thing, not even when my family looked at me with hot, teary eyes and cold judgemental faces. What could I say, except *I'm sorry. I'm so sorry*?

As the last few stretchers and the last few plastic bags disappeared inside, Molly finally stirred and leaned in close to me. 'Don't you have any body bags?' she said quietly. 'For disasters and emergencies like this?'

'There's never been a disaster like this before,' I said. 'We never needed body bags because we never lost this many people.'

'We didn't lose the battle,' said Molly. 'We destroyed the Loathly Ones' Nest, and their tower. We stopped the Bad Thing from coming through. Hell, we saved the world, Eddie.'

'If this is a victory, I'd hate to see a defeat,' I said. 'Whatever temporary success we achieved, we paid for with our dearest blood. Those people followed me into battle because they believed in me. They were the chosen ones, who'd earned their place through merit and hard work. I promised them victory and glory, and a chance to be heroes. This . . . this was supposed to be a demonstration of Drood power. No one was supposed to get hurt. Now most of those brave souls are gone and the family will seem more vulnerable than ever.'

'So what are you going to do?' said Molly.

'I have no choice any more. Every Drood must have a torc and the armour that goes with it. Whether I think they can be trusted or not. The family must be protected. If need be, even from me and my stupid ideas.'

'Don't!' Molly said sharply. 'Don't start doubting your judgement because one battle went against you. You did everything right. You weren't to know there were so many drones hidden inside the tower, or about their weapons.'

She broke off as Harry strode over to confront me. He held his head high, striding like a soldier, his every move full of the arrogance of the utterly self-justified. He knew the whole family was watching. He slammed to a halt in front of me, struck a condemnatory pose, and raised his voice so everyone could hear.

'This is your fault, Edwin. All of it. I told you your attack force wasn't big enough. I told you we needed torcs if we were to defeat the Loathly Ones. But no, you wouldn't listen. You knew best. You had to prove yourself as leader. And now, because of you, because of your pride and arrogance, all those good men and women are dead. Sacrificed on the altar of your ambition!'

'Nice speech, Harry,' I said. 'Been practising it on the way home, have you? I had to go with the information I had. None of this could have been predicted. We've never faced anything like this before.'

'Just what I would have expected from you,' said Harry. 'Excuses! Face facts, Eddie: you're not up to the job. You never were. Even as a field agent you were deemed so second rate you were never allowed outside London! If you had any real pride, if you really cared about what was best for the family, you'd step down and let someone more qualified take over.'

'Got someone in mind, have you, Harry?' I said. 'Yourself, perhaps?'

'Typical of you, Eddie, to try and make this about personalities,' Harry said grandly. 'I don't want to lead this family; I just want you gone. The Matriarch knew about you. Knew you weren't to be trusted with anything that really mattered. That's why she let you run away from home, because you wouldn't be missed. We should have hunted you down like any other rogue.'

'I was never a rogue! I worked for the family!' I stepped forwards, my hands clenching into fists.

'Don't,' Molly said quickly. 'It's what he wants.'

'Yes, listen to your better half,' said Harry, sneering openly now. 'You showed your true colours when you shacked up with her. When you had the sheer nerve to bring the infamous Molly Metcalf into our home. The bitch in heat of the wild woods!'

I hit him hard, right in the mouth. He staggered backwards, but didn't go down. The watching crowd made a series of shocked noises, but no one moved. They were waiting to see what would happen next; and their eyes were very bright. Harry turned his face so they could see the blood on his mouth and chin, and then he armoured up. The silver swept over him in a moment and he stood tall and proud before the family, like an avatar of vengeance. I'd done what he wanted. He'd goaded me into losing my temper and striking him first. He'd had a long time to plan this on the way back, to work out how to manipulate me before the family. I knew all that, knew I was playing his game; and I didn't care. I needed to hit someone, and Harry would do fine. I armoured up and we stepped forward to face each other, both of us reflected in the other's armour.

'Come on,' said Harry. 'Show me what you've got. Show me the dirty tricks you used to murder my father.'

'Love to,' I said. I raised my hands, and long silver cutting blades grew out of my fists.

'Stop this!' said the Armourer, forcing his way forward through the crowd. 'Stop this right now, both of you! Sarjeant-At-Arms, do your duty, dammit!'

Then, and only then, the Sarjeant came forward to separate us. The Armourer was quickly there too, slamming a liver-spotted hand flat against my silver chest, and glaring fiercely into my featureless silver mask. The Sarjeant glared at Harry, and of course Harry immediately armoured down. Like a good little boy, a respectful member of the family. He'd played me, right from the start. He'd never expected to actually have to fight. He knew someone would step in to stop it. What mattered was that he'd made me look bad in front of the family. He flashed me a brief triumphant smile, and then strode off into The Hall along with the Sarjeant-At-Arms. Probably to make his report to the Matriarch. No one actually applauded him, but there was a general murmur of support within the crowd.

I armoured down and nodded shame-facedly to the Armourer. He growled something under his breath and shook his head.

'Get inside, boy. The situation's beyond saving here.'

I looked around me, at the watching family. It wasn't that long ago they'd gathered together together to cheer my name, as the family's saviour. And now they regarded me as some kind of war criminal. It wasn't just that I'd lost so many people in battle. I'd disappointed them by not being their perfect hero after all. I took out the Merlin Glass, shook it to full size, and stepped through into the Armoury. Molly and the Armourer hurried through after me and I shut the Glass down again. The weight of the family's disapproving eyes was gone, and we were alone.

'You know, Eddie,' said Molly. 'It seems to me that you're getting a bit too dependent on that mirror.'

'Nonsense,' the Armourer said briskly. 'That's why I gave him the Glass, to get him out of close scrapes. Devices are meant to be used. How about I make us a nice cup of tea? And I'm pretty sure there's an unopened box of Jaffa Cakes around here somewhere.' He stopped abruptly and stared at me. 'You know, you look like shit, boy. Are you hurt? Injured?'

'No,' I said. 'All that slaughter and butchery, and I came through it without a scratch. Of course I did; I had the family armour. The others didn't, and the Loathly Ones tore them apart.'

'Never look back, boy,' the Armourer said gruffly. 'Concentrate on what you're going to do next. Doesn't matter if you lose a battle, as long as you win the war. Take a look at the family record: we've known our fair share of defeats. Of course, you have to go back quite a way to find anything like this . . . But that's because the family's grown soft and complacent and cautious down the years, leaving the dirty work to the field agents. Only picking the small battles, the small victories we were sure we could win. That's why the Loathly Ones have been able to stick around this long, and build up their numbers. Never would have been allowed, not even a century ago.

So stop feeling sorry for yourself, Eddie, and think! Did you learn anything useful from this first encounter? Anything you can use the next time you go up against the bastards?'

'Maybe,' I said. I felt suddenly tired and sat down on the nearest chair. Molly looked worried, and I gave her a reassuring smile. Though it couldn't have been that reassuring because she looked even more worried. I fished inside my jacket pocket and brought out the Kandarian stone amulet Molly had recovered from the wreckage of the tower. I handed the ugly thing over to the Armourer, who studied it closely for a while and then sat down beside me and studied the thing even more closely under a powerful magnifying glass. Molly pulled up a chair and sat down beside me. I barely noticed. I was focused on the amulet. I needed it to be something, something important, to justify what we'd been through to get it. The Armourer prodded and rubbed at the grey stone amulet with his broad, heavy engineer's fingers, muttering to himself all the while.

So, Kandarian all right. In remarkably good condition given that it's almost certainly over three thousand years old, judging by the style of the markings. But then, most Kandarian artefacts are very enduring. They were built to last, using processes we can only guess at now. Kandar . . . Vile place, by all accounts. Demon worshippers. Gave themselves up voluntarily to possession by Beings from Outside. Subjugated every other culture they came in contact with and did terrible things to them. Slavery, torture, ritual sacrifice; slaughter and suffering were meat and drink to old Kandar. Finally they went to war with themselves, and their whole civilisation was wiped out in the course of one terrible blood-soaked night. Not a trace of their cities remains today. Their culture and their people utterly extinct. Probably just as well. All we ever see now is the odd amulet or weapon, preserved long after they should have crumbled into dust by the energies trapped within. We only understand the language because so many spells and incantations were originally written in it.'

'What about this particular glyph?' I said, pointing at the amulet. 'I translated it as "Invaders".'

'Hmmm? Oh yes, quite right, Eddie. Good to see you paid attention during some of your classes, at least. Yes. Invaders. Quite definitely plural. And the surrounding glyphs suggest that this was a summoning, to bring these Invaders through into our world. I think we have to assume that the Presence you felt on the other side of the Nazca gateway was just one of many. Which in turn suggests—'

'That there must be other Nests,' I said. 'More gateways built by the Loathly Ones to bring through a whole invasion force of these Beings.'

'Oh shit,' said Molly. 'It was hard enough taking one down. How many could there be?'

'Who knows?' said the Armourer. 'Hundreds, thousands; hundreds of thousands? Nests set up in countries across the world and all of Humanity under threat. A threat we would have known nothing about if you hadn't launched your attack on the Loathly Ones, Eddie.'

'This is major league stuff,' said Molly. 'The whole world under threat? What do we do?'

'We stop them,' I said. 'That's what this family does. Uncle Jack, do we need to unlock the Armageddon Codex again?'

'Certainly not,' the Armourer said firmly. 'I opened the Codex for you once, and that was one time more than I ever expected to see it opened in my lifetime. No, those superweapons are only supposed to be used as a last resort, when reality itself is under threat. And things aren't that bad. Yet.'

'But if the world's about to be invaded by Beings from Outside—' I said.

'No, Eddie. The family can deal with this. We have before. Read the records. I swear we don't teach nearly enough family history any more. The Codex weapons are for when everything else, including tears, swearing and prayer, have failed us. Not to salve your pride after it's taken a beating in the field.'

'You weren't there,' Molly said sharply. 'You didn't see what we did. Sense what we sensed . . . It was bad, really bad. Whatever it was, trying to force its way into our reality, it was worse than anything I've ever encountered. I've dealt with demons and devils in my time, and forces from Above and Below our reality, but these Invaders . . . They scare the shit out of me. Remember, Eddie, when you said there were two kinds of enemy: demons and gods? Well, the Loathly Ones may be demons, but whatever they're trying to summon most definitely aren't.'

'The family can handle this,' the Armourer said. 'I have developed weapons here beyond your worse nightmares. You have no idea what the Droods are capable of, Molly, when they finally go to war. We've been drowsing too long, coasting on our past victories. About time we got stuck in again and got our hands bloody. We were warriors once, and will be again.' The Armourer smiled, and his usual kindly, absent-minded manner vanished, replaced by a cold and focused malice. I should never have forgotten that this man had once been a first-class field agent during the coldest part of the Cold War, and lauded almost as much as his famous brother James.

Licensed to kill, in hot blood or cold, so long as they got the job done.

The Armourer turned to Molly and was immediately his old gruff self again. 'Don't you worry, my dear, all will be well. You'll see. Now, Eddie, how did you get on with that new short-range teleport bracelet I gave you? Work okay? Any problems?'

'Ah,' I said. 'Yes, well . . . Actually, in the heat of battle, with so much going on, I sort of forgot I had it with me.'

The Armourer sighed heavily. 'Lean forward, will you, Eddie.' I did so, and he smacked me hard round the back of the head.

'Hey! Dammit, Uncle Jack, that hurt!'

'Good. It might help you remember next time. I give you these things to give you an edge in battle! To keep you alive! I expect you to use them. I expect you to—' A nearby comm unit began to bleep insistently and the Armourer broke off to answer it. 'What? I'm busy!'

The Sarjeant-At-Arms's face appeared on the monitor screen. He nodded brusquely to the Armourer, and then stared right past him at Molly and me.

'I thought you might go to ground in the Armoury. I'm calling an emergency meeting of the Inner Circle in the Sanctity. Right now. There are urgent matters to be discussed.'

'Oh, yes?' I said. 'And when did you get the authority to summon the Circle together?'

'Be there,' he said. 'Or we'll start without you.'

And he closed down the screen before I could answer.

'If it's not one thing,' said Molly, 'it's another. And I thought my family was bad.'

'Your family?' I said.

'Don't ask.'

*

Molly and I left the Armoury and headed for the Sanctity. I could have transported us both there with Merlin's Glass, but for once I was in no hurry. I wanted time to think, plan what I was going to say. The Armourer said he'd be along soon, and I really hoped Jacob would show his ghostly face this time. I knew I was going to need all the support I could muster at this meeting. And then Molly suddenly stopped dead in her tracks and announced that I'd have to go on without her.

'I'm sorry, Eddie. Really. But I can't stay inside this oppressive old pile any longer. I just can't. I have to get out, into the open air, before I start to wither.'

'But this is Inner Circle business, Molly. It's important. I need you to be there with me.'

'I can't help that. I have to get out of here before I start screaming. You have no idea what this place does to me, Eddie. You can come and look for me in the grounds when you've finished. I need time to myself anyway, to recharge my powers and rebuild the energies I used up on the Nazca Plain. Right now, I don't have a spark of magic left in me. And I can't live like that.'

I grabbed her by both shoulders and made her look at me. 'I need you with me this time, Molly. They're going to crucify me in there. I can't face them alone.'

'Yes, you can. You don't need me nearly as much as you think you do. You're a lot stronger than you believe, Eddie. Than you allow yourself to be. I'll see you later.'

She pulled herself out of my grip and hurried off down the corridor, heading for the front entrance and the freedom of the grounds. I called after her, but she didn't look back once. So I went on to the Sanctity alone, wondering what the hell I was going to say.

When I got there, somehow the Armourer had contrived to arrive ahead of me. He raised one wrist to show off a teleport bracelet and waggled it at me meaningfully. I deliberately ignored him, and looked around. Gathered together in the presence of the softly glowing Strange were Penny, the Sarjeant . . . and Harry. He folded his arms across his chest and gave me a smug smile. The Sarjeant stood beside Harry, being ostentatiously supportive. Penny looked at me thoughtfully. There was no sign of Jacob. Strange's crimson glow didn't feel nearly as comforting as usual. I gave everyone there my best hard stare.

'Well, well, this is a surprise. Harry Drood present at what is supposed to be a private meeting of my Inner Circle. What are you doing here, Harry?'

'I was invited,' he said easily. His mouth was still swollen and bruised from where I'd hit him. He could have had that fixed easily, but right now it was more useful as it was. As visible proof of my temper and brutality. It certainly didn't stop him smiling triumphantly at me.

'Harold has a right to be heard,' said the Sarjeant-At-Arms.

'I see,' I said. 'And is that what all of you feel?'

'He was there with you when it went wrong,' said Penny. 'We need an independent witness as to exactly what happened. You must see that, Eddie.'

'Oh, I see a lot of things,' I said. 'I should have remembered that betrayal and back-stabbing are just business as usual in this family.'

The Armourer stirred uneasily. 'Don't be like that, Eddie. You know I'm on your side. But we need the facts as to what happened. And we have to be seen to be impartial if our decisions are to be accepted by the family as a whole. It may be that Harry can tell us things about the battle that you can't. We're going to need all the information we can put together if we're going to take on more Loathly Ones in their Nests. We're not here to judge you—'

'Aren't you?' I said. 'No, perhaps not you, Uncle Jack. But they are. They've already made up their minds. I don't have time for this, people. There are things I need to be doing. For the good of the family.'

'Don't you dare walk out on us!' said the Sarjeant-At-Arms.

'Oh, blow it out your ear, Cyril,' I said.

And I stalked out of the Sanctity without looking back, even when first the Armourer and then Penny called my name. I was so angry my hands had curled into fists again, clenched so tight they were actually painful. My heart was pounding like a trip hammer, and I could feel the angry flush in my face. I had to walk out. I couldn't let them goad me into saying the wrong thing, making the wrong decision. There was no point in staying; the hanging judges had already made up their minds. And without Molly to back me up, and the Armourer dithering, I would have been out-voted or shouted down no matter what I said. By my own Inner Circle. I couldn't believe they'd invited Harry without even checking with me first.

I strode through the corridors and connecting rooms of The Hall, fuming to myself and glaring at any member of the family who got in my way. Most had the sense to keep well back. None of them spoke to me, just watched silently as I passed. Which suited me. One snide comment and I would have knocked them down.

Still, mad as I was, a part of me stood back, shaking its head and saying, *This isn't like you. You always believed in don't get mad, get even*. When the Matriarch denounced me as a rogue and sentenced me to death, I didn't lose my rag; I went straight into planning how to bring her down. But then I'd known I was innocent; that I hadn't done anything wrong. That kept me going, despite the obstacles put in my path. This . . . was different. There wasn't room in me for anything but anger, most of it aimed at myself.

Because I screwed up. I got my people killed. My family. And nothing else mattered.

By the time I got to the front door the anger had died down to a dull throb and I was thinking more clearly. Or at least clearly enough that I was more concerned about Molly than myself. I hadn't taken her seriously enough when she said she *couldn't* live in The Hall; that she needed to be among living things, in the wild. I knew she was having trouble adjusting, but I thought she'd get over it. Now I had to wonder if she ever would. If she ever could. This was a woman used to living in her own private forest, after all. While I had to stay here, in The Hall, or risk losing control of the family.

Martha had already told me to my face that she was only waiting for me to make a mess of things so she could come sweeping back and restore the Matriarchy. And what then? The restoring of the old ways? Gold armour instead of silver, paid for by the sacrifice of children? Back to the family running the world instead of protecting it? No. I couldn't let that happen. My duty to the family outweighed my duty to myself. It always had. I couldn't turn my back on my family, not even for Molly. It's always the family ties that matter, whether we like it or not.

I could lose Molly. The only woman I had ever loved.

I came to the front entrance, strode through the front door and then stopped and looked down the long gravel path as an ambulance materialised suddenly out of thin air. This rather caught my attention, as nothing is supposed to be able to materialise in our grounds unless we give permission well in advance. Which mostly we don't. The ambulance came roaring up the path to The Hall and then skidded to a halt right in front of me, spraying my shins with flying gravel. The sign on the side of the ambulance said 'Dr Syn's Fly By Night Delivery Service'. The cab door opened and the driver got out. A cheerful sort in the traditional starched white uniform. He strode over to me, thrust a clipboard and pen into my hands, and saluted briskly.

'Sign here, squire. One looney to go, and no I don't answer questions. I just drop people off and leg it before they can turn nasty. Sign there, please, on the dotted line. You are acknowledging delivery of one William Dominic Drood, also known as Oddly John. And get a move on, squire. I've got this American gentleman and his giant rabbit to drop off yet.'

I signed Harry's name where indicated, and handed back the clipboard. I've always been a cautious sort. The driver saluted me again, went round to the back of the ambulance, unlocked a very heavy padlock and pulled open the doors with a hearty cry of, 'Come on out you lovely looney, you're home!' William Drood stepped out of the ambulance, blinking in the bright summer light, and the driver took him firmly by one arm and brought him over to me.

'Here you are, squire. One headbanger, as ordered. Hours of fun for the whole family. Try not to lose him; you wouldn't believe the paperwork if I have to chase him down again. Have a nice day! Forgetting you already!'

One more salute and he was back in the cab. The ambulance tore off down the gravel path and disappeared in mid screech. The day seemed suddenly, blessedly, quiet.

'What an appallingly cheerful person,' said William. 'I really must remember to send him a note of thanks. Inside a letter bomb.'

'Welcome back, William,' I said. 'Welcome home.'

He nodded vaguely and looked around him. He didn't seem particularly happy to be back. He did look better than the last time I'd seen him, alone in his cell at the Happy Daze sanatorium. They'd dressed him up in a good suit before sending him home, though he looked distinctly ill at ease in it. In fact, he looked generally uneasy. His face seemed somehow in between expressions, and his eyes were as haunted as ever. As though he was still seeing strange worlds and alternative realities out of the corner of his eyes. And given who he was . . . I said his name again and his gaze slowly returned to me. I put out my hand, and after a pause he shook it solemnly.

'Do you remember me?' I said.

'Of course I remember you, Edwin. I'm not completely gaga. You came to see me in . . . that place. You got a message to me, saying it was safe to come home again. So here I am. I do hope you're right, Edwin.'

'It's good to have you back, where you belong,' I said.

'Is it?' he said vaguely, looking at The Hall behind me as though he'd never seen it before. 'It doesn't feel like home. But then it didn't, even before I left. I found something out, you see, and then nothing seemed the same any more. I can't even say I feel like William Dominic Drood, either. I think I was happier as Oddly John. Nobody ever expected anything of him. I think perhaps I left William here, when I went away. Maybe now I'm back, he'll come back too. If it's safe. I saw something, you see, in the Sanctity . . .'

'It's all right, William,' I said quickly. 'I know what you saw. What you found out. Everyone knows now. The Heart is dead, destroyed; and all its evil with it. We have new armour now, from a new source. There's nothing here to be afraid of any more.'

He looked at me sadly. 'That would be nice. But we're Droods. So there's always something to be afraid of. Comes with the territory. I've been afraid of so many things for such a long time now.'

'Is there anyone particular in the family you want to see?' I said, carefully changing the subject. 'Anyone you've missed?'

'No,' said William, after a moment. 'Never had any family of my own. And old friends . . . so long ago, it seems. I don't think I want them to see me like this Not properly myself yet. Whoever that turns out to be.'

'I know what you need,' I said firmly. 'You were the best Librarian the family ever had; and I've got a wonderful surprise for you. We have rediscovered the Old Library, after all these years. We need someone like you to put the place in order.'

William looked at me sharply, his face intent and focused for the first time. 'The Old Library? But that was destroyed by fire, centuries ago!'

'No,' I said, grinning. 'Just hidden away, waiting to be found. And you're not going to believe some of the treasures it contains. Come along.'

I took him back through The Hall, and he gawked around him like a tourist, as though he'd never seen any of it before. Perhaps he'd forgotten it in his efforts to forget what he'd seen in the Sanctity. He'd had to forget, to survive. He'd put himself in the asylum, hiding from the family and what he'd discovered about it. He pretended to be mad to get in, but as the years went by he had to pretend less and less. He'd been gone so long that none of the people we passed along the way recognised him, and he showed no interest in talking with any of them. I took him through to the Library and he brightened immediately. He walked back and forth among the stacks, smiling as he recognised this book or that, and tut-tutting at the state of the place. He was standing straighter now, his gaze was sharper, and he walked with more confidence. Back on his own ground more of who he used to be was coming back to him.

Already he was looking and sounding more like the Librarian I remembered as a child.

When I thought he was ready, I took him to the portrait of the Old Library hanging on the rear wall, opened it up with the right Words, and we stepped through the portrait and into the Old Library itself. The huge depository of ancient family lore and forgotten world history. William took a deep breath, staring at the miles and miles of shelves with eyes as wide and delighted as a child. Stacks and stacks of books, manuscripts, scrolls and even a few stone tablets, stretching away into the distance for as far as the eye could see. William smiled suddenly, and it was like his whole face came alive at last. I smiled too, glad I'd finally done something right. The Hall might not feel like home to him, but the Old Library certainly did.

'To get you started,' I said casually, 'you might like to do a little research for me. I need everything you can find on Kandarian culture, and in particular any old summoning rites concerning Beings called the Invaders. Take your time. End of the day would be fine.'

'I know, I know,' he said, in a typically snotty Librarian's voice. 'Nothing changes. You want the impossible, and you want it to a schedule. Am I expected to do this by myself, or do I have any staff?'

'You have a staff of one,' I said. 'Namely, the current Librarian. Rafe? Rafe, where are you?'

A head popped out of the stacks further down, a hand waved cheerfully, and a pleasant young chap with a bright beaming face hurried over to join us. I liked Rafe. The previous Librarian had resigned his post when I took over. Not just a Zero Tolerance member but also one of the Matriarch's cronies, he refused to serve under me. I was forced to promote his assistant to full Librarian. He hadn't done too badly. It helped that he loved his job and practically went into ecstasies when he first saw the Old Library. He was currently trying to track down an Index so we could get some idea of what we had on our hands.

'Hi!' he said to William, shaking his hand enthusiastically. 'I'm Rafe. Short for Raphael, which I never use. I am not a turtle. You must be William. You're a legend, in Librarian circles. Which, admittedly, aren't as big as they might be. But! Here you are, back again, just in time to help me make sense of this mess. No one's used this place in centuries, and it shows. I said I needed expert help, but you could have knocked me down with a feather when Edwin said he could get you! And here you are! Really looking forward to working with you!'

'Don't worry,' I said to William. 'He calms down a bit once he gets used to you. And the Ritalin in his tea helps.'

'Let's get to work,' said William.

And he strode off into the stacks, not looking back at either of us. Rafe nodded quickly to me and hurried off after his new mentor. I grinned and shook my head as William sent Rafe running from stack to stack, searching out ancient volumes and sacred texts, shouting after him like a shepherd with his dog.

With any luck, putting the Old Library in order would help William put himself back in order too.

*

When I stepped back through the portal into the main Library, Penny was waiting for me. I turned my back on her to shut down the portrait and then walked right past her without speaking. A little childish, perhaps, but I wasn't in the mood to be messed with. Penny strode along beside me, cool and collected as always.

'You're not an easy man to track down, Eddie. If someone hadn't happened to mention they saw William Drood in the corridors, I'd never have thought to look here. Has he really been in a madhouse all these years? Never mind; you were right about the tutors so hopefully you'll be right about the rogues too. Will you please slow down, Eddie! We need to talk!'

'No, we don't,' I said, not slowing down.

'Yes, we do! In your absence, the Inner Circle has voted Harry in as a full member. Everyone agreed. Even the Armourer, though that was probably only because Harry is James's son . . . Anyway, the point is the Inner Circle then voted unanimously that you not be allowed to make any more decisions of a military nature without consulting the Inner Circle first. And that you should not implement any such decisions without the full support of the Circle. You do see what that means? Do slow down, Eddie, I'm getting a stitch in my side. Well? Have you nothing to say?'

'Trust me,' I said. 'You really don't want to hear what I feel like saying.'

'Eddie . . .'

'None of this matters,' I said flatly. 'I put the Inner Circle together to advise me. Nothing more.'

'I see,' Penny said coldly. 'So you're the Patriarch now, is that it? You're running the family on your own, answerable to no one?'

'Change the subject,' I said, and she must have heard something in my voice, because she did.

'I've finally managed to make contact with the rogue known as the Mole. Thanks to some rather imaginative work by our communications staff, who turned out to be far too au fait with underground information systems for my liking. You did say you wanted the Mole brought back into the fold?'

'He could be very useful to us,' I said, a little defiantly. 'When he went rogue he went underground, literally, and put together an information network unmatched anywhere else in the world. He knows things; things no one else knows. And he's in contact with all kinds of powerful groups and individuals who wouldn't even dream of talking to us directly. We need the Mole, and his sources.'

'Well, unfortunately the Mole refuses to leave his hole,' said Penny. 'Even though we did everything we could to reassure him of his safety here. He's made it very clear he won't leave his refuge for any reason. But you must have impressed him, because he has agreed to help us search out information on what the Loathly Ones are up to, and the possible locations of other Nests. Right now he's teleconferencing with some of our brightest technogeeks, and no doubt teaching them all kinds of unfortunate new tricks.'

I nodded and slowed my pace a little. Penny was starting to puff. 'That's about the best we could hope for with the Mole,' I said. 'I'll talk to him later. Any other rogues surfaced yet?'

'We've put the word out,' said Penny. 'But it's up to them to contact us. And many of them have good reason to be . . . cautious. So. That's my news. I'm off. Things to see, people to do.'

'Anyone in particular?' I said. There must have been something in my voice because she looked at me sharply.

'Not that it's any of your business, but yes. I'm going to see Mr Stab.'

'You really don't want to talk to him,' I said. I stopped, and she stopped and faced me. She had a fierce, defiant look, so I chose my words carefully. 'You don't know what he is, Penny. I've seen some of his victims, or what was left of them. Cut open, gutted. I once saw a cache of his old victims, sitting together round a table, propped up and mummified so he could visit his old kills and glory in them. Savour the memory of their horror, and their screams. He's not human, Penny. Not any more. He made himself over into something else entirely, back in 1888.'

'You don't know him like I do,' said Penny. 'You've never taken the time to talk with him, listen to him, like I have. There's more to him than you think. He needs help, someone who cares enough to help him change. Anyone can be redeemed, Eddie.'

I was still struggling for something to say when she turned on her heel and strode away. I could have gone after her, but I didn't. It wouldn't have done any good. Some people simply won't be told. They have to find out for themselves, often the hard way. And what man ever understood what a woman sees in another man? And just maybe she was right. Maybe Mr Stab could be saved. Molly believed in him. I didn't. This was Mr Stab, murderer and ripper of women for over a century. A century of slaughter of women who also probably thought they understood him, right up to the point where he drew his knife.

So I went off and found a private place, locked the door, and called on Merlin's Glass to show me what Penny and Mr Stab were up to.

You're getting a bit too dependent on that mirror, Molly said. But I was doing what I had to. For the family.

Penny and Mr Stab went walking through the grounds, down by the lake. The sky was very blue, the trees were bowing slightly under the urging of the gusting wind, and pure white swans sailed majestically over the dead still waters of the lake. Penny made encouraging noises to them but none of them would come close while she had Mr Stab with her. The two of them walked on together, smiling and talking like old friends.

'So,' Penny said, 'did you have a good time killing the Loathly Ones?'

'Not really,' said Mr Stab. 'They didn't die like people do. There was no real suffering, no horror in their eyes; and such things are meat and drink to me.'

'Was the whole thing as big a disaster as Harry keeps saying?'

'No,' said Mr Stab, after a thoughtful pause. 'We stopped the Loathly Ones from bringing their unholy master through from Outside. Destroyed their tower, killed most of them and scattered the others. Edwin came up with the plan that made that possible. If he hadn't, if that Being had come through, that would have been a disaster, and the whole world would have paid for it. Humanity itself might have been wiped out . . . even me. It was an interesting sensation, to find myself face to face with Something worse than I am.'

'Do you still feel the need to kill?' Penny said abruptly. 'Or are you . . . satisfied, now?'

'I still feel the need,' said Mr Stab. 'I always do.' He looked at her bluntly. 'Why do you seek me out, Penny? You know what I am.

What I do to women. Do you want me to do it to you?'

'Of course not!'

'Then why, Penny?'

'No one's ever as bad as they're painted,' she said, after a while.

'I am.'

'Perhaps. I've heard the stories. But I wanted to meet the man *behind* the stories. Something draws me to you.' Penny looked into his face, meeting his cold gaze unflinchingly. 'Everyone can be saved. Everyone can be brought back into the light. I've always believed that.'

'What if they don't want to be saved?'

'If that were true,' said Penny, 'you would have broken your word to Molly by now. You live here with us, surrounded by temptation, but you do nothing. Molly said you were a good friend to her.'

'Molly believes . . . what she wants to believe,' said Mr Stab.

'So do I,' said Penny. 'Enough talk of dark and unpleasant things! Let me take your mind off such things, for a while.'

Mr Stab nodded slowly. 'Yes. You might be able to, at that.'

'I thought a picnic,' Penny said cheerfully. 'I've got a hamper set out in that little grove over there. Shall we?'

'Why not?' said Mr Stab. 'It's been a long time since I did anything so civilised.'

'We need to get to know each other better,' said Penny. 'How long has it been since you could talk freely to anyone? How long since anyone would just sit and listen to you?'

'A long time,' said Mr Stab. 'I have been alone a very long time.'

'I can't keep calling you Mr Stab,' said Penny. 'Don't you have a first name?'

He smiled. 'Call me Jack.'

'Oh, you,' said Penny.

And they walked on together, arm in arm.

I put the Merlin Glass away and headed for the front entrance at speed. I didn't want Penny alone with Mr Stab, far away from help. I didn't think he'd dare hurt a Drood right in the shadow of Drood Hall, but . . . I hurried through the hallways and connecting rooms, and all the way my family drew back and gave me plenty of room. Some glared, some muttered, but none of them had anything to say to me. Just as well. I had nothing to say to them. When I finally got to the front entrance, Molly was there waiting for me, along with one familiar face and one strange one. She had them both in vicious ear holds, putting on enough pressure to keep them quiet and grimacing at her sides.

'Look what I found!' Molly said cheerfully. 'Sneaking around in the grounds.'

'We were not sneaking!' protested the familiar face with as much dignity as could be managed when someone is twisting your ear into a square knot. 'We were . . . taking our time about making our presence known.'

'Hello, Sebastian,' I said. 'Been a while, hasn't it, since you betrayed me to Manifest Destiny, and then tried to kill me. Who's your wriggling friend?'

'Hold still!' snapped Molly. 'Or I'll rip them off and make you eat them.'

'It's all right, Molly,' I said soothingly. 'You can let go now. Even a notorious thief and con man like Sebastian Drood has better sense than to start any trouble at Drood Hall. Right, Sebastian?'

'Of course, of course! Leave off, woman, before my ear is permanently malformed! I'll be good. I promise.'

'Damn right you will,' growled Molly.

She let go, reluctantly, and Sebastian and his companion straightened up and felt gingerly at their reddened ears. Sebastian's usual air of sophistication was in tatters, but he still looked very prosperous in his expertly cut suit, and in excellent shape for a man in his sixties. Even if his thinning hair was obviously dyed.

'I am not any old thief,' he said haughtily. 'I am a gentleman burglar. I steal beautiful objects from people who don't appreciate them, and pass them on to people who can. For a percentage. I only steal the very best, from the very best. I have standards.'

'How did you get into the grounds unnoticed?' I said. 'We've completely reworked The Hall's security systems since I came back. Alarms should have gone off all over the place the moment you even thought about breaking in.'

Sebastian gave me his best supercilious smile. 'I am a professional burglar, old thing, and an expert in my craft. And I called in a few favours. You know how it is.'

'Not even remotely,' I said. 'Enlighten me.'

'Do you tell me your secrets? Suffice it to say it was a one-time deal, and highly unlikely to be repeated. And as to why I chose the less obvious way in, let's just say I wasn't entirely sure of my welcome. Given our past history. Your message to the rogues did say "All sins forgiven", but I'm afraid I've grown terribly cynical in my time away from the family.'

'You have so many sins to be forgiven,' I said. 'Including those against me and Molly. But don't sweat it, Seb, because you betrayed me to my enemies. We take that kind of thing for granted in the family these days. But you seemed to be doing so well, out in the world. Why leave your little lap of luxury in Knightsbridge after all these years? And don't even mention the word duty; I know you, Seb.'

'I want my torc back,' Sebastian said flatly. 'I've made too many enemies in my time to survive long without one.'

'Fair enough,' I said. 'But if a single precious heirloom goes missing in The Hall while you're here, I'll know it was you. And I will have Molly turn you into something even more slimy than you already are.'

'Something truly viscous and oozy, with exposed eyeballs and testicles,' Molly said gleefully. 'I've been practising.'

'And they say you can't come home again,' said Sebastian. 'This is exactly how I remember the family: coldly judgemental and extremely threatening. Worry not, Edwin; I'm not here to make waves. I just want my torc. Even if I have to, and I can't believe I'm saying this, earn the damn thing.'

'That's the spirit,' I said. 'You'll fit in nicely.'

'I understand you're looking for tutors,' said Sebastian. 'There are any number of useful tricks I could teach to the . . . more open-minded young Droods. Subjects and skills they probably never even dreamed of.'

'I should hope not,' I said. 'Or they'd have been kicked out, like you.'

Sebastian sniffed, hurt. 'There isn't an ounce of charity in you, is there, Edwin?'

'Not a bit,' I said. 'I had it removed surgically. Now. Who's your friend?'

'Oh, I'm Freddie Drood, darling!' said the young man on Molly's other side. 'Fabulous to meet you!'

Freddie was tall and dark and handsome, with coffee-coloured skin and close-cropped, jet-black hair. He wore a snakeskin jacket over a silk shirt open to the navel, and Levi's so tight he must have shrunk them on in the bath. He had mascaraed eyes, a bushy moustache and a big toothy grin.

'Freddie,' I said. 'Can't say the name rings a bell.'

'How unkind,' said Freddie, pouting. 'I was absolutely notorious in my time, darling. But of late I found myself a teensy bit financially embarrassed, so I teamed up with Sebbie here, as partners in crime. I got him into the best parties, so he could case the joint, and then we came back later and robbed the poor dears blind.'

'And why did the family find it necessary to kick you out?' I said.

'Oh, I've always been big and flamboyant and larger than life, honey,' said Freddie, throwing back his head and striking a dramatic pose. 'I started out as a field agent, but once away from dreary family restraints, I blossomed! I was practically a celeb, darling, and positively in demand for every little bash where the famous and infamous gathered. The family approved at first, because I picked up the most wonderful gossip about our putative lords and masters. But I couldn't bring myself to stay under the radar. I was getting noticed, so the family told me to come back home. I refused, and they cut me off without a penny. The heartless swine.

'Fortunately, I was already living with the first of a long line of sugar daddies, all of them quite prepared to keep me in the style to which I was determined to become accustomed, so for a long time it was party, party, and let the good times roll! Until I made the mistake of trying to set up a little private income of my own, through some discreet blackmail. The very first person I chose committed suicide, the poor dear, and left a very revealing letter behind. After that I was persona non grata in the better circles for ever such a long time. Which is how I ended up with Sebbie. I had a very large lifestyle to fund, darling: dancing and drinking and debauchery, all night long!'

'And what are you doing back here?' I said, when Freddie finally paused for breath.

'I really do need a torc, sweetie. There are too many diseases out there these days. Don't worry. I'm quite prepared to sing for my supper. A girl in my position does tend to hear things. I'm sure I can tell you all sorts of things you need to know.'

'I'm sure you can,' I said. 'All right. You both appal me beyond my ability to describe, but unfortunately right now you're probably just what the family needs. Go on in and report to the Sarjeant-At-Arms, and find a way to make yourselves useful. Seb, I think we'll keep you nice and busy with a series of lectures and tutorials. Like how to use a torc in illegal ways, for breaking and entering, and so on. Freddie, try and keep busy, and out of trouble.'

'Honey, I've never been that busy in my life,' said Freddie.

And with a wave and a wink he sauntered off into The Hall with Sebastian trailing dolefully after him.

'Was that wise?' said Molly. 'One'll get you ten they only came back to loot The Hall.'

'Maybe,' I said. 'Hopefully the Sarjeant will keep them under his thumb. It's either that, or kill them. And we need the rogues. We need their different viewpoints, knowledge, skills.'

'Even if it means welcoming back pond scum like Sebastian?'

'Everyone deserves a chance,' I said. 'I need to believe that anyone can be redeemed.'

At which point Freddie returned, without Sebastian. 'I've had a thought!' he said brightly. 'As I understand it, the family has put out a call for all rogues to come home, but hardly any are taking up the offer. Am I right? Thought so, darlings. Quite understandable, I'm afraid. Not everyone trusts the new regime to be terribly different from the old one. But I've bumped into all manner of rogues in my time, some long forgotten, or even thought dead, by the family. How would it be if I were to go out into the world, track these elusive fellows down and use my many charms to persuade them to come home? For a generous bounty on each head, of course.'

'Oh, of course,' I said. 'Sounds good to me. Do well, and I guarantee you a new torc. Didn't take you long to get tired of the old homestead, did it?'

'Honey, I'd forgotten how oppressive the old pile is,' said Freddie. 'I could never live here. It would crush my spirit. I would wither, darlings, positively wither! I must have my freedom.'

'You've got it,' I said. 'You can leave right now.'

'And the extent of the bounty?'

'Depends on who you can deliver,' I said. 'You can find your own way out, can't you?'

'I always do, honey,' said Freddie.

He sauntered off down the long gravel pathway, swaying his hips that little bit more because we were watching. Somehow I just knew Freddie was always happiest in front of an audience.

'Your family never ceases to amaze me,' said Molly.

'They can surprise me too, sometimes,' I said. 'My own Inner Circle has turned against me, because you weren't there to back me up.'

'Eddie, that's not fair,' said Molly. 'If you can't control them, you certainly can't expect me to.'

'I don't want to control them,' I said. 'Not as such. I just want the stupid bastards to understand that I'm right. I need them to believe that my way is the right way. Or everything I've done, to save the family's soul, could be undone.'

'You don't need me for that,' said Molly.

'Yes, I do! I do need you, Molly. I'm stronger, more confident, when you're with me.'

Molly smiled and moved in close, putting her hands on my chest. 'That's very sweet, Eddie. But I can't always be with you. I just can't. Not here. Not in this place. I told you: I'm never going to fit in here. I belong in the wild. I'm beginning to think I made a mistake in coming here with you. I love you, Eddie, you know I do. You matter to me in a way no one else ever has. I want you, Eddie; but I don't want this.'

She looked at me for a long moment, her dark eyes deep and unfathomable. 'You're starting a war, Eddie. A war I'm not sure you can win. The Loathly Ones were bad enough; but that thing they were summoning? Major league bad. I signed on to fight demons, not gods. You need to start with something smaller, more manageable. Like Manifest Destiny. Truman's still out there, putting his nasty little organisation back together again. And this time he won't have the Zero Tolerance people pulling his reins and holding him back. Start with him, Eddie. With a fight you can win.'

'I'll consider it,' I said. 'Now, please, come back inside. Be with me, if only for a while. I'm tired. I need to crash. Get some sleep, forget the world and its problems. It's going to be a hard day tomorrow.'

'Of course, sweetie. Come and lie down with me and I'll take your cares away. And you can help me forget mine. But what's so special about tomorrow? What's happening then?'

'The funerals,' I said.

Next morning came round all too quickly, and the insistent clamour of a bullying alarm clock made sure Molly and I were up bright and early to greet the coming day. And the pressures and problems it promised. Molly and I went down to breakfast in one of the big dining rooms. Rows and rows of tables covered with bright white cloths, a long sideboard with every kind of breakfast you could imagine, and huge windows looking out over the lawns. There were braised kidneys and kedgeree and even porridge, though you couldn't get me to eat that stuff no matter how much salt you put on it.

I'm not really a morning person, never have been, and I'm not that keen on breakfast, but this day of all days I needed to be seen, so that no one could accuse me of avoiding the funerals. My absence would have been interpreted as an admission of guilt.

So I nursed a cup of strong black coffee while Molly tucked into a full fry-up, complete with liver and mushrooms and more scrambled eggs than was good for her arteries. I'd never realised what a noisy eater she was, unless it was the terribly early hour. Everything sounds louder and more oppressive first thing in the morning. There were a lot of other people around us, breakfasting and talking animatedly. None of them had anything to say to me, or Molly.

'Why are we up this early?' said Molly, attacking her mound of steaming scrambled eggs with quite appalling vigour.

'Funerals here are always held early in the morning,' I said. 'It's tradition. Probably for the best, this time; we've got a lot to get through. All the people I lost—'

'Don't start,' Molly said sternly, threatening me with her fork. 'None of what happened was your fault. If it was, I'd tell you. Loudly and violently and where everyone could hear me.'

I considered that. 'You would, wouldn't you?'

'So why are we holding the funerals so quickly? It's not like they're going to go off.'

'We don't hang around, where funerals are concerned,' I said. 'The family has too many enemies who might try to use our own dead against us.'

Molly chewed on a crispy bit of bacon. 'What kind of funeral does your family put on?'

'Oh, it'll be a big ceremony,' I said. 'My family has a ceremony established for practically everything. We're very big on tradition. Helps discourage the rank and file from thinking for themselves. And I'll have to make a speech at the end. It's expected of me.'

'What are you going to say?' said Molly.

'I don't know,' I said. 'I suppose I could throw myself on the family's mercy . . .'

Molly shook her head. 'I wouldn't.'

After breakfast, I led Molly to the back of the main house and out through the huge French windows on to the long sloping lawns where the funeral was to be held. The coffins gleamed brightly in the early morning sun, rows and rows of them stretching away before us. Closed, of course, to hide the fact that most contained only parts of bodies, and some contained nothing at all. Two hundred and forty wooden boxes. I didn't know we kept that many in stock. Or perhaps someone used a duplication spell. Two hundred and forty fewer Droods, to stand between the world and the evils in it.

Family loss always matters. But my family matters more than most.

Everyone, or so it seemed, turned out for the funeral. They came from all over The Hall, standing in groups according to their calling or status. No one wanted to stand with Molly and me, not even the other members of my Inner Circle. Ranks and ranks of the living lined up before the rows of coffins, while hidden speakers pumped out consoling music. The Armourer was off to one side, fussing over a remote control panel. Keeping an eye on the energy field that protected us from enemy attacks and spying eyes.

The music finally ended with a stirring rendition of 'I Vow To Thee My Country', which we've pretty much adopted as our anthem, and then a Drood vicar came out to start the service. He was a Christian; nothing more. The family has never bothered with the various schisms that have split the Protestant Church down the years.

We'd probably still be Catholic, if the Pope hadn't ordered us to assassinate Henry VIII when he split England away from Rome. The Pope really should have known better. No one orders Droods around.

The vicar took us quickly through a stripped-down service, not even pausing for hymns or homilies, and then he stepped back and nodded to the Armourer. Uncle Jack hit a large red button with the flat of his hand, and two hundred and forty coffins disappeared, gone, leaving only faint indentations in the grassy lawn. Molly looked at me inquiringly.

'Transported directly into the heart of the sun,' I said. 'Instant cremation. Ashes to ashes, and less than ashes. Nothing left behind to be used against the family. I told you we all get cremated; we're a bit more dramatic about it than most. Now, if you'll excuse me, I have to make my speech. Good thing I don't suffer from stage fright; looks like everyone's here, except the Matriarch.' I frowned. 'She should be here. She shouldn't let private arguments get in the way of family duty. Ah well. Wish me luck.'

'Anyone even looks like heckling, I'll set fire to their underwear,' said Molly.

'How very fitting,' I said.

'I thought so,' said Molly.

I walked unhurriedly forward to where the coffins had been, and then turned and faced my family. So many Droods, all in one place, watching me with uncertain faces, waiting for me to say the words that would make everything all right again. If I could have, I would . . . But when in doubt, tell the truth. It may not be comforting, or reassuring, but at least then everyone knows where they are. So I told them what we found, down on the Nazca Plain. The Loathly Ones working through their drones, the insane structure they built, and the Awful Being they tried to summon through into our reality. Told them how my force fought bravely and well, against unexpected overwhelming numbers, and how we triumphed in the end. Those of us who remained.

'This is exactly the kind of threat the family was created to oppose,' I said, my voice ringing out loud and clear on the still morning air. 'To be shamans, protecting the Human tribe against threats from Outside. Those who came with me, and fell so valiantly, gave their lives to save Humanity. Be proud of them. And yes: we paid a high price for our victory. Which is why we must never be caught off guard again. My Inner Circle and I have decided that every member of the family will be presented with a new torc, and as soon as possible. We must be strong again. There is a war coming, not just against the Loathly Ones and the Invaders from Outside, but against all our enemies who would seek to divide and destroy us.'

I had hoped I'd get a cheer, or at least a round of applause, when I announced new torcs for everyone, but no one made a sound. And when I finished, they just stood there, looking at me blankly, as though to say *Is that it? Is that all?* And then Harry strode forward out of the crowd and every eye turned to him. I should have known. Should have known he'd seize the occasion to stick another knife in my back.

I looked quickly for Molly, and shook my head. I couldn't afford for anyone to think I was afraid to let Harry speak.

'There is a war coming,' Harry said, his voice loud and confident. 'The Nests of the Loathly Ones must be destroyed, and the Invaders prevented from entering our reality. But we can't wait around for new torcs . . . coming *as soon as possible.* We need them now. Right now! What's to prevent our many enemies from launching an attack, while we're perceived to be weak and vulnerable after such a setback? What's to stop the Loathly Ones from hitting us right now, in retaliation for the destruction of their tower, or to prevent us from attacking other Nests? We need our torcs. The family must be protected. It must be made strong again. And for that . . . we need a new leader.'

He stared right at me, his face cold and unyielding. 'I demand that Edwin step down! His half-baked ideas and incompetent leadership have cost us too much already. He's a threat to us all. He has proved himself a failure in the field, got most of his people killed, and doesn't even have the decency to apologise or admit his fault. It's time to undo the damage he's done to the family, and return us to traditional control. We must restore the Matriarch to power. She alone has the experience to wage a war successfully.'

'No,' I said flatly, and my voice stopped him dead. All faces turned back to me again. I tried to keep the anger out of my voice. 'Are your memories really so short? The Matriarch betrayed this family. Have you forgotten the price she made you pay for your old armour? The deaths of your twin brothers and sisters? Babies sacrificed to the Heart? She sanctioned that practice, and kept it a secret from you, because she knew you'd never go along with it once you knew the truth. Will you sell your souls again so easily? The torcs I will provide you, from Strange, will have no price tag attached. The armour I will give you, you can wear proudly.'

I looked at Harry. 'I can guarantee the family new torcs. Can the Matriarch do that? Can you, Harry?'

'So, Strange belongs to you, does he?' said Harry.

'Strange belongs to no one,' I said. 'But he knows an aresehole when he sees one.' I looked back at the sea of watching faces. 'It's up to you. Make your own decision. Don't be told what to do, by the Matriarch, or Harry, or me. I can't lead you into a war against your will, and I wouldn't if I could. I'm not your Patriarch. I'm a Drood, determined to do what's right. To be what I was raised to be. To fight the good fight against the enemies of Humanity.'

There was a long pause, during which I could almost hear my heart hammering in my chest. I had nothing else to say. At last, in ones and twos, and then in groups, my family applauded, accepting my words. They bowed their heads to me and then turned away and dispersed, heading back into The Hall. Not an overwhelming response, but it would do. For now. I looked around but Harry had already disappeared. Running off to report to the Matriarch, no doubt. I did see the Armourer taking time out for a quiet cigarillo, and he gave me a cheerful thumbs up. I nodded, and went to join Molly.

'Fight the good fight?' she said. 'As opposed to the bad fight, I suppose. What the hell's a bad fight?'

'The kind where you lose two hundred and forty good men and women,' I said. 'I can't do this alone, Molly. I need help. Professional help. People who know how to fight a war.'

'The clock's ticking,' said Molly. 'Where are you going to find these people in time?'

'Precisely,' I said.

CHAPTER NINE
Out of time

Penny came marching towards us with a determined look in her eyes. 'Keep going,' I said to Molly.

'We could run,' she said.

'Lacks dignity.'

By which time Penny had caught up anyway. She planted herself in front of us, hands on hips, glaring at me. I smiled pleasantly back, like I hadn't a care in the world; knowing that would annoy her the most.

'We have a problem,' Penny said flatly.

'Really?' I said. 'You do surprise me. And let me guess. It's my fault – right?'

'Maybe,' said Penny. 'Janissary Jane has gone missing. Disappeared without trace. There isn't even any record of her leaving the grounds, which is supposed to be impossible with the new security systems we've had put in place since your return.'

'Jane's a professional,' I said calmly. 'She comes and goes as she pleases. Still, it's odd she should disappear without saying anything. Any clues?'

'Just the one. A note pinned to her door with a knife. It said "Gone to get really big guns."'

'Yeah,' I said. 'That sounds like Jane, all right.'

'She must have taken the losses at Nazca personally,' said Molly.

'Jane's a soldier,' I said. 'She's fought in demons wars, seen whole civilisations die around her. If Janissary Jane thinks we need bigger guns, we must be in even more trouble than we thought. Still, she'll be back.'

'Hopefully with really big guns,' said Molly.

'Anything else?' I said to Penny.

'While I'm here, I would like to remind you about the decisions the Inner Circle made in your absence.'

'I hadn't forgotten,' I said.

Penny sighed. 'I told them you'd take it personally. Look, Eddie, this really isn't about you. It's about what's best for the family. No one's talking about deposing you; we just want you to consult us more.'

'Trust me, Penny,' I said. 'I understand.'

Penny sighed again. 'If you did, we wouldn't be having this conversation. So, in the interests of peace and goodwill and not smacking you round the head in public, I will change the subject. Nice speech you made. You said the right things. And unlike Harry, what you said clearly came from the heart. Keep that up and you might take the family with you after all.'

'Only might?' I said.

'There's more to being a leader than being right,' said Penny. 'You have to inspire, to motivate . . . and to know when to play politics with the right people.'

'And there I thought you were changing the subject,' I said. 'Let me try. How's Mr Stab?'

She looked at me sharply, immediately on guard. 'He's doing well. Settling in. His lectures are always standing room only, though as yet no one's worked up the nerve to attend a personal tutorial. He's a fascinating man. Very deep. Why are you asking me, Eddie?'

'Because you've been spending a lot of time with him,' I said.

'I won't even ask how you know that,' Penny said coldly.

'Best not to,' I agreed.

'What I do in my private time is my business, Eddie. Don't go poking your nose in where it isn't wanted or needed. Or Mr Stab might cut it off.'

She stalked away, her stiff back radiating anger. Molly looked after her.

'What was that about?'

'It seems that Penny and Mr Stab are something of an item these days.'

'You're joking! Really? Doesn't she know who he is? How can she not know who and what he is?'

'She knows,' I said. 'She doesn't want to believe it. She thinks she can change him. And maybe she can. You always said he was a good friend to you.'

'Well, yes, but only because he knows I can kick his arse in a dozen different ways . . . Oh hell, I'd better get after her. Time for some serious girl talk, and perhaps even an intervention. See you later, sweetie.'

A quick peck on the cheek, a waggle of the fingers, and she was off after Penny, moving at speed. I hoped the intervention worked. I could use one less thing to worry about.

I wandered through The Hall, not going anywhere in particular, just thinking. If I couldn't trust the advisors in my own Inner Circle any more, then I'd have to get some new ones. Preferably ones who understood more about the realities of fighting a war. And I had a really great idea on where to find them, made even more fun by the certain knowledge that this was one idea the Inner Circle definitely wouldn't approve of. I was still grinning at the thought when my left jacket pocket started jumping around like a wild thing. I grabbed at it with both hands, wrestled it still, and finally pulled out Merlin's Glass, shaking and shuddering like a vibrator in heat. It jerked itself out of my hands, grew rapidly in size, and then hung there on the air before me, a gateway through which I could see the Old Library. Shelves and shelves of books, in a warm golden glow, accompanied by the definite sound of someone muttering to themselves. William Drood appeared suddenly in the frame and nodded brusquely to me.

'Don't panic, it's only me. I needed to talk to you privately, so I activated the Glass from a distance.'

'I didn't know you could do that,' I said.

He snorted loudly. 'Lot of things you don't know about the Merlin Glass, boy, and I haven't enough time to warn you about all of them. Suffice to say that this is a device constructed by the infamous Merlin Satanspawn. The clue is in the name.'

'Next time, ring a little bell or something,' I said. 'Scared the hell out of me.'

'You're lucky I was able to improvise a vibrate mode,' said William. 'The original version called for a really loud gong sound. Now pay attention, Edwin. I need to talk to you. Here, in the Old Library, where we won't be overheard. Come on, step through the doorway. I haven't got all day.'

I sighed inwardly. It didn't seem that long ago when I was the one giving orders around here. I stepped through the opening, into the Old Library, and the Glass immediately shrank down to normal size again and tucked itself back into my pocket. I didn't know it could do that, either. I resolved to spend more time reading the instruction manual, first chance I got.

William heaved an oversized leather-bound book on to a brass reading lectern, and leafed through the pages rather more quickly than was probably safe for such ancient paper. He soon found the right page and began reading it to himself in a fast murmur, following the line of words with a fingertip. I waited for him to fill me in on whatever was so important that he'd had to summon me so urgently, but he seemed to have forgotten I was even there. I found a chair, and sat down to wait.

Every time I thought William was getting better, he fell back into Oddly John mode.

The younger Librarian Rafe appeared from between the towering stacks with a cup of steaming tea, which I accepted gratefully. Rafe looked fondly at William, and leaned forward to murmur in my ear:

'You have to make allowances for the old codger. We've both been up all night searching for the information you wanted. The Old Library has copies of books I never dreamed still existed, some of them so dangerous we had to perform low-level exorcisms before we could even get near them. William is a marvel, he really is. Jumping from one clue to the next, following the trail from volume to volume, from parchment scrolls to palimpsests to one ancient treatise actually inscribed on thin plates of beaten gold. I've been trying to get him to take a rest, but he's been a driven man ever since you showed him that Kandarian artefact.'

'Damn,' I said. 'It wasn't that urgent. Has he really been up all night and this morning?'

'Yes, he has,' said William, not looking up from his reading. 'And actually, it is that urgent. I'm not deaf, you know. I can hear everything you're saying. Now then, Eddie, I've turned up a great many references to Kandar and the Invaders. Most of them distinctly worrying, and all things you need to know right now. Which is why I brought you here. Rafe, where's that cup of tea I asked for?'

Rafe looked at me, but I'd already drunk most of it.

'I'll go and get another cup,' said Rafe.

'Never mind, never mind; stick around, Rafe. I want you to hear this as well as Edwin. Make sure I don't miss anything out. I'm not as sharp as I once was . . . Pay attention, Edwin! This is important! The whole family needs to know this.'

His voice was getting querulous. Rafe brought forward a chair and William sank gratefully into it. He rubbed tiredly at his forehead. He looked suddenly older, distracted, and worryingly vague about the eyes. When he lowered his hand, it was shaking visibly.

'I meant to go to the funeral,' he said suddenly. 'Rafe?'

'We missed it,' said Rafe. 'I did tell you, but you said the work was more important.'

'And so it is! I did mean to go, but . . . What was I saying?'

'Perhaps you should go to your room and have a little lie down,' I said. 'Get your strength back.'

'No!' William said immediately. 'Nothing wrong with me! And there's no time, no time! Besides I like it here. I'm not really . . . ready to meet people yet.'

'But you're home now,' I said. 'Among family.'

'Especially not family,' William said firmly. 'I don't want any of them to see me like this. I'm not . . . all the way back yet. I wore Oddly John as my cover for a long time and he's very hard to put down. Sometimes I wonder if he's the real me now and William is a memory of someone I used to be, long ago. I don't want to go to my room. I like it here. I find the books comforting. And Rafe. You're a good boy, Rafe. Make a fine Librarian, one day.'

'You'll be fine, William,' I said reassuringly. 'You just need a little time to adjust.'

He didn't seem to hear me, looking around him in a vague, troubled way. 'I hear things. See things. Always off to one side, where I can't pin them down. I thought that would stop once I left Happy Daze. Maybe they followed me here.' He put his hands together in his lap, to stop them trembling, and then he looked at me. 'I think the Heart did something to my mind. To keep me from telling what I knew. And I think . . . whatever it did . . . it's still happening.'

'The Heart is gone,' I said. 'Gone and destroyed. It can't hurt you any more.'

He shook his head slowly, wringing his hands together and muttering under his breath. I started to get up. Whatever information William had found, or thought he'd found, clearly couldn't be relied on. Maybe Rafe could dig some sense out of it later. And then I stopped short as William rose abruptly to his feet and glared into my face.

'And where do you think you're going, boy? Just because I have a bad moment? You wanted to know about the Kandarians, and the Invaders, and I know everything you need to know. Everything the family needs to know. So you sit down and listen.'

His eyes were clear and sharp again, and his presence was almost overwhelming. As though some inner switch had been thrown, and the old William had woken up and resurfaced. I sat back down, and William took up a lecturer's stance.

'The Kandarians made themselves powerful by voluntarily giving themselves over to temporary possession by forces from Outside,' he said crisply. 'As a result their warriors were inhumanly strong, and fast, and incredibly resistant to pain or injury. Remind you of anything? Yes, just like our family, the Kandarians made a deal with a greater power; but they were never satisfied. Always wanting more, always making new deals with new hosts. As they conquered the lands and civilisations around them, and spread their vicious empire of slaughter and torture and terror over wider and wider territories, the stronger they needed to be, to hang on to what they'd taken. In the end, their enemies banded together to put a stop to Kandarian expansion. The Kandarians found that unacceptable. They were having far too much fun. And so they determined to become even stronger and more powerful. Whatever the cost. They wanted to be gods on earth. So they made one more deal, with what we now know as the Loathly Ones, who in turn introduced the Kandarians to the Invaders. Very powerful Beings, from outside Space and Time. And that was the Kandarians' first mistake. Contact with the Invaders drove the Kandarians insane. All of them. They turned on each other, and wiped out their entire race and civilisation in one terrible night of death and destruction. Doing to themselves what they had spent so many years doing to everyone else.

'Not one of them survived.

'They didn't know what we know now. That there aren't really any Loathly Ones, as such. Not as separate entities. They're just the protrusions into our reality of much bigger entities. The fingertips, as it were, of the Invaders. Think of the Loathly Ones as Trojan Horses, through which the Invaders can gain a foothold in other realities. The Invaders have many names, in many cultures, and are feared by everyone with two brain cells to rub together. The Many-Angled Ones, The Horror From Beyond, The Hungry Gods. Beings from a higher reality than our own, who descend into lesser realities like ours in order to feed, to consume us. They feed on life, on every living thing, from the biggest to the tiniest. They eat worlds, wipe out whole realities, always moving on to the next, like cosmic locusts.

'When our family first made a deal with the Loathly Ones, bringing them through into our world as a weapon to use against the Nazis, we unknowingly brought our world, our reality, to the attention of the Invaders. And though we were careful to bring through only a small number of Loathly Ones, small enough to control, we thought . . . still we opened a door that was never properly closed. And of course the Loathly Ones did break free from our control, and down the years have grown in numbers and power until finally they're ready to summon the Invaders through. So they can feed on us. On everything. All life, all creation. We have to stop this, Edwin, because we started it.'

William finally stopped, standing straight and tall, gazing at me expectantly. I looked at Rafe.

'He's not exaggerating,' said Rafe. His voice was steady, though his face was pale and sweating. 'I've checked the references. It's all there, in the books. It's just that no one ever put it together, before William.'

'All right,' I said, a bit unsteadily. 'This is much bigger than we thought. How do we fight these . . . Invaders?'

'You don't,' William said flatly. 'If they ever break through, it's over. You have to prevent the Loathly Ones from building their towers. Wipe them out, down to the last one. Or we'll never be safe.'

'And . . . there are some books missing,' said Rafe. 'Important books. I'm assuming the Zero Tolerance fanatics removed them, maybe to hand them over to Truman and Manifest Destiny. Or maybe they destroyed them so no one would know the truth. You see, these books described the original deal the family made with the Loathly Ones. What we promised them, and they promised us.

And just maybe, some knowledge on how to undo the deal.'

'How many books are missing?' I said.

'We're still compiling a list,' said Rafe. 'One whole section of family history is missing. Including, not surprisingly, those volumes that might have told us who originally suggested we contact the Loathly Ones, and why.'

'I always assumed that was down to the previous Matriarch,' I said slowly. 'Great-grandmother Sarah.'

'I think it was more complicated than that,' said Rafe. 'I've been ploughing through some of the associational texts, unofficial family history, personal diaries and the like, and it does seem that other more sensible alternative choices were put aside in favour of the Loathly Ones.'

'Like who?' I said.

'The Kindly Ones,' said William. 'The Infinity Brigade, the Time Masters. All the usual suspects, all far more friendly to Humanity than a bunch of degenerate soul-eaters. But someone high up in the family insisted on the Loathly Ones, against all reason. I have to wonder if there was a traitor in the family. Perhaps someone already infected by the Loathly Ones.'

My skin crawled. 'An infected Drood, at the very heart of the family? Could there be others, still moving among us?'

'It's possible,' said Rafe. 'We've grown complacent down the years. Maybe the Armourer could come up with something we could use as a test.'

'I'll talk to him,' I said. 'A traitor in the family . . . maybe that's why there were so many drones waiting for us at Nazca. They knew we were coming. Someone tipped them off.'

'Has anyone gone missing since you returned?' said Rafe.

'Only Janissary Jane, but . . . No. Wait a minute.' I scowled, not liking where my thoughts were leading me. 'She'd got back from a demon war when I found her. She said she was the only survivor. And now I have to wonder why.'

Our heads snapped round sharply as we heard a faint furtive noise among the stacks, not far away. I was on my feet in a moment, plunging through the towering shelves, with Rafe and William not far behind. And there, not even trying to hide or run away, was the Blue Fairy, caught with a pile of books in his arms. He smiled quickly at the three of us, while being careful to stand very still.

'Hello!' he said. 'Don't mind me. Just here to pick up a little light reading.'

'This is the Old Library,' I said. 'Off limits to everyone, but especially you.'

'How very unkind,' said the Blue Fairy. 'Anyone would think you don't trust me.'

'Those are forbidden texts,' growled William. 'Rare and important and very valuable. Put them down. Carefully.'

'Of course, of course!' said the Blue Fairy, still smiling his bright and easy smile. He lowered the pile of books slowly and cautiously to the floor, and then held up both hands to show they were empty before stepping back from the pile. 'Can we calm down a little, please? I mean, we're friends here, aren't we? All on the same side?'

I gave him my best withering glare. I'd always assumed the Blue Fairy mostly came to The Hall because he felt in need of protection from his many enemies. Like the Vodyanoi Brothers. And only secondly to do good works for the redemption of his chequered soul. After all, the Blue Fairy was still half elf; and you can never trust an elf.

'What, precisely, where you looking for?' I said.

'I was interested in your family's past dealings with the elves,' the Blue Fairy said immediately. 'I don't really know much about Daddy's side of the family. Full-blood elves don't talk to half-breeds. Our very existence is taboo to them. But seeing you here, Eddie, among your own kind, made me sort of curious about mine. You know your roots, who and what you came from. I never have.'

I would have believed anyone else, but this was the Blue Fairy, so . . .

'Next time, ask permission first,' I said. 'How did you get in here, anyway? The shields I had put in place around the portrait should have eaten you alive.'

'Oh, please,' said the Blue Fairy, with an airy wave of one slender hand. 'I am a professional. I've been getting in and out of better-guarded places than this since before you were born.' And then he hesitated, and looked at me oddly. 'I couldn't help overhearing the Librarian's fascinating discourse on the Kandarians. It seems to me that I read something about them, and their connection with the elves. The Fae Court was already ancient when the Kandarians began building their very unpleasant empire, and it is said that the elves introduced the Kandarians to the Loathly Ones, as a way of destroying them. Beware of elves, Eddie; they always have a hidden agenda.'

He turned and walked away. I watched him go, and wondered whether he'd been trying to tell me, in his own indirect way, something very important about himself.

I left the Old Library with a lot on my mind. I'd learned many important things, most of which horrified me, all of which made me that much more determined to go ahead with my secret plan. If I was going to have to fight a war against Hungry Gods, with nothing less than reality at stake, I wanted some seriously heavy backup. First, I needed a place where no one would bother me, where I could use Merlin's Glass in a way I was sure absolutely no one in the family would approve of. So I left The Hall and went to the old chapel tucked away round the side of the house. Jacob's haunt, before I brought him back into the family. The chapel had been officially off limits to the family for centuries, because Jacob was there, and while he might have left no one had got around to reversing the ban.

I approached the chapel cautiously, but the thick mat of ivy half covering the heavy wooden door didn't even twitch. While Jacob was in residence, the ivy had acted as his early warning system, to ensure he remained undisturbed. But now he was gone, the ivy was just ivy. The door was stuck half open, as always, and I had to put my shoulder to the heavy wood to shift it. The door scraped loudly across the bare stone floor, raising acrid clouds of dust. I coughed a few times and called out Jacob's name. I still half hoped . . . but there was no reply.

Jacob was gone.

The pews were still stacked up against the far wall, shrouded in dusty cobwebs. The huge black leather reclining chair still stood in front of the old-fashioned television set. It was only too easy to remember Jacob, slouched at his ease in the chair, watching the memories of ancient television programmes on a set with no working bits in it. The refrigerator still stood beside the chair, but when I opened it, it was empty. I closed the door and sat down on the chair. The leather creaked mournfully under my weight.

I wished Jacob was around. I could always talk to him. And maybe he would have been the only one I trusted enough to talk me out of what I intended to do. I wasn't up to running a war. I didn't have the experience. The Nazca Plain Nest had proved that. I was damned if I'd see any more of my family killed because of me. I needed expert help and support from real warriors and tacticians to help me plan the battles in the war that was coming. And since it didn't seem likely that I'd find such experts here in the Present, I'd have to look for them in the Past and the Future.

The Armourer had forbidden me to do that. But I never was any good at listening to what my family told me.

I took out Merlin's Glass and looked at it for a while, turning it over and over in my hands. I wasn't blind to the risks of what I was planning. But the family had to be protected. I shook the mirror out to full size, and it hung before me on the air, its surface a shimmering blank.

'Open yourself to the Past,' I said firmly. 'And find me the best warrior, the best planner, to help me in the war that's coming. Find me a man good and true, someone I can trust. Find me the one perfect individual, to do what's needed.

The mirror snapped into sharp focus, showing me a clear image of . . . Jacob Drood. At first I thought the mirror had misunderstood me, and located the ghost of Jacob because he was most on my mind. But the more I looked at the image, the clearer it became that this wasn't any ghost. This was the real Jacob, the living man from long long ago. He looked so much younger, and . . . less complicated. As I watched, the image burst into movement and I was looking through a window into the Past as the living Jacob chased a giggling young woman around the chapel. Grinning cheerfully, he pursued her in and out of the properly positioned pews, the girl staying just enough ahead to encourage him. Their clothing suggested late eighteenth century, though I was never very good on dates and history.

I must have made some kind of noise, because they both stopped what they were doing and looked sharply in my direction. They didn't cry out, or seem particularly scared or startled; they were Droods, after all. I could see the gold collars round their throats.

Still, Jacob moved quickly to put himself between the young woman and the man staring at them through a hole in mid air. I held up my hands to show they were empty, and gave them my most reassuring smile.

'It's all right, Jacob,' I said quickly. 'It's all right. I'm family. I'm Edwin Drood, speaking to you from the Future. The twenty-first century, to be exact. The family has need of you, Jacob.'

'If thou be family, show me thy torc,' said Jacob.

I pulled open my shirt to show him the collar round my neck. Jacob raised an eyebrow.

'A silver torc, and not gold. Has the family's mettle become so debased, in your future time?'

'There have been some changes,' I said. 'But the family goes on. You'd recognise who we are, and what we do. The world still needs protecting, from many dangers.'

Jacob nodded slowly, then turned the young woman round, smacked her firmly on the bottom and urged her towards the chapel door. 'Get thee gone, girl. This is man's business.'

She giggled again, gave him one last saucy wink and trotted quite happily out of the chapel. I made a mental note to tell this Jacob not to try that in my time.

'Best bit of bum in The Hall,' Jacob said cheerfully.

'That may be,' I said, 'but why the chapel?'

'Because the family's chased me out of everywhere else,' said Jacob. 'It seems the morals of this age are changing, and fun is out of fashion.' He looked at me shrewdly. 'From the Future, you say. Might I inquire how it is that thou art are here, speaking with me?'

'Merlin's Glass,' I said, and Jacob nodded immediately.

'I had thought that devious and dangerous device long lost, and rightly so. Thy need must be desperate indeed, to put faith in such a thing.' Jacob regarded me thoughtfully. 'How is it that a man of such future times recognises my face, and hails me by name? Am I to become famous, and a legend in the family?'

'Sort of,' I said. 'I need you to come to me, Jacob; into the Future, to help the family. Will you?'

'Time travel is forbidden, without the express order of the Matriarch,' Jacob said slowly. 'But tell me, young sir, how goes the world, in your time? What new wonders and marvels?'

'Come and find out,' I said.

'Tempter!' said Jacob, smiling. 'And yet it must be said the family is not entirely happy with me just now. I am out of sorts with my own times – so perhaps some time apart might enable the family to look on me more happily, through the kinder eyes of absence . . . So! Anything for the family, young Edwin!'

I reached out my hand, through the gateway, across the years, and Jacob took it. It was actually a shock, to be able to feel his flesh and blood hand in mine. I brought him through Merlin's Glass, out of his time and into mine, and the gateway immediately snapped shut. Jacob let go of my hand and looked around him, clearly shocked at the state of the chapel, gone (for him) in a moment from the tidy sanctuary he knew to the grubby abandoned derelict of now. He started to say something . . . and the ghost of Jacob appeared out of nowhere: a fiercely glowing presence with wild eyes hovering above us. He pointed a shaking shrivelled hand at me, his voice howling inside my head like a damned soul.

What have you done? What have you done!

He vanished. Jacob grabbed me by the arm. 'What in sweet Jesu's name was *that*?'

'I don't think I'm going to tell you,' I said, after a moment. 'I think . . . I'm going to have to work up to that.'

I prised his fingers off my arm, and then used the Merlin Glass to open a gateway between the chapel and the Old Library. I called for Rafe, and he came trotting up immediately.

'This is Jacob Drood,' I said briskly. 'Yes, *that* Jacob. I brought him forward, out of the Past, to help us. I need you to look after him, bring him up to speed, tell him anything he needs to know. And no, I'm not going to answer any questions at this time. Just do it, all right?'

'You love making trouble for yourself, don't you?' said Rafe. 'Why don't you shoot an albatross and get it over with? Come with me . . . Jacob, and I'll do my best to explain the unholy mess you've been dropped into.'

'Ah brave new world, that has such secrets in it,' Jacob said drily. 'It would appear the family of this time is not so different from the family I know, after all.'

I pushed him through the gateway and shut down the Glass

before either of them could ask any awkward questions. I'd asked the Glass for the most suitable candidate, and it chose Jacob. So he had to be the right man for the job. He just had to be. I sighed heavily, looked round the empty chapel, and raised my voice in the dusty silence.

'All right, Jacob, you can come out now.'

And there he was, sitting slouched in his reclining chair, a skinny spectral presence in a grubby T-shirt and baggy shorts. His flyaway hair floated around his bony head as though he was underwater, and his eyes were dark and brooding. He glowered at me, but his heart wasn't in it. For the first time since I'd known him, he looked old and tired and defeated.

'Why did you do it, Edwin? What did you think you were up to? Why didn't you tell me you were planning to snatch my living self out of the Past?'

'The Merlin Glass said you were what the family needed to fight this war,' I said. 'But you must have known I was going to do it. Why didn't you tell *me*?'

'Because I didn't remember!' The ghost of Jacob looked sadly at his empty television set, and brief images flickered across the dusty screen of the living Jacob in his own time, doing the simple everyday things the living do . . . a jumble of memories, gone in a moment.

'So much of my past is lost to me,' Jacob said softly. 'My life is so long ago now. After I died I spent centuries here, sitting and waiting, waiting for the important thing I had to do, waiting for so long I finally forgot what it was I was waiting for. I knew you were important, from the first day I set eyes on you as a child. I remembered, eventually, that I had to help you seize control of the family away from the Matriarch; but I still didn't know why. There's more to me being here, Eddie, than the destruction of the Heart. There's something I have to *do*, something *important* . . . but I don't know what!' He looked up and fixed me with a steely glare. 'But I do remember one thing now, Eddie. You brought me here, to this time, to die. You made me, or will make me, what I am.'

'How?' I said. My throat was dry, my voice a whisper.

'I don't know. Let's just hope it's a good death. For the family.'

'No,' I said. 'I won't let that happen.'

'You can't prevent it. In fact, you mustn't.'

'I could send you back. The living you. Open the gateway and—'

'But you won't. Because you need me.'

'Jacob . . .' I said.

He nodded gruffly. 'I know, boy. I know.'

'You were my first real friend,' I said. 'And apart from Uncle James, the only family I ever had. You and James were the only ones I ever cared for. And now you tell me I'm going to be responsible for your death too? No. No, I can't let that happen. Not again. I killed one father; I can't kill another!'

'Time isn't fixed,' Jacob said kindly. 'But if I don't die, like I'm supposed to, I won't be here to be your . . . friend, when you need it. Won't be here to help you take down the Heart. The family always comes first, Eddie. I'm glad I got to meet you, boy. You were worth waiting for. You are the son I never had. Now dry your eyes, and do what you have to. There is a purpose in this, a destiny we have to fulfil. I remember that much.'

'Why have you been hiding from me?' I said, when I could trust my voice again.

'Because I had the feeling something bad was about to happen. And because I need time alone, undisturbed, to make myself remember what it is I'm supposed to do. Before it's too late. Don't come looking for me, Eddie. And don't tell the living me about . . . me. Just in case you think of a way out.'

He grinned, winked a glowing eye and vanished from his chair, leaving me alone in the chapel.

Considering how my first attempt at meddling with Time had gone, I wasn't sure I wanted to try again. But need and duty and Jacob's encouragement drove me on. I still needed help, perhaps now more than ever, and the only place left to look was among the future descendants of my family. And besides, I always was stubborn. So I fired up Merlin's Glass again and instructed it to show me the Future.

'Show me how The Hall will look, a hundred years from now,' I said. That seemed safe enough.

The doorway opened, showing me a view of The Hall, standing tall and proud in its extensive grounds. The house looked a hell of a lot bigger. Whole new wings had been added, and a tall stone tower on each corner. Airships of an unfamiliar design buzzed like sleek black wasps around the landing field at the back, and there were children, hundreds of children, running free and happy across the sloping lawns. And then the image changed abruptly, showing me another Hall. It was a ruin, broken stone and crumbling brick, and the windows dark. The grounds were a rioting jungle of strange and alien plants, lapping right up against the sides of The Hall like a solid green tide. Creepers hung out of windows, trees burst through broken walls. And no sign of the family anywhere.

The image changed again. This time The Hall I knew was gone, replaced by a magnificent high-tech structure, all gleaming steel and silver and huge flashing windows. Swirling energies coalesced around tall shimmering towers, and strange machines hopped across the neatly manicured lawns. And the whole place was surrounded by flying angels, full of a terrible beauty, singing songs of war, shining brighter than the sun . . .

The images before me kept changing, flashing by faster and faster. All of them potential, possible futures. All equally real, equally likely or unlikely. I commanded the Glass to stop, thought for a while, and then told it to show me an image of The Hall in a future where the family failed to stop the Invaders.

This time, The Hall stood alone and abandoned on an endless blasted plain. No signs of life anywhere, from horizon to horizon, and the cloud-covered sky was empty. Dust fell slowly, endlessly, undisturbed by even the slightest breath of a breeze. No sign of any living thing. Nothing moved. The sky was a dark and sullen purple, like a bruise.

A dead world.

I felt cold. Chilled right down to the bone; to the soul. This was what would happen if the family failed. If I failed.

I told the Glass to show me how this had happened. What the Invaders would do, when they came. Images came and went before me, but I couldn't understand any of them. It was too strange, too different, too *other.* There were great shapes, living things big as mountains, radiating through more than three physical dimensions. Looking at them made my head hurt, made me feel sick. Time seemed to slow down and speed up, landscapes rose and fell like tides, cities burned and the moon fell out of the sky. People and other living things ran screaming through distorted streets, transforming and mutating into things that shouldn't have been able to survive in a rational world. But still they persisted, still horribly alive and aware and suffering. A black sun, huge and awful, dominated a sky set on fire, until suddenly it shattered, blown apart, spitting out the dreadful things that had been gestating inside it.

The strangeness accelerated, until I couldn't look any more. I turned away, and suddenly fell sick and shaking to the cold stone floor. Behind me, there were terrible sounds. I yelled for the Glass to stop, my eyes squeezed shut, tears leaking past screwed-up lids. And immediately a blessed silence filled the chapel. When I finally dared to look again, there was nothing in the mirror hovering before me but my own reflection. I looked like hell. I looked like I'd already been through a war, and lost.

I rose slowly to my feet, a cold determination forcing the weakness out of me. I wasn't going to lose. I couldn't afford to. I was going to get my help from the Future, whatever the cost. Because the alternative was so much worse.

I instructed the Merlin Glass to go as far into the potential futures as necessary to find me the one descendant best suited to helping me win the war against the Invaders. A warrior, to lead the family into battle. A leader of men, to inspire them. A man who would be everything I was not.

The Glass showed me a new scene, strange enough to take my breath away. A battlefield on an alien planet. Three suns blazed in a garish pink sky, looking down on a great snowy waste littered with hundreds of broken bodies and splashed with blood. Huge broken war machines lay half buried in the snow, so alien in design I couldn't even guess what they were supposed to do. But the bodies in the snow were quite definitely men and women, though their strange jade-green armour was unfamiliar. It boasted crusted accumulations of jagged technology, punctuated with jewels that glowed like radioactive eyes. The bodies bore the marks of sudden and brutal death, some actually torn apart and dismembered. War had come and gone here, and these people had lost.

And then one man came running across the snowscape, his booted feet sinking deep into the snow with every step, forcing himself on through brute strength. He plunged through the snow with desperate speed, not bothering to look back at what he knew was coming after him. He wore the same kind of armour, though most of his jewels were no longer glowing, and he carried some kind of gun in one hand and a long sword in the other. As he drew nearer, I could see he was about the same age as me, though his brutal, blood-spattered face made him seem older. He wore his jet-black hair in a long mane, held out of his eyes with a golden circlet round his forehead. And yet, for all his desperate situation, he was grinning; as though he was playing a game. The only game worth playing. He was tall and lithely muscular, and I knew that none of the blood dripping from his armour was his.

More armed men came spilling over the snowy horizon. They ploughed through the snow after the running man, whooping and howling, sounding more like beasts than men. They fired their guns, but somehow he was never where the energy beams hit. Snow exploded behind him, superheated water flying in steaming droplets though the cold air. But finally he seemed to decide that there was no more point in running and he turned abruptly to face his pursuers, holding one arm up before him. The energy beams immediately targeted him, only to be soaked up by an invisible force shield apparently radiating from his raised arm.

The pursuing men closed in on the warrior, and he stood patiently, waiting for them to come to him. To my surprise, they put away their guns and went for him with swords the moment they were in reach. The fight that followed was swift and savage, like nothing I'd ever seen before, every move cold and clinical and utterly without mercy. The warrior fought well and fiercely, handling the long steel blade as though it was weightless. Blood and guts and hacked off limbs decorated the snow around him, and none of his enemies even came close to touching him. He stamped back and forth in the crimson snow, slicing and cutting and avoiding the blows coming at him from every direction with almost feline grace.

There must have been twenty men and more against one lone warrior; and he killed them all in just a few minutes.

As the last man fell into the snow in a flurry of spurting arterial blood, the warrior looked calmly about him, not even breathing hard. He nodded once, as though satisfied with his performance, and then lowered his sword. He was starting to relax when another man rose up from the snow behind him. He'd been hiding under another body, completely hidden, waiting for his chance. He raised his unfamiliar gun to shoot the warrior in the back, and I drew my Colt Repeater and shot the man in the head, through the doorway. A bullet from the Past, to kill a man in the Future.

The sound of the Colt was loud and coarse after the brief hum of the energy weapons, and the warrior spun round incredibly fast, his sword at the ready. Just in time to see the man who would have killed him collapsing into the snow with half his head blown away. The warrior saw me watching him through a hole in the air, and his gaze was dark and cold and thoughtful. He strode unhurriedly through the bloody snow to stand before the gateway, and then considered me pensively for a long moment. He still hadn't put away his sword. Blood dripping from the blade steamed in the chill air I could feel blowing through the opening. He said something, his breath clouding on the air, but I couldn't understand him. It didn't sound like any human language I'd ever heard. I quickly ordered my torc to translate and his words began to make sense.

'Thanks for the help,' said the warrior. 'Didn't expect to find a friend in this God-deserted place. I owe you a debt of honour, stranger.'

'Where are the rest of your people?' I said.

He shrugged. 'Dead. Every last one of them. We knew it was a suicide mission when the Emperor sent us here; but it wasn't like we had a choice. Man proposes, and the Emperor disposes. Especially when you're no longer in favour at Court.' He stopped and looked sharply around him, listening for something I couldn't hear. 'My enemies are coming again. Can you get me out of this mess, stranger? I am the only survivor of my command, and the size of the opposing force is far greater than I was given to understand.'

'You're taking my appearance very calmly,' I said. 'Or are such things as this common, in your time?'

He shrugged again. 'I've seen stranger shit than this, out on the Rim. Get me out of here, stranger, and I vow to serve you as I would my Emperor. Not for ever; my vow to the Imperial Throne must take preference. But a time away from Court might help the blood to cool a little . . . on both sides. Shall we say service to you, in return for my rescue, for a year and a day?'

'Sounds fair to me,' I said. But when I tried to reach through the opening, the Glass wouldn't let me. I'd been afraid of that. 'Look, I'm not really a stranger. I'm speaking to you from far in your Past. I don't know exactly how far. Centuries, certainly; maybe more. You are a descendant of my family. And my family needs a warrior's guidance. But I can't bring you through. You're too far off from me. But I have another way of reaching you.'

'Better be quick,' he said dispassionately. 'My enemies will be here soon. What's your name?'

'Edwin Drood,' I said. 'And yours?'

The warrior smiled. 'Deathstalker. Giles Deathstalker.'

CHAPTER TEN
Various voices, prophesying war

Sometimes it seems to me that the whole of my time at The Hall consists of people marching up to me, determined to tell me things they already know I'm not going to like. There's a certain look I've learned to recognise: equal parts determination and it's-for-your-own-good glee. This time it was Callan Drood, emerging from a side room as I wandered back into The Hall. He looked not so much sunburned from his trip to South America as sun-roasted. He headed straight for me, already scowling furiously. Didn't mean it had to be bad news: Callan always looked that way. Even at the best of times, he gave the impression of someone perfectly prepared to walk through anything that got in his way, including walls, regulations and quite possibly people. I knew I didn't want to hear what he was so determined to tell me, but short of clubbing him down with the nearest blunt instrument and walking over him, there was no way of avoiding the man. So I stopped, heaved a heavy sigh to show I wasn't at all happy, and let him get on with it.

'The Inner Circle wants to talk to you,' Callan said bluntly.

'It's nice to want things,' I said. 'I want several large drinks and a meat pie, followed by a nice lie down, and I think I'll go and get them right now.'

'Let me rephrase the message,' said Callan. 'The Inner Circle needs to see you at this moment, and I have been instructed not to take *No, go to hell,* or even *Fuck off and die* for an answer.'

'The Circle has already demonstrated that it can make decisions without me,' I said flatly. 'Let it carry on.'

'Sulking doesn't become you,' said Callan. 'So cut it out or I'll slap you somewhere painful. Right here, in public. This is important.'

'This bluff but honest act of yours is really starting to get on my tits,' I said. 'How important?'

'Sphincter-clenching, testicle-shrivelling, end-of-the-world and everything-turning-to-shit important,' said Callan. 'They're waiting for you in the War Room. Probably crying and wetting themselves and trying to hide under things.'

'Oh,' I said. 'That important.'

So we went down to the War Room, threading our way through the security checks until finally we passed through the specially reinforced doors and into complete bedlam. The usual hushed air was gone, replaced by a tense, charged and very noisy atmosphere, in which people ran from work station to work station, held rapid conversations, threw up their hands and then hurried on somewhere else. The giant display screens covering the black basalt walls, showing maps of every country in the world, were thickly dotted with flashing red lights, indicating real-time emergencies and disaster spots. The farcasters and computer technicians were shouting into their hands-free headsets while waving sheets of paper for messengers to pick up and take wherever necessary.

I actually stopped and stared for a moment. The War Room was always the cold, calm and collected heart of family decision-making. I'd never seen the place so distracted, so openly close to panic. What used to be my Inner Circle was standing around the main mission table, waiting impatiently for me. Or, at least, most of it. There was no sign of Jacob, of course, nor of Molly or Penny. Presumably those two were still off somewhere private, having their girl-to-girl chat. The Sarjeant-At-Arms was there, and the Armourer, and Harry . . . and Roger Morningstar. I did wonder whether I should object to a known hellspawn being allowed into the Drood family War Room but that was, after all, the kind of thinking I was trying to overturn. If he had anything useful to contribute, I'd listen to him.

We could always kill him later.

Still, with Molly and Penny absent, and both the living and the dead Jacob off about their business, it meant the only real ally I had in the Circle was the Armourer. Good old Uncle Jack. Who was, to be fair, glowering at Roger.

'What is that half-breed demon doing here?' he demanded as I approached the main mission table with Callan at my side.

'Roger's with me,' said Harry.

The Armourer sniffed loudly. 'Don't know what the family's coming to.'

'Hi, guys,' I said. 'What's happening?'

The Armourer immediately turned his glare on me. 'Where the hell have you been, Eddie? Look at the world maps! Information has been flooding in ever since your little exercise in South America, all of it bad. There are brush fires breaking out across the globe because there aren't any agents left in the field to stamp them out. The staff here are being run ragged trying to keep track of what's going on.'

'I've brought in some extra people, from Intelligence and the Media Pit, and basically anyone else who didn't look too busy or who couldn't run away fast enough,' Callan said briskly. 'We're just about staying on top of things, for the moment. But events are definitely accelerating as world leaders give spectacularly good impressions of lemmings with a really bad hangover and no inhibitions.'

I had to raise an eyebrow at him. 'Since when have you been in charge of the War Room, Callan?'

'Since you and your precious Inner Circle decided you'd rather spend your time squabbling with each other instead of getting your hands dirty with the day-to-day running of the family. I used to work here before I had delusions of being a field agent, and when I got back from that major clusterfuck in South America, I felt a need to be doing something useful, so I looked in here and was appalled to see how lax things had become in my absence. So I walked right in, rolled up my sleeves and took over. No one else was volunteering. The people here were actually grateful for someone to tell them what to do. You don't like the way I'm running things, fine, boot my arse out of here – if you can find anyone dumb enough to take over. I'll bet you lot don't even know the precedence protocols, do you? And what are you smiling at, Edwin?'

'For a moment there,' I said, 'you reminded me of me.'

'Now you're just being nasty,' said Callan.

'These tough guy bonding rituals are very sweet,' said Harry, 'but, Callan, as lord and master of the War Room, do you think you could lower yourself to brief us on what's happening now?'

Callan flared his nostrils. 'Don't push your luck, new boy. You and brimstone boy are only here on sufferance. Okay, everyone: bottom line. Politicians of every stripe and flavour are currently threatening each other with war, invasions, and all sorts of economic terrorism, because they believe the family is currently incapable of stopping them. Word of our lack of field agents, and maybe even lack of torcs, has clearly got around. So across the world lots and lots of old grudges, hatreds and blood feuds are finally being paid off, with age-old enemies gearing up for some serious and long-delayed blood-letting.

'Added to that, the usual unusual suspects are itching to take advantage of the situation. While the cat's away, the mice will inevitably get uppity. All the familiar nasty organisations and individuals are operating more and more openly, daring us to try and stop them. We've been enforcing the peace so long, we've forgotten how much bad stuff was bubbling under the surface.'

He stopped to glare at me accusingly. Everyone else joined in. I glared back at them.

'The more they come out into the open, the easier it will be for us to step on them,' I said. 'They'll get what's coming to them. Anything else, Callan?'

'Oh, loads. All of it bad, bordering on unnerving. Elf sightings are up. Significantly up. Current thinking from Intelligence is that the elves may be planning to use the weakening of dimensional barriers by the Invaders to return at last from their long exile. Intelligence thinks we should try and make contact with the Fae Court, try and get them on our side, as allies against the Invaders. Because it's not in the elves' interests for the Invaders to destroy the very world the elves hope to return to rule.'

'Elves will never side with Humanity,' I said flatly. 'They hate us too much. They might side with the Invaders, just for the joy of seeing the Invaders do the one thing the elves never could: murder Humanity.'

'Then there's the aliens,' said Callan. 'Most of the species we're currently monitoring have disappeared. Presumably going while the going's good.'

'Rats leaving the sinking ship,' growled the Sarjeant-At-Arms.

'Well, quite,' said Callan. 'Do feel free to chime in and interrupt my briefing whenever you feel like it, Cyril. Finally, there is patchy but convincing evidence that Heaven and Hell are taking a direct interest in what's going on. There are reports of angels. From Above and Below.'

We stared at Roger, who shrugged. 'No good looking at me. Neither side would confide in a half-breed. In fact, they'd probably fight each other for the privilege of killing me.'

'I know how they feel,' I said.

At which point, the terrible sound of an enormous gong slammed through the War Room, so loud people clapped their hands to their ears to try and keep it out. Everyone looked frantically round, bracing themselves for an attack; but all that happened was the Merlin Glass hopped out of my jacket pocket, grew to full size while hanging in mid air, and formed a gateway between the War Room and the Old Library. William Drood stared out of the opening at the panicked War Room and smiled weakly.

'Sorry about that. I thought I'd disabled the gong function.'

I sighed heavily. 'I'm a bit busy at the moment, William. Is this really important?'

'Of course!'

'Of course,' I said. 'Everything's important these days. Always breaking news, and never any time for the heart-warming stuff about a badger that's learned to skateboard. Don't mind me, I'm babbling because it's either that or start throwing things. What do you want, William?'

He smiled distantly, looking, it had to be said, even more twitchy and distracted than usual. 'Rafe is taking care of your friend. I have some new and quite probably vital information on the nature and intentions of the Loathly Ones. You need to hear this, Edwin, before you go making any plans.'

'All right,' I said resignedly. 'The Inner Circle's here with me. Fill us in.'

The Armourer stepped forward suddenly, standing beside me to stare into the opening. He smiled broadly at the Librarian. 'William!' he said. 'My God, but it's good to see you again! I didn't know you were back in The Hall. Why didn't you come and find me? You're looking . . . good. Come on through and join us here! We'll have a good long talk about old times, once this is over.'

William gazed sadly at him. 'I'd rather not come through. I'm not ready yet. It's Jack, isn't it? Hello, Jack. It has been a while, hasn't it? Though I couldn't tell you how long. I rather lost track of things, like time and . . . things.'

The Armourer looked at me, lowering his voice. 'What's the matter with him? I thought you said he was—'

'Cured?' said William. 'A bit optimistic, that, I'm afraid. And I'm crazy, not deaf. Let's just say I'm slowly getting back to who I used to be.'

'Why did you stay away for so long?' said the Armourer. He was trying to talk calmly, naturally, but it was clear how much his old friend's condition was affecting him. 'Why didn't you say goodbye to anyone? To me? You didn't even leave a note! Didn't you realise how worried we'd be? I spent years trying to track you down, long after everyone else had given you up and labelled you a rogue. *I* never gave up on you. Why didn't you tell me you were going, William? We'd been friends since we were kids.'

'The Heart drove me out,' said William. You could tell he was trying hard to concentrate, to hold his straying thoughts together. 'It hurt me. Bad Heart. I had to run, get away from The Hall, and the family, run for my life and what was left of my sanity. Yes. I had to go to ground where no one would think to look for me, and then hide deep inside myself, so even the Heart couldn't find me. I went so very deep inside, Jack, and coming back is . . . difficult. We'll talk later, Jack. Yes. Catch up, the two of us. Just . . . not yet.

'For now, I need you all to listen to what I have to tell you. And pay attention. I don't think I'm up to going through this twice.'

His face firmed, his voice becoming clearer and more authoritative as he took on his old role as expert lecturer. Perhaps because it was another role he could hide behind, that required nothing of him but his expertise.

'The family knows the Invaders of old. We fought them long ago, when the Druidic Droods were still supporting the Romans in their occupation of old Britain. According to the Latin texts, it took the whole might of the Roman Empire, along with the first Drood field agents, to destroy towering structures being built across the known world by *possessed* primitive peoples. The Roman military stamped these early Nests out with their usual brutal efficiency, but more kept springing up. There is evidence to suggest that in the end the Heart stepped in and intervened directly, destroying the remaining structures and preventing the Invaders from entering our reality. Presumably because it wasn't prepared to lose its new property. This was the Heart's world, and it didn't feel like sharing. Anyway, many centuries later, the last Matriarch but one, Sarah Drood, took the knowledge from those times from the "lost" Old Library, and used it to summon the Loathly Ones back into our reality, supposedly to be used as weapons against the Nazis.'

'Supposedly?' said the Sarjeant-At-Arms sharply. 'I've seen the records. The soul-eaters made excellent weapons against the Nazi war machine, before the Vril Force came in on the other side and balanced the scales again.'

'I'm sure they did a lot of damage,' said William. 'But I don't think that was why they were brought back.'

'I've never understood why we chose them,' said the Armourer. 'I mean, soul-eaters? There had to have been better, safer, options we could have pursued.'

'Oh, there were,' said William. 'But someone, someone fairly high up in the family, insisted on the Loathly Ones. The more I read in the unexpurgated records, the more I am forced to the conclusion that someone in the family was a traitor. Perhaps already possessed by some demon.'

'But how was that possible?' spluttered the Sarjeant. 'The torcs protect us from all forms of possession or soul peril!'

'Only one way it could have happened,' said William. 'Someone gave themselves up willingly to possession. Just like the Kandarians.'

That stopped us in our tracks for a while.

'A traitor in the family,' I said finally. 'That's easier to believe now, after all we've discovered about the Heart, and the Matriarchs and the Zero Tolerance faction, but still . . . a Drood giving themselves up to a demon and allying with soul-eaters? Why? What could they hope to gain?'

'More importantly,' Harry said slowly, 'could there still be traitors, or possessed Droods, operating inside the family? That could explain how we were so easily ambushed on the Nazca Plain.'

William nodded sadly. 'I was better off when I was crazy and didn't know what was going on. One thing seems regrettably clear. Ever since the Loathly Ones were let back in, for whatever reason, sixty years ago, they've been possessing victim after victim, slowly building their power and influence to the point where they could start building their structures again, and summon the Invaders.'

'There are reports coming in of more of these structures, in various stages of completion, from across the world,' said Callan. 'It's like they're not even trying to hide them any more.'

'How many?' said the Sarjeant-At-Arms.

'Hundreds, so far. Wouldn't surprise me if we ended up with thousands.'

'Let us discuss what we know of the Loathly Ones,' said William, in full lecture mode now. 'They don't move in and take over their victims like most demons, or devils from Hell.' There was a slight pause while everyone looked at Roger, but he had nothing to say. William sniffed a few times and then plunged on. 'No, these demons infect their victims through simple proximity. They implant a mental/spiritual embryo into the human body and soul. The invading presence then uses the human as food while the embryo gestates, before finally hatching into a complete Loathly One.

'Demonic cuckoos, as it were.

'First come physical changes. Warpings of the flesh, strange mutations in the body, all concerned with making the host strong enough to hold and contain the embryo that's forming. As this grows inside the host it eats into the mind and soul, changing the thoughts and personality of the human host, who can feel themselves going mad, becoming alien, but are helpless to stop or even slow the change. We can only imagine the kind of hell these poor unfortunates go through. Thoughts, emotions, beliefs, all change . . . until nothing is left but a new Loathly One drone. The human is gone, replaced.'

'So essentially,' I said, 'once infected, their victims die by inches, day by day, losing every bit of themselves to become the thing that infected them. Another drone for the Invaders. Right, that's it. Kill the poor bastards on sight. No exceptions. We'll be doing them a favour.'

'The really worrying thing,' said William, 'is that there exists a small but definite possibility that some, perhaps even all, of those who survived the battle of the Nazca Plain could themselves have been infected. And are now becoming traitors within the family. They might not even know themselves; they could have been made to forget. The Drood armour should have been protection, but we don't have enough data yet to know if the new silver torcs are as powerful as the old gold ones.'

Harry frowned. 'Shouldn't we be able to see the infection in a person, using our Sight, or through our mask?'

'We should,' said William. 'But the records say no. It would seem the infecting presence is too . . . *other*.'

I looked at the Armourer. 'We need a test; some way to find out the truth. Something that can detect an infected person. We have to be sure of who's who. And what's what.'

'I'll get on to it,' said the Armourer.

'We need a test that can be applied to the whole family,' said Harry. 'We need to know who we can trust.'

'Couldn't agree more, Harry,' I said, looking straight at him. 'Anything else, William?'

'The next logical step for the Loathly Ones has to be a full summoning,' William said heavily. 'Once enough of the structures have been completed, they will attempt to bring the Hungry Gods through into our world. To consume everything that lives. I think we can assume that our destruction of the tower on the Nazca Plain has shown them the dangers of trying to do this with one isolated structure, so that should buy us some time. But how much—'

'Ready for some more bad news?' said Callan. 'Intelligence seems pretty sure, thanks to some intercepted communications, that to get this far the Loathly Ones made use of a judas goat. They made a deal with Truman, and his Manifest Destiny organisation, for money, technical supplies, concealment and so on. Apparently Truman believes he can use the Invaders to take control of our world, and then force them out again. The idiot actually thinks *he's* using *them*.'

'Shows how desperate he is,' I said. 'Well, we wanted a big battle to show off our renewed strength and power to the world, and now we're facing the biggest fight of our lives with the whole world watching and the whole world at stake. Be careful what you wish for . . . All right. That's it. Everyone in the family gets a new silver torc. As soon as possible, no exceptions. I've already talked with Strange, and he doesn't see any problems. He's just waiting to be asked. If this family is going to war, I want us all in armour. Because we're going to need every fighter we can muster. Sarjeant-At-Arms, you'll have to take sole charge of the training, at least until Janissary Jane shows up again. I have to say a lot of them looked pretty good, even without armour.'

'The family will be ready,' said the Sarjeant. 'I'll see to that, Edwin. No damned cosmic locusts can hope to stand against the Drood family in its armour.'

'Very rousing, I'm sure,' said Harry. 'But I have to ask: is this wise? Putting us in armour before the Armourer's had time to come up with his test for possible traitors within the family? Do you really want to give Drood armour to a potential traitor or assassin?'

'You've changed your tune,' I said, a little amused. 'Only this morning you were calling me every name under the sun because I hadn't already made the armour available to everyone.'

'That was then,' said Harry. 'This is now. And I'm not convinced we can properly train so many people in time anyway. The Sarjeant can be very . . . inspirational, but untrained agents in the field can be a danger to themselves and their companions, never mind the enemy.'

'This family has more trainers and tutors on hand than ever before, thanks to me,' I said. 'And we won't launch another attack until I'm sure we can win it. I won't lose any more good men and women. Fortunately, I've already made certain . . . arrangements, to bring in expert help. Advisors in the art and practice of war.'

'Oh, God,' said the Armourer. 'I know that look on your face. You think you've done something really clever. What have you done, Eddie? And why do I know I'm not going to like it?'

'Probably because you know me so well, Uncle Jack,' I said. 'You all said I didn't have the relevant experience to lead this family into the war that's coming, and you were right. But since no one else in the family does either, I was forced to go further abroad to find people who did have the experience and the expertise. I asked the Merlin Glass to find me the two most suitable members of the family, one from the Past and one from the Future. And it did.'

'You did this without consulting the Inner Circle first?' said Harry. 'How dare you?'

'I didn't tell you because I knew you'd try and talk me out of it,' I said calmly. 'And I didn't intend to be talked out of it. And anyway, it worked. William, have Rafe bring our visitor here, so everyone can meet him.'

'I've got him standing by,' William said dourly. 'I knew you'd get to this point eventually.'

The living Jacob stepped into view beside him and smiled cheerfully at the dumbfounded faces before him. He had a glass of wine in one hand, and he must have found some food because he'd spilled half of it down his front. 'Greetings to my noble descendants! I am Jacob Drood, soldier, philosopher and bon vivant!'

The Armourer and the Sarjeant-At-Arms, both of whom had good reason to know the ghost of Jacob, looked equally shocked and appalled. Harry and Roger and Callan recognised the name and looked at me sharply. The Sarjeant, not surprisingly, put it into words first.

'*Have you gone stark staring mad?* Does he know about—?'

No, he doesn't,' I said quickly. 'And I really don't think we should tell him yet. It's the kind of thing you need to work up to.'

'Tell me what?' said Jacob, immediately suspicious.

'Does the other Jacob know?' said the Armourer. 'How's he going to take it?'

'He does know,' I said. 'And he's taking it . . . as well as can be expected. He approves, though. He says it's necessary.'

'What other Jacob?' said the living Jacob. 'Edwin, is there something thou'rt keeping from me?'

'Oh, lots,' I said. 'You know how it is in this family.'

Jacob sniffed, and drained his wine glass.

I stared steadily at the Armourer and the Sarjeant. 'The Merlin Glass chose this man as the best and most suitable candidate out of the whole Past family. That ought to tell you something. Jacob, all will be made clear to you, in time. Now please, say a few words about yourself.'

'I have fought in many wars,' the living Jacob said, a little grandly. 'Those secret and invisible wars the Droods have always specialised in, for the protection of the world. I can help thee deal with the practical and political sensibilities, those being my area of expertise in my day. The principles of waging war are really quite simple: divide and conquer, identify and strike at weak spots and, most of all, get everyone else so confused they don't dare do anything for fear of doing the wrong thing.'

'The world has changed since your day,' said Callan.

'But the hearts of politicians have not, I'll warrant,' said Jacob.

'He's got a point,' said Callan.

'Thank you, Jacob,' said the Armourer. 'I'm sure your experience will prove invaluable. Now, if you and William will excuse us, we have private matters to discuss.'

William nodded and gestured, and the Merlin Glass shrank to normal size again and tucked itself into my jacket pocket. Thankfully without the bloody gong sound this time. The Armourer glared at me.

'All right, Eddie. You're still looking dangerously smug. Drop the other shoe. Who or what did the mirror find for you in the Future?'

'Ah,' I said. 'This is where it gets a bit complicated. I have located a superb future warrior, and distant descendant of ours, called Giles Deathstalker.'

'Deathstalker?' said Harry. 'What kind of a name is that?'

'It suited him,' I said. 'The point is, I've seen the man fight and he's death on two legs and nasty with it. Just what we need. He's quite ready to help us. Unfortunately . . .'

'I knew there'd be a catch,' said the Armourer.

'Unfortunately, he's so far ahead of us in the potential timelines that the Merlin Glass couldn't bring him through. I'll have to go and get him. And that means using the Time Train.'

The Armourer didn't actually sink to the floor and bury his face in his hands, but he looked very much like he wanted to.

'The Time Train? Have you finally lost every last little bit of your senses, Eddie? You can't use the Time Train! It's far too dangerous!'

'By all means, try it,' Harry said generously. 'Either way, we win.'

I ignored him. 'I know what I'm doing, Uncle Jack,' I said.

The Armourer snorted loudly. 'Be the first time. Well, if you must go, be sure and bring back as many future weapons as you can.'

'Deathstalker,' said Roger Morningstar. 'Hell of a name.'

CHAPTER ELEVEN

About time

When it came to my using the Time Train, the Inner Circle were right behind me. Fortunately, I was able to shake them off thanks to some fast running and my superior knowledge of The Hall's short cuts and side passages. They should have known better than to order me not to use the Time Train under any circumstances. I've always had this problem with authority figures, even now I am one. I left their raised voices behind me and headed quickly for the rear of The Hall, and the old hangar where the family keeps those past mechanical marvels we have more sense than to try and use nowadays.

I reached out with my thoughts through my silver torc and made mental contact with Strange.

'Hi there!' said Strange. 'Did you know the Sarjeant-At-Arms is looking for you? And the rest of your Inner Circle?'

'The fact has not escaped me,' I said. 'I need you to run a diversion for me. You game?'

'Of course! I could use a little fun. Your family are very worthy, Eddie, but a lot of them are very solemn.'

'Trust me; I had noticed. All right, I need you to broadcast the news that everyone in the family is to get their new torcs. The Inner Circle and I just decided. You okay with that?'

'Oh, sure. The more the merrier, I say.'

'Great. Then spread the good news, and tell everyone they need to come to the Sanctity right now.' I grinned. 'That should block the corridors nicely, and keep the Circle from interfering with what I've got planned.'

'Oh, dear,' said Strange. 'Are you about to do something desperate and dangerous again?'

'Of course. Mind the store while I'm gone, Strange.'

'Please, call me Ethel.'

'Over my dead and lifeless body.'

To my surprise, when I finally got to the rear of The Hall, avoiding the main corridors that were already filling up with cheering family members, Molly was already there waiting for me. She greeted me with a fond embrace and a smug smile.

'How did you know I was going to be here?' I said.

'Honestly, sweetie, I am a witch, remember? Sorry it took me so long to get away, but Penny needed a lot of talking to. I think I finally managed to beat some sense into her pretty little head. There's no one more stubborn than a secret romantic. Especially one who's taken it on herself to redeem the unredeemable.'

'Has she agreed to stop seeing Mr Stab?' I said.

'Well, not as such,' said Molly. 'The best I could get out of her was an agreement never to meet him alone.'

I nodded reluctantly. 'Penny always was stubborn. Runs in the family. Baffles me what she sees in him anyway.'

'I suppose it's like those sad, desperate women who want to marry serial killers in prison,' said Molly. 'Women always believe they can change a man, bring out the good in him through the power of their love. Some like more of a challenge, I suppose. And Mr Stab does have that dark, dangerous, vulnerable thing going for him. I know, I know . . . he's been slaughtering and butchering women for over a century . . . but there is more to him than that, Eddie. I have seen him do good things. So have you.'

'He's Mr Stab,' I said. 'He kills women. That's what he does. If he hurts Penny—'

'He won't,' said Molly. 'He's never hurt a friend of mine.'

'If he kills her, I'll kill him. Friend of yours or not.'

'If it comes to that, I'll help you,' said Molly. 'So, why are we here, Eddie?'

I gestured at the long steel and glass hangar, standing tall and proud at the rear of The Hall, though set a discreet distance away. It was a wide, steel-girdered construction, with an arching glass roof big enough to hold several football matches in simultaneously. The family never does things by halves, even when it comes to museums hardly anyone visits any more. I took Molly's arm in mine and led her towards the open entrance.

'I've located a very useful ally in the Future,' I said. 'Unfortunately, he's so far ahead of us that we're going to have to go and get him in person. And for that, we need the Time Train.'

'Just the two of us?' said Molly.

'Well,' I said, 'I did ask for volunteers, but the response was disappointing. Apparently everyone else had more sense. Time travel is always dangerous, and no one's actually used the Time Train in ages. Probably with good reason. It's not the most reliable device the family ever built. If you'd prefer to stay behind, I'd quite understand. I'd stay behind if I could find anyone daft enough to go in my place.'

Molly hugged my arm firmly to her side. 'Do you really think I'd let you go anywhere without me?'

I grinned at her. 'I like this being an item thing.'

'You romantic devil, you. Flatter me with your silver tongue, why don't you?'

'Together, for ever,' I said. 'How about that?'

'For ever and ever and ever,' said Molly.

I led her into the long hangar. It's a huge place, packed full of the early technological wonders produced down the ages by family Armourers with a bee in their bonnet. It had to be said, both the museum had known better days. The inner walls were cracked and discoloured, and dull yellow sunlight fell through glass panels left cloudy and spotted by age and neglect. It was a storage space now, for things whose time had moved on. Strange and wondrous artefacts that had once been ahead of their time overtaken and forgotten.

Like the 1880s Moon Launch Cannon, only used once. And the oversized Moleship, basically a steel cabin with a bloody big diamond-studded drill head mounted on the front. It had been constructed to investigate the interior of the earth in the days when people still believed in the Hollow Earth theory. The hulking exhibit before us was actually Mole II, built so the family could go looking for whatever had happened to Mole I. In the end it never got used, because we had to fill in and block off the original tunnel after something Big and Nasty from the lower depths tried to crawl up it.

'And we used to have a giant mechanical spider,' I said, leading Molly through the exhibits. 'We confiscated it from some mad

American genius in the Wild West. Not entirely sure what happened to it. I think it ran away.'

'Boys and their toys,' said Molly, smiling sweetly. 'You'll be boasting about the size of your engines next. Why keep this stuff if you never use it any more?'

'Because the family never lets go of anything that belongs to it,' I said. 'Besides, this is history. It's interesting. Not to mention instructive. And you never know when you might need something again. Better to have a thing and not need it, than need it and not have it. Like the Time Train . . . I only remembered it was here because I used to love reading about things like that when I was a kid sloping off from my lessons.'

We weren't alone in the hangar. A dozen or so men and women in scruffy overalls fussed around various exhibits, tinkering with the machinery or polishing and cleaning them to within an inch of their lives. None of them looked at us, as long as we were careful to maintain a respectful distance. Molly gestured at them, and raised an eyebrow.

'Enthusiasts,' I said. 'They volunteer to work here in their spare time. All obsessed with a particular period or device. They keep the exhibits in order, just for the joy of it. Express the slightest interest in their particular pride and joy, and they'll talk your ear off.'

'Now, let me be sure I've got this right,' said Molly. 'This Time Train you want to use: no one's actually taken it out of the hangar in ages, it's pretty damned dangerous even when it's working properly, and the only guarantee we have it'll work at all is some dedicated amateur technician. Have I missed anything? You are not filling me with confidence here, Eddie.'

By now we'd reached the Time Train, and the sheer size of the thing dwarfed the other exhibits. The Train itself was a big, black, old-fashioned steam engine, gleaming and glistening like the night, with luxurious silver and brass fittings buffed and polished to a cheery warm glow. Half a dozen luxury Pullman coaches, in the familiar milk chocolate and cream livery, stretched away behind the coal tender. A quick peek through the coaches' curtained windows revealed a whole other world of seats and fittings whose quality would have shamed the Orient Express in its heyday. The family never did believe in doing things by half. The huge black engine towered over us like a sleeping beast, only waiting to be roused. A tall gangling individual appeared suddenly in the cab and smiled bashfully down at us.

'Oh, hello,' he said. 'Visitors – how nice. We don't get many visitors, old Ivor and me. Ivor is the engine, you see.'

'Yes,' I said. 'I had a hunch it might be. Molly, allow me to present to you the family's one and only expert steam train engineer, Tony Drood. Latest in a long line of such enthusiasts. Right, Tony?'

'Oh, yes,' he said, clambering agilely down the gleaming steel ladder on the side of the cab to join us. He had to be in his late fifties, though his hair was still suspiciously jet black. He wore a set of grubby overalls, and his hands and face were covered with dirty smudges from whatever he'd just been working on. He finally stood before us, smiling and bobbing his head a bit shyly. 'An honour to meet you both, Edwin and Miss Molly. Can't remember the last time anyone of quality came to see us, eh, Ivor old thing?'

He reached up and fondly patted the bulging black steel chamber.

'Ivor really is very impressive,' said Molly, and Tony beamed at her as though she'd taken a thorn out of his paw.

'Impressive he is indeed, Miss Molly, and that is no lie. I have made it my business to see that he is kept spotless and in perfect working order, ready to go at a moment's notice.'

'Ready to go anywhere, anywhen?' I said. 'Even into the far Future?'

'All of Time is at your disposal,' said Tony grandly. 'Ivor can take you back to the dawn of the world, or up any of the future timetracks. You do understand about parallel future histories? . . . Of course you do, everyone's seen *Star Trek*. Though I always preferred the original series. Where was I? Oh, yes, Ivor is fully functional and raring to go! He can do the Kessel run in under five centuries!'

'He's still a bit . . . ancient, though, isn't he?' said Molly.

Tony glowered at her. 'Do not listen to her, Ivor! She is a philistine, and knows no better. I will have you know, Miss Molly, this engine was built back in the days when they valued skill and craftsmanship as well as efficiency. This is no modern soulless device, this is Ivor the Time Train! A comfortable and civilised way to travel in Time. I tell you, Miss Molly, Ivor could still do the family proud, given half a chance.'

'Funny you should say that, Tony,' I said. 'As it turns out, you are in a position to do me and the family a great service. I think it's well past time Ivor was allowed out for a little trip.'

Tony grinned so broadly it must have hurt his cheeks, and actually wrung his hands together in his enthusiasm. 'Just say the word, Edwin! I've waited all my life for a chance to take the old boy out and show what he can do! No one in the family's authorised use of the Time Train since my grandfather took her out at the end of the nineteenth century.' His face fell, and he looked at Molly and me a little guiltily. 'An unfortunate business, that . . . Bit of a disaster, really. The last Matriarch but three, Catherine Drood that was, got a bee in her bonnet that one of the Old Ones was waking up, down on some obscure little island in the southern hemisphere. And nothing would do but that Grandfather take the newly invented Time Train back into the recent past, with a team of expert specialists, to shut the Old One down before it could properly awaken. Of course it, went horribly wrong. Turned out that it was the energies generated by Ivor's arrival that woke the Old One up in the first place. One thing led to another, and in the end grandfather and his team had no choice but to blow up the whole damned island and seal the Old One in its tomb.

'Krakatoa, the island was called. Anyway, Ivor got the blame, which was really quite unfair, and he's been out of favour ever since.'

'Hold everything,' said Molly. 'If no one's taken the train out since the nineteenth century, does this mean you've never actually driven the thing yourself?'

'Well, no, not as such,' said Tony. 'But I know all I need to know! The care and handling of Ivor is a sacred trust, miss, handed down from father to son for generations. A family within the family, you might say. Rest assured that I have read every one of the manuals, and my grandfather's journals, and I know the workings of Ivor inside and out. Don't you worry, miss! Old Ivor's straining at the traces, raring for the off! Aren't you, old boy?'

He slapped the black steel familiarly, and Molly and I both jumped a little as Ivor let loose a sudden blast of steam from his funnel, as though in response. Maybe it was. Wouldn't be the first time the family built something that turned out to have a mind of its own.

Don't even get me started about the sentient water cooler that was supposed to know when you were thirsty; drowned three people before we could wrestle it to the ground.

'Let's get going,' I said briskly. 'Build up your pressure, or whatever it is you need to do, and full steam ahead to the Future!'

Tony looked at me blankly. 'You mean right now?'

'No time like the present,' I said. 'And . . . there are a few people who might want to have a word with us before we go, and I really don't feel like talking to them, so the sooner we can get under way the better. That isn't going to be a problem, is it?'

'Oh no, Edwin! Not at all! In fact, the principles of time travel will allow us to return a few seconds after we depart, and that way you won't have to miss out on talking to anyone!'

'Oh joy,' I said. 'Let's go, Tony.'

'Say no more, sir!' said Tony, saluting me enthusiastically. He scrambled back up the ladder into the cab, all but exploding with pleasure and nervous energy. This was his moment, his great chance come round at last, and he couldn't wait to get under way. I'd rather been counting on that. Anyone less enthusiastic might have asked a whole bunch of awkward questions, to which I didn't have any good answers. I felt a bit guilty at taking advantage of Tony, but only a bit. I had too many other things to feel guilty about. I needed the warrior called Deathstalker, the family needed him; and that was all that mattered. Molly and I followed Tony up the narrow steel ladder and into the surprisingly spacious cab. We stood well back as Tony hurried from one long steel lever to another, throwing them back and forth with infectious enthusiasm and good cheer. Nothing like watching an enthusiast show off at what he does best. He leaned forward to check a row of old-fashioned gauges on the main bulkhead, and tapped a few with a forefinger before turning round to smile brightly.

'I always maintain a good working head of pressure,' he said proudly. 'Partly because it's good for the boiler, partly just in case the call should ever come . . . Allow me a few minutes to shovel in some more fuel, and then we can be on our way! Oh yes!'

'Where are the tracks?' said Molly, leaning dangerously far over the side of the cab before I pulled her back.

'As I understand it, there aren't any,' I said. 'Ivor travels in Time, not Space.' I looked at Tony. 'You can leave the carriages behind. We won't be needing them.'

His face fell. 'But they're very comfortable! Downright cosy, in fact. Polish the brass every day, I do!'

'Nevertheless,' I said firmly.

Tony pouted, and then went back to unhitch the carriages. I took a look at the various gauges, but they meant nothing to me. And yet, I could feel something . . . a sense of pressure building, of controlled power gathering itself. Standing in Ivor's cab was like standing in the mouth of a great beast as it finally came awake. Tony jumped back into the cab, opened the tender door, and started shovelling what looked very like coal into the open chamber. Molly and I watched for a while.

'Excuse me,' said Molly, 'but how exactly does building up a head of steam help us to travel in Time?'

'Oh, this isn't coal, miss,' said Tony, shovelling energetically. 'This is crystallised tachyons.'

Molly's scowl deepened. 'But tachyons are particles that can't travel any slower than the speed of light, so—'

'Don't ask,' I said kindly. 'I always find it better not to ask when faced with something like this. The answers will only upset you. Merely considering the problems involved with Time travel makes my head hurt. I really don't want a lecture on quantum steam mechanics, and neither do you.'

It didn't take long to build up a full head of what passed for steam, and Tony finally put away his shovel, slammed the chamber door shut and wiped the sweat from his forehead with a red-spotted handkerchief.

'All clear, sir and miss. But now we need an exact destination, Ivor and I, if we're to navigate the Future timelines. We need proper spatial and temporal coordinates.'

I took out the Merlin Glass, and instructed it to show Ivor where and when to find Giles Deathstalker. The Glass immediately pulled itself out of my hand and shot through the air, growing in size as it went, until finally it hung hovering at the end of the hangar, filling the whole entrance.

'I think it's trying to tell us it knows the way,' I said.

'That thing is really starting to creep me out,' said Molly. 'Nothing should be able to do the things that hand mirror can do. Not even if it was made by Merlin Satanspawn.'

'Hush,' I said. 'It might hear you.' I turned to Tony. 'Aim Ivor at the gateway the Glass has opened up; it should give him the coordinates he needs.'

'I don't know,' Tony said dubiously.

'Just do it,' I said. 'What's one more crazy thing in the midst of all this weirdness?'

'A man after my own heart!' said Tony. 'Full steam ahead, Ivor! Warp Factor Six and don't spare the tachyons!'

The Time Train lurched forward, sending us staggering for a moment. Ivor chugged loudly with effort, venting something very like steam from his funnel, and Tony darted around agaom throwing the levers this way and that, while keeping a watchful eye on the various gauges. There was no real feeling of forward movement, but slowly the hangar began to slip away behind us as we moved forward into Time. Molly and I clung to the sides of the cab and looked out past Ivor's purposeful prow as we headed inexorably toward Merlin's Glass, still hovering before us and seeming to grow larger and larger, far past the point where the hangar should have been able to contain it. There was nothing in the mirror's surface; no reflection, no sign of the future we wanted . . . only an endless night, untouched by moon or stars. And then the Time Train surged forward, Tony hooting loudly with excitement, and we plunged into the Merlin Glass, which swallowed us up in a moment.

At first, it was like being in a tunnel. Darkness all around, while a single old-fashioned spirit lamp filled the cab with a warm golden glow. The only sound was the roar of Ivor's powerful engine as we plunged on into darkness. And then, one by one, the stars began to come out; in ones and twos, then in dozens, then in thousands, until we were surrounded by great surging oceans of light. It was like passing through outer space, but nowhere any astronaut had ever seen. Instead of familiar constellations, there were great seas of stars, blazing with a light almost too pure and beautiful to bear. Comets sailed past Ivor, brightly coloured, like the sweets we loved as children, sweeping past in elegant arcs that contrasted sharply with the steady surging progress of Ivor the Time Train.

Strange planets passed us by, weird and uncanny, that had no place in any natural solar system.

'If this is outer space,' Molly ventured, 'and I'm quite prepared to be told that it isn't, how come we're able to breathe?'

'Ivor has many talents and many secrets,' Tony said expansively. 'You are quite safe, Miss Molly, as long as you stay inside the cab.'

'But where, exactly, are we?' I said.

Tony shrugged. 'I've read the books, but I have to say no one seems too sure of exactly what it is Ivor travels through. My grandfather, the last man to actually take Ivor out, said that this is what Time and Space look like, seen from the other side. Whatever that means. There are other theories, suggesting that Ivor travels through the universe below ours. Or possibly the one above. Believe whatever makes you feel safest, that's what I say.'

I looked at Molly. 'Conversations like this are why the family prefers to leave time travel strictly alone.'

'Pah!' said Tony. 'They have no sense of adventure!'

'Hold everything,' said Molly. 'What is *that*?'

We looked where she was pointing. A enormous shape was sweeping rapidly through the starry night, heading straight for us. As it grew closer, it revealed itself to be a huge dragon. Disturbingly large, a hundred times the size of Ivor, it was a garish banana yellow in colour, with sickly pink markings up and down its long body. The head was blunt and bony, with a row of glaring red eyes set above a gaping maw packed with jagged shark-like teeth. Vast membranous yellow wings bellowed out on either side of the bulging midsection. It had short grabbing arms set on the neck below the mouth, armed with vicious curving talons. The dragon shot past us, silent as a nightmare, the massive wings barely flapping. The head turned to follow us, on the end of a long serpentine neck, and up close the head alone was bigger than Ivor.

'I'm still waiting for an answer,' said Molly. 'Any answer. What the hell is that thing?'

'Well, blow me,' I said, a trifle testily, 'I didn't think to bring my *Observer Book Of Space Dragons* with me. It's obviously something that lives here, and it doesn't look too happy to see visitors. Let's hope very fervently that it's eaten recently.'

'That is one big bastard,' said Tony. 'Do you think it might try and harm my Ivor?'

'Maybe it's never seen tinned food before,' said Molly.

'It's bigger than us, and it's got really nasty teeth and claws,' I said. 'I would lay good odds on its not being a vegetarian.'

'Is Ivor armed?' said Molly. 'Do you have any weapons aboard?'

'There are any number of defence systems,' said Tony, looking at me. 'Unfortunately they are situated back in the carriages.'

'Somehow I knew it would turn out to be my fault,' I said.

The dragon swung around and came flying straight at us again, the huge jaws grinning wider and wider, as though it planned to swallow Ivor whole. It might have been roaring or howling, but I couldn't hear anything. The utter silence made the situation even more nightmarish. I drew my Colt Repeater and fired the gun again and again, aiming for the massive head. Every shot hit home, but the bullets were too small to do the monstrous creature any real harm. Tony slammed a long steel lever all the way home, using both hands to do it, and Ivor lurched forward with a new burst of speed. The dragon shot past us, impossibly large, and one yellow hand raked down Ivor's black steel side. Great showers of silent sparks flew off into the darkness as diamond-sharp claws dug long furrows in Ivor's side.

He vented a long blast of steam like a scream.

The cab rocked from side to side, and Molly and I had to cling on to keep from being thrown out. Tony shouted obscenities, and worked his levers furiously. Molly yelled at me,

'Distract the bloody thing while I work on a spell!'

'Distract it? What do you want me to do, drop my trousers and moon it?'

'*Just do something!*'

I grabbed the side of the cab with both hands and leaned out for a better look. The huge yellow dragon was already turning round and heading back for another attack. I drew the Colt Repeater again, aimed carefully, and shot out the dragon's glowing eyes, one after another. The terrible jaws stretched even wider in a howl of rage and pain I could sense, even if I couldn't hear it. It was like fingernails down the blackboard of my soul. The dragon shook its head back and forth, as though trying to shake off the sudden pain and blindness, but still it kept coming, heading right for us. It got bigger and bigger, blocking off the view ahead, until its great yellow form filled the view before us.

And then Molly leaned out over her side of the cab, stabbed a single finger at the dragon, and pronounced several very unpleasant Words of Power. The awful sound of the Words seemed to echo endlessly on the quiet, and the dragon suddenly didn't seem quite so big or imposing. In sharp jerks and shudders, it shrank rapidly in size, becoming smaller and smaller, until by the time it reached Ivor's cab it was no bigger than an insect. It fluttered around our heads, buzzing angrily, until Molly reached out and crushed it between two fingertips. And that was that.

Molly wiped her hand on her hip and smiled sweetly at me. 'You should have remembered,' she said. 'In space, size is relative.'

'You scare me sometimes,' I said.

We carried on, through the space that wasn't space, and saw many strange and wondrous things. Planets came and went. One opened like an eye, and stared at us coldly as we passed. Another had a dozen rings spinning around it, all circling madly at different speeds and in different directions. It looked like a vast clockwork toy set in motion at the beginning of the universe, slowly winding down. Another planet opened up like a flower, and hundreds of long tentacles burst out of it, groping and grasping at Ivor, trying to lock on and pull us in. Tony sent Ivor plunging this way and that, with judicial use of his long steel levers, and skilfully evaded every tentacle that tried to curl around us. A few slapped harmlessly against Ivor's sides, and he seemed to shudder at the touch. But we soon left the planet behind, and it closed slowly up again, sulkily pulling its feeding tentacles back inside.

Another planet disappeared entirely as we approached, only reappearing after we were safely past.

I couldn't tell you how long the journey took. There were sights and incidents enough to mark the passing of time, but there was no real sense of duration. It might have been minutes or days or weeks. I never felt tired or hungry or bored. But finally the stars ahead of us began to dance, and swirl, churning around us in complicated patterns, finally coalescing into a giant rainbow below us of such rich and vivid colours they dazzled the eye. There were hues and shades that had no counterpart in the dull and ordinary everyday world. It was the most beautiful thing I'd ever seen. Molly and I clung together for comfort in the face of something so inhumanly glorious, while Tony clung to Ivor.

'What is it?' Molly said finally, breathlessly.

'It's the Starbow,' said Tony, his voice faint and awed. 'I read about it in Grandfather's journal, but I never imagined . . .'

'I've heard of it,' I said. 'But never expected to see it. They say you can follow it to the end of the universe, and maybe even to your heart's desire.'

'Oh, Eddie,' said Molly. 'Could we . . . ?'

'Yes,' I said. 'We could. But we have somewhere else we have to be. We have duties and responsibilities.'

'Yes,' said Molly, not looking away from the Starbow. 'If only—'

'If only,' I said. 'Always the cruellest words. Tony, get us out of here.'

He poured on the speed, and slowly we left the Starbow behind. And sometimes I think that was the hardest thing I ever had to do.

Finally Merlin's Glass reappeared before us, and we roared through it. And just like that we were back in the reality we knew, in the Future I'd seen before. The Time Train seemed to drop like a stone for a long moment, then a great icy plain rose up beneath us and the next moment Ivor was churning along through thick snow. Molly and Tony and I were thrown this way and that as Ivor's speed cut back in vicious shocks and jerks. Tony wrestled his controls with both hands, shouting and cursing, and finally the Time Train slammed to a halt.

It was suddenly very cold, our breath steaming thickly on the air before us. My bare face and hands smarted from the sudden exposure, and I peered out the side of the cab, looking for familiar details. We were actually on the alien world this time, with its pink sky and three fiercely shining suns. The snowy wastes stretched away as far as I could see in every direction. Thin twists of mist turned this way and that on the freezing air.

'You bring me to the nicest places, Eddie,' said Molly, beating her frozen hands together and blowing on them.

'Hey, this is a whole new alien world!' I said.

'You couldn't have picked a warmer one?'

'Well, we're in the right place,' I said.

'How can you be sure?'

'Because I recognise the bodies,' I said.

They were as I remembered them, dozens of dead men and women scattered across the blood-stained snow.

'Giles Deathstalker's work,' I said. 'He's a hell of a fighter.'

'Could be a hell of a mass murderer, for all you know,' said Molly. 'Where is he, anyway?'

I looked around, but there was no sign of the future warrior. I had to wonder how accurate Ivor and Merlin's Glass could hope to be. We'd come a long way, and just a few day's difference after who knew how many centuries was only to be expected. A lot could happen to a man on the run in a few days; most of it bad. But Ivor and the Glass were all I had, so I was in no position to complain. Molly and I climbed down from the cab and strode out across the blindingly white plain, our feet sinking deep into the thick snow with every step. It was bitterly cold, almost unbearable, away from the protection of Ivor's cab, but the sheer effort involved in forcing my way through the snow soon had me sweating. Every breath seared my lungs, and my forehead ached like someone had punched it.

But it was still an alien world, with three suns burning bright in the garish pink sky. I pointed this out to Molly, but she grunted, unimpressed, and hugged herself tightly, as though to keep any warmth from leaking out. I waved cheerfully at Tony in the cab, and he waved back, but showed no sign of wanting to leave his beloved engine.

I trudged through the drifts towards the dead bodies. They were everywhere, hundreds of them, lying sprawled in awkward poses in the blood-soaked snow. Some were missing limbs, some were missing heads. Some had been gutted, hacked open. But up close, it soon became clear that my earlier identification had been wrong. These weren't men in futuristic armour; their armour was a part of them. These people were some kind of cyborg. Man – machine composites. Steel cables and jagged pieces of technology projected from dead white flesh. Cameras in eye-sockets, guns built into the hand. No two bodies were exactly the same, but they were all clearly the result of the same process. They looked ugly as sin. Whoever had put them together had valued function over aesthetics. The faces seemed human enough, and the blood was all too familiar.

'Nasty injuries,' said Molly, lurching to a halt beside me. She leaned over one body for a better look, careful not to touch. 'But no bullet wounds. These poor bastards have been hacked to pieces. If I didn't know better, I'd say Mr Stab had beaten us here.'

'Giles does seem to prefer the sword, believe it or not,' I said. 'He was carrying a bloody big one the last time I saw him.'

'They're using swords in the future?' said Molly, incredulously. 'When they have the technology to produce cyborgs like these?'

I shrugged. 'Who knows what's normal around here?'

I spotted a discarded gun lying in the snow and bent down to pick it up. It was eerily light in my hand, for all its bulky size. It was mostly a dull green metal, crusted with glowing crystals and blinking coloured readout lights. But it had a barrel, and a trigger, so I aimed it out across the plain and fired. A searing bolt of energy blasted from the gun and blew a massive crater out of the snow a good hundred yards away. The ground shook under our feet for a moment, and Molly grabbed at my arm. All the snow above the crater had been vaporised, leaving thick spirals of mist twisting in the air.

I hefted the energy gun, grinning. 'Oh, Uncle Jack is going to *love* this.'

'If you can keep from blowing us up,' Molly said drily. 'Put it away, Eddie. You can play with it later.'

I looked for a safety catch, but the gun didn't seem to have one so I slipped it carefully into my jacket pocket. Molly knelt down beside one of the cyborg bodies.

'Do you think we should take one of these back with us? The Armourer could probably learn all kinds of things from the technology.'

I considered it, but shook my head. 'Feels a bit too much like body-snatching, I think.'

'Wimp,' said Molly. She started to straighten up, and the cyborg grabbed her suddenly by the arm with one dead hand.

Molly yelled, despite herself. She tugged fiercely, but the cyborg had a death grip on her arm. I stepped quickly forward, and stamped hard on the cyborg's chest. The armour bruised my heel even through my shoe, but the impact tore the cyborg's hand away from Molly's arm. It grabbed for my leg, but I'd already stepped back. Molly back-pedalled away from the cyborg as fast as the thick snow would let her, cursing loudly. The cyborg sat up and looked at us both with a dead, expressionless face. Silvery circuit patterns covered his brow and trailed down one cheek. He raised an arm and pointed at me, and a thin black barrel slid smoothly out of the back of his hand. I threw myself down into the hard-packed snow, and an energy bolt flashed through the air where I'd been standing, close enough that all the hair on my body stood up at once.

I rolled to one side and struggled to my feet. The cyborg rose up out of the snow in swift, jerky movements, already turning his head back and forth, checking for a new target. And yet, despite this, I never once got the feeling that the cyborg was alive. The man was clearly dead, his eyes fixed and unblinking; it was the built-in machinery that kept him going, probably set off by Molly's proximity.

I subvocalised the activating Words and armoured up, the silver strange matter flowing over me in a moment. At once I was insulated from the alien world's cold, and I felt stronger, faster, sharper. I ran easily through the deep snow, heading towards the cyborg. It turned quickly and shot me at point-blank range. The energy beam hit me square in my armoured chest and ricocheted harmlessly away. I relaxed a little. I'd been pretty sure the armour would protect me, but it was nice to know. I reached out, grabbed the cyborg's gun arm and ripped it out of the socket with one burst of armoured strength. The cyborg rocked on its feet, but didn't cry out and didn't fall. It started to raise the other arm, so I tore that one off too. It still didn't fall, so I grabbed its head with both hands and yanked it clean off.

The eyes stared up at me, unblinking. The mouth moved a few times, and then was still. I looked at the cyborg body. It stood in place, unmoving. I threw the head away.

Molly applauded, the sound flat and small in the empty quiet. 'Hardcore, Eddie.'

'He was already dead,' I said. 'Or at least, I hope so. Tell you what, let's give the other bodies plenty of room, okay?'

Molly sniffed loudly, still hugging herself against the cold. 'I don't like this place. Really. My senses are supernaturally attuned to the natural world, to the energies generated by living things, and I'm not getting anything. I know, I know, this is an alien world, but even so

. . . I ought to be picking up *something*. I'm telling you, Eddie, there's not a living thing here. Nothing. And not just here, in this place . . . you've brought us to a dead world, Eddie. These cyborgs, or whoever they were fighting, killed everything on this planet.'

'You can't know that,' I said. 'Might have been a dead world before they got here.'

'No,' said Molly. 'I can tell. They killed every living thing here so they could use this world as a battlefield. What kind of Future have you brought us to, Eddie? And what kind of man would it produce?'

I shrugged uncomfortably. 'I don't know! You can't judge a whole Future civilisation by just one world.'

'I wonder who these people were,' said Molly. 'And who they were fighting?'

'Giles said something about serving an Emperor,' I said.

'Then I suppose these must be the Rebel forces,' said Molly, smiling slightly for the first time.

'Didn't know you were a *Star Wars* fan,' I said, glad of a chance to change the subject.

'Only the original trilogy.'

'I never really understood about the Rebel forces in those films,' I said. 'I mean, they had rebel bases on rebel worlds, and starships and armies and weapons, but who was paying for it? Where was the funding coming from? They couldn't have had volunteers standing around on street corners, rattling collection tins and saying, "Please support the rebellion". Darth Vader would have had them shot.'

And then we both looked round sharply as the sound of approaching engines caught our ears. We gazed out over the snowy waste, to where the horizon disappeared in the mists, and there was Giles Deathstalker, plunging through the snow towards us at a terrific pace. Faster than I could have managed, even with my armour's help. And above and behind him came a dozen airships, strange elegant craft bristling with unfamiliar weapons, all of them aimed down at the running fugitive. But though crackling energy beams stabbed down from the airships again and again, somehow they never even came close to hitting the frantically dodging figure below. Giles Deathstalker was always somewhere else.

The airships swept past him, streaking through the soft pink sky, and pulled around in a wide arc that would bring them back again for another strafing run. Giles hadn't seen me, or the Time Train yet. He had his head down, concentrating on running and evading his enemies. Out of the mists behind him came a small army of jade-green armoured figures, trudging determinedly through the heavy snow, firing vivid energy beams after the man fleeing before them. They had no better luck than the airships, but craters were appearing around Giles now, filling the air with a mist of vaporised snow.

I yelled at Giles, using the silver mask to amplify my voice. His head snapped round and he changed direction to come straight for me and the Time Train, ploughing through the deep snow like it wasn't even there. His movements were almost inhumanly fast. But even with his speed and determination, it was clear that at least some of his pursuers would cut him off before he could reach us. And the airships were returning.

'Get back to Ivor, I said to Molly. 'Protect the Time Train, whatever happens. It's our only way home.'

'Damn right,' said Molly. 'This is a lousy place to visit, and I wouldn't want to live here.'

She headed to the engine, forcing her way through the drifts, while I set off across the frozen plain towards Giles. My armoured legs sent the snow flying through the air to either side of me. The pursuing army saw me coming, and yelled to each other. God knows what they thought I was. A few fired energy guns in my direction, but they didn't even come close. And then there was an explosion behind me, and I stopped abruptly to look back.

The airships had spotted the Time Train, and were attacking it with their energy weapons. A whole bunch of craters had been blasted out of the snow around Ivor, getting closer and closer. A shimmering protective screen suddenly appeared around the train, and I grinned. Molly had got her act together. Energy beams glanced away from the screen, but every blow hit the screen like a hammer, sending ripples through the protective energies. And then several beams targeted the screen at once . . . and one got through. It sliced across Ivor's black steel side, and he screamed shrilly through his funnel.

I turned my back and ran on. There was nothing I could do to help. Either Molly would find a way to strengthen her shield, or she wouldn't. I trusted her to do her job, so I got on with mine. I had to get to Giles and escort him safely back to the engine. I forced on the speed, my silver arms pumping at my sides, moving so quickly now I couldn't even feel the obstruction of the snow I was slamming through. Up ahead, Giles had come to a sudden stop. A whole group of his armoured enemies had manoeuvred to get between him and the Time Train. More were catching up from every side. There seemed to be hundreds of them, yelling triumphantly, their voices high and thin in the bitter cold air. Giles looked around him, calmly and unhurriedly, and then drew his long sword. He was surrounded by a whole army who clearly wanted him dead, but I couldn't see the slightest trace of concern on his face.

Just something that might have been pleasant anticipation.

I charged forward, smashing my way through the weakest part of the circle, sending armoured men flying through the air. I finally crashed to a halt beside Giles, and he looked at me curiously, his sword at the ready.

'Hi,' I said. 'Edwin Drood, at your service once again. Told you I'd be back.'

'Yes,' said Giles, 'but that was two days and three nights ago. I've been dodging my enemies ever since, waiting for you to show up.'

'Yeah, well, sorry about that,' I said. 'Things to do, you know how it is. And Time Travel isn't the most exact of sciences.'

'We know,' said Giles. 'That's why it's forbidden.' He studied my armour. 'Nice outfit. How do they get you out of it, with a can opener?'

'Show you later. Your carriage awaits; shall we go?'

Giles looked around him. 'These gentlemen might have other ideas.'

'Hell with them,' I said.

Giles grinned. 'My sentiments exactly.'

The armoured men finally got fed up listening to us talk, and surged forward. There were ranks and ranks of them, but strangely they were all holding swords and axes now, instead of their energy guns. I was going to have to talk to Giles about that later. At least these definitely were men in armour this time, and not cyborgs. So they should stay dead when I killed them. I grew long silver blades from my armoured hands, and Giles and I went to meet them.

There had to be over a hundred of them, heavily armed, pressing in from every direction at once. They never stood a chance. Their swords and battle-axes glanced harmlessly away from my armour, and my strange-matter blades cut easily through every protection they had. I hacked about me with inhuman speed and strength, and blood flew on the freezing air, steaming in the moments before it hit the snow. Men fell screaming, dying, to every side of me, and I kicked them out of the way to get to my next victim. Giles stamped and spun and sliced about him with a speed and strength very nearly equal to my own. His long blade flashed through the air as he cut men down with almost clinical precision. No one could even get near him. We fought back to back, and sometimes side by side, and we were unstoppable. The dead piled up around us, the churned-up snow crimson with blood and guts. Screams and horrified cries filled the air, but always from them, not us.

It wasn't a fight, for all their superior numbers. It was a slaughter.

I don't usually kill on missions. Usually I don't have to. The armour gives me all the edge I need. I've always thought of myself as an agent, not an assassin. The last time I had to fight and kill, on the Nazca Plain, I didn't hesitate because the Loathly One drones weren't human any more. Killing them had felt like stepping on insects. This, here, was different. Giles and I were surrounded by a small army of enemies, intent on killing us. They'd already injured Ivor. In such circumstances, family training takes over. I did what I had to, I cut men down and ran them through and did my best to feel nothing, nothing at all. I might have to kill, but no one had ever been able to train me to enjoy it.

Giles enjoyed it. He grinned cheerfully throughout, sometimes laughing aloud when he executed a particularly successful or graceful attack. Giles was a warrior, doing what he was born to do. That was what I'd come here for, after all.

The armoured men began to fall back, and resort to their energy weapons at last. They were losing, and they knew it. But the searing beams ricocheted harmlessly away from my armour, often taking out their own men, and none of them could hit Giles. He danced and pirouetted in the heart of the enemy, striking out with deadly grace, now and then catching an energy beam on his arm-mounted force shield. I'd never seen a fighter like him. And in the end the last of the armoured men broke and ran rather than face us. They scattered across the snowy plain, running in a dozen different directions, and we let them go. Giles calmly lowered his sword, and I retracted my blades back into my silver hands. We stood together, both of us breathing heavily from our exertions. Giles flicked heavy drops of blood from the end of his sword. The front of his armour was splashed with blood, none of it his. There was no blood on my armour, but only because it couldn't stick to the strange matter. Giles nodded to me cheerfully.

'So. Fun, wasn't it? Laugh, Edwin. The enemy is dead and we are alive, and there is no greater feeling in the world! You have the makings of a warrior, Edwin Drood. A bit slow and deliberate, but efficient enough for all that.'

'If you'll follow me to the Time Train,' I said, a bit breathlessly, 'I think we ought to get out of here.'

'Sounds good to me,' said Giles. 'I could use a break.'

We headed back towards Ivor, which was still encased in Molly's protective shield. The airships flew back and forth overhead, energy beams stabbing down on and around the engine. None of them seemed to be getting through. The snow around the Time Train was gone now, blasted away right down to the bedrock.

'The sooner we can get out of here, the better,' Giles said conversationally. 'The Emperor will send reinforcements as soon as word gets back that I am still alive. He'll send a whole army, if that's what it takes to bring me down.'

'I thought you said you served the Emperor?'

'I did,' said Giles. 'But I am currently out of favour at Court. It's . . . complicated.'

'Somehow I knew it would be,' I said. 'Is there by any chance a woman involved?'

'Yes. How did you know?'

I had to smile. 'There's always a woman involved.'

Once we were close enough to the Time Train for Molly to spot us, she set about distracting the airships by broadcasting illusions. A dozen different Ivors appeared scattered around the real thing, each with its own apparent protective shield. But the airships must have had some kind of sensors, because they weren't fooled for a moment. They kept pounding away at the screen surrounding the real Ivor. A dozen huge yellow dragons appeared above us, clashing horribly with the pink sky. They launched themselves at the airships, which fired back reflexively. Energy beams flashed right through the illusions, and actually took out some of the other airships. There were explosions in the sky, and broken airships fell out of the air like burning birds.

By now Giles and I had reached the Time Train, and Molly opened a door in her protective screen long enough for the two of us to hurry through. I armoured down, and then paused as I reached for the ladder leading to the cab. The one energy beam that had punched through the screen had gouged a deep furrow all the way along Ivor's black steel side, and steam, or something very like it, was venting furiously from the open wound. I scrambled up into the cab, with Giles close behind me. Tony was bouncing from one gauge to another, worriedly studying the shifting readings, while Molly sat cross-legged on the floor, working on maintaining the protective screen.

'Greetings to one and all,' Giles said cheerfully. 'Allow me to present myself. I have the honour to be Giles VomAcht Deathstalker, Warrior Prime to the Emperor Ethur, at your service.'

'Wonderful,' said Molly, not looking up. 'Now shut up and let me concentrate on the only thing keeping us from being blown to shit.'

'Ah,' said Giles. 'You're an esper!'

'No, I'm a witch.'

'Oh,' said Giles. 'One of *those* . . .'

Given the way he said it, and the look on Molly's face, I knew this conversation wasn't going to go anywhere useful. I turned to Tony.

'How bad is the damage to the engine?'

'Bad enough, bad enough. God alone knows what it's done to Ivor's containment fields.'

'Can you get us out of here, and back home?'

'I don't know! If we try, and the fields buckle, they'll be finding bits and pieces of us all across history.'

'Never mind the *if*,' I said. 'See those shapes, emerging from the mists on the horizon? They look very much like reinforcements to me, and lots of them; and I really don't think we should still be here when they arrive. We need to go *now*, Tony.'

He glared at me, and then slammed home the long steel levers, one after the other. Ivor shook and shuddered. Tony started shovelling his crystallised tachyons into the fuel chamber. Giles considered this thoughtfully.

'I hadn't realised you came from so far back in the Past.'

'One more word out of you, and you can get out and push,' said Tony, shovelling for all he was worth.

'Don't bother the engineer while he's working,' I said to Giles. 'He'll get tetchy.'

A whole bunch of energy beams hit the protective screen at once, and Molly cried out in pain, her eyes squeezed shut with the strain of maintaining the field. A trickle of blood burst out from under her left eyelid. Tony slammed the fuel chamber door shut and threw the throttle all the way open, muttering a mixture of prayers, obscenities and encouragements to Ivor under his breath. Ivor lurched forward, sending us staggering, and then headed for the Merlin Glass, which was once again hovering in the air before us. One of the airships shot at it, and the energy beam rebounded straight back to blow the airship out of the sky. I figured that anything built by Merlin Satanspawn would be able to defend itself.

The other airships increased their fire on Ivor as he began to move, chugging unevenly through the thick snow, but none of the attacks got through, even as Molly's face ran with sweat, and more blood leaked from her clenched shut eyes. Ivor slowly built up speed, the snowy waste slipping away behind us, until the Merlin Glass seemed to sweep forward and swallow us up; and we left the alien world behind us, plunging back through the other side of Space and Time, heading for home.

Molly relaxed with a great shuddering sigh, and leaned exhausted against the inner cab wall. Her eyes were still closed, but the bleeding seemed to have stopped. I sat down beside her and gently cleaned the sweat and blood from her face with my handkerchief. She smiled slightly, to let me know she was glad I was there.

Ivor was clearly straining. His speed seemed to rise and fall, and his insides made strange and worrying noises. Tony fussed endlessly over the various gauges, making constant small adjustments to his levers while keeping up a monologue of encouraging soothing words to his beloved engine. Giles stood patiently on his own, his arms folded across his chest, looking interestedly out at the oceans of stars around us. After a while, Molly was able to open her eyes again, and once I was sure they weren't damaged I got up to talk with Giles. I thought I ought to try and make him feel welcome. But it wasn't easy. Although our translation was still working well enough, there was a hell of a lot of history between us, and it was sometimes hard to find words or even concepts we had in common. We couldn't even be sure how many centuries separated us.

'I'm taking you back to Earth,' I said. 'At the beginning of the twenty-first century AD.'

Giles shrugged. 'Sorry. Means nothing to me. I'm from the centre of the Empire: Heartworld, in the thirty-second century of the New Age. And before that, from a small colony world out on the Rim.'

'And you used to work for the Emperor?' I said carefully.

'Well, still do, officially. I am Warrior Prime, by popular acclaim leader of the Emperor's Host in battle. The Emperor will take me back, once we've put this little . . . misunderstanding behind us.'

'Won't he miss you?'

'Ethur? He'll be glad to be rid of me, for a time. Give him a chance to cool down, let my supporters make reparations behind the scenes . . . and then he can summon me back to Court without losing face. Some emergency will arise that only the Warrior Prime can deal with; something always does. And then he'll welcome me with open arms. He'll have to. He needs me. He might rule the Empire, but I'm the one who keeps the peace.' He looked at me thoughtfully. 'You can get me home again, can't you?'

'Oh sure,' I said immediately, trying hard to sound confident. 'That's the joy of time travel. We can return you to your exact departure point in Space and Time, give or take a few seconds.'

'I'd rather you allowed a few months,' said Giles.

'No problem,' I said. 'Right, Tony?'

But he wasn't listening to me, he was still crooning to his engine. I searched for something else to say, to change the subject.

'So . . . why a sword, Giles?'

'Because it's an honourable weapon,' said Giles, as though the answer should have been obvious.

'Oh, wonderful,' said Molly. 'We've picked up a loony.'

After various incidents and adventures, we arrived home. The Time Train came roaring out of Merlin's Glass and screeched to a halt inside the hangar at the rear of The Hall. Home again, in a cloud of something very like steam. The engine shut itself down, shaking and shuddering, and was finally still, the black steel ticking loudly as the metal slowly cooled. The Merlin Glass shrank down to its usual size and tucked itself almost coyly into my jacket pocket. I had to wonder which of us was making the decisions these days. I really needed to read the instruction manual, once I had a minute to myself. I helped Molly descend from the cab, and she leaned tiredly against me. Tony was already down, worriedly studying the long rent in Ivor's side. The engine was making sad little parp-parp noises from his funnel. Giles jumped down from the cab, and looked curiously about him. I started to explain what the hangar was, and then stopped as I realised the place was even more quiet and deserted than usual. No enthusiasts working on their projects, no one fussing around a particular device; no trace of anyone, anywhere.

Which strongly suggested we hadn't returned to the hangar a few seconds after we left, after all.

Two men appeared in the hangar door and headed for us. They both looked very familiar, and then a chill ran through me as I realised they both had the same face. It was the living Jacob and the ghost of Jacob, walking side by side. Someone had clearly taken the living Jacob in hand and introduced him to modern clothes. He was now wearing faded drainpipe jeans, a T-shirt bearing the legend *I'm Not Dead Yet*, and a black leather motorcycle jacket. It seemed to suit him. The ghost of Jacob had given up his suit, and was back to baggy shorts and a T-shirt saying *Ghosts Do It With Spirit*. He looked pretty solid, but bits and pieces of him seemed to fade in and out, and his flyaway hair still drifted as though he was underwater. Both the living and the dead Jacob seemed very serious. They came to a halt before me, and I looked from one to the other.

'Okay,' I said. 'This is seriously creeping me out.'

'What?' said the living Jacob, scowling. 'Oh, us. Turns out I'm the only one I can trust around here.'

'Right,' growled the ghost of Jacob. 'Things have seriously deteriorated in your absence, boy.'

'Where the hell have you been all this time?' said the living Jacob.

'How long have we been gone?' I said.

'Eighteen months,' said the ghost.

'*What?*' I spun round and glared at Tony. 'You swore you could get us home only a few seconds after we left!'

'It's not Ivor's fault!' Tony yelled. 'He was injured by the energy beam! It's a wonder he got us back safely at all!'

'I'll talk to you later,' I said. I turned reluctantly to the two Jacobs. 'Eighteen months? Really? Jesus wept . . . All right, fill me in on what's been happening. No, wait a minute; what do I call you? You can't both be Jacob.'

'We worked that out ages ago,' said the ghost. 'I'm Jacob. He's Jay. And since you left, everything has gone to hell in a handcart. The Loathly Ones have worked with Truman's new and invigorated Manifest Destiny organisation to build Nests and towers across the world. There are thousands of them now. The family, under Harry's leadership, has been working hard to stamp them out, but for every one we destroy a dozen more spring up to take its place. Soon the Loathly Ones will begin their mass summoning, and bring the Hungry Gods through into our reality.'

'And then we're screwed,' said Jay.

'Hold it, hold it,' I said. 'What was that about "under Harry's leadership"?'

'With you gone, he took control of the family,' said Jay. 'With the backing of the Matriarch. They dismissed the Inner Circle, and Harry's been running things pretty much single-handed ever since. Him and his friend, the hellspawn.'

'And the family is losing the war,' Jacob said grimly. 'Tell me at least you brought powerful new weapons from the Future.'

'I've got an energy gun,' I said, a bit defensively. 'The Armourer should be able to reverse engineer something useful from it . . . And I have brought this gentleman to advise us: the Warrior Prime, Giles Deathstalker. He knows a lot about fighting wars.'

'Never lost one yet,' Giles said cheerfully. He nodded to Jacob. 'Pretty good hologram, that. Though I think your focus needs fixing.'

'Don't tell him,' I said quickly. 'We need to introduce him slowly and carefully to the stranger parts of our family. Now, how bad are things, really?'

'Really bad,' said Jay. 'The family is scattered all over the world, stamping out Nests as fast as we can locate them, but there are too many of them. Even with our new armour, it's a hopeless task. We had no idea how many Loathly Ones there were, or how many underground Nests. They've been planning this for decades.'

'How long before they can begin their summoning?' said Molly.

'Three, four days, tops,' said Jacob. 'You got here in time for the end.'

'Well, couldn't we use the Time Train again, go back in Time another eighteen months?' said Molly. 'Stop this happening?'

'Ivor's not going anywhere,' Tony said flatly. 'I've got months of work ahead of me before he'll be fit to go out again.'

'So,' I said. 'I am left with just a few days to stop the bad guys from destroying the world, and save the family from itself. If I hadn't already done this once before, I might be seriously worried.'

CHAPTER TWELVE
A circle full of secrets

'Sorry, Giles,' I said. 'But it looks like you're going to have to hit the ground running. I don't have time to give you a proper briefing and a guided tour of The Hall. So do your best to pick it up as we go along.'

He smiled coldly: a tall, dark and dangerous presence in his futuristic armour. 'I've experienced enough alien worlds and cultures in my time; I think I can cope with anything you have here. Do people still drink wine? Do they still have sex? Are there still braggarts and villains and people who need killing? Then I believe I'll fit in fine.'

'The man has a point,' said Molly.

'Well, I'm going to have to love you and leave you,' Jay said briskly. 'I have work that must be attended to, with Rafe and William in the Old Library. When it comes to the Loathly Ones, information is ammunition, and we're pitifully short on both.'

He bobbed a quick bow to Giles, and left the hangar at something approaching a dead run.

'And you have work to be about too,' said the ghost Jacob, scowling ominously at me. 'Harry, bad cess to the man, and the useless bunch of toadies and yes-men he appointed to replace your Inner Circle, are currently deciding important matters in the Sanctity, and making a right dog's breakfast of it. You need to be there, boy, before Harry drops this family in it any deeper.'

'You seem a lot more . . . together,' I said. 'More focused, in body and soul.'

The ghost shrugged quickly, little blue balls of ectoplasm bobbing up off his shoulders. 'Having my living counterpart around certainly helped remind me of who I used to be, and there's nothing like a major emergency and the almost certain death of the whole damned world to concentrate the mind wonderfully. On the other hand, my memories of this shared time are almost non-existent. I think I may have done this to myself deliberately. Perhaps so I wouldn't have to tell my living self how he's going to die.'

'You still think he's going to die here, in this time, helping us?' I said.

'Oh, yes. A glorious death . . . but no peace for the wicked. He will die and become me, and I will linger on for centuries, to reach this place, this point in time. And all I can say is, there had better be a bloody good reason for it.'

'You still don't know why you're here?' said Molly.

Jacob favoured her with his usual nasty smile. 'Hell, does anybody?'

'You're not a hologram, are you?' said Giles.

'Wouldn't lower myself,' said Jacob. 'I am one hundred per cent ectoplasm, and proud of it. I can walk through walls on a good day, though mostly I don't because it's very disconcerting. What's the matter, warrior? Don't they have ghosts in the future?'

'No,' said Giles. 'We're civilised.'

'Let's get to the Sanctity,' I said. 'If only because this conversation is starting to make my head hurt. Molly, Giles, stick close to me, and don't kill anyone unless you feel you absolutely have to. Jacob, you coming?'

'Wouldn't miss it for the netherworld,' said the old ghost, grinning unpleasantly.

I used the Merlin Glass to transport us to the corridor outside the Sanctity. It seemed even a Glass made by Merlin couldn't break through Strange's other-dimensional protective barriers. So we stepped through the enlarged mirror into the corridor and immediately found ourselves facing half a dozen men standing guard outside the doors. They were big muscular types, who might as well have had the word 'thug' tattooed on their low foreheads. There's always a few, in every family. I blame bad toilet training. The guards moved quickly to block our way, scowling in their best intimidating manner. One actually flexed his muscles at us.

'No admittance,' the head thug said coldly. 'The Patriarch is not to be disturbed.'

'What a pity,' I said. 'Because I feel like disturbing him. You don't recognise me, do you?'

'No,' said the head thug flatly.

'How soon they forget,' murmured Molly.

'Don't care, neither,' said the thug. 'Doesn't matter who you are. No admittance, no exceptions. Now piss off, or we'll hurt you.'

'No one does decent threats any more,' said Molly. 'They just can't be bothered to make the effort to be decent henchmen.'

'I really don't have the patience for this,' I said. 'Jacob, do you think you could—'

The ghost thrust his ancient grinning face forward, his eyes blazing, and the thugs took one involuntary step back. Jacob drew his awful aspect around him, and the corridor was suddenly full of the presence of death and horror, and the cold inescapable embrace of the grave. It was like waking up and finding a corpse in bed with you, like suddenly knowing when everyone you loved was going to die.

It was sometimes too easy to forget what Jacob really was: a dead man walking, only held together by an inhuman effort of will.

He took a step forward, and the thugs broke and ran, departing screaming down the corridor. Jacob laughed softly and I winced. There was nothing human in the horrid sound. And then suddenly he was Jacob again, my old friend and support. But after seeing what he really was, or could be, I had to wonder if I'd ever be able to look at him the same way again.

He must have sensed something, because he turned and looked at me uncertainly. He tried to smile, but it wasn't very convincing.

'Sometimes I feel I'm the tip of an iceberg, Eddie, and that if I ever found out how much more of me there is, I wouldn't be me at all. That's why I need to keep my living self close; he reminds me of what it is to be human. To be only human.'

'Wonderful,' I said, deliberately keeping my voice light. 'Another thing to worry about.'

Jacob managed something like his old grin. 'It's not easy being a ghost. Or everybody would be doing it.'

'Fascinating,' said Giles. 'You people have taken psychological warfare in a whole new direction.'

'Can we please burst in on Harry?' said Molly. 'I'm feeling an increasing need to hit someone.'

'Yeah,' I said. 'It's been that kind of a day.'

I kicked in the Sanctity doors and we stormed into the great open chamber. Strange's rich crimson glow had expanded to fill almost half of the massive hall; but it no longer projected the old comfort and reassurance. Harry broke off from shouting at his advisors and spun round to face us. He recognised me immediately, but instead of the surprise I expected, after eighteen months away and no guarantee I was ever coming back, all I saw in his face was a cold, calculating anger. Behind him, his advisors' jaws dropped in a quite satisfactory manner; though I didn't think much of Harry's choices. The Sarjeant-At-Arms was there, of course, and Roger Morningstar, and Sebastian and Freddie Drood. The latter pair doing their best to hide behind the first two. Still, to give Harry his due, he recovered quickly. He adjusted his wire-rimmed glasses as though to see me more clearly, and glared haughtily at me.

'Where the hell have you been?' he demanded. 'Typical of you, Eddie, not to be around when you're needed. And where are my guards? They're supposed to keep out . . . unnecessary people when I'm working.'

'Your guards will be back,' I said. 'Eventually. There's only so far they can go before they run out of grounds. One of them called you Patriarch. When did that happen, Harry?'

'Someone had to take charge after you abandoned us to play with your Time Train.' Harry looked disparagingly at Giles. 'It took you eighteen months to find . . . him? A barbarian with a sword?'

'I am Giles Deathstalker,' said the future warrior, and there was something cold and very dangerous in his voice that shut Harry up immediately. 'I am Warrior Prime to the Emperor Ethur, commander of his armies and conqueror of worlds. Do but say the word, Edwin, and I will make him kneel to you. Or I could cut off his head. I'm quite good at that, and it might stop him yapping.'

'A nice thought,' I said. 'But leave it for later. You can forget that Patriarch crap, Harry; I'm back, and you can return to the substitutes' bench.'

'You really think it's going to be that easy?' said Roger, stepping forward to stand at Harry's side. 'Harry's been running this family for over a year. The family has accepted him. What makes you think anyone wants you back in charge?'

'When I walked in, this room was full of barely suppressed hysteria and panic,' I said calmly. 'Not what I'd expect from a Patriarch. And really, Harry, is this the best you could do for advisors? I wouldn't take their advice on how to pick my nose. I swear, I take my eye off this family for five minutes, and everything goes to hell.'

'Five minutes?' said Harry. 'Eighteen months! We didn't know whether you were dead or alive, or captured, or gone over to the enemy, or ever coming back! And now you swagger in here with a smug smile and a condescending word – and what have you got to show for it? One man!'

'One Deathstalker,' said Giles. 'And that makes all the difference.'

'He's big,' said Sebastian.

'I had noticed,' said Freddie.

'And he's got a really big sword.'

'Best kind.'

'What happened to my Inner Circle?' I said loudly. 'I chose them carefully, to represent all the voices in this family. I'm not surprised to see the Sarjeant here, hello Cyril, and Molly and Jacob are with me, but where, pray tell, are the very sensible Penny and our extremely experienced Uncle Jack?'

'The Armourer is in the Armoury, where he belongs,' said Harry. 'And Penny is busy looking after those tutors you so graciously inflicted on the family. They're popular enough, I suppose, if not especially useful. If I had to be in charge, and there was no one else, I decided I wanted my own advisors. People I could trust to see things my way, and carry out the policy I set. There's no room for arguments during an emergency. Don't think you can walk back in and take over, Eddie. You had your chance, and you blew it.'

'Whereas you have done so much better?' I said. 'Do tell.'

'You weren't here! You don't know everything that's happened in the last year and a half! I've been fighting a war against an enemy that threatens the whole world. Not one Nest, one tower, but thousands of the bloody things. Hundreds of thousands . . . we can't even keep count any more, they're spreading so fast. Look at you, standing there, sneering at me. You have no right to judge me! You have no right to walk in and expect us all to fall at your feet, and plead with you to save us! I run the family now. By right. I've earned this. I am the Patriarch. If you want it, you're going to have to take it from me.'

'You see, that's the difference between us right there, Harry,' I said. 'I never wanted it. But I've always known my duty to the family. And that's why I have to replace you: for the good of the family.'

Harry armoured up, and to my surprise the metal that flowed from his torc was golden, not silver. He laughed at the expression on my face, his own hidden behind the featureless golden mask.

'I never liked the silver look. I talked to Strange, and he saw no reason why the strange matter shouldn't be gold so I had him change it. Gold is the colour of tradition, of continuity, a reminder of the days when our family was strong. And will be again!'

'Strange!' I said. 'Are you listening?'

'Yes, Eddie.' The voice emanating from the crimson glow sounded muted and far away. 'It's good to see you again. You've been a long way; I can see it on you. And the world . . . has moved on while you were away. Even I am not what I was, being spread so thin. Only my protections keep the family safe. It's the Loathly Ones, Eddie. They infect the living world like a virus, like a cancer. And the more they take over, the more their presence limits me. I provide armour for the Droods, and power for the family's weapons and defences, but every day I find it that little bit harder. The Hungry Gods are coming and not even I can hope to stand against them once they manifest in all their awful glory.'

I'd never heard Strange sound so tired, so beaten down. Almost defeated. He'd always seemed so powerful, so far above Humanity, it had never even occurred to me that there might be other forces, other Beings, as far above him. I looked at Harry, standing proud and tall in his golden armour.

'Put that away,' I said. 'We don't have time for this shit. We have important business to discuss. Family business.'

'No,' he said immediately. 'There's nothing more important than this. Nothing can happen, nothing can be decided until we know who's in charge. I notice you haven't put on your armour, Eddie. What's the matter? Haven't you got the balls for a fair fight?'

'A duel?' I said. 'In the middle of this, you want to fight a duel?'

'It is the traditional way,' said the Sarjeant-At-Arms, smiling just a little bit.

'Another reason why I never got along with the traditional ways,' I said. 'But if it'll make you happy, Harry . . .'

I subvocalised the activating Words, and the armour poured out of my torc to encase me. I immediately felt stronger, sharper, more confident. A quick glance down showed me my armour was now as golden as his. I flexed my golden fists slowly, and then started towards Harry. He came to me, and we circled each other cautiously. Everyone else fell back, to give us plenty of room. I saw Molly holding Giles by the arm and murmuring urgently in his ear, making it clear he mustn't interfere. He nodded. He looked like he understood about duels.

The Sarjeant-At-Arms took a step forward, perhaps to say something in support of Harry, or perhaps to try and distract me; and Giles swept forward impossibly quickly, crossing the width of the hall in a moment. His long sword leapt into his hand as he slammed the Sarjeant up against the wall and set the edge of the long blade against his throat. It all happened so fast the Sarjeant didn't have a chance to call up his armour. He looked into Giles's cold eyes, so close to his own, and stood very still, saying nothing. A slow trickle of blood ran down his throat from where the razor edge of the sword just parted the skin over his Adam's apple.

'Don't,' said Giles.

Harry seized the moment while my attention was elsewhere and threw himself at me. We went head to head, both of us too angry to think of subtlety. We traded blows that would have killed ordinary men, but neither of us felt them. We grappled with each other, swaying back and forth as we wrestled, but we both knew all the tricks. We slammed together again and again, our superhuman strength and speed equally matched. I pushed him away from me, and extruded long golden blades from my hands. Harry grew blades from his hands too, and we cut viciously at each other, thrusting and hacking and swirling around each other too quickly for the human eye to follow. We were in the grip of the armour now, our passion and hate transformed into superhuman action.

I slammed his left blade aside through brute force, and lashed out at his chest. The supernaturally sharp edge cut through his armour to reach him; the only thing that could. I heard him grunt, in pain and surprise, and then I had to duck quickly as his backhand response almost took my head off. We spun and danced, stamping our golden feet so hard we cracked the wooden floor. We fought on, golden blurs in the crimson light. But we were too evenly matched, trading superficial cuts and wounds that never came close to ending the duel.

But I'd been through a lot more than he had, and I was tired. My arms ached, and I could feel blood trickling warmly down my skin inside my armour. I had to end this, while I still could. So I used an old trick, the one I used to beat his father. I parried both his blades with mine, forced them up and out of the way, and went for his throat with both hands. My blades withdrew into my golden gloves so I could get a good grip on his neck. The impact sent us both crashing to the floor, and I ended up on top, both my hands bearing down on his throat. His hands discarded their blades as he instinctively grabbed at my wrists, trying to force my hands away. The armour around his neck should have been a match for my armoured hands; but at such close proximity, under the force of my will, his armour and mine melded together, so that my bare hands were suddenly at his bare throat, inside the armour.

He made some sound of shock and surprise, and then my grip closed, and I cut it off. He bucked and struggled under me, but he couldn't shift my hands. He choked and convulsed, and I wouldn't let him breathe.

Until finally he stopped fighting me and slapped the ground at his side. The old signal of a fighter who yields. I let go, and he started breathing again. I stayed crouched over him, ready if he was faking. For a while we stayed there, him on the floor, me over him, both of us breathing hard. I would have killed him if he hadn't yielded; and he knew it.

'Was that how you killed my father?' he said finally.

'Typical of you, Harry,' I said. 'Always fixated on the past. A leader has to look to the future. I could have killed you; but I didn't want to. First, because it would probably have caused more problems than it solved and, secondly, the family needs experienced field agents like you. Now more than ever. So, forget this Patriarch crap. Go back to being part of my Inner Circle. Give me your word that you'll follow me, obey my orders, for the good of the family . . . and this is over.'

'And if I say no?'

'You know the answer to that. It's all or nothing, Harry. Deal?'

'Deal,' he said quietly, bitterly. 'For the good of the family.'

We both armoured down. I gave him my hand and helped him to his feet.

'No!' Roger said suddenly, stepping forward. 'You don't have to give into him, Harry! You don't have to take any crap from anyone, not while I'm here!'

And he took on his Infernal aspect, wrapping it round him like a cloak; and he didn't seem in any way human any more. Shadows gathered around him, a living darkness that seemed to eat up the crimson light. There was a thick stench of blood and sulphur on the air, and a rush of almost unbearable heat sent all of us stumbling back, even Harry. Roger smiled, and his mouth was full of pointed teeth. His eyes were black pits in his face. His presence was heavy in the Sanctity, like an unbearable weight pressing down on the world. He looked like what he really was: something from the Pit. Even Harry couldn't bear to look at him directly. Roger laughed softly, an evil, hateful sound that had no human humour in it, and we all winced. Roger rose up towards the ceiling, defying the natural laws of the world as though they were nothing, and hung on the air with his arms mockingly outstretched; as though nailed to an invisible cross.

'Jesus doesn't want me for a sunbeam,' he said, in a voice like an animal grunting. 'You think you're so much, Eddie Drood . . . Let me show you true power.'

Before I could say anything, Molly flew up to face him, levitating effortlessly. Her face was set and cold, as she put herself between me and the hellspawn. I wanted to call out to her, but I had no voice. Unnatural energies coalesced around both of them, felt as much as seen, spitting and crackling like beads of water on a hot surface. Something was gathering between them, something awful . . . Being this close to the two of them felt like razor blades slicing into my soul. Mortals weren't supposed to see things like this, feel things like this. Forbidden magics and inhuman practices . . .

Roger waved a hand and a hole opened in the floor of the Sanctity. The wooden floorboards seemed to rot away into nothing, and the hole grew steadily, like a cancer in the body of the world. Barbed brass tentacles, already slick with spilled blood, shot up out of the hole and snapped around Molly, pinning her arms to her sides. She cried out, as though fouled by their touch, and struggled fiercely, blood spurting on the air as the metal barbs dug into her flesh. And then the tentacles snapped back into the hole, taking her with them, and the hole disappeared. The floor was solid again, untouched, as though nothing had happened. Roger turned slowly, still hanging unsupported on the air, and smiled his awful smile at me.

'I am of Hell,' he said, 'and I carry it with me everywhere. So I'm never far from home. I just sent your girlfriend to Hell, Eddie Drood. Damned her for ever to eternal suffering, to the lake of flames and the torments of the Pit. How do you feel about that, Eddie Drood?'

'After I've killed you, I will go down into Hell and bring her back,' I said. 'Whatever it takes, whatever it costs. But first I will break your body with my golden hands and make you scream, and after all the terrible things I do to you, falling back into Hell will seem like a relief.'

'Wow,' said Molly. 'Hardcore, Eddie.'

Everyone looked round, startled, and there she was, standing untouched and unharmed where the hole had been. I ran over and took her in my arms, and we held each other tightly, and nothing else mattered.

'I really thought I'd lost you,' I said.

'You really think I'd go anywhere and leave you behind?' she said.

When we finally broke apart and looked around, Roger was staring at us incredulously. And for all his Infernal presence, he didn't look half as threatening any more.

'You can't be here!' he said. 'You can't! I sent you to Hell!'

'Been there, done that,' said Molly.

She snapped her fingers crisply, and a hole opened in the high ceiling above us. A celestial light slammed down through the hole, shouldering its way into the mortal world like a holy spotlight, transfixing Roger where he was like a bug on a pin. He screamed horribly, thrashing helplessly in agony in the grip of that Heavenly beam, and we had to turn our heads away. The glare was too dazzling, too pure, for human eyes to look on. Being in the same room with it hurt, as though it was burning away my imperfections. Molly snapped her fingers again, and the light snapped off, the hole in the ceiling gone in a moment. Roger fell to the floor and lay still, breathing harshly. He looked like just a man again. Harry hurried forward to kneel beside Roger and take him in his arms. He rocked him back and forth like a hurt child, murmuring soothing words. Roger's face was blank with shock and suffering and an indescribable horror. I looked at Molly.

She shrugged. 'I've been around. You'd be surprised who owes me favours. Really.'

'We'll talk about this later,' I said. 'Everybody else okay?'

I looked around. Sebastian and Freddie were huddled together in a far corner, trying to climb into each other's pockets. The Sarjeant-At-Arms looked pale and shaken, but not even the sight of Heaven and Hell could break his composure. Jacob the ghost had disappeared. And Giles Deathstalker . . . was grinning widely, as though he'd watched a really good show.

While I was considering that, the Sanctity doors flew open and a whole bunch of Droods came running in, led by the thugs who used to guard the doors. They seemed to have got their second wind and, emboldened by reinforcements, they were back to teach us a lesson. Unfortunately, they made the tactical error of bursting in unarmoured. Giles was off the spot and heading for them the moment they appeared, moving impossibly quickly for someone who didn't have Drood armour. He didn't bother to draw his sword; just slammed into the newcomers, stopping them in their tracks, and took them down with swift, almost clinical precision. He struck about him with amazing skill, and every blow sent a man flying. In a few moments he was the only man standing, surrounded by moaning and unconscious bodies. He wasn't even breathing hard.

'Now that is what I call a fighter,' said the Sarjeant-at-Arms. I'd never heard him sound impressed before. 'You did well, Edwin. This is exactly what we need.'

'Thank you for not killing them,' I said to Giles. 'They're family.'

He nodded briefly. 'I know. I saw the collars round their necks. I only kill when necessary. And these poor specimens definitely weren't worth it.'

'That is partly why you're here,' I said. 'I need you to train my family, turn them into warriors, to fight a war against impossible odds and the most powerful enemy even you've ever seen.'

'I can do that,' said Giles. 'I've made armies out of worse. I can take the most unprepossessing material and turn them into fighting men. I am a Deathstalker. We win wars. It's what we do. How long have I got?'

'Good question,' I said. I looked at the Sarjeant-At-Arms. 'Talk to me, Cyril. I need to know exactly what's been happening while I've been away. Just the high spots, for now; I'll pick up the details later.'

The Sarjeant nodded slowly. 'Welcome back, Edwin. The family has missed your . . . decisiveness. You have to understand: Harry had the support of the Matriarch. I had no choice—'

'Tell me what happened,' I said. 'We can spread the blame around later. You can start with: how did everything go so wrong? When I left we were winning. Sort of.'

'Manifest Destiny had some of their people at the Nazca site,' said the Sarjeant. 'Long before you and your team arrived. Truman wanted to keep a close eye on his new allies. But everyone he sent there ended up possessed, or infected, by the Loathly Ones. They returned to Truman, to spread the gift that keeps on giving. They infiltrated his organisation and penetrated his new base, infecting others in their turn. They became his closest advisors, and whispered poison in his ear. They persuaded Truman to support the establishing of new Nests, and fund the building of new towers.

'Backed by Manifest Destiny's resources, and under Truman's protection, the Loathly Ones spread their influence across the world, embedding their infected agents in organisations and governments in every country. Ostensibly they spoke for Manifest Destiny, representing it as an alternative to Drood rule. Of course, once they were invited in, they quickly moved up to high positions and set about spreading chaos and indecision, dividing Humanity from within. There are Nests everywhere now, in every country, often hidden away inside ghoulvilles to hide the building of their towers. Once these have reached a specific number, known only to them, the great summoning will begin; and the Invaders will come through.'

'Wait a minute,' I said. 'They haven't infected Truman himself? Why not? Then they'd run his organisation.'

'It seems they can't,' said the Sarjeant. 'After all the operations he's had carried out on his brain, it would appear he is immune to their touch.'

'Maybe we can use that,' I said. 'If we could reach him, make him see the truth . . . we might even learn from him a way to make everyone immune—'

'Perhaps,' the Sarjeant said kindly. 'If I might continue . . . ?'

'Oh yes, you go ahead, Cyril. Don't let me stop you.'

'We know that those infected by the Loathly Ones become Loathly Ones,' said the Sarjeant. 'They work together like insects, a hive mind, where each of them knows what every one knows. The Nests communicate, ghoulville to ghoulville, in a way we can't understand or intercept. We invade and destroy every Nest we locate, and burn down their towns, but they're better at hiding than we are at finding. We're winning the battles, but losing the war.'

'Sorry to interrupt,' said Strange. 'But the War Room has just received a significant communication. Callan is on the line; he says he's finally located Truman's new base of operations. Shall I patch him through?'

'Damn right,' I said. 'First good news I've heard . . . Callan! This is Edwin Drood; I'm back. What have you found?'

'Well it's about bloody time,' said Callan, his unmistakable voice emerging from Strange's crimson glow. 'You picked a hell of a time to go on vacation. Did you bring me back a present? No one ever brings me back presents. Look, I'd love to chat but I don't know how long I dare remain in contact. Truman's new base is crawling with security people, and some things that very definitely aren't people. You wouldn't believe the layers of protection he's put in place.'

'Understood,' I said. 'Where is he?'

'You're not going to believe this. I'm here looking at it, and I don't believe it myself. To be exact, I'm outside Stonehenge, keeping what I fervently hope is a safe distance from the outer ring of Stones. Truman has set up his new base in the bunkers set deep underneath the Stones. Once again, he's taken advantage of an old mothballed Government installation dating back to World War Two, I believe. The bunkers were put in place as a last redoubt, to which the Government could retreat if the Nazis invaded and forced them out of London.'

'Hold it,' I said. 'I thought as long as the Soul of Albion was safely in place at Stonehenge, no one could invade England?'

'Maybe the Government of the day didn't trust it,' said Callan. 'Are you ready for the really bad news? Truman's got his hands on the Soul. He's dug it up from under the main sacrificial stone, and locked it away in his private office.'

'Callan,' I said carefully, 'how sure are you of your information?'

'I went in and had a look for myself, and I am here to tell you right now that I am not doing it again. Sneaking past his protections and very heavily armed guards has taken ten years off my life, and positively cured that slight but definite touch of constipation I was suffering from. If I were shaking any more you could mix cocktails in me. See if I ever volunteer for field work again.'

'How could Truman have got to the Soul?' I said. 'The family's been adding layers of protection around it for centuries.'

'I know,' said Callan. 'There's only one answer, and it's not a very nice one. Someone in the family must have given him the necessary Words to unlock the guards. And that someone would have to be *very* high up. A traitor in the family—'

'Impossible!' said the Sarjeant. 'It's unthinkable!'

Not after the Zero Tolerance debacle,' I said. 'They were ready to destroy the family in order to rebuild it in their own image.'

'Just like you,' said Harry.

'Shut up, Harry,' I said. 'This is grown-up talk. Recommendations, Callan?'

'Put together a major strike force, transport it straight here, and I will use it to hit Truman where it hurts, right now, while we've got the element of surprise.'

'No!' I said quickly. 'I know your idea of tactics, Callan: everything forward and trust in the Lord. You hold your position, keep watching, and report back if there are any new developments. I'll work out a plan of attack and get back to you. Until then, *stay put*. That's an order.'

'You can go off people, you know.'

'Strange, cut him off and then talk to me.'

'Yes, Eddie. Callan is still talking to the War Room. He is not happy.'

'Wouldn't recognise him if he was,' I said. 'Tell me about the Soul of Albion, Strange.'

'I only know what the family knows, Eddie. According to your records, an unnatural, other-dimensional crystal fell to earth from the stars thousands of years ago. Long ago, so long ago that history shades into legend, someone carried out a major Working with the Soul, harnessing its power to ensure that England could never be invaded. As long as the Soul stayed in position, under Stonehenge.'

'Could we use the Soul to stop the Invaders coming through?'

'I don't know,' said Strange. 'Its full capabilities have never been tested. It might protect England, if it was replaced in time.'

'All right,' I said. 'How about you, Strange? Could you stop them? There's some evidence in the Old Library to suggest that the Heart intervened to stop them back in Roman times.'

'No,' said Strange. 'You must understand, Eddie, there is so little of me here, relatively speaking. Even with the extra strange matter I brought through to make your armour. In order to put up a barrier that could keep out the Many-Angled Ones, I'd have to manifest my whole self in this reality; and that would be just as disastrous as the Invaders coming through. Strange matter doesn't belong here; it upsets the natural balance. You have no idea how far removed I am from what you think of as life.'

'How long do you think it will be before the Loathly Ones are ready to summon the Invaders?' said Molly, to show she wasn't being left out of the discussions.

'Three, four days,' said Strange. 'I can feel the strain the completed towers are putting on the natural dimensional barriers. I can feel the Hungry Gods gathering around this little universe and making their terrible plans.'

'I'm beginning to wish I'd never asked you,' I said. I looked at Giles. 'How about it, Warrior Prime? Can you put together an army in three or four days?'

'Normally, no,' said Giles. 'But this clearly isn't a normal family, or a normal world. I like it. It's so . . . extreme. If the rest of your family are anything like you, I might manage something interesting in a few days.'

'Actually, you don't even have that long,' said Sebastian.

We all looked round. Sebastian was no longer cringing in his corner. He stood alone, smiling at us, and there was something in his smile and in his eyes that closed a cold hand around my heart. He didn't look like Sebastian any more.

'Seb?' said Freddie, still in his corner. 'What are you doing, darling? This is no time to stand up and be noticed. This really isn't like you, Seb.'

'You don't know me,' said Sebastian. 'None of you really knows me. But then, Sebastian was such an easy part to play. Unfortunately, now his time is up. And so is yours.'

'My God,' said Harry. 'He's infected. He's a Loathly One. How did we miss that? He's the traitor in the family!'

'Not the only one,' said Sebastian, still smiling his inhuman smile. 'I'm afraid you've been very naïve. Now it's time for you to die.'

He shook and shuddered, his whole body convulsing and twisting in sudden spurts of growth. He rose up to be eight feet tall, broad at the shoulders and barrel-chested, his torso packed with thick cables of muscle, his angry red skin stretched almost to bursting point. Two more arms burst out of his sides, and all four hands now boasted heavy curving claws. His face was wide and monstrous, with no trace of humanity left in it.

'The Hungry Gods condemn you to death, Edwin Drood,' he said in a horribly normal voice.

'Hit him,' I said.

Harry, the Sarjeant-At-Arms and I armoured up and threw ourselves at what used to be Sebastian. We hit him with our golden fists, and he just stood there and took it. Harry and I extruded long blades from our golden hands and hacked at him, but the cuts closed up as fast as we made them. The thing that used to be Sebastian laughed at us, and struck out with his four heavy fists, and even with the speed our armour gave us, we were hard put to avoid them. It was the torc, you see. Sebastian still had his torc. He couldn't wear the armour over this monstrous form, but it still protected him. Why hadn't it protected him from infection by the Loathly Ones? Why had it hidden the infection from the rest of us?

'Don't kill him!' I yelled to the others. 'We need him alive, to answer questions!'

'Don't kill him?' said Harry. 'I can't even hurt the bastard!'

Giles stepped forward out of nowhere, swinging his sword. The huge blade came sweeping round in a long arc and slammed into Sebastian's thick muscular neck. The steel blade rebounded helplessly, leaving the neck undamaged, and the vibrations almost jarred the sword out of Giles's hands. He shrugged, sheathed the sword, drew his energy gun and shot Sebastian in the head at point-blank range. There was a bright flare of discharging energies, and when we could see again, half of Sebastian's head had been blown away. Sebastian lurched sideways, and almost fell. Bits of charred brains fell out of his head. The Sarjeant and Harry and I grabbed him and wrestled him to the ground, using all our armoured strength to restrain him and pin him to the floor. He bucked and heaved under us, even with half his head gone. Molly and Roger stepped forward, bathing him in soothing spells and stupefying enchantments. Sebastian relaxed with a great sigh, and lay still.

And only I saw what happened next.

Molly got in too close, concentrating on her magics, and one clawed hand swept out, just touching Molly's side in passing. It didn't cut her, or damage her, but through my golden mask I saw *something* pass between them. Something came out of Sebastian and entered Molly; all done in a moment. Molly cried out, in shock more than pain, and fell back clutching her side. I cried out something too, because I knew what had happened even though I didn't want to admit it. I leaned over and punched Sebastian right in his exposed brain. Blood and charred materials flew out of his head, and he howled miserably in pain. I drew back my spiked golden fist to hit him again but the Sarjeant grabbed my arm with his armoured hand.

'Easy, boy,' he said. 'I understand; but you wanted him alive, remember?'

I nodded briefly, not trusting my voice. Sebastian was quiet now, and the Sarjeant and Harry held him easily to the floor. He'd shrunk back down to human size and form, and his damaged head was already slowly healing. Giles stood by, gun in hand, ready to fire again if necessary. I yelled at Strange to summon some security people, and then I went to see Molly. She was standing a little apart, hugging herself tightly with both arms, as though trying to hold something in, or hold herself together. I spoke to her, but she didn't seem to hear me.

Sebastian laughed, and I turned to look at him. He wasn't struggling, but he'd raised his damaged face to look at me.

'My torc is real, Eddie,' he said, in a high, taunting voice. 'It couldn't protect Sebastian, and yours won't protect you, or your people. I passed unnoticed among you, and no one hid anything from me. Oh, the secrets I know! The secrets I've told! The Droods who went to their deaths because of me!' Harry punched him in the face, breaking his nose with a flat crack. Sebastian paused to spit out blood, but he was still grinning at me. 'The Hungry Gods are coming, and there's nothing you can do to stop us!'

'Get him out of here,' I said. 'Put him in a cage, somewhere secure, and get the truth out of him. Take him apart if you have to, right down to the genetic level if need be, but find out what makes him tick. I want to know everything there is to know about him.'

'You're authorising extreme measures,' said the Sarjeant. 'Not that I'm arguing, but . . . this isn't like you, Eddie.'

'Do it,' I said.

Sebastian had infected Molly. Something alien and awful was growing within her, gestating in her mind and soul, to make her into a Loathly One too. I knew it, but I couldn't tell anyone else. I daren't. They'd want to put her in a cage, and take her apart; and I couldn't allow that. Not Molly. So I didn't tell anyone. Interestingly, neither did Sebastian. Perhaps he thought no one had noticed.

The extra security men came rushing in, already armoured, and the Sarjeant and Harry handed Sebastian over to them. He didn't fight them, but even as they dragged him away he shouted back at us, his voice full of a terrible laughter:

'When we come in our glory, you will love us! We will make you love us! And worship us, and work for us, even as we consume you and your world! You'll love us and adore us, and walk willingly into the slaughterhouse! Everything that lives will become us!'

'Who infected you?' said the Sarjeant-At-Arms. 'You know we'll get it out of you eventually. Was it someone in the family?'

But Sebastian just laughed and laughed, until the doors slammed behind him.

For a while, none of us in the Sanctity said anything. We were all shocked, for our various reasons. Freddie came out of his corner, his face pale and drawn, looking at us as though we might have some answers for him.

'He was my friend,' he said. 'We worked together. How could he be infected and I couldn't see it? How could he pretend to be Sebastian so closely that I couldn't tell?'

'The touch of the Loathly One corrupts,' said the Sarjeant. 'Part of him was still Sebastian, and wanted to collaborate. But by the end there, Sebastian was probably like a coat the drone could put on and take off.'

I looked at Molly. I still didn't say anything.

'We need to know exactly when he was infected,' said Harry. 'So we can figure out how long he's been spying for the enemy. How much he might have told them. How much of our plans and Intelligence are compromised.'

I glared at him. 'I ordered the Armourer to work out a test to determine who among us might be infected!'

'So you did,' said Harry. 'The Armourer came up with a test; we went through it and we passed. So either Sebastian was infected after he was tested—'

'Or the test is no damn good,' I said. 'The Armourer's worked so many miracles for us down the years that we tend to forget he does fail, from time to time. Sebastian suggested there were others like him in the family. Maybe right here in The Hall. Maybe even the original traitor, who arranged for us to bring the Loathly Ones through in the first place. And he said his torc worked for him, protecting and hiding him once he was infected . . . Strange?'

'Don't look at me,' said Strange. 'It shouldn't have been possible. I designed your new torcs and armour to duplicate exactly the properties of those provided by the Heart. I can only assume he was already infected before I handed out the new torcs, and that it was . . . affected by his infection. Remember, the Loathly Ones are the intrusions into our reality of the Hungry Gods themselves. And they are vast and powerful and terrible enough to frighten even me.'

'We need to test everyone again,' I said. 'I'll talk to the Armourer, see if we can boost the test some.'

'Test everyone?' said Harry. 'Including you?'

'Everyone,' I said. I didn't look at Molly. 'We need to know who's who.'

'Sebastian said there were many of his kind among us,' said Freddie. 'Hiding behind familiar faces, watching us.'

'The Devil always lies,' I said.

'Except when a truth can hurt you more,' said Molly.

'Are you all right, Molly?' said Strange. 'You seem—'

'She's fine,' I said.

'Yes,' said Molly. 'I'm fine.'

'So,' I said. 'Truman has the Soul of Albion. For that, he must have had the active cooperation of someone in the family. Any ideas, Sarjeant?'

'There are still members of the Zero Tolerance faction working openly within the family,' the Sarjeant said slowly. 'Some could be maintaining ties with Truman. There are those within the faction who see him as a means of reclaiming power and position within the family.'

'Including the Matriarch?' I said, and he nodded reluctantly.

'And where do you stand on the matter, Sarjeant?' said Harry.

Cyril drew himself up to his full height, his scarred, disfigured face cold and forbidding. 'I protect the family against anything that threatens it.'

'The Matriarch,' I said. 'Dear Grandmother Martha . . . she could have provided Truman with the necessary Words to unlock the protections around the Soul.'

'She could have,' said the Sarjeant. 'But I have no evidence to that effect, or I would have done something. In my opinion, Truman sees the Soul as his ace in the hole, to protect him from the Invaders should they turn against him.'

'I'm getting more from Callan,' Strange said abruptly. 'I think you need to hear this, Eddie.'

'Okay, patch him through,' I said. 'Callan, this had better be good.'

'Depends on your definition of good,' said Callan. 'Truman's found out we're here. And rather than destroy us immediately, he wants me to pass on a message to you. Namely, that he is ready to destroy the Soul of Albion unless the Drood family puts itself under his control. Specifically, he wants access to and control of the forbidden weapons held in the Armageddon Codex. Apparently he believes he can use them to force the Invaders out of our reality, once he's used them to take control of the world. The idiot . . . I really would like permission to withdraw now, please. I don't like him knowing exactly where we are. I can practically feel the vultures gathering.'

'You stay right where you are,' I said. 'Talk to Truman, promise him anything, stall him. As long as he thinks there's still a chance, he won't do anything. I'll get back to you as soon as we've made a decision. Strange, cut him off.'

'Yes, Eddie . . . he's still talking to the War Room,' said Strange. 'Though shouting is probably more accurate. Dear me, such language!'

'First things first,' I said. 'We have to find out who the traitors are in the family.'

'We don't have time for a witch hunt,' said Harry. 'Not when we have so many more important decisions to make.'

'Well, you would say that, Harry,' I said. 'I think I'll start by having a nice little chat with the Matriarch. I expect she'll talk to me, once I tell her about Sebastian.'

'You can't see her,' said Harry. 'She's ill. She's not seeing anybody.'

'She'll see me,' I said. Now, Strange, show me what the family's been doing to fight the Invaders during my unintended absence. Just the highlights, for now. I'll catch up on the details as we go along. Show me what I need to know.'

Visions appeared, emerging from Strange's crimson glow. Shifting scenes of golden-armoured family in running fights with Loathly One drones in the nightmarish streets of ghoulvilles. I saw dozens of armoured forms taking on hundreds of drones, and killing everything that moved that wasn't family. The drones were often horribly misshapen, monsters with only the barest touch of humanity left in them. The Droods beat them down with golden fists, and tore the drones limb from limb. A quick death was the only mercy they had left to offer. They stormed through the narrow streets, their golden armour shining bright in the sharp, painful light of the ghoulville. They destroyed buildings, tearing them apart and pulling them down through brute strength, to be sure they hadn't missed anyone hiding inside; and afterwards they set fire to the ruins.

Whole towns went up in flames. They say fire purifies.

Sometimes the drones were already dead and decaying, only kept moving by the unnatural energies within them. Sometimes they looked just like you or me. They came out into the streets, pleading and crying and protesting their innocence. But they were so far gone they'd forgotten how to sound and act as people do. Especially the children. The armoured Droods killed them all. They had to be Loathly Ones, or they wouldn't be in a ghoulville.

Sometimes the family dropped their armour, to vomit, or cry, or simply sit on a pavement holding themselves and rocking back and forth.

We've never seen ourselves as killers. That's not the Drood way. We've always preferred to operate behind the scenes, making small changes here and there to prevent the family as a whole having to do things like this. Secret wars are one thing; mass slaughter quite another. But we're Droods; and we've always been able to do the hard, necessary things. To protect Humanity.

I hoped we didn't get a taste for it.

I saw my family destroy towers in the ghoulvilles: huge unnatural alien structures, part technological and part organic. Sometimes the towers screamed as they fell. They fell and they fell, and yet somehow there were always more of them . . .

The visions stopped. I stood silently, thinking. The Sarjeant cleared his throat in a meaningful way.

'We are further handicapped by our need to keep this secret from the general populace. They can't be allowed to know what's happening. We're keeping politicians and governments informed, to a point, and they're all cooperating. To one extent or another. World-wide panic and chaos is in no one's best interests.'

'Now you've seen how bad it is,' said Harry. 'The odds we've been facing. Maybe Truman's right. Maybe we should open the Armageddon Codex.'

'No,' I said. Not yet.'

'Tell me you've got a really good plan,' said the Sarjeant.

'Well,' I said. 'I've got a plan.'

CHAPTER THIRTEEN

Truth, and other things, will out

I threw everyone out, as fast as I could without being too obvious about it. I sent Giles Deathstalker away with the Sarjeant-At-Arms to discuss new training programmes for the family. Between the two of them, I'd bet on our army against anyone else's. Harry and Roger stalked off on their own, no doubt to stir up new mischief somewhere else. Neither of them looked back at me as they left. And after a discreet pause, Molly and I said goodbye to Freddie, and to Strange, and we went looking for some empty place where we could talk safely together, in private.

People looked at us as we walked through the corridors. No one actually cheered or booed, they just watched us and kept their thoughts to themselves. Most looked like they were waiting for someone to tell them what to do for the best. I knew exactly how they felt.

Molly and I ended up in the main dining room at the back of The Hall. It was completely deserted, in between shifts, the rows of tables standing silent and waiting under their pristine white tablecloths. It was hard to believe that eighteen months had passed since we were last here. Molly and I sat down facing each other, and I suddenly realised I didn't have a single clue what to say. What do you say when the woman you love is dying?

'It's not like we haven't been here before,' Molly said. 'Remember when you were infected by the strange matter, and we both thought you only had a few days to live? We didn't sit around crying our eyes out; we got on with business. We survived that. We'll survive this.'

'How do you feel?' I said. 'I mean, *really*. Do you feel any different?'

'I can feel . . . something else inside me,' she said slowly. 'Like after a large meal. A feeling of heaviness. As though there's more of me now. My standard magical protections are containing it, for the moment.' She smiled briefly. 'But then I would say that, wouldn't I? If I were already a Loathly One drone, in mind as well as body.'

'No,' I said. 'I'd know the difference. I could tell if you weren't you.'

'Yes,' she said. 'You probably could.'

'Let's talk about something else for a while,' I said. 'Give us a chance to sneak up on the main subject, maybe catch it by surprise.'

'All right. What did you have in mind, Eddie?'

'Well . . . what was that business with Heaven and Hell, and "*I've* been *around*"?'

'Ah,' said Molly. 'Yes. I suppose that had to come out eventually. You've been very good, Eddie, really you have, not asking too many questions about what I did, and what I promised, to gain my magical powers. Possibly because you were afraid of what the answers might be. Well relax, sweetie; I haven't sold my soul to anyone. I made a series of pacts and deals down the years, with various Powers. Some Infernal, some Heavenly, a few alien . . . And I paid for my magic with years off my life. Don't look like that, Eddie; I never wanted to grow old anyway. Now, of course, it would appear the whole question has become irrelevant. My various debtors were paid with years from my putative old age; and now it seems more than likely I won't get that far. The thing growing inside me will take me long before my allotted time.'

'Not while I'm here,' I said. 'I'll never give up on you, Molly. There must be something we can do. This is Drood Hall; we work miracles for the world every day. I have the right to expect one small miracle, just for you. You know . . . I could get you a torc. Strictly speaking, it's forbidden for anyone not of Drood blood, but I'm sure Strange would help. I probably wouldn't even have to explain why. He's very understanding, for an inexplicable other-dimensional being.'

'It's a nice thought, Eddie, but I don't think it would work. The torc didn't help Sebastian – except to help him hide his condition.'

'Okay, scratch that idea. How about the Armourer? He's created enough wonders for the family, he can create one more for me. For you.'

'But then we'd have to tell him everything. How much can we trust him? I don't want to end up in a cage like the others. Not while there's still work to be done.'

'Do you feel up to fighting in the field?' I said.

'When I don't, then you'll know there's something seriously wrong. Physically, I feel fine. No different at all. My magic is insulating me from whatever changes are beginning. Mentally . . .' Molly cocked her head slightly on one side, as though listening. 'It's like there's another voice in my head, me but not me, distant but distinct, faint but insistent.'

'What's it saying?' I said, as casually as I could.

'Smoke crack and worship Satan. No, I can't tell. It's too far away. It doesn't sound like anything bad.'

A sudden rush of helplessness ran through me. I wanted to get up and run around the room, overturning the tables and kicking the chairs out of the way. I needed to be doing something, anything . . . but I made myself sit there, quiet and calm. I couldn't let Molly see how worried I was. So we just sat there, together, facing each other across the empty table.

'What are we going to do?' I said finally. 'We can't tell anyone. We can't trust anyone. Not with this.'

'We stay calm and focused,' said Molly. 'Actually, I think I'm coping with this rather well, don't you? I thought I'd be having panic attacks by now, and hyperventilating into a paper bag. You're the one who looks like you might break down in hysterics at any moment.'

I smiled briefly. 'Never could hide anything from you, could I?'

Molly put out her hands to me, and I took them both in mine. She looked at me earnestly. 'I need you to be strong for me, Eddie, so I can be strong. We can beat this. We can.'

'You know,' I said wistfully, 'when I saved the family from the Heart and put an end to the old evils, I really thought things would improve. I should have known better. What are we going to do, Molly?'

'We destroy the Loathly Ones and all their works,' Molly said firmly, squeezing my hands hard. 'And along the way, we keep our eyes open for something we can use as a cure. Failing that . . . you kill me while I'm still me. Before I become something we'd both hate.'

'I couldn't do that,' I said.

'You have to, Eddie. In case I'm not strong enough to do it myself.'

We looked at each other for a long time, holding on to each other the way drowning men clutch at straws.

'Why haven't you turned me in?' Molly said at last. 'Why haven't you told everyone that I'm infected, and a danger to the family? You know you should. It's your duty.'

'I'll decide what's my duty and what isn't,' I said. 'The most important thing for me is to save you. I brought you here, made this possible, so it's my fault.'

'Oh, Eddie. I never knew anyone so ready to blame themselves for everyone else's problems.'

'I will do whatever it takes to save you, Molly. If you believe nothing else, believe that. There has to be an answer.'

'And if there isn't?'

'Then I'll make one.'

We talked some more, but didn't really say anything. Only the normal, reassuring things you say when you're afraid in the dark. And in the end we had to leave, so I could go about my business. My whole family was depending on me; not just Molly. And I've always known my duty to my family. Damn them. I sent Molly down to the Armoury, to Uncle Jack. She could talk about the problem to him, in general terms, and see what he had to say.

And I went to see my Grandmother.

According to Harry she was ill, too ill to see anybody, but that was an old trick where the Matriarch was concerned when she didn't feel like talking to anybody. So I made my way up to her private suite on the top floor and wasn't that surprised to discover two more of Harry's over-muscled thugs standing guard outside the door. They took one look at me approaching and both of them armoured up immediately. It would seem word had already got around as to what I'd done to the other bullyboys. I strolled to the two guards, armour down, doing my best to radiate casual unconcern. They both moved slightly but definitely to block my way.

'Sorry,' said the one on the left. 'The Matriarch is not to be disturbed. We have our orders.'

'Not to be disturbed at all,' said the one on the right. 'Under any circumstances.'

'I just said that, Jeffrey,' said the first guard.

'Well, I never get to say anything,' said the second. 'You're always leaving me out of things, Ernest.'

'Look,' said Ernest, 'can we please talk about this later?'

'You never want to talk about anything, you.'

Ernest sighed loudly behind his golden mask. 'You're not still mad about that party, are you?'

'Party? What party?'

'You are; you're still mad about it.'

'You went off and left me on my own!' Jeffrey said hotly. 'You knew I didn't know anyone else there!'

'I've said I'm sorry, haven't I? What else can I say?'

'You could let me do the threats. You never let me do the threats.'

'That's because you're no good at them,' Ernest said patiently.

'I could be! A bit of practice and I could be very good at them!'

'All right! All right, then. You go ahead and do the threats. I'll stand here and watch. Maybe I'll pick up a few tricks.'

'Excuse me,' I said.

Jeffrey turned to confront his partner. 'You're going to make remarks, aren't you? Loud and sarcastic remarks.'

'No, I won't!'

'Yes, you will! You're always criticising, you. You never let me do anything fun!'

'I'm letting you do the threats, aren't I? Look, I'll even let you hit him first. How about that?'

'Really?' said Jeffrey. 'I can hit him first?'

''Course you can! Go ahead, enjoy yourself!'

'Thanks, Ernest. That means a lot to me. You're a good friend.'

'Oh, get on with it, you big softy. Kick his head in.'

I decided I'd heard about as much of this as I could stand. I took out the Merlin Glass, shook it to full size, activated the teleport function and then clapped the mirror over both of the guards in turn, sending one to the Antarctic, and the other to the Arctic. Then I shook the mirror down, put it away and smiled at the empty corridor.

'If you bump into the Vodyanoi Brothers,' I said. 'Say hi for me.'

I knocked politely on the Matriarch's door and tried the handle, but it was locked. I waited for a while, but no one opened it. I knocked again, putting a bit more effort into it, and then the Matriarch's voice came from the other side of the door.

'Who is it? Who's there?'

'It's Eddie, Grandmother. I'm back. Can I come in and talk with you?'

'The door is locked. And I don't have a key.'

I raised an eyebrow at that. 'All right, Grandmother. I'll soon have the door open. Stand back.'

'Don't you dare break my door down, Edwin Drood! It's a valuable antique!'

I sighed quietly to myself. 'All right, Grandmother. Give me a moment.'

I knelt down and studied the lock. Old-fashioned, sturdy, no problem. I armoured up my right hand, concentrated, and a thin extension of the golden strange matter slipped forward into the lock, shaping itself to fit the interior exactly, moulding itself into a key. The tasks and skills of a Drood field agent are many and varied. I unlocked the door, armoured down, pushed the door open and entered into the Matriarch's waiting room.

She was standing in the centre of the antechamber, alone. The room seemed very big and empty without the usual attendant crowd of family and friends and well-wishers. The Matriarch herself seemed somehow smaller, diminished. She was doing her best to stand tall and proud, as always, but for the first time I could see the effort. She was dressed formally, but her long mane of grey hair hung carelessly down, instead of being piled up on top of her head. She nodded stiffly to me, a stick-thin old lady with nothing much left but her dignity.

'Edwin. It's good to see you again.'

'And you, Grandmother. May I ask how you came to be locked in your own rooms?'

'I have been held prisoner!' she said angrily, almost spitting out the words. 'Harry has kept me under guard for months, forbidden to communicate with the rest of the family.'

'Why would he do that?' I said.

'Because I found out what he is.' Martha looked at me suspiciously.

'Did you know, Eddie? You always know things you're not supposed to . . . No, of course not. You would have told me something like that. Come into my private rooms, Edwin. I don't feel safe talking out here; you never know who might be listening these days.'

She led me through into the bedroom. The curtains were drawn, keeping the room comfortably gloomy. Alistair was lying flat on his back in bed, still wrapped up in bandages like a mummy. A single blanket covered him, hardly rising as he breathed. He didn't react as Martha and I came in and shut the door. Martha looked at him expressionlessly.

'Don't worry, he's asleep. Doesn't even know we're here. He sleeps most of the time, now. It's getting harder and harder to wake him long enough to take his nourishment. He really should be down in the Infirmary, but I hate to think of him there alone with tubes in him. Everyone else is waiting for him to die, but they don't know my Alistair. He's strong. A lot stronger than anyone ever gave him credit for. You'll see. One day he'll wake up and be himself again, like a butterfly emerging from his cocoon. Sit down, Edwin.'

We sat down on comfortable chairs by the empty fireplace, facing each other. The Matriarch studied me intently for a long moment.

'You look different, Edwin. Older. But then you've been through so much, haven't you? You've grown up. I knew it would happen eventually. It looks good on you . . . But so much has happened while you were away. A year and a half, Edwin! Where have you been, all this time?'

'Travelling in Time, Grandmother. I went into the Future, and found a mighty warrior to bring back to aid the family. I was supposed to return only a few seconds after I left, but—'

The Matriarch sniffed. 'The Time Train. I might have known. There are good reasons why we never use the stupid thing. I could have told you it wasn't dependable, but you didn't ask anyone, did you? You were so sure you knew better. I should have ordered it dismantled years ago, but for this nagging feeling that some day the family might need it.'

'What happened to you, Grandmother?' I said patiently.

'I have been kept prisoner in these rooms practically from the day you disappeared. Harry came to see me. He said it was necessary for him to take command of the family, in your absence, and I was quite prepared to give him my blessing. You have to understand, Edwin: he said the right things, promised me the right things. He made me believe he embodied the old traditional values of the family. Unlike you . . . But even though he was saying the things I wanted to hear, I still didn't entirely trust him. I've run this family too long to take anything or anyone at face value.

'So I had a quiet, very discreet, word with the Sarjeant-At-Arms. Just to be sure. The Sarjeant didn't want to tell me what he knew, but I made him. And that was when I found out the truth about Harry. That he was a deviant, and an abomination! Bedding his own hellspawned half-brother! And he dared look me in the eye and tell me he believed in the old family values! I summoned him here, and confronted him with what I knew. He didn't try to defend himself. Just sighed and shrugged, and said it didn't matter. He had control of the family and he didn't need me any more. He locked me in my own rooms, put his own guards at my door. They took care of my needs, saw that Alistair and I never wanted for anything . . . but nothing I said or promised or threatened would sway them. They were Harry's creatures. I haven't spoken to another living soul in over a year.

'Oh, Harry sees that I'm kept informed about everything that's happening. I get regular reports, and I'm invited to make useful comments, which I do. My duty to the family hasn't changed. But you have to get me out of here, Edwin! Harry isn't up to the job. The family is losing this war! You need my expertise and experience!'

'Yes,' I said. 'We do. But I'm back, and I'm running things again, Grandmother. Running them my way. Are you ready to work with me, now?'

'Of course. I've had a lot of time to think . . . You and I are never going to agree on many things, but the needs of the family must come first. And right now, it needs both of us.' She glanced at the still form on the bed. 'He won't miss me. He doesn't even respond to my voice any more. Any nurse will do, until he wakes.' She looked back at me. 'I haven't forgiven you for what you did to him. I never will. But duty comes first. I've always known that.'

'Then I think you and I should go down to the War Room,' I said.

'So you can take charge there. You know how to run it far better than I ever could. And they need some direction.'

The Matriarch's eyes met mine. 'I'll run the War Room, you run the war. We can discuss the rest after we've won.'

I grinned. 'Looking forward to it, Grandmother. But let's be clear with each other. You need me, now that Harry has . . . disappointed you. That's the real reason you're going along with this. You haven't forgiven me for removing you from power and changing the way the family does things. And I haven't forgiven you for those children sacrificed to the Heart down the years. We can work together, and we will, because the family and the world needs us to. But understand, Grandmother: you make one move to undermine my authority, or try and seize control again, and I'll have you marched straight back here and locked in again. For the duration.'

She smiled at me, that old familiar cold smile. 'You see, Edwin: you do understand how this family needs to be run. I'll make a Drood out of you yet. I agree to your conditions. For the duration.'

I shook my head slowly. 'Even when I win an argument with you, it feels like I lost. One last question, before we go. It's becoming increasingly clear that there has to be a long-standing traitor set deep inside the family. Someone possibly infected by the Loathly Ones, perhaps even the person responsible for bringing them here in the first place. Do you have any idea who that might be? Any name come to mind?'

She stared at me for a long moment. I think she was actually shocked. 'A long-term traitor? Unsuspected since World War Two? Impossible!'

'Unfortunately not, Grandmother. Are you sure no one comes to mind?'

'No. It's unthinkable . . . But then so much has happened that I would once have considered unthinkable. I will consult the old family records. See if anything jogs a memory.'

'Okay. Let's go. The War Room awaits.'

'No,' said Martha. And just like that, all her old stern command was back in her voice. 'There is something that must be done immediately, for the good of the family. You must order the expulsion of Harry, and the execution of his hellspawn lover. They cannot be allowed to contaminate the family with their presence any longer.'

'No,' I said, my voice as cold and stern as hers. 'Harry's a good field agent, with a lot of experience. We still need him. I won't declare him rogue just because . . . I mean, come on, Grandmother, we've had gay people in the family for ages. You must have noticed.'

'Of course I've noticed! I don't care that he's a homosexual! Your generation thinks it invented sex and all its possibilities. I don't give a damn that Harry is gay; I care that he's taken his half-brother as a lover! Incest like that is strictly forbidden in the Droods, Edwin. It has to be, or we would have become dangerously inbred by now. The vitality and vigour of the Drood bloodline must be strictly maintained; that's why marriages are always so carefully considered and, if need be, disallowed. And above all, to take as his lover a thing from the Pit! I can't believe you allowed a hellspawn into The Hall, Edwin!'

'Roger is James's son,' I said carefully. 'He's your grandson too, just like Harry and me.'

'He is a demon, and never to be trusted,' Martha said flatly. 'Kill him, Edwin. For the good of the family and the sake of the world.'

'I'll think about it,' I said.

'That's what I used to say to you, when you were a child and I had no intention of doing what you wanted,' Martha said dryly.

'Maybe you're right,' I said. 'I am growing up, after all.'

We both stood. The Matriarch stepped forward, and for a moment I thought she was going to shake my hand formally. Instead, she put her hands on my shoulders, squeezed them gently, and smiled at me.

'Make me proud, Eddie.'

'I'll do my best, Grandmother.'

'I know you will.'

'Grandmother . . .'

'Yes, Eddie?'

'It was you who told the Prime Minister where and when to find me when I went back to my old flat, wasn't it?'

'Of course, dear. You see? You're thinking like a Drood leader already.'

We summoned a nurse to sit with Alistair, the Matriarch put on her stern finery and then she and I went down to the War Room; and all along the way people stood and stared, and then broke into spontaneous applause. Some even cheered. No one had seen Martha in public for a year and a half, and now here she was walking by my side. Word went swiftly ahead of us, and by the time we'd descended to ground level crowds were lining the rooms and corridors to cheer our progress. The Matriarch ignored them all, her back stiff and her head held high, and they loved her for it. Some of the cheers and applause was for me, and I made a point of smiling and nodding, while being very careful not to let it go to my head.

When we finally strode into the War Room, an almost palpable wave of relief swept through the huge chamber. Men and women stood up at their consoles and work stations to cheer and clap us. A few actually whistled. Martha bowed once to the room, and then made a quick cutting gesture with one hand; the applause stopped immediately. I don't think I could have managed that, on the best day I ever had. The Matriarch cracked out a series of brisk commands, her voice sharp and authoritative and above all calm and business-like, and soon people were back at work, bent over their various stations with a new confidence and enthusiasm. Runners charged back and forth like mad things, gathering the latest information to bring the Matriarch up to date, while others made sure she was supplied with a fresh pot of tea and a new packet of Jaffa Cakes. Sometimes I think this family runs on tea and Jaffa Cakes.

I stood back and watched. It's always a pleasure to observe a real professional at work.

The communications people soon had her in contact with world leaders, every government, country and powerful individual who mattered. Display screens around the War Room were filled with scowling faces, and translation programs ran overtime as the Matriarch addressed them all with her usual cool authority. Many of the faces seemed relieved to see her back. Martha strode from screen to screen, speaking to everyone individually, and through a carefully calculated combination of calm reason, sweet talking, basic bullying and the occasional reminder that she knew where the bodies were buried, she soon had the most important people in the world falling over themselves to agree to work together on dealing with the Loathly Ones. They committed money, manpower and military resources and, most importantly, they agreed to keep the hell out of our way while we did what was necessary. Martha cut them off one by one, and then stretched slowly, luxuriously, like a cat. She seated herself with royal dignity at her command station and smiled briefly at me.

'And that, Edwin, is why the family has to be in charge. Because we're the only ones equipped to see the really big picture and remain independent enough that people will accept our advice as impartial. We can persuade anyone, regardless of politics, on what must be done for the good of all. You can never trust politicians to do the right thing, Edwin, because at heart all they really care about is staying in power. They live in the present; it's up to us to take the long view.'

I smiled, nodded, and said nothing. There would be time for philosophical arguments later, once we'd made sure there would be a later. I hung around long enough to make sure she had things firmly under control, and then I left the War Room and went to the Armoury where Molly was waiting for me.

I was happy to find the Armoury back to its usual raucous and very dangerous self, complete with bangs, bright lights and the occasional unfortunate transformation. Happy chaos and mayhem went on around me as I wandered through in search of Molly and Uncle Jack. Now that the lab interns had their armour back, they had once again embraced their old daredevil practices and were clearly in their usual productive and self-destructive mind sets.

In the firing range, half a dozen armoured forms were taking it in turn to test new guns on each other. The armour soaked up every kind of punishment from projectile guns, curse throwers and hand-held grenade launchers. The noise in the confined space was appalling.

I remembered the time the Armourer created a gun that fired miniature black holes. It took six people to wrestle him to the ground and sit on him, and then prise the damned thing out of his hand before he could demonstrate it.

One young lady was trying out the latest version of a teleportation gun. I stopped to watch. The family's been trying to get the bugs out of that for years. The basic idea is very simple: you point the gun at something and it disappears. In practice, it tended to backfire a lot and we lost a lot of interns. This particular intern was chained firmly to a bolt in the floor as she fired her gun at a target dummy. The dummy's left leg disappeared and it fell over sideways. The intern whooped in triumph, did a little victory dance, and then the leg reappeared, flying straight at her with some force. Wherever the teleport gun had sent the leg, they clearly hadn't wanted it.

Someone else was trying to get an invisibility cloak to work, but all it was doing was making the wearer partially transparent so we could see his insides working. Beauty really is only skin deep. A large explosion sent half a dozen armoured figures flying through the air. No one looked round. Two of the braver, or perhaps more suicidally minded, interns were duelling with atomic nunchucks behind a portable radiation shield. Rather them than me. And one guy with a third eye in the middle of his forehead was flipping urgently through his notes trying to figure out what had gone wrong.

Business as usual in the Armoury.

I found Molly talking with the Armourer at his usual work station. Or, at least, Molly was listening while the Armourer talked. Apparently Uncle Jack was taking it very badly that his test to uncover drones in the family had failed. He broke off to glower at me as I joined them.

'About time you got back. I warned you nothing good ever came of messing about with time travel.'

'I brought you back an energy gun,' I said.

He harrumphed. 'I've seen it. It's rubbish. I've dreamed up more destructive things during my tea break. And I don't care what anyone says; my test was perfectly competent!'

'How did it work?' I said patiently.

'Oh, like you'd understand, even if I explained it to you in words of one syllable accompanied by a slide show.'

'Try me.'

'It checked, very thoroughly, for the presence of other-dimensional energies in the test subject. Basically, looking for anything that didn't belong in our reality.'

I nodded. 'Yeah, that should have worked.'

The Armourer scowled, fiddling absently with an oversized grenade on the table before him until I took it away from him.

'We'll have to run everyone through the test again,' he said unhappily. 'And this time, make allowances for the new torcs. Being other-dimensional things themselves, I should have realised they could be used to hide or distort the results.' He shook his head slowly. 'I must be getting old. I never used to miss things like that.'

'You still build the best toys in the world, Uncle Jack,' I assured him.

He smiled briefly. 'So did you get a chance to try out my new teleport bracelet, this time?'

'Ah . . .' I said.

'It's not fair,' the Armourer said bitterly. 'I work every hour God sends, and a few he doesn't know about, creating weapons and devices for this family, and then no one can be bothered to give them a decent bloody field test!'

'Look, I've been busy, all right?' I said. 'There were an awful lot of people trying to kill me, in the Future.'

'Good,' said the Armourer.

'The important thing,' I said quickly, before he could slide into one of his sulks, 'is why didn't Sebastian's torc protect him from the Loathly One in the first place? Even if it happened before he received his new torc, it should still have detected the infection within him and worked to destroy it. Instead, it seems Sebastian was able to use the torc to hide his infection from your test and the rest of the family.'

'Don't look at me,' the Armourer said stiffly. 'The family armour has always been a mystery. No one's ever been too sure exactly how it does the things it does. The old or the new. The Heart wouldn't talk about it. Maybe Strange would. You should ask him, Eddie.'

'I already did,' I said. 'He wasn't much help.'

'Hmmm.' The Armourer leant back in his chair, scowling thoughtfully. 'Well, theoretically the infection by a Loathly One is as much mental and spiritual as it is physical. The mind is changed, reprogrammed if you like, and the body adapts to accommodate the changed mind's needs. The torcs have always protected us from telepathic attack and demonic possession . . . but this is something else. The Loathly Ones are, after all, merely the three-dimensional protrusions into our reality of much more powerful entities. The Many-Angled Ones, or Hungry Gods, come from a place where the rules of reality are very different, perhaps even superior to ours. If the Loathly Ones really are from a higher reality, so to speak, their presence might be enough to actually *overwrite* our natural laws with their own – though of course only in a limited way. You could see each new infection as a beach-head into our reality; every new drone helping to weaken local laws in favour of their own . . . Hmmm. Yes. A very worrying thought, that. But it does give me some new ideas I can add to my test. Now I know what to look for.'

'We don't have much time, Uncle Jack,' I said.

'I know, I know! You always expect me to work miracles to an impossible deadline! It's a wonder I've got any hair left at all. I'd have an ulcer, if I only had the time. You'll have the new test by the end of the day. Now go away and bother someone else.'

'Actually,' said Strange, his voice booming suddenly out of somewhere close at hand, 'now that I know what to look for, I can perform the test for you.'

'Jesus, Strange, don't do that!' I said, as we all jumped. 'Have you been listening in again? Even after we had that long chat about human concepts like *privacy, good manners* and *minding your own business so as not to royally piss off everyone else*?'

'But this is important, Eddie, really it is! I promise! I've already checked your whole family and its guests, and identified a number of infected drones.'

'How many?' I said, a sudden premonition sending a chill running through me.

'Twenty-seven,' said Strange.

Molly and I looked at each other, and then at the Armourer. He seemed to shrink in on himself. 'That can't be possible,' he said numbly. 'I couldn't have missed that many.'

'Are you sure, Strange?' I said. 'You have to be really sure about this.'

'It's not something I can be wrong about,' Strange said sadly. 'The other-dimensional impact is really quite distinct. My torcs couldn't protect you because the Hungry Gods come from a higher reality than mine. They scare me, Eddie. They could eat me up like a party treat.'

Will everyone please stop panicking?' I said. 'It's very unnerving. I am in charge, therefore I am officially the only one allowed to panic. Everyone else, I'll tell you when. Get a grip on yourself,

Strange, or I'll start to think you aren't as important an entity as you like to make out. What matters is we can still win this. Now, Strange, talk to the Sarjeant-At-Arms, give him the relevant names and have him take the drones into custody. Very secure custody. Tell him to do it quietly and discreetly; no public violence unless absolutely necessary. We don't want the rest of the family upset. I want all twenty-seven taken alive, and capable of answering questions.'

'Yes, Eddie. About Molly . . .'

'Not now, Strange,' I said steadily. 'We'll talk about that later.'

'Yes, Eddie.'

'Is something wrong with you, Molly?' said the Armourer. 'You look very pale. And Strange sounded worried about you.'

'Oh, it's just something that happened during our trip through Time,' Molly said easily.

She distracted him with details about the yellow dragon and the Starbow while I wandered off to do some thinking of my own. I'd hoped to find some way of discussing Molly's problem with Uncle Jack, but this new emergency had to take precedence. Twenty-seven infected family, all working secretly to undermine and betray us? No wonder the war had been going so badly in my absence. There had to be an original traitor, embedded deep within the family, passing on his infection . . . Or could it be a Typhoid Mary, not aware of what they were doing? Something in that thought reminded me of an old worry that I hadn't checked in on since I returned. I looked around me. Molly had Uncle Jack chuckling at her stories. The lab interns were engrossed in their own dangerous business. So I found a quiet corner, hidden away behind a blast shield, and took out Merlin's Glass. I commanded it to show me the Present.

'Show me Penny Drood and Mr Stab,' I said. 'Where are they, right now?'

My reflection in the mirror vanished, replaced by a view of Penny in her room. She was sitting elegantly on the edge of her bed, idly kicking her long legs. She was wearing her usual tight white sweater over tight grey slacks, and looked her usual cool and collected self. And then the view seemed to pull back, showing me Mr Stab, standing on the other side of the room, considering Penny thoughtfully. He was wearing a casual dark suit, and looked almost normal and everyday; until you took in his face, and his eyes. Even in repose, Mr Stab looked like what he was. He might as well have had the mark of Cain branded on his brow. But Penny smiled at him, as though he was just another man.

'You don't need to stand so far away. I trust you.'

'You shouldn't,' said Mr Stab.

'After all the time we've spent together? If you were going to hurt me you would have done it long ago. But you've been here in The Hall for nearly two years, and you haven't hurt anyone. You're stronger than you think you are; I wish I could make you believe that.'

Mr Stab smiled briefly. 'If anyone could, it would be you.'

'Why won't you tell me your real name? Mr Stab isn't a name; it's a title, a job description.'

'You could always call me Jack.'

'No, I couldn't,' Penny said firmly. 'That's who you used to be, not who you are. I don't think you realise how much you've changed during your time here. You have students and followers, your lectures are always packed; you have a place here, with us. With me. You've shown me sides of yourself you've never shared with anyone else. You've let me get closer than anyone else.'

'Yes,' said Mr Stab. 'I have.'

He moved over and sat down beside her on the bed. His back was straight and stiff, and he kept his hands together in his lap. Penny forced an arm through his, hugged it to her side, and then leant her blonde head on his shoulder. He sat very still.

'I do care for you,' he said. 'In my way.'

'It's all right for you to care,' said Penny. 'You're allowed to care; to love.'

'Yes,' said Mr Stab. 'I can love. I have. But it always ends badly.'

Penny lifted her head and glared playfully at him. 'You are the gloomiest person I know! It doesn't always have to end badly. We're the Droods; and we exist to make sure things don't have to end badly! That's our job.'

'My job is very different,' said Mr Stab. 'I have done . . . such terrible things, Penny.'

'Anyone can change,' said Penny. 'Anyone can be saved. I've always believed that. The Mr Stab I've come to know, and love, is very different from the stories I've heard. I love you, and you can love me.'

'I wish it was that simple, Penny.'

'It is that simple! And part of being in love is being together. Like this. How long has it been since you allowed yourself to be close to a woman?'

'A long time. I don't want to hurt you, Penny.'

'You won't! This is love, two people together. Just . . . let yourself go. Do what you want to. I want you to. It's all right, really.'

'I love you, Penny,' said Mr Stab. 'Let me show you how much I love you.'

Penny smiled and turned to take him in her arms, and then stiffened and looked down at the long blade Mr Stab had eased into her gut. There was hardly any blood yet. He turned the blade and pulled it across, cutting deeper, and she cried out and grabbed his shoulders with both hands. The expression on her face was pure disbelief. She tried to push him away, but she didn't have the strength so she hung on to his shoulders as he pulled the long blade out and stabbed her again. Blood spurted from the first wound, soaking the front of her sweater and splashing across the front of Mr Stab's jacket. His face was . . . quietly sad. Penny convulsed and cried out again. Blood flew from her mouth, spraying across Mr Stab's face.

I had grown the Merlin Glass to full size the moment I first saw the knife, and I was through the Glass and heading for Mr Stab by the second attack; but already I knew I was too late. Mr Stab let go of Penny and backed away as I headed for the bed. I let him go, intent only on Penny. I was already screaming mentally to Strange for help, and he was telling me help was on the way; but I knew it wouldn't do any good. I leant over Penny and tried to close the wounds with my hands. Blood quickly soaked my arms to the elbow. She looked at me, jerking and kicking, and tried to say something, but the only thing that came out of her mouth was more blood. The bed was soaked in it. She died in my arms, still trying to say something. I let her go. I stood up and moved away from the bed. I was covered in blood. I looked at Mr Stab, standing silently by the door. He could have left, could have run, but he hadn't.

'I tried to tell her,' he said. 'Tried to warn her. That . . . is the only pleasure I can know of a woman now. Part of what I bought, along with my immortality, from my celebration of slaughter when all of London knew my name. That . . . is all the love I can show. All that's left to me. I tried so hard to stay away from her. But I am . . . what I am.'

'I told you,' I said, and I could hear the cold rage in my voice. 'I told you what would happen if you didn't control yourself.'

I armoured up, grew a long golden blade from my hand, stepped forward and cut off his head with one savage blow. He didn't move, didn't try to evade the blow. My golden blade sheared right through his neck, and the head fell to the floor and rolled away, the eyes still blinking and the mouth working. I stood before the headless body, breathing harshly from the rage and grief burning within me, and only slowly realised that the body hadn't fallen. It stood there, by the door. No blood spurted from the neck stump. And as I watched, the body stepped slowly forward, reaching out with its hands. I backed quickly away, but it wasn't interested in me. One hand grabbed the severed head by its hair. I made some kind of sound. I don't know what. The body lifted up the head and put it back on the stump, and the wound healed in a moment, leaving no trace behind.

Mr Stab looked at me expressionlessly. 'You think no one ever tried that before? I've been beheaded, shot, poisoned, staked through the heart. I can't die. That is what I bought with the deaths of five whores in 1888. Immortality, whether I want it or not. I'm Jack, Bloody Jack, Jack the Ripper, now and for ever. And the only love I can ever know, the only pleasure I can ever have of a woman, is through the knife. Send me out into battle, Eddie. Maybe the Loathly Ones can find some way to kill me.'

The door burst open as the medics arrived and rushed in, too late. Mr Stab walked away as they clustered round the body, not looking back even once.

There was nothing I could do, so I transported myself back to the Armoury. It wasn't as though I had anywhere else to go. Molly cried out when she saw the blood soaking me, and hurried forward, running her hands over me to see where I was hurt. Uncle Jack started to shout for the Armoury's medical staff until Molly assured him I was okay. I couldn't speak. I couldn't say anything. I held Molly tightly to me, and she let me, even though the blood soaked her too. I buried my face in her hair, in her shoulder, and she murmured soft soothing words to me. Until finally I was able to let her go and stand back.

Molly took me by the hand and led me like a child to the nearest chair. I sat down heavily. I felt tired, drained. And finally, in a voice that didn't sound like mine, I was able to tell them what had happened. Uncle Jack found me some medicinal brandy, and patted me awkwardly on the shoulder while I drank it. Then he moved away to call the Sarjeant-At-Arms to get the details. Molly sat beside me holding my hand.

After a while, Uncle Jack came back with some lab coats for me and Molly to change into so we could get out of our bloody clothes. Molly had to help me undress. My hands were shaking. We left the clothes in a heap on the floor. The lab coats were fresh and clean, and smelled of disinfectant.

'Talk to me,' I said. 'Tell me something. Anything. I don't care. I need something to do, so I don't have to think about Penny.'

'Well,' said Molly, glancing at Uncle Jack. 'There is a problem with the Blue Fairy.'

'When isn't there?' I said. 'What's he done now?'

'He's been kept under constant but covert surveillance by the Sarjeant-At-Arms ever since he got here,' said the Armourer. 'And don't look at me like that, Eddie; I know you vouched for him, but his reputation went before him. Anyway, it seems he spent a lot of time in the Old Library, having a series of what he thought were casual and unobserved conversations with Rafe and William concerning the origins, powers and capabilities of the Drood torc. When he'd pumped those two dry of everything they knew, he went to the source and continued his questions with Strange. Very detailed questions. In fact, he's in the Sanctity right now, according to the Sarjeant-At-Arms.'

'All right,' I said. 'Let's listen in.'

I used the Merlin Glass again, and as my reflection disappeared from the mirror I thought for one moment it would show me Penny and Mr Stab again, and my heart almost stopped; but then the Glass showed me the Blue Fairy, standing alone in the Sanctity, calmly addressing the crimson glow of Strange. Blue was doing his best to seem entirely relaxed and at his ease, and perhaps only someone who knew him as well as I would have detected how tense he really was. Molly and Uncle Jack crowded in behind me, watching the scene over my shoulders.

'But what is it you want from me?' Strange was saying patiently. 'We have had many fascinating conversations, Blue, and I have enjoyed them, but I really can't keep going round in circles with you. Not when so much is happening. Tell me what you want. I assure you, I have no human sensibilities to be offended.'

'Very well,' said the Blue Fairy. 'If straight-talking is to be the order of the day, I want a torc. A golden torc for my very own, like everyone else.'

'But you are not family,' said Strange. 'You are not of the Drood bloodline. And it has been made very clear to me that only they can wear the torc. No exceptions. Why would you want a torc, Blue? You are half elf, with powers and abilities of your own.'

'Yes,' said Blue. 'I have. I hoped it wouldn't come to this, but . . .' He moved his hands in a certain way, the long elegant fingers tracing unnatural patterns on the crimson air. 'An exception has been made in my case. Give me a torc.'

'That was a very intriguing compulsion spell,' said Strange. 'But of no avail against such as I.'

The Blue Fairy moved his hands more urgently, this time muttering in old elvish under his breath. The air seemed to shudder under the impact of the ancient Words, and shimmering trails followed the Blue Fairy's gestures, spitting discharging magics. And then something unseen picked up the Blue Fairy and threw him the length of the Sanctity. He slammed into the far wall with enough impact to kill a simple human, and then he slid slowly down it, ending up in a crumpled heap on the floor. He was breathing harshly, his hands limp at his sides.

'Oh dear,' said Strange. 'And we were getting on so well, too . . . But no one compels me. What am I going to do with you? Something suitably unpleasant, I think, *pour disourager les autres*. Maybe I'll turn you inside out, keeping you alive, of course, and then put you on display. That should give you a whole new way of looking at things.'

I decided I'd seen enough. I opened the Merlin Glass and transported myself into the Sanctity. Molly followed me through quickly before the doorway closed itself down.

'Ah, Eddie,' said Strange. 'Eavesdropping again? And after all you had to say to me on the subject?'

'I'm in charge,' I said. 'I'm allowed to be contradictory. In fact, I think it's a job requirement. What was that about turning the Blue Fairy inside out? I've never heard you sound threatening before.'

'He tried to compel me,' said Strange. 'No one compels me. I help because I choose to. No other reason.'

'Of course,' I said. 'But in the future, if punishments are to be handed out, I'll do it. Clear?'

'You're no fun any more,' said Strange.

I walked over to the Blue Fairy, who was slowly and painfully rising to his feet. He glanced at the door, but Molly had already moved to put herself between him and it. He sighed briefly, and tugged vaguely at his clothes to try and make himself look more presentable.

'Hello, Eddie,' he said calmly. 'Molly. Didn't know you were back.'

'Clearly,' I said. 'Why were you trying to force Strange to give you a torc?'

He shrugged, and tried his best charming smile. 'Reverting to nature, I fear; my old self coming out again. You know how it is.'

'I'm really not in the mood for civilised chit-chat,' I said, and there must have been something in my voice, because he stood a little straighter. 'Talk to me, Blue. Tell me the truth. Or I might let Strange have you.'

'Your time away has not mellowed you,' said the Blue Fairy. 'Very well. I'm afraid I wasn't entirely honest with you when I arrived. I only came here to help myself, not you. I wanted a torc. I wanted a golden Drood torc so I could take it to the elves. Present it to the Fae Court, and bargain its secrets for admittance to the Elven realm. I'm tired of trying to live as a human in the human world. I've never been very good at it. And after my near-death experience, I thought a lot more about the other side of my heritage. And it seemed to me that they might be kinder than you. In the end, it's about family, Eddie. The need to belong. You should understand that.'

'Your very existence is an abomination to the elves,' said Molly.

'Breeding outside the fae blood is their greatest taboo. They'd kill you on sight, torc or no torc.'

'He knows that,' I said. 'But hope springs eternal in the deluded heart. No torc, Blue; not for you. Not now, not ever.'

He nodded slowly. 'And you're not going to kill me?'

'I should. But I've already lost one friend today.'

'I did try to warn you, Eddie. Even half-elves always have an agenda.'

'That's right, you did. So here's your choice. You can go, or you can stay.'

'That's it?' said the Blue Fairy, after a moment.

'Yes,' I said. 'I don't have the energy to be mad at you. But if you stay, and fight alongside us in the war that's coming, you could win acceptance. And a place here. Friends can be a kind of family.'

'You shame me with your generous spirit,' said the Blue Fairy. 'I'll stay, and I'll fight. Now, if you'll excuse me?'

I nodded to Molly and she stepped aside from the door to let him leave. She waited until the door was firmly closed behind him, and then looked at me.

'Are you crazy? You can't trust him! He's half elf.'

'I know,' I said. 'That's why I want him close, where I can keep an eye on him.'

'You humans, with your subtleties,' said Strange. 'You're far more frightening than I could ever be.'

Next, Molly and I went to visit the isolation wards in the Infirmary, in the North Wing. Neither of us wanted to, but we had to see how the infected Loathly One drones were doing. Twenty-eight now, including Sebastian. Twenty-nine, including Molly. I was ready to go on my own, but Molly insisted on accompanying me and I couldn't say no. Not when she was fighting so hard to hang on to her humanity.

The family has always trained its own doctors and nurses to staff its own hospital. Partly because we don't want the world to know that Droods can be hurt, even with their marvellous torcs, and partly because only we are equipped to deal with the kind of problems faced by Droods, in and out of the field. Our doctors have to be able to diagnose and treat all kinds of physical, spiritual and unnatural accidents, everything from werewolf bites to long-distance curses to post-possession stress disorder.

Our Infirmary equipment is extremely up to date, and sometimes even a bit beyond, but the place itself is still the traditional pale paste-coloured walls, snotty matrons and the faint but pervasive smell of boiled vegetables. Molly and I strode quickly through the wards, nodding briskly to the staff on duty. A few looked as though they would have liked to object to our presence, but we were come and gone before they could put their objections into words. Most of the ward beds were occupied; far more than normal. Some were clearly dying, despite all the doctors could do for them. A small cold part of me was glad to see that Harry had been as bad a leader as me, but I pushed the thought aside.

The isolation wards are tucked away in their own private annex. Essentially, they're a series of heavily armoured, pressurised holding tanks, with steelglass walls, designed to contain the more problematic patients; like field agents who've brought back a disease from some other dimension, or the seriously possessed. The only entry point to each tank is a closely guarded airlock, whose combination code is changed daily, just in case. There are only six tanks; we've never needed more. Now they were packed from wall to wall with the recently rounded-up drones.

Molly and I moved slowly down the row of isolation tanks, nodding to the armed guards at each airlock door. Some of the drones came forward to beat on the heavy steelglass with their fists. Their voices came clearly to us through the built-in speakers, saying they were innocent, uninfected, this was wrong, there'd been a terrible mistake. They called me by name and pleaded for my help. Others shouted threats and curses. But most sat or stood quietly, their faces expressionless, waiting to see what would happen next. Waiting for us to drop our guard, just for a moment.

In the very last tank, Sebastian Drood came forward to stare mockingly at us as we stopped before the airlock. As the most dangerous, he had a cell to himself. He looked normal enough now, though there was something wrong with his face, as though he'd forgotten how to look human. Or perhaps he didn't feel the need to bother any more. He nodded politely to me, and smiled at Molly.

'Dear Molly,' he said. 'How does it feel to be one of us?'

'I'll never be one of you,' she said steadily. 'Whatever it takes.'

'Ah,' he said, shrugging easily. 'You say that now . . . but we all start out feeling that way. We don't turn ourselves in, like we know we should, because we're different. We're strong, we can beat this. We'll never give in; no, not us. But after a time you won't want to fight it. In fact, you'll embrace it. Because being human is such a small thing to leave behind.' He turned abruptly to look at me. 'You haven't told anybody about her, have you, Eddie? I counted on that. And by the time you realise how hopeless it is, it'll be too late. Is that why you're here, Eddie? To kill me before I can tell anyone what I did to dear Molly? Am I to be destroyed while trying to escape?'

'Say what you like,' I said. 'No one will believe you. A drone would say anything, tell any lie, to try and undermine the family.'

'Then why are you here?' said Sebastian. 'Hoping for a cure, perhaps? Don't waste your time and mine. There isn't one. Once someone is one of us, they're one of us for ever.'

'You could do yourself some good,' I said. Win yourself some better treatment by agreeing to answer a few questions.'

'And don't waste any time on lies,' said Molly. 'I'd know.'

'Yes,' said Sebastian. 'You would. Very well. Ask your questions.'

'Who was the original traitor?' I said. 'Who worked to persuade the family to bring the Loathly Ones back in 1941?'

'Haven't a clue,' Sebastian said cheerfully, leaning on the steelglass with his arms folded. 'And in case you were thinking of threatening me with truth-spells or cattle-prods or whatever we use for interrogation these days: yes, I know we're a hive mind, but we're kept strictly compartmentalised. Each drone only knows what it needs to know, when it needs to know it. Basic security. I might have known who the traitor was once, but I am currently cut off from area of knowledge. Or indeed any area that might help you. Same with the other drones here.'

'There are ways of digging out the truth,' I said. 'Old ways. Of course, they can be very destructive, to the body and the mind . . .'

'Dear me,' said Sebastian, smiling widely. 'Threats of death and torture to a helpless prisoner? What are the Droods coming to?'

'The safety of the world has to come first,' I said.

'Oh it does, it does. But can you save the world by damning yourselves? Can you fight monsters by becoming monsters?' Sebastian's tone was openly mocking now, though his face was utterly expressionless, not even trying to seem human any more. 'The Hungry Gods are coming, Eddie, and there's not a damned thing you can do to stop us. No one's ever stopped us. Hello, Freddie.'

Molly and I looked round sharply as Freddie came uncertainly forward to join us. He nodded briefly to Molly and me, but his attention was fixed on Sebastian. I hardly recognised Freddie. All his usual glamour and flamboyance was gone, stripped away by events. He looked smaller, diminished, staring at Sebastian with an awful fascination.

'Hello, Seb,' he said finally. 'Are you still Seb? Do you remember me? Do you remember being my friend?'

'Of course I remember you, Freddie. I haven't changed, not really. I'm just being more honest about what I am. I remember our friendship, the good times we had together; I simply don't care any more. Never did, really. All part of the job. You were a means to an end, I'm afraid, a plausible way of gaining entry to The Hall. I knew it would go easier if I had you there to vouch for me. Eddie might have called all the rogues home, but he had good reason not to trust me.'

'Were you infected, even back then?' I said.

'I'm not going to tell you. Now hush, I'm talking to Freddie. I couldn't believe it when you went dashing off again, Freddie, right after I'd brought you here. I needed you, and your extreme personality, to distract people from me. That's why I made such a point of calling you back here, to be one of Harry's advisors. You never had a useful thought inside that pretty head of yours in your entire life. But I made a point of seducing you, to make sure you'd stay this time. You're so larger than life that no one ever looked at me when you were around.'

'Did you ever feel anything for me?' said Freddie, almost whispering.

'Oh, I don't know,' said Sebastian. 'Perhaps. Sometimes. Sometimes . . . I'm more human than at other times. But it doesn't matter. That's all over now. There will be no room for real human emotions in the world that's coming. You'll love us because we'll make you love us, to make the transition easier. But we won't care. We are the Hungry Gods, the Many-Angled Ones. And you are food.'

Freddie turned away, as though Sebastian had hit him, and walked off down the row between the isolation tanks, not looking back.

'That was cruel,' I said to Sebastian.

'Have to be cruel to be kind,' Sebastian said briskly. 'Now go away. I have nothing else to say to you. If there's anything else you want to know about being a drone, ask Molly. Of course, you may not be able to trust her answers . . . as time goes on.'

He laughed at us. I took Molly by the arm and pulled her away, and we walked back through the isolation ward. The drones came forward to the front of their tanks and watched us intently through the steelglass, and all their expressions were exactly the same. They watched Molly, not me. She was staring straight ahead, lost in her own thoughts, and I don't think she noticed. I hoped not.

'I didn't know Sebastian and Freddie were gay,' she said finally.

'I don't think Freddie's ever been that discerning,' I said, glad of a chance to talk about something else. 'He'd stick it in mud, if he thought it would wriggle. And Sebastian . . . would probably do whatever he thought was necessary. Freddie was always a serial romantic, couldn't stand not to be in a relationship with someone. Anyone. Sebastian used that, so he could use Freddie as cover. Poor bastard.'

'Sebastian knows about me,' said Molly. 'Sooner or later, he will talk. When he thinks it's to his advantage. And sooner or later, someone will listen and believe. You know that.'

'It will take time,' I said. 'And we only have three, four days till the Invaders come through. The family is going to be too busy to care about Sebastian's ravings.'

We stopped as one of the armed guards approached us. Molly tensed, and grabbed my arm. I did my best to look casual and unconcerned.

'We've had word from the man guarding Sebastian,' said the guard. 'Apparently he has something else to say to you. Something important. But he'll only say it to you two.'

'Probably a trick,' said Molly. 'Distract us with false information.'

I could tell how much she wanted out of the isolation ward, but I couldn't just leave. Sebastian did know things; there was always the chance he could be manoeuvred into saying more than he intended. So we went back to Sebastian's isolation cell, with Molly walking stiffly at my side. When we got there, he smiled sweetly at us, leaning at his ease on the heavy steelglass wall.

'I was infected long ago,' he said, without even bothering with any pleasantries this time. 'You have no idea what it feels like, when the change really starts to kick in. It's like being part of something bigger, something far more important and significant. I felt a real sense of purpose, of destiny, for the first time in my life. Being human is such a limited thing. Why should I regret leaving it behind, when I will become so much more? When the Hungry Gods come through I shall be part of them, and glory in your destruction.'

'But you're losing yourself,' I said. 'Giving up everything you've made of yourself. That used to mean so much to you, Sebastian.'

'I never knew how small I was, until I was touched by the gods,' said Sebastian. 'Why stay a caterpillar, when you can become a butterfly?'

'Butterflies don't normally kill everything else in the field,' said Molly.

Sebastian smiled at her. 'They would if they could. And so will you, Molly dear.'

'You said you had something important you wanted to tell us,' I said. 'Spill it, or we're leaving.'

'Oh yes . . . You've been very clever, Eddie, discovering and rounding up the drones we infected during the battle on the Nazca Plain . . . But from now on, every time you come into contact with us, you'll lose more people. No matter how many battles you win we'll take more of you, until there's no one left. You don't dare fight us, because if you do we'll make you just like us.'

I smiled right back at him. 'Well, you would say that, wouldn't you?'

I took Molly to our room. We both needed some down time. Time to think. I stretched out on the bed, but instead of joining me Molly stood by the window, looking out over the grounds. The silence in the room seemed to grow stronger and heavier the longer it went on, but neither of us knew how to break it. I'd said I'd help her, said I'd save her; but I didn't know what to do. I'd said I'd protect her from my own family if necessary; but we both knew the fate of

Humanity had to come first. We both knew a lot of things; but neither of us wanted to be the first to say them.

'How do you feel?' I said at last, just to be saying something in that awful silence.

'I can feel the first changes,' she said, still looking out of the window. 'Physical changes. My body feels different. Uncertain. And there are strange thoughts in my head that seem to come out of nowhere. My magics are keeping things under control, for now. I know so many spells, so many forbidden magics and secrets; but I never thought I'd need a weapon I could use against myself.'

'There must be someone who can help you,' I said. 'All the places you've been, the contacts you've made.'

'The price they'd ask would be worse than the affliction,' said Molly.

'Then someone in the family,' I said. 'We need to stop or slow the changes till after the war. Till we can really go to work on it.'

'Who could we ask?' said Molly. 'Who could we trust with a secret like this?'

'The Armourer,' I said. 'Uncle Jack would understand. We had to kill his brother James, and he understood about that.'

'That was to save the family,' said Molly. 'And I am becoming a real and present danger to the family. Who else is there?'

'I don't know! How about the Blue Fairy? He owes me. Maybe he could fish for a cure. He found one for himself.'

'We can't trust him. He's half elf.'

'Well . . . maybe Giles could take you with him, back to his future,' I said desperately. 'Who knows what kind of cures and medical technology they have then?'

'You heard the man,' Molly said sadly. 'His is a strictly scientific future. His people probably wouldn't even be able to recognise what was wrong with me. And anyway, we can't unleash the Loathly Ones and the Hungry Gods on the future. They must be stopped, here and now.'

I had to smile. 'Am I hearing this right? The infamous Molly Metcalf, developing scruples and morality at this late stage?'

She turned around, and managed a small smile for me. 'Everyone has to grow up eventually. All it took for me was an other-dimensional parasite infecting my body and eating my soul.'

I sat up on the bed and looked at her. 'Now you're one of them, are you part of their hive mind yet? Can you hear them? Can you listen in on the Loathly Ones' communications?'

Molly frowned, concentrating. 'There is something on the edge of my thoughts. Far away, a background sound. But it's babble, a meaningless gabble of noise. Not human . . . alien. Perhaps I'll come to understand it, as I become . . . more like them. Will my thoughts come to sound like that? So alien, so intrinsically *other*, as to be beyond human comprehension?' She looked at me intently. 'We have to stop them, Eddie. While I'm still me. Maybe if we drive them out of our reality, the infection will go with them.'

'Yes,' I said kindly. 'Maybe.'

'I'm scared, Eddie. Scared of becoming less and less me, and becoming something that won't even care what it's lost. I won't care that I don't love you any more . . . If there is no cure, if there is no hope left, kill me, Eddie, while I still know who you are. If you love me, kill me.'

'Yes,' I said. 'I can do that.'

CHAPTER FOURTEEN
Peace and war

All Droods are fighters. It's in the blood, and the training. We're born to the torc and raised to fight from childhood on, even if most of us never get to leave The Hall or see a hand raised in anger. Because the family has always known that a day like this might come, when the Droods must go to war in defence of Humanity, and the world.

Cry havoc, and let loose the Droods of war.

Janissary Jane taught us a lot, but Giles Deathstalker taught us something else. When Jane was running things, she put us through war games. Giles ran his manoeuvres like the real thing, with half the family set against the other half, so we could learn how to fight as part of a group. It wasn't enough for us to be warriors any more, nor even heroes; we had to be an army. Giles taught us strategy, and tactical thinking, instead of relying on our usual one-on-one philosophy. To think of the operation as a whole, and not just our own individual part of it. We caught on quickly. We're used to training.

And so there we were, out on the great grassy lawns, shining bright and savage in our golden armour as we did our level best to kill each other. Every Drood man and woman, save for the absolute minimum specialists necessary for running Operations, the War Room and the Infirmary, charging this way and that under Giles's strict commands. We slammed together, body against body, pushing our muscles and nerve to their limits. The sound of combat was deafening, as golden blades sought golden chests, and armed fists hammered into armoured heads, and voices rose in fury and passion and eager exhilaration. The gryphons hauled themselves off their haunches and sulked away in search of somewhere more peaceful, soon followed by the peacocks and other wildlife. Even our resident undine poked her head up out of the lake to see what was going on before quickly disappearing again. Ranks of children excused from lessons watched us make war, and cheered and applauded excitedly from a safe distance. They were there so they could learn too.

Because we all knew, though no one ever said it out loud, that even if we won this war a hell of a lot of us probably wouldn't be coming back. And the next generation of Droods might have to step into our shoes a lot earlier than any of us had intended.

I was there, right in the middle of the action, training alongside everyone else. Running back and forth on the increasingly churned-up lawns, taking turns leading and being led in the various battle groups. I was far too used to being a lone wolf, and that was a luxury I could no longer afford. So I charged again and again, running madly till my lungs ached and black spots flickered in front of my eyes, growing long golden blades from my armoured hands and throwing myself into yet another savage, brutal mêlée.

I ached in every limb, and my heart pounded so hard I thought it might leap out of my chest. And this was only a rehearsal for the real thing.

Apparently Giles had known something very like living battle armour in his far future time, because he had all kinds of ideas on how to make our armour a weapon in itself. During the short breaks between his carefully choreographed campaigns, he lectured us on how limited the family had always been in its thinking, where the armour was concerned. It didn't have to be only a defence, a second skin to protect us and boost our strength and speed; James's trick with the blades showed the armour could be made to respond to our thoughts and needs. If a sword, then why not a battleaxe? If I could raise spikes on my knuckles, why not all over my body? The armour was the shape it was only because it had never occurred to us that it could be anything else.

If you already have a miracle, why try to improve on it?

It took an outsider like Giles to make us see the armour's true capabilities; that the possibilities were limited only by our lack of imagination. Once the idea took hold, there was no stopping us. It took a lot of concentration, but the strange matter of our armour moulded itself under the force of our various desires. Golden hands grew all kinds of weapons, and gleaming faces became scowling gargoyles, howling wolves, monsters and angels. Pliable body shapes twisted and transformed, taking on mystical shapes and legendary forms. A few even grew golden wings from their backs and flapped awkwardly into the air. We couldn't hold our new shapes for long, not yet; it took too much concentration. But who knew what might become possible, after long practice?

I watched the fierce shapes and impossible transformations strut before admiring audiences, and wasn't sure I entirely approved. Right now we needed an army with every weapon at its command. But what would become of us, after the war? When there was no more need for golden monsters and gleaming gladiators? Under normal conditions, all the family ever needed to keep the peace was a limited number of specially trained field agents, like I used to be. Would these golden soldiers be ready to retire to The Hall and oblivion?

And what if . . . what would happen if the armour itself started responding to unconscious impulses, as well as conscious commands? Might we become monsters from the id, ravening creatures driven by personal demons? Perhaps even trapped inside our own armour as it responded to deep unconscious needs and ignored our conscious, horrified pleas to stand down?

Nightmares for another day. Right now, my job was to make sure the world would see another day. First win the war, then worry about the peace. So back to battle I went, armour clashing against armour, all through the long hot day. And before my eyes the Drood family quickly became something else, something fiercer and finer and more concentrated in its purpose. Giles Deathstalker was cranking the family up to eleven.

And we loved it.

During another brief break, I sat exhausted on the grass drinking a wonderfully chilled Becks straight from the bottle. The Matriarch had come out to observe how the manoeuvres were going, and had very thoughtfully brought a picnic hamper with her. I got first crack at it because rank has its privileges. So I chewed on cold chicken legs, enjoyed my nice Becks, and ostentatiously ignored the cucumber sandwiches. Sometimes I think Grandmother takes the whole county aristocracy bit far too seriously.

She sat beside me, perched confidently on a shooting stick in her usual tweeds and pearls, watching everything with great interest. She made a point of consulting me at regular intervals, and agreeing with everything I said. This was for public consumption, of course, so that the family could see I had her full backing. After a while, Giles Deathstalker came over to join us. He'd been working himself harder than any of us but didn't seem to be sweating or even out of breath. He looked like he did this every day, and for all I knew maybe he did. He was a Warrior Prime, whatever the hell that was. Giles bowed courteously to the Matriarch and nodded cheerfully to me.

'Doing good, Eddie. Strong form and a fierce will to win. I'm impressed. So. Why don't you and I put on a bit of a show, demonstrate to your family what two experienced fighters can really do? Nothing too strenuous, just a mock duel. What do you say?'

I sighed inwardly, while carefully keeping my face calm and composed. It seemed every time I brought someone new in, they had to fight me to see if I was fit to lead them. To test themselves against me; preferably in full view of everyone else. Everyone always wants to know if the legendary gunslinger really is as fast as his legend. And I was getting pretty damned tired of it. If Molly had been there, she would have snorted and said, '*Men!* Why don't you both just get them out and measure them?' in a loud and carrying voice.

But Molly wasn't there. She was off wandering the grounds again, communing with her inner self. Whoever or whatever that might be these days.

'Of course,' Giles said easily, 'if you're too tired, Eddie, or don't feel up to it, I'd quite understand. And so would everyone else.'

'That's quite enough of that,' the Matriarch said briskly. She rose smartly from her shooting stick, leaving it standing there looking a little lost and abandoned. She advanced on the startled Giles, fixing him with her cold stare. 'I don't know how they run things in your time, Giles Deathstalker, but we don't choose our leaders through right of challenge. We're all warriors here. You have to be more than a fighter to lead the Droods. But if you're really so desperate for a duel, I'll oblige you.'

'You?' said Giles, not even bothering to hide his surprise. And then he smiled condescendingly at her.

'Oh, no,' I said quietly. 'Don't smile.'

'I'm sure you were quite the warrior woman, in your day,' said Giles, and Martha cut him off right there.

'I am the Drood Matriarch,' she said, every word chipped out of ice. 'And any Drood is a match for some jumped-up future mercenary.'

Giles raised one hand in a conciliatory gesture. Martha grabbed his arm, spun him round into an armlock, and then slammed him face first down on to the grass. He hit hard enough to force a groan out of him. And then she kicked him so hard in the ribs that people twenty feet away winced. Giles scrambled away from her and rose quickly to his feet. He wasn't smiling any more. He started to say something, and then broke off as Martha advanced purposefully. He took up a standard defensive pose, and a hell of a lot of good it did him. Martha beat the crap out of him, parrying his increasingly desperate blows with casual skill, threw him this way and that and made the whole thing look easy. All of it without even having to armour up.

Giles really should have known better. You don't get to be Matriarch of the Droods just by inheriting it. Martha had taught unarmed combat for thirty years, and only gave up because she finally found someone better at it than she was.

Giles wasn't stupid. Once it became clear he couldn't hope to beat her, or even hold his own, he surrendered. Martha immediately stepped back and allowed him to rise painfully to his feet.

'I take your point, Matriarch,' said Giles, wiping blood from his mouth with the back of his hand. 'I'm impressed.'

'You should be,' Martha said coldly. 'I do hope we don't have to do this again. And Giles, if you were entertaining any ambitions, you could never hope to lead us. You're not family.'

She turned her back on him, dismissing him, and he was smart enough to accept it. He yelled at everyone watching to get back to their training, and they did. Martha retrieved her shooting stick and looked at me consideringly.

'I defeated three sisters to claim my position as Matriarch. Don't you ever forget that, Eddie.'

'Of course, Grandmother,' I said, and she strode off back to The Hall. I watched her go, and when I was sure she was out of earshot I said, 'There are more ways of fighting and winning than throwing people around, Grandmother.'

'I heard that!' she said, not looking back.
'Yes, Grandmother.'

The organised mayhem resumed, with Giles barking his orders perhaps a little more loudly than before, but I felt I'd earned myself a rest. I raided the abandoned picnic hamper for some caviar and toast, and wandered off to find some peace and quiet. I ended up in the old Chapel again. Quiet and peaceful, and no sign of the ghost Jacob. I was beginning to worry about that. He was up to something. I sat down in his cracked leather chair and fished the Merlin Glass out of my pocket. Using the thing to see what was going on around me, and find out things I wasn't supposed to know, was becoming addictive. But they were always things I needed to know, for the good of the family, so . . . I commanded the Glass to show me the Present, and reveal what Molly was doing. I wanted to trust her, to believe in her instincts and self-control, but she wasn't simply Molly any more. There was something else inside her now, something alive – and enemy. I had to be sure of her. For all our sakes.

Even in the few hours since yesterday, I'd noticed physical and mental changes in Molly, almost despite myself. She looked taller, stronger, her movements somehow stranger, though that could have been my imagination. But there was no denying she held herself differently, and now and then I caught her standing unnaturally still, blank-faced, as though listening to some inner voice. She said she was getting glimpses of the Loathly Ones mass mind, on the edge of her thoughts. It was still mostly a gabble, she said, but she was starting to understand parts of it. She began identifying specific locations for Loathly One Nests, including some we'd never suspected before. I passed these new coordinates on to the War Room, and they quickly confirmed them and told me to press Molly for more. (I told them she was finding these Nests through her magics, and with her reputation they had no trouble believing it.) And every time Molly found a new Nest she would look at me almost challengingly, as though to say, *See? I'm still me. Still Molly. Still on your side.* And what could I do but nod and smile and congratulate her; even as it proved that her mind was changing, to understand more and more of the alien gabble of the mass mind.

She was having serious mood swings too, but I didn't know if I could blame that on the infection.

The Merlin Glass showed her to me, standing in a small copse of trees looking out at the old abandoned waterwheel on the far side of the lake. Her face was drawn and thoughtful, her dark eyes far away, ignoring the swans that circled hopefully before her on the calm waters of the lake, hoping for breadcrumbs. I gazed at her for a long time. She still looked like Molly. My Molly. But I had to wonder how long that would last. How long before the inner Molly changed so much that she couldn't pass for the real thing any more. I felt so helpless. Sick with it. Here I was, leader of the most powerful family in the world, and there wasn't a single damned thing I could do to save the woman I loved. Except lead her into battle and hope she died honourably.

So I wouldn't have to kill her myself, when she turned. Could I do that? I thought so. It was what she wanted, what she'd asked me to do. And besides, I'd done worse, in my time, for the family.

As I watched, Harry Drood and Roger Morningstar wandered along the bank of the lake to join her. Harry was smiling cheerfully, as though he was out for a stroll and had just happened to bump into Molly. Roger smiled meaninglessly, his eyes dark and watchful as always. The grass scorched and blackened where he put his feet, and the swans headed hurriedly away. A bird flying overhead fell suddenly dead out of the air, and landed at his feet. Roger picked it up and bit into it thoughtfully, as though it was a snack. Blood ran down his chin. Harry looked at him reproachfully and Roger immediately threw the dead bird aside. Molly had to know they were there, but she ignored them until they were almost upon her. And then she stopped them both in their tracks with a single hard look.

Their voices came clearly to me, from far away.

It was obvious from the way she was looking at them that she was wondering if they knew about her. After all, Roger had more than human senses, and Harry had years of experience as a field agent. But she quickly decided they didn't, and nodded briefly to Harry, ignoring Roger.

'Molly,' said Harry, smiling easily. 'You're looking good.'

'What do you want, Harry?'

'What I always want,' said Harry, still smiling, absently adjusting his wire-framed glasses. 'I want what's best for the family. Which these days means my being in charge of things, and not Eddie. The family needs my calm, considered decisions; not Eddie's mad impulsiveness. He'll screw it up, get us all killed. You must know that, Molly; you know him better than any of us. Can you really trust him to do the right thing, under pressure? And if we go down . . . who's going to be left to save the world?'

'What do you want, Harry?' Molly said again.

'You are our only means of getting to Eddie,' said Roger. 'If we could win you over to our cause, that is, Harry's reclaiming of the family leadership, we feel there's a very good chance Eddie would fall apart without you.'

Molly smiled suddenly. 'You really don't know Eddie at all. He's always been stronger than people think. He's had to be. He doesn't rely on me. He doesn't need me. And he'll carry on just fine when I'm gone.'

Harry and Roger glanced quickly at each other. 'Are you planning on leaving us, Molly?' said Harry.

'Don't say you've finally had enough of Eddie's goody-goody ways,' said Roger. Well, it's about time. You and I were close once, but I never did understand what you saw in him.'

'You and I were never that close,' said Molly.

'How can you say that?' said Roger, pouting playfully. 'It hit me ever so badly when you walked out on me. Took me weeks to get over you.'

'I walked out on you because you tried to sacrifice my soul to Hell!'

'Details, details. We all have our little family obligations.'

Molly sniffed. 'So, you're with Harry now. Bit of a surprise; you were always such a major tit man. Am I to take it you're gay?'

Roger shrugged. 'I'm half demon. I don't accept any human limitations, least of all in my sexuality. I want to try everything . . . and mostly I do.'

Molly looked at Harry. 'And you're not in the least jealous of what Roger and I used to have?'

'The only thing you ever had in common was a bed,' said Harry. 'Roger and I are in love.'

'Love?' Molly said incredulously. 'He's a hellspawn! A thing of the Pit, dedicated to dragging all Humanity down into eternal damnation!'

'Criticism?' said Roger. 'From the infamous Molly Metcalf? The woman who once laid down with demons in the Courts of Hell to buy power she couldn't acquire any other way? Does Eddie know about that? Have you told him *all* the things you used to do, O wild and wicked witch of the woods? Do you think he'd feel the same way about you if he did know?'

Molly met his gaze squarely, chin slightly lifted. 'I was a different person then. I had sworn vendetta against the Droods for the murder of my parents. I needed all the power I could get to take them on. But that was then, and this is now, time changes all things . . . pick whichever cliché you prefer. I'm not the person I used to be.'

'You think Eddie will care about that?' said Roger. 'I think you'll find he's still very traditional, very old-fashioned, about certain things.'

'He doesn't have to know what we know about you,' said Harry. 'We don't have to tell him. Not if you could find it in your heart to help us a little.'

'In return for your guaranteed silence?' said Molly.

'Exactly,' said Roger. 'Speak on our behalf. Support our position. Help persuade Eddie that it is in everyone's best interests for him to step down and allow Harry to replace him as family leader. No big speeches, no big deal. Just a word in his ear, at the right moments.'

And then he broke off because Molly was smiling at him, and it really wasn't a very nice smile. Molly took a step forward, and Roger fell back a pace. Harry moved quickly to put himself between the two of them.

'Once,' said Molly, 'It might have mattered to me, what you might say to Eddie. But things have changed. Tell him anything. I don't care, and I don't believe he will, either. Neither of us are concerned with the past any more; only the future. But even so, Harry, Roger: I'd be very careful about doing anything that Eddie might perceive as a threat to me. He's become very protective of me, the sweetie. And you really don't want him to kick your arse in front of everyone again, do you, Harry?'

'We're going to war!' said Harry. 'The family needs me as leader!'

'No,' said Molly. 'You had your chance, and you blew it. You let things get this bad. If I were Eddie, I'd kill you for what you've done to the family. And you know what? I might kill you both anyway. On general principles. I could use something to cheer me up.'

She smiled brightly at Harry and Roger, and then turned and walked away. They watched her go.

'Women,' said Roger, and Harry nodded.

I closed down the lakeside scene, but I wasn't finished with the Merlin Glass. Part of me wanted to go and find Molly, and hold her to me, and tell her . . . nothing mattered. Nothing mattered to me, except her. But I had responsibilities to the family, and there were things I needed to know. So I told the Glass to show me where Mr Stab was, and what he was doing. I should have remembered that not only do eavesdroppers rarely hear good of themselves, they also rarely hear anything good about anyone else.

To my surprise, the Merlin Glass showed me Mr Stab sitting at his ease among the towering book stacks of the Old Library, while the under-Librarian Rafe served him tea. Mr Stab had changed out of the casual suit he'd been wearing the last time I saw him. Presumably because it was soaked with Penny's blood. Instead, he was back in the formal dress of his original Victorian times. He sat quietly and calmly as Rafe added milk but no sugar, and then handed him the delicate china cup. Mr Stab blew gingerly on the tea to cool it, but his eyes never left Rafe's face as the young Librarian sat down opposite him.

'You're not drinking your tea, Rafe,' said Mr Stab.

'I'll let it cool a bit first. You go right ahead.'

Mr Stab looked at Rafe almost sadly, and then took a long drink from his cup. He made a slight moue of civilised distaste, and put the cup down on a bookshelf beside him.

'If you're going to work with poison, Rafe, you need to make the tea a lot stronger, to disguise the taste. And you put enough strychnine in that cup to see off a dozen normal men. But I haven't been that easy to kill for a long time now. Poison is as mother's milk to such as I. Why, Rafe? Is it Penny? Was she a friend of yours? Or perhaps something more?'

Rafe stood up abruptly, throwing his cup aside. He stood towering over Mr Stab for a long moment, his hands clenched into fists at his sides. Mr Stab rose easily to his feet to face him. Rafe couldn't get the words out at first, he was breathing so hard. His face was twisted with hatred and loathing.

'We were never close,' Rafe said hoarsely. 'But we might have been. She never knew I cared about her. And now, thanks to you, she never will. Damn your soul to Hell.'

'Already done,' said Mr Stab.

Rafe attacked him, throwing himself at the calm and unmoving immortal. He beat at Mr Stab with his fists, while hot tears ran down his face, and Mr Stab just stood there and took it. Rafe armoured up, and his golden fists hammered at Mr Stab's impassive face. The armoured strength behind the blows must have been hideous, but Mr Stab took no obvious damage from them. And if he felt any pain, he didn't show it. In the end, Rafe stood before Mr Stab with his arms hanging heavily; he armoured down, his face wet with sweat and tears. Mr Stab looked at him.

'Cry, boy,' he said. 'It's all right. I would too, if I could.'

William Drood came along then, to see what the noise was about, and took in the scene in a moment. He looked fiercely at Mr Stab, who immediately stepped back, and William came forward and took Rafe away. Mr Stab stood very still, not even looking around him, until William returned on his own. I watched Mr Stab's face the whole time. It never changed once. I had no idea what he was thinking, or feeling. If he felt anything. There were times when I wished I could be like that, and not have to feel the things that hurt me. William gestured for Mr Stab to sit down, and he did so. William sat opposite him. He looked sadly at the discarded tea things.

'Don't drink the tea,' Mr Stab said.

'So I gather,' William said drily. 'Sorry about that. He's young. They take things so personally at that age. Still, nothing you haven't encountered and deserved before, I expect. What do you want here?'

'Molly Metcalf said I might find answers here,' said Mr Stab. They might have been discussing the weather. 'Old knowledge, unavailable anywhere else. Perhaps even the means to a cure for my condition. Or at least to ameliorate certain aspects of it.'

William considered him thoughtfully. 'You chose to make yourself what you are. Have you now come to regret it?'

'You know this Library better than anyone,' said Mr Stab. 'Can you help me?'

'Why should I?' William said bluntly. 'After all you've done, why shouldn't I delight in the prospect of your inevitable descent into Hell?'

'To save future lives?' Mr Stab said calmly. 'So that there might be no more Pennys, and no more Rafes.'

'I suppose there might be something here,' William said. 'We have books on every subject under several suns, from the unusual to the improbable, the unlikely to the downright impossible. I'm pretty sure you're in there somewhere. It depends on exactly what it is you want me to find.'

'I made myself what I am,' said Mr Stab. 'Everything I am and everything I have ever done is my responsibility. But for the first time . . . I wish to change things.'

'That would depend on who or what you made your original deal with,' William said carefully. 'Some deals can be . . . renegotiated. Do you wish to become human again?'

'I've always been human,' said Mr Stab. 'That's the problem. I want something else. I want to find a way to bring back my victims. All of them. To raise from the dead the women I have slaughtered down the many years, and give them life again. Including those five poor women who made it possible, back in that unseasonably hot autumn of 1888.'

'I'm sorry,' said William. 'But it can't be done.'

Mr Stab surged forward impossibly quickly, a long gleaming blade suddenly in his hand. Before William could even react, the razor-sharp edge was pressed against his throat, just above his Adam's apple. Mr Stab stared coldly into William's face, his cold breath beating on William's wide open eyes. The blade pressed against the skin of his throat, and a single slow trickle of blood ran down his neck as the skin parted a little under the sharp edge. William sat very still.

'That is not the answer I wanted to hear,' said Mr Stab.

'We all have things in our life that we would wish undone,' William said carefully. He clearly wanted very much to swallow, but didn't dare. 'But sins can never be undone. Only pardoned.'

'It's not enough,' said Mr Stab.

'I know,' said William. He kept looking into Mr Stab's unwavering gaze, unnerving as that was, because it was better than looking down at the blade at his throat. 'But there's nothing here in this Library, no book or knowledge, that will let you bring the dead back to life. Only one man could ever do that, and I think we can definitely agree that you're not him. I could help you raise the spirits of those poor unfortunate women, so you could commune with them, or raise up their bodies as zombies; but that isn't what you want. What you need.'

Mr Stab thought about that for a long moment, while William scarcely breathed, and then he stepped back abruptly and made his long blade disappear again. William put a hesitant hand to his throat, and breathed more easily as he saw only a few drops of blood on his fingertips.

'What else is there?' said Mr Stab. He wasn't looking anywhere in particular, and William clearly wondered if Mr Stab was still talking to him.

'Else?' said William.

'I can't undo what I did, can't stop being who I am. Can't even stop or escape through death. What does that leave?'

'There's always atonement,' said William. 'Perform enough good deeds to balance out your sins.'

Mr Stab considered that. 'Would killing in a good cause count?'

'I would say so, yes.'

Mr Stab smiled for the first time. 'Good thing there's a war on, then.'

He turned and walked away. William watched him go, and then looked again at the blood on his fingertips.

Some time later, I stood in the rose-coloured glow of the Sanctity with the Matriarch at my side, waiting for the others I had summoned to arrive. I didn't know whether it was me, or the times, but Strange's ruddy glow no longer calmed or comforted as it once had. Strange himself was very quiet. Perhaps he didn't approve of the things I was having the family do, with the armour and power he so selflessly provided. I couldn't allow myself to care. I had a war to win. I'd care later, if I was still alive.

Or, at least, I hoped I would.

'It's never easy,' Martha said suddenly, her harsh, cold voice echoing in the great empty chamber. 'Never easy, sending agents out into the field, possibly or even quite probably to their deaths. We do it because it's necessary, for the good of the family and the world. But it never gets any easier.'

'Thanks for the thought,' I said. 'But knowing that doesn't help.'

'It will,' said Martha. 'In time. I'm glad you came home, Edwin. Who could have known we'd have so much in common?'

'Eddie,' Strange said abruptly. 'Sorry to intrude, but your meeting will have to wait. I've just been informed by the security people at the holding cells that Sebastian has been murdered.'

'What?' said the Matriarch. 'That's impossible! Not under our security!'

'What happened?' I said, cutting across the Matriarch. 'Did he try to escape?'

'No,' said Strange. 'He was found dead in his cell.'

'How could this have happened?' said the Matriarch. She sounded honestly outraged. 'Our security is the best in the world. It has to be.'

'Details are still coming through,' said Strange. He sounded subdued, almost distant. Not his usual exuberant self. I suppose a constant supply of bad news will do that. And I couldn't help thinking that our material world must have been such a disappointment to him. I made myself concentrate on what Strange was saying. 'At first the guards thought it might be suicide. Until they got inside the isolation tank, and discovered the extent of his wounds, which are . . . extensive. It seems he's been cut open, from throat to crotch. But there's no record of anyone entering the tank. No sign that anyone entered or left. The security cameras show nothing. Which I gather is supposed to be impossible.'

'Keep us updated on the investigation,' I said after a moment. 'And double the number of guards at the doors of the holding tanks.'

'That's it?' said Martha. 'Edwin, we need to go down there and see this for ourselves!'

'No, we don't,' I said. 'We'd be in the way. Let security get on with their job. They're very good at it.'

'But—'

'They already know how impossible it is. They don't need us looking over their shoulders. We have to concentrate on what's really important, not let ourselves be distracted. That could be why Sebastian was killed now – to distract us on the eve of launching our attack. After all, why kill Sebastian? What could he possibly have told us?'

'The identity of the long-term traitor in the family,' said Martha. 'Only one of us could have evaded our security. Someone who knew it, inside and out. But you're right, Edwin. We can't let ourselves be distracted from what really matters.'

One of us. Yes. I wanted it to be one of us, bad as that was. Because it could have been Molly. I didn't want to think that, but I couldn't stop myself. Molly could have got to Sebastian, using her magics. She wanted him dead because of what he did to her. Or could the thing inside her have influenced her thoughts, and had her kill him for the Loathly Ones' own purposes?

'Strange,' I said. 'Where's Molly, right now?'

'I'm afraid I've no idea, Eddie,' said Strange, after a pause. 'I don't seem able to locate her anywhere. Which is odd.'

'It doesn't matter,' I said. 'It's not important. I'll talk to her later.'

The meeting finally got under way as the various necessary people arrived. Giles Deathstalker was first, of course, with a soldier's sense of punctuality. He looked calm and relaxed and incredibly dangerous, as always. He bowed to me and to the Matriarch, and it would have been hard to say which was the more respectful nod. I was beginning to think that maybe I should have duelled with him after all. Soldiers only respect strength. But if I'd lost . . .

Next to arrive were Harry and Roger, both smiling easily and innocently, as though they hadn't just been trying to persuade my Molly to betray me. The Matriarch glared daggers at them both, but restricted her acid tongue for the good of the family. I could think of lots of things I wanted to say, but I restricted myself to a polite nod. I needed Harry and Roger. The family needed them.

Mr Stab strolled in, accompanied by the Sarjeant-At-Arms, and it felt like the temperature in the Sanctity dropped several degrees. We all looked at him, but none of us had anything to say. Mr Stab smiled coolly back at us, as though he was used to awkward situations like this. He had volunteered for the mission I was putting together as soon as I explained it to him, and I was glad to have him on board. As long as the Sarjeant-At-Arms was there to keep an eye on him.

The next to arrive was another volunteer, the Blue Fairy. Who might have agreed in order to make up for his plan to steal a torc, but still didn't have the grace to look in any way guilty. He was dressed in his best, all flashing colours and elaborate cuts, and he had a smile for everyone. It was hard to dislike the man; but worth the effort.

The Armourer wandered in and stood off to one side, his hands thrust deep into the pockets of his charred and stained lab coat, fidgeting and avoiding eye contact with anyone. He knew the mission I planned was dependent on the new weapon he'd devised, and clearly resented spending time here explaining it to the meeting when he could have been working to perfect it. Ever since he retired from fieldwork, Uncle Jack had not so much lost his people skills as thrown them away.

And the last to arrive, as always, was Callan Drood. For him, showing up on time was something other people did. He wore a long leather duster and a floppy wide-brimmed hat, and looked like he'd come straight from a cattle roundup. Callan always liked to give the impression that you'd dragged him away from something far more important that he couldn't wait to get back to.

'Right,' I said loudly, once they were assembled. 'This is it. The big attack, the big push, to stop the Loathly Ones in their tracks and prevent them from bringing the Invaders through into our reality. With Molly's help, Intelligence has finally pinpointed the location of every Nest throughout the world. We have to hit them all, and destroy them and their towers. And we have to get this right first time, people; because the odds are we won't get a second chance. You will be leading carefully selected strike forces of our best fighters against the biggest and most important ghoulvilles – those whose towers Intelligence believes are closest to completion. Once they're wiped out, we will proceed from ghoulville to ghoulville, Nest to Nest, wiping them out in order of importance. Until they're gone. Not one Nest, not one tower, not one drone can be allowed to survive. And we have to do this fast, people. Once we begin, the news will flash from Nest to Nest, transmitted through the Loathly Ones' mass mind, and after that they'll be expecting us. Uncle Jack, tell the nice people about the nasty new thing you've developed for them to play with.'

The Armourer stepped forward, scowling. He'd done everything he could to try and persuade me to let him lead one of the strike forces, but despite his field agent experience he was too valuable to put at risk. He didn't take kindly to me pointing this out, and had used language quite unbefitting a man of his age and position.

'I have developed a new kind of bomb,' he said flatly. 'A whole new kind, that basically turns a tower's other-dimensional energies against itself. The result is a massive explosion that destroys the tower completely, and every living thing within a hundred-mile radius. So make damn sure you're outside the ghoulville before it detonates. All you have to do is set the bomb at the base of the tower, set the timer, and run like hell. Be sure to guard every way in and out of the ghoulville; we can't let any drones escape. I'm sorry, Eddie. I know you were hoping I could come up with some way of curing the infected, but there's nothing I can do. Nothing anyone could do. Once someone is infected, they're lost to us. To Humanity. We know the drones are the innocent victims in this, but we have to concentrate our efforts on saving those we can: the rest of the world.'

I didn't say anything. I didn't want to believe what he was saying. Didn't want to believe my Molly was hopelessly lost. But for now I nodded, and went along. What else could I do?

'Your job is to cut a path through the drones to the tower, and activate the bomb,' I said to the others. 'Don't get distracted. Don't waste time killing drones when you should be getting to the tower. This about destroying whole Nests, not individual drones.'

'No need to rub it in,' said Harry. 'We're not stupid. I notice you aren't down to lead one of these strike forces, Eddie. Why is that?'

'Because he's needed here,' the Matriarch said flatly. 'As am I. Someone has to take the overview. Something, I am told, you were always remarkably bad at.'

'Of course,' murmured Harry. 'I knew it would be something like that.'

Then we looked round sharply as Subway Sue burst into the

Sanctity. It had been so long since I'd last seen her I'd actually forgotten about her. She was even more of a mess than usual, which took some doing. Her long, flappy coat was torn and tattered and covered with assorted filth, and her hair was a mess of greasy strings. But her mouth was firm, and her eyes burned fiercely. She marched up to me and planted herself in front of me.

'I've been searching for something useful to contribute,' she said, in her rough, scratchy voice. 'Something to justify Molly's faith in me, and my presence here. And I think I've found it. I know more about hidden ways than anyone else – the secret paths, dimensional short-cuts and forbidden doors. In my various lives as luck vampire, subterranean and down and out, I've had occasion to use most of them more than once. But I've found you something new; or at least something so old and disused it's new again.

'It's taken me some time, travelling through the darker regions, talking with old friends and enemies and allies, but I've found a whole new secret way for you to use. An approach your enemy will never suspect because no one's used it in ages. Mostly because it's too dangerous. But you're Droods; you laugh at danger, right? You can use this way to get anywhere in the world from anywhere in the world, arriving entirely undetected. It's the underside of the Rainbow Run. The Damnation Way.'

She finally stopped for breath, and looked at me expectantly.

'The name doesn't exactly fill me full of confidence,' I said carefully. 'Might there be a reason why no one's used it for so long? Something . . . specific that makes it so very dangerous?'

'No one knows for sure,' said Subway Sue, doing her best not to sound defensive. 'People just stopped coming out the other end when they used it. The best bet seems to be that Something lives there now, and eats travellers. Something really bad.'

'"Who's that trot-trotting across my bridge?" said the troll,' murmured Harry.

Sue glared at him. 'I will slap you in a minute, and it will hurt.'

'Well, thank you for your time and efforts on our behalf, Sue,' I said. 'But we already have our own instantaneous, undetectable means of transporting ourselves into the ghoulvilles. But should any problems arise, I'm sure we'll feel better knowing we have your Damnation Way to fall back on.'

I was being kind, and everyone there knew it. Including Subway Sue. She nodded stiffly, turned her back on us and stalked out of the Sanctity. I looked at the others.

'End of briefing. You know everything you need to know. Stop off at the Armoury and pick up your bombs, and then get to know the people in your various strike forces before reporting to the War Room for the off.'

'I have a few questions,' said Harry.

'Yes,' I said. 'I thought you might have. What is it, Harry?'

'Well, to start with, where is the infamous Molly Metcalf? Shouldn't a witch of her undoubted talents be one of the lucky people leading a strike force?'

'Oh, she's around,' I said. 'Making herself useful.'

Molly had wanted to go into the Nests and work her infamous mayhem, but I had to say no. I couldn't risk her infected nature suddenly surfacing so close to a tower. She said she understood. I hadn't seen her since.

'And this remarkable new means of transport,' said Harry. 'Have you some new miracle device, hidden in your pocket?'

I had to grin. 'Funny you should say that, Harry . . .'

Molly was waiting for us in the great stone cavern of the War Room when the Matriarch and I arrived some time later. She smiled at us, but not with all her attention, as though she was thinking of something else. I deliberately looked away. The War Room was pretty much deserted, by normal standards; I hardly recognised the place. Most of the work stations and display screens had been shut down, so the War Room could operate on a skeleton crew. It was strange to see the world maps without their usual glowing coloured lights, but we no longer cared about what was going on in the rest of the world.

The Matriarch went straight to her operations table and was immediately surrounded by a dozen runners bearing the latest reports and Intelligence updates. I wandered round the room, checking out the remaining communications staff. Most of them had joined the thousands of armoured figures waiting more or less patiently in the corridors outside, preparing themselves for the battles to come. Normally every agent operating out in the field could count on having hundreds of people at The Hall to back them up, ready to provide information, advice or support; but we couldn't afford that now. Everyone had to fight. This was to be slash and burn, cold killing, butcher's work.

I circled the War Room and ended up back beside Molly. She looked taut, under strain, like a piece of wire stretched so thin it might break at any moment. I wanted to put my arm around her, but I knew she wouldn't want that. Molly always had to appear hard and confident, in public. She would have hated even the thought that anyone might see her as weak. So I stood as close to her as I could, and kept my voice calm and easy, as though we did this whole battle-for-the-fate-of-Humanity bit every day.

'So,' I said. 'Looks like it's kicking off at last. Marching into Hell for a Heavenly cause, and all that. Where have you been?'

'In the grounds,' she said. 'It's very peaceful out there.'

She didn't say anything about Harry and Roger, and I didn't feel like pressing her. But it did make me wonder if she might be keeping other secrets from me too. She could have killed Sebastian, for all kinds of reasons. How could I protect her, if I didn't know what to protect her from?

'Listen,' she said abruptly, still not actually looking at me. 'Don't get yourself killed, all right?'

'I'm not going out with the strike forces,' I said. 'I'll be running things from here. Safe and sound, far from any harm.'

'I know you, Eddie. The first time anything goes wrong, you'll be off and running to play the hero one more time. You can't help yourself. It's who you are. So watch yourself out there. Watch your back. There are traitors everywhere, these days. And . . . I don't know what I'd do with myself, if I didn't have you any more.'

'It's going to be all right,' I said. It didn't sound convincing even as I said it, but I didn't know what else to say. I took her hand in mine and squeezed it. She squeezed back, still not looking at me.

We stood together, watching the main display screens as they showed constantly shifting views of the golden army continuing to assemble in the corridors outside, standing in their ranks for as far as the eye could see. There was surprisingly little chatter; everyone seemed taken up with their own thoughts. The old and the young stood watching in the background, no doubt silently wondering if they'd ever see their loved ones again. I never got to see my parents off, on their last, fatal mission. Teacher wouldn't let me out of class. By the time I managed to sneak out, it was too late; they'd already gone. I never saw them again.

It's mattered to me more and more of late: that I never said goodbye.

Anything, for the family. Damn the family. And damn the world that makes us necessary.

The various strike force leaders turned up, having checked their people; the stress and the strain making them act like exaggerated cartoons of themselves. Giles Deathstalker strode in like the soldier he was, and crashed to attention before the Matriarch's desk. She acknowledged him with a flick of an eyebrow, and went back to work. Harry and Roger sauntered in, ostentatiously hand in hand. The Matriarch wouldn't even look in their direction. I don't know quite when Mr Stab arrived. I looked up and there he was, a Victorian anachronism amidst so much twenty-first-century technology. The Sarjeant-At-Arms came rushing in a few moments later, clearly annoyed at Mr Stab having slipped his leash. He glared hard at his elusive responsibility, and moved forward to stand beside him. Mr Stab nodded politely.

The Armourer bustled in, carrying a big bag full of useful bits and pieces, with half a dozen lab techs scurrying after him like eager puppies. And Callan Drood arrived late, of course, complaining bitterly over something inappropriate with the Blue Fairy, who pretended politely to be listening.

And that was that. These people would lead the four main strike forces, dealing with the most dangerous situations and the most nearly completed towers. The other strike forces were being led by our most experienced field agents. I should have been leading one of the forces. Preferably with Molly at my side. But I had taken on the duties of leadership when I took command of the family, and that included standing by and watching helplessly as others went off to fight and die at my command. Martha said it never got any easier.

Which made it a lot simpler to understand how she'd ended up the way she was.

Harry strolled over to join Molly and me, Roger close at his side. Harry pointedly ignored Molly to smile at me.

'Well now, Eddie,' he said, making a brave stab at casual, 'when are you going to whip your latest miracle out of your hip pocket and amaze us? How are we going to burst into these Nests and ghoulvilles without being detected? I know you love to keep your brilliant save-the-day ideas to the very last moment, but we are getting terribly close to the off.'

I grinned, took the Merlin Glass out of my pocket, and shook it up to full size. It stood on end in the middle of the War Room, like a door to absolutely everywhere. Which, technically speaking, it was. Everyone crowded together before the Glass as I gave a brief run-down on its capabilities, and we stared dubiously at the frowning faces of our reflections. We didn't look much like the people who were going to save the world.

'The Merlin Glass sees the Present,' I said. 'Anywhere and every-where. And it can function as a gateway to anywhere it sees. That is going to be our way in, people. We tell the Glass to tune in on a Nest, it shows us the interior of the ghoulville, and then we, or rather you, go through the Glass with your strike force and kick the shit out of the Loathly Ones. What could be simpler?'

The Armourer and his lab crew scurried around the base of the Merlin Glass, connecting it up with a whole mess of rainbow colour-coded cables to the communication desks and the display screens, so we could follow what was going on in more than one Nest at once. Molly hovered over them, beefing up the connections with an overlay of magical supports. Harry looked at me abruptly.

'This is how you knew about Mr Stab and Penny before anyone else. You were watching. You pervy little Peeping Tom, you. Who else have you been secretly observing, all this time?'

'I lead the family,' I said calmly. 'I watch everyone.'

Harry glanced at Mr Stab, standing off to one side. 'We're going to have to do something about him, Eddie.'

'When you've worked out what, and how, let me know,' I said. 'For now, we need him.'

'We won't always need him,' said Harry.

'No,' I said. 'We won't.'

'It's time,' said the Matriarch, and we turned. She stood tall and commanding before us, every inch the grey-haired warrior queen. She fixed her cold gaze on me. 'The troops are assembled and ready to begin. All preparations have been made. Give the word, Edwin.'

'Yes,' I said. I turned to the Merlin Glass. 'Show me the Present,' I said. 'Show me the interior of the ghoulville with the most nearly completed tower.'

Our reflections disappeared from the mirror in a moment, replaced by swirling patterns of energy that hurt the eye to look at, and then the Merlin Glass punched through the dimensional barrier separating the Loathly Ones' Nest from the rest of the world, and there the infected town was, clearly visible through the Glass. I'd never seen one before, only heard descriptions and read reports. It wasn't enough to prepare you for the real thing. For what had once been a human town, a human place, but wasn't any more.

The light in the ghoulville was painfully bright, fierce, almost intolerable to human eyes. It didn't seem to bother any of the drones as they scurried and scuttled through the narrow streets. They didn't talk to each other, or even look at each other. They didn't need to. All their thoughts originated in the Nest hive mind, the mass mind. They didn't look human any more, didn't move in human ways. Either because they didn't need to pretend, away from outside eyes, or because they'd forgotten how to. Even the buildings of the ghoulville seemed alien, infected. They slumped at odd angles, the wood and stone and brick rotten, diseased, crawling with its own purulent life. Strange lights blazed in the windows, unhealthy lights, and alien silhouettes did awful alien things.

'The gravity fluctuates too,' said Callan, standing beside me. For the first time he sounded subdued, almost unnerved. 'Up and down, left and right, can snap back and forth without any warning. Directions mean nothing. Streets writhe and twist with a life of their own, and suddenly turn around and dump you back where you started. Doesn't affect the drones. Probably because they don't think like us any more. The air is barely breathable, even when filtered through the golden mask, and it stinks of blood and offal and decay. The drones here are dead or dying, burnt by the energies within them. When I finally die and go to Hell for all the terrible things I've done for this family, at least it'll look familiar.'

'You haven't been taking your medication again, have you, Callan?' said the Blue Fairy. 'Have some of mine, dear. Peps you up nicely.'

'There's nothing wrong with me!' Callan said angrily. 'It's the ghoulvilles that are wrong! And you have to be prepared for them; for everything they can throw at you. Or you'll never get to the bloody towers.'

'The armour will help,' the Armourer said gruffly, having finished his work with the Merlin Glass. 'Trust in the armour, and your training, and you'll do fine. Nerves are normal before a mission. When I was a field agent, I used to puke my guts up every time I had to go over the Berlin Wall into East Germany. I swear I once saw one of my kidneys floating in the toilet bowl.'

'Thank you, Uncle Jack,' I said.

'Intestine, I thought, that can't really be intestine, can it?'

'Thank you, Uncle Jack!'

He sniffed, and looked the Merlin Glass over with professional approval. 'Whatever else you might say about Merlin Satanspawn, and whole books have been written on the subject, he did do good work.'

'The drones can't see or hear us, can they?' said Mr Stab. 'They have no idea we're watching?'

'None at all,' the Armourer said cheerfully. 'I have given you the perfect element of surprise. Don't waste it.'

Giles Deathstalker drew his great sword, and almost unconsciously everyone fell back a little to give him more room.

'It's time,' he said. 'Let's do it.'

'Not exactly El Cid, is he?' said the Blue Fairy. 'Whatever happened to inspirational speeches? I very definitely feel I could do with a little inspiring right now.'

Giles glared at him. 'Don't screw this up or I'll have you flayed.'

'He's a Drood,' said the Blue Fairy.

I commanded the Merlin Glass to open a gateway into the four main Nests; and one by one the display screens flared into life, showing views inside the ghoulvilles. The Armourer's connections were working. I looked round once, silently saying goodbye and

Godspeed, and then Giles walked straight into the Merlin Glass and through into the ghoulville beyond. Two hundred golden figures followed him, filing quickly through the War Room, and then Harry and Roger went, followed by their strike force, and so on and so on. It didn't take nearly as long as I thought, to send the leaders and their strike forces through, though my voice went harsh yelling commands to the Merlin Glass to lock on to new locations. The stamp and clatter of armoured feet was deafening in the War Room, and I had to shout above it to be heard. All the display screens were up and running now, showing strike force after strike force slamming into unsuspecting drones. And then the last Drood went through; and there was nothing more to be done, except watch.

The various attacks on the Nests happened simultaneously, spread over the many display screens. You couldn't watch them all if you tried. Too much was going on. But this is how it happened, battle by battle, backed up by survivors' tales.

The first thing the Armourer did was to help Molly seal off the Merlin Glass, so that Droods could still pass through but no drones could get out. We couldn't allow any of the Loathly Ones to escape. They all had to die. Even though what happened to the drones wasn't their fault. They didn't ask to be infected. No, it was our fault, the Droods' fault, for bringing the Loathly Ones through into our reality in the first place.

Our mess, for us to clean up.

Giles Deathstalker's ghoulville used to be a small town in New Zealand, called Heron's Reach. A very small town, surrounded by sheep country, so far off the beaten track no one had even noticed it was missing yet. We knew. We're Droods. We know everything. It looked like it might have been a nice place, originally. Now infected drones streamed through its narrow streets like maggots in a wound, under an alien light so harsh it blasted away any trace of a shadow. Many of the drones were malformed, twisted and turned by the other-dimensional forces burning within their flesh, and they moved with eerie syncopation, like flocking birds.

They stopped what they were doing the moment Giles and his strike force appeared out of nowhere, slamming into the nearest drones and cutting them down without a moment's hesitation or mercy. The drones surged forward as one, throwing themselves at the invading force. They all had the same horrid alien look on their faces as they swarmed over the golden armoured figures, trying to drag them down through sheer force of numbers.

Giles led from the front, swinging his long sword with impressive skill and strength. The heavy blade cut off heads, thrust into chests, sliced through flesh and bone without even slowing. He cut down drones or swept them aside, always pressing forward, trampling bodies under his bloody boots. Golden armoured men and women surged forward after him, striking down drones with heavy fists, or extruded golden blades. Blood flew on the air, offal splashed in the streets. The drones didn't scream as they fell, or beg for mercy. They just kept coming until their bodies failed them, and even then they tried to clutch at golden legs or feet until they died. Giles hacked and sliced and stabbed, swinging his sword in long deadly arcs as though it was weightless. He laughed and cried out happily as he killed, and blood soaked his armour and spattered his grinning face. The Deathstalker was a warrior, doing what he was born to do, and loving every minute of it.

Not all his strike force felt the same. Though most fought on with the professional skill of their training, concentrating on the goal of their mission, some simply couldn't do it. They weren't killers, and no amount of training could make them that way. They did what they could, and then turned away from the slaughter and came home. No one said anything as they lurched back through the Glass. Medical staff were there to lead them off to the Infirmary. We understood.

Some didn't make it. Drones swarmed over them the moment they left the main force and buried them under sheer numbers, beating on their golden armour with misshapen fists.

The strike force couldn't turn back to rescue them. Speed was of the essence in this operation. They had to reach the tower and take it out with the Armourer's new bomb before the drones could come up with some new alien weapon to stop them, as they had on the Nazca Plain. So: get in, do the job, and get out. Nothing else could be allowed to matter. The Droods pressed forward, killing everything that wasn't them, guarding each other's sides and backs.

We could see the tower, on the far edge of town. A hundred feet tall and more, jagged and asymmetrical, built to alien specifications from strange technologies and organic components. It stood high and arrogantly proud against an incandescent sky, blazing with unnatural lights. It seemed alive and aware, as though it knew we were coming, and was struggling to perform its awful function before we could stop it. To bring the Hungry Gods through, just to spite us.

The Loathly Ones drones were clogging the streets now, packing them shoulder to shoulder as they surged forward to attack the Droods. Giles and his people were having to cut and hack a path through them, like forging a path through thick jungle. Blood and bodies covered the ground and slowed the strike force's advance even further. But still Giles led the way, something almost inhuman in his fierce refusal to be stopped. He encouraged his people on with far-future battle cries that meant nothing to them but stirred their blood anyway. They stuck behind him, striking down the enemy with dogged determination.

The drones fought us with every weapon they had, from tools and axes they had picked up, to clawed and barbed distorted hands, to a handful of rifles and shotguns. None of them were any use against Drood armour, and Giles was too good at what he did to be hurt. Blades couldn't cut the gold, bullets were absorbed by it, and clawed hands scrabbled uselessly at golden face masks. But when Giles finally came in sight of the base of the tower, all that changed.

Up close, the tower seemed to be coming alive, like some great beast waking from a long slumber with murder on its mind. Powerful energies coalesced around it, as though other-dimensional aspects of the construct were imprinting themselves on our reality from outside. The tower appeared . . . more real than its surroundings. More real than the Droods. Several of the golden figures had to turn away, unable to face what was happening. Giles stood firm. Nothing in the ghoulville had fazed him so far, even though he had none of the armour's built-in protections. I had to wonder if the Deathstalker had far-future technology implanted within him that he hadn't got around to telling us about.

Giles glared up at the tower, reached inside his armoured jerkin and brought out the bomb the Armourer had created for him. It didn't look like much: just a steel box with a simple timer built into the lid. Giles brandished the box at the tower, shaking it fiercely as though to taunt it, and everyone in the War Room winced. It was never wise to shake things the Armourer had built. But even as Giles bent down to place the bomb in position at the base of the tower, he had to straighten up suddenly as a whole army of new drones emerged from an opening in the base of the tower that hadn't been there a moment before.

There was something different about these drones. They were all clearly dead, flesh rotting and falling away as they ran jerkily forward, only driven on by the alien will working within them. Their faces were eaten away, some of them didn't even have eyes any more; but they headed unerringly towards Giles and his people. Each of the drones was carrying a rough sword of some unfamiliar metal that glowed disturbingly even in the harsh ghoulville light.

'We're getting long-range readings on the swords,' said the communications officer. 'They're giving off massive amounts of radiation, but nothing we can easily identify. Best guess is, the metal for those swords comes from the same dimension as the Invaders. The radiation level is rising dramatically and being so close to the drone bodies is just eating them up.'

'Will the armour protect our people?' said the Matriarch, to the point as always.

'Unknown, Matriarch. Technically, since the strange matter of the new armour is also other-dimensional in origin—'

'If you don't know, you're allowed to say so,' said the Matriarch, not unkindly.

'We don't know,' said the communications officer. 'But the Deathstalker hasn't got any protection. We should pull him out—'

'No,' said the Matriarch immediately. 'He has to plant the bomb. He knew the risks when he went in.'

'And it's not as if he's family,' muttered Molly.

We watched the display screens. The whole strike force had come forward to stand between the Deathstalker and the drones, so he could concentrate on planting the bomb and setting the timer. The first drone to reach a Drood swung his glowing sword round in a rough, unpractised arc. The Drood put up a golden arm to block the blow; and the blade sheared right through the arm. The armour didn't even slow it. The Drood screamed shrilly as his severed arm fell to the ground at his feet. Blood spurted from the stump for a moment, before the armour closed automatically over it, sealing off the wound. The Drood staggered backwards, moaning incoherently, and the drones pressed forward.

The Droods tried fencing with their extruded golden blades, but the glowing swords cut through those too. The Droods adapted quickly, using their superior strength and speed to avoid the sword blows, and closed in to wrestle with the drones. They ripped arms off, and heads, but more and more armed drones came streaming out of the opening at the base of the tower, overwhelming the strike force; and one by one the Droods fell, cut down by dead men with alien swords.

Giles worked as fast as he could, but he kept having to leave his work on the bomb to defend himself. His skill with his long sword was enough to keep the drones at arm's length, but it was clear he was getting tired. For all his skill, he was just a man, without our armour to support him. He was slowing down, missing opportunities, and it was clear from his grim expression that he knew it. And around him, the Droods were dying.

A few broke, and tried to run. The drones in the town swarmed over them and dragged them down, holding them to the ground until the armed drones could reach them.

The last half dozen Droods, the six left alive out of the two hundred who had followed the Deathstalker in, formed a tight circle around him, and yelled at him to finish working on the bomb while they held back the drones. Giles nodded reluctantly, sheathed his sword and knelt down beside the bomb, concentrating on the timer. The Droods fought fiercely, holding the armed drones at bay through sheer strength and speed; but we knew the armour couldn't support that level of exertion for long.

'He's not going to make it,' said the Matriarch. 'They'll get to him before he can finish. Armourer, can we detonate the bomb from here?'

'Of course,' said the Armourer. 'But he still has a chance. Don't write him off yet. We have to give him every chance . . .'

I started towards the Merlin Glass. This had been my idea, my plan. I couldn't leave Giles to die when perhaps I could save him. But even as I started moving, Molly sprinted past me and threw herself through the Merlin Glass gateway. I cried out, but she was already gone. She reappeared on the display screens, deep within the New Zealand ghoulville, flying through the bright unbearable air with dazzling speed. She shot over the town in a moment, and dropped out of the overbearing sky like an avenging angel, and the impact of her landing broke apart the ground before the tower. Hundreds of drones fell this way and that. She rose up, lightning swirling and snapping around her hands, and blasted away every drone she could see. They exploded where the lightning touched them, scattering rotting flesh and body parts in a hundred different directions. The beleaguered Droods raised a ragged cheer for her, and she grinned fiercely.

Giles stood up abruptly. 'It's done! We have ten minutes to get the hell out of here.'

'Allow me,' said Molly. She picked up Giles and the six remaining Droods with her magic, and flew them away through the painfully bright air towards the Merlin Glass gateway.

Behind them, drones fell upon the bomb and tried to tear it apart, but the Armourer's work defeated them. They beat at it with their rotting fists, and cut at it with their glowing swords, but the Armourer always did good work. On the top of the box, bright red numbers counted inexorably down to zero.

Molly flew Giles Deathstalker and the six Droods back over the ghoulville, her face a mask of desperate concentration. She dropped down to where the gateway hung unsupported on the open air, and flew them through and into the War Room. I moved quickly to seal off the gateway to that particular location. Molly touched softly down beside me, and looked proudly, almost triumphantly, at me, as though to say, *See? I'm still me, still on the side of the angels. You can still trust me.* I smiled reassuringly back at her. What else could I do? Even though her time in the ghoulville hadn't affected her. Even though she didn't even narrow her eyes against the unbearable light, or so much as cough at the unbreathable air.

The communications officer shouted that the bomb had exploded and the Heron's Reach ghoulville was destroyed, and we all raised some kind of cheer. It didn't feel like a victory, with so many Droods dead.

Doctors and nurses rushed the six survivors away to the waiting emergency wards, to treat them for shock and check them for radiation damage. A couple tried to say they were ready to fight on in other Nests, but you could see their hearts weren't in it. The Matriarch ordered them to stand down, and I think they were secretly grateful. I knew how they felt. I remembered the carnage on the Nazca Plain. It's hard to fight an inhuman foe with only human resources.

Of course, I could almost hear Martha say. *If it was easy, everyone would be doing it, and the world wouldn't need Droods.*

Harry Drood and Roger Morningstar took their two hundred armoured Droods and went to Siberia. Tunguska, to be exact, where Something crashed into the Earth in 1908. The impact was so devastating it flattened trees for hundreds of miles in every direction, and the light generated by the impact was so bright that Londoners could read a newspaper in the streets at midnight. There are lots of theories about what it was that hit Tunguska all those years ago, everything from a meteor to a crashing alien ship to a miniature black hole . . . but no one knows anything for sure. Except us. We know. We know everything, remember?

As far as we could work out, the Loathly Ones' presence in Tunguska was a coincidence. They had no idea what was still sleeping there, deep and deep under the permafrost, and we were happy for things to stay that way. 'What if the drones should wake it up by accident?' Molly had asked. 'Then we'd really be in trouble,' I said.

The Loathly Ones had taken over a secret Soviet science city, X37, one of the highly classified research communities set up to run the kind of experiments the USSR knew the rest of the world wouldn't approve of. That's why this was in Siberia – so that if things did go very badly wrong there'd be hardly anyone around to object. X37 wasn't on any official map, then or now, and had been pretty much deserted in recent years by the scientists and their families after the funding dried up. When the drones came, there was only a single troop of Russian soldiers guarding a handful of scientists working on a new kind of food flavouring. They never stood a chance. X37 became a ghoulville, and no one even noticed. Except us.

Harry and Roger and their strike force passed through the Merlin

Glass and arrived in a great open square in the middle of the secret city. The surrounding buildings seemed to have evolved, transformed themselves, in disturbingly organic ways. Wires and cables wriggled through the walls, threading through brick and stone like pulsing veins. More cables hung across the streets like spiders' webs, or exposed nerve structures, pulsing slowly on the bright air. Strange combinations of technology and living things protruded from burst-out doorways and shattered windows, as though the buildings' insides had grown too big for them. With the stark, fierce light and air so thick with unbreathable elements, it seemed the whole city was underwater. The armour protected Harry and the Droods, Roger didn't seem to notice it.

They could see the tower from where they were, standing tall and grotesque and defiant above the blunt utilitarianism of the old Soviet architecture. Strange energies were crackling up and down the length of the tower, as though it was trying to force itself awake.

Harry and Roger looked quickly around as a horde of demons came running at them from every direction at once. They'd been alerted by the attack on the New Zealand ghoulville, and they were ready. But here, in this Nest, all the drones were freaks and monsters. Whether it was a legacy of the forbidden sciences practised in X37 during the Cold War, or strange emanations from what lay sleeping under the permafrost, every drone here was over sized and monstrous. Terribly misshapen, with huge bones and long strings of muscle, stretched faces with slit mouths full of shark teeth, clusters of eyes and even waving barbed antennae. They might have been human once, but they had left all that behind. The drones surged forward with fangs and claws and improvised weapons, and Harry and Roger and the Droods went forward to meet them.

Fang and claw were no match for golden armour, and the Droods' enhanced strength and speed made them a match for any monster. Harry wore the gold and fought alongside his people, striking down his enemies with brutal efficiency. Roger hung back from the main fighting, watching carefully. He was waiting. And when the first drones appeared with glowing swords clutched awkwardly in malformed hands, he was ready for them. He pointed a finger, and they exploded. He looked at them in a certain way, and blood burst from their mouths and eyes and ears. He spoke certain Words, and their rotting flesh melted and ran away down their bodies. Roger Morningstar wore his Infernal aspect openly, and even Harry couldn't bear to look at him directly any more.

For all the drones' overwhelming numbers, without the radioactive swords they were no match for Drood armour and Hell magic. Harry and Roger took the point, and slowly but inexorably they fought their way out of the open square and headed for the tower. Every drone in the Nest came running or sliding or hopping through the city streets, pressing together in the narrow intersections to block off the way to the tower but it didn't even slow the strike force down. They cut and hacked and hammered their way through the drones, killing everything that wasn't them.

Harry stayed at the head of his people, proving himself a magnificent fighter. The golden blades in his hands swept back and forth with supernatural speed, too fast for the unaided human eye to follow. Blood gushed over his gleaming chest, and sprayed across his golden face mask. Drones attacked him singly and en masse, and never so much as slowed his advance. He had learned everything the Deathstalker could teach him about fighting with blades, and nothing could stop him now.

Roger strode along beside him, embracing his Infernal aspect, and the drones fell dead just for getting too close to him. Roger looked at last what he really was: a thing from the Pit walking arrogant and unleashed in the world of men, and poisoning it merely by his presence. Wherever he looked, bodies exploded or burst into flames. Some he turned inside out and left to lie in the gutters. When he spoke, drones turned on themselves and tore each other apart.

He smiled a devilish smile; home at last.

The Droods forced their way along behind their leaders and killed everything that came within reach. The tower loomed up before them, a door opened at the base, and a whole new army of drones came staggering and lurching out, bearing hundreds of the glowing swords. Roger spoke a single dreadful Word and they all exploded into flames, bright crimson fires that stank of blood and brimstone, and consumed the drones as fast as they could appear.

Harry put the bomb in place, set the timer for a comfortable margin, and then he and Roger led the way back through the ghoulville to the Merlin Glass. They trooped through into the War Room, and I shut down the gateway. The bomb went off, X37 was destroyed, and everyone in the room went mad all over again. Harry and Roger hugged each other, Roger's aspect now safely suppressed again. The Droods armoured down and clapped each other on the shoulder and on the back, and there were even some tears and kisses.

Victory can feel oh so fine. While it lasts.

Mr Stab and the Sarjeant-At-Arms led their strike force into the Punjab, in India. A narrow fertile valley surrounded by mountains supporting a small population; a perfect target for the Loathly Ones. The quiet settlement became a ghoulville and no one noticed. It was, after all, the kind of place where one tribe wouldn't lower themselves to speak to another, and none of them would speak to outsiders because authority was never to be trusted. They might want you to pay taxes.

When the strike force passed through the Merlin Glass, the ghoulville turned out to be a collection of squat stone houses, half overgrown with slowly stirring vegetation, strangely mutated by the town's other-dimensional energies. There were cracks in the bare stone ground that seemed to fall away for ever, and the light was so bright it washed the details out of everything.

It was a scene out of some bare abstract hell; and Mr Stab seemed quite at home there.

The drones were waiting again, but this time when they came surging forward to attack the invading force, the crowd seemed to split apart at the last moment, broken in two by an immovable object. They surged around this object and did their best not to touch it, though they fell on the Sarjeant-At-Arms and the other Droods with their usual ferocity. But they couldn't touch Mr Stab. Something about his no-longer-human nature actively appalled them. They couldn't bear to be close to him.

So he walked straight forward into the roiling mob, and began killing with an elegant grace, using a long shiny knife that had appeared in his hand out of nowhere. He walked unopposed through the surging drones, and did awful, terrible things to them, and they couldn't even touch him. Mr Stab smiled slightly, possibly remembering other times . . .

The Sarjeant-At-Arms moved quickly in behind Mr Stab, backing him up, and the strike force followed. The Sarjeant had never been one for swords and blades; he used the aspect granted him by the family to summon weapons. All he had to do was gesture in a certain way and a fully loaded gun would pop into his hand. And the Sarjeant used these guns to shoot down any drone who showed up with a glowing sword, long before they could get close enough to do any damage. When a gun ran out of bullets, he tossed it aside and summoned another. The rejected gun would disappear in mid-air, and there was never any shortage of replacements.

Mr Stab sliced up the drones, and the Sarjeant mowed them down, and the strike force moved inexorably forward, towards the tower on the horizon. They almost made it look easy. Mr Stab danced through the slaughter, killing with a touch, the Sarjeant emptied gun after gun, and the armoured Droods struck down anything that came within reach. They soon came to the base of the tower, and more drones appeared from within, bearing an assortment of entirely unfamiliar weapons. The Sarjeant-At-Arms took no chances and shot them all down from a distance. The few that couldn't be stopped by bullets, protected by strange glowing armours or energy fields, proved no problem for the smiling Mr Stab.

The Sarjeant planted the bomb, set the timer, and then led his people safely back home. Another Nest destroyed, another tower gone, with no losses or casualties. I started to relax. We'd had a bad beginning. It looked like we were starting to get the hang of things now. Maybe we could pull this off. I said as much to Molly, and she nodded, smiling. I should have known better.

Callan and the Blue Fairy took their strike force into a small settlement just north of San Francisco. Officially, the Blue Fairy was there as a volunteer to support Callan, and watch his back. In practice, I'd had a quiet word with Callan, and told him to watch the Blue Fairy. I still wasn't ready to trust Blue yet.

Their ghoulville had once been an integral part of the Summer of Love in the sixties: a central point for more sex, drugs and rock and roll magic than any reality could comfortably bear. In these more hard-headed materialistic days, the small town of Lud's Drum was a haven for shaggy old hippy types, burnt-out casualties of the drugs war, and a whole industry had grown up devoted to trading on the town's disreputable past. Only people like us still kept a watchful eye on Lud's Drum, because dimensional barriers in and around the town had been dangerously weak ever since Timothy Leary dropped an heroic dose of LSD and peyote there and tried to perform a remote exorcism on the Pentagon. As a result, the Loathly Ones took the town with hardly an effort. Lud's Drum was one of the few places where drones could walk around openly without being suspected. Now it was a ghoulville, and one of the last remnants of the sixties dream was a living nightmare.

Callan led his strike force through the harshly lit streets, cutting down drones with cold, almost clinical precision. He didn't allow himself to be distracted by the crumbling candy-coloured houses, the soft undulating streets, or the endless waves of drones who fell upon his people with vicious, malevolent glee. He cut a path through them, heading with stern resolve straight for the nearly completed tower in the very centre of the town. Callan might have a smart mouth and an irreverent attitude when dealing with authority figures, but nothing distracted him from his focus when he was out in the field.

The Blue Fairy stuck close to him, guarding Callan's back with surprising skill and purpose. He didn't have a sword or a gun, only a slender wand that he'd produced out of nowhere. *Oh, this old thing,* he'd said airily. *Been in the family for ages.* In the ghoulville he produced a series of small but surprisingly effective magics that kept the drones at arm's length. It shouldn't really have surprised me that Blue knew how to fight. He couldn't have lasted all these years, with the kind of enemies he'd made, without having developed some survival skills.

Callan led his people by example, always pushing forward, not allowing himself to be stopped or even slowed by anything the demons could throw at him. His golden blades rose and fell, and blood flew on the air. Always moving doggedly forward, he brought them closer and closer to the tower through sheer martial expertise and an almost brutal determination. Watching him made me feel proud to be a Drood. This was what we were for: to strike down the bad guys in Humanity's name.

The drones had their glowing swords, and other equally awful weapons, but the Blue Fairy saw to it that they never got close enough to do the Droods any harm. He stabbed the air with his wand, a slender length of bone carved with elven glyphs, and wherever he pointed it things went wrong for the drones. Over and over again. Blue scowled fiercely as he concentrated, skipping this way and that to ensure he never came close to being in danger himself; but I got the feeling he was enjoying himself, none the less.

He was half elf, after all, with an elf's ingrained talent for death and destruction.

They made it to the base of the tower before everything went wrong. The tower rose up before them, like a jagged lightning bolt of alien technology and organic components driven into the ground with godly force. Its shape made no sense, as though it had more spatial dimensions than the human mind could cope with, and once again there was a definite sense that the thing was in some way alive and aware, and knew they were there. Callan planted the bomb at the base of the tower, with the Blue Fairy looking over his shoulder, while armoured troops formed a barrier to hold back the swarming drones.

Callan set the timer, stood up and nodded to the Blue Fairy, and then every single member of the strike force stiffened suddenly, crashed to the ground, and lay still. No warning, no obvious reason, no drone with a new weapon. Just two hundred armoured Droods lying motionless on the ground. I couldn't even tell whether they were dead or alive. Callan glared about him, sweeping his golden blades this way and that. And then the Blue Fairy elegantly tapped him on the shoulder with his wand, and Callan fell to his knees.

'Sorry, old thing,' said the Blue Fairy. 'But I never was very good at playing with others. And you have something I need.'

We watched helplessly as Blue put his wand to Callan's neck, and then somehow . . . whipped the torc away from Callan. His mouth stretched wide in a scream, but no sound came out of it. He was still kneeling, but now he was just a man again, ripped from his armour. The Blue Fairy looked at the torc in his hand, turning it back and forth, and then he looked out of the display screen at us, smiling almost sadly.

'I know, Eddie,' he said. 'You trusted me. Which was very nice and all that, but this torc will buy me entry into the Fae Court. I told you: in the end, it's always about family. And never, ever, trust an elf. We always have an agenda.'

He turned sideways, and kept on turning until he had disappeared from sight. The Droods snapped back to life again, save for Callan, who collapsed, twitching on the ground. The drones surged forward.

Somehow the Droods got Callan home. They battled their way out of Lud's Drum, with the drones making them fight for every yard. And all the time the bomb was ticking. They came streaming back through the Merlin Glass, carrying an unconscious Callan, and I slammed the doorway shut just as the bomb went off. There was a moment of light so bright I could feel it, and the whole War Room shook; but the gateway closed in time to protect us. Lud's Drum was gone, and with it the Nest and its tower.

They took Callan away to the Infirmary. Shock, they said. God knows what having his torc ripped from him felt like. I asked Strange if the elves could make the torc work for them, and he said, 'What are elves?' Which didn't exactly help matters. We would be revenged on the Blue Fairy later. No one steals from the Droods and lives to boast of it.

After that drama, everything else went pretty much as planned. The strike forces went into ghoulville after ghoulville, using the tactics we'd developed, and Nest after Nest was destroyed along with their towers. The Armourer's bombs never failed, and we didn't lose one more Drood to the drones. No more nasty surprises, no more appalling new weapons, just Droods doing their job, making the world safe. The hours trudged slowly by, with golden figures constantly coming and going through the Merlin Glass. The drones still fought savagely, making us work for every victory. But still, step by step, we were winning. Fresh men and women came forward to replace those Droods exhausted by too many raids, and the work went on. The whole family was ready to fight, if need be. The Infirmary coped well. Overall, losses were actually fewer than expected, and planned for. We had the end in sight when it all went to rat shit again.

A communications officer stood up abruptly to shout his new information to the Matriarch, and the whole War Room went quiet to hear it.

'It's Truman!' he shouted. 'He's had Loathly One drones in his new underground base, building a tower, hidden behind his protective screens! It must be almost complete, because its presence just punched right through the screens! It's so powerful Truman can't hide it any longer. It's almost ready to open a door and bring the Invaders through! This has all been for nothing!'

'Be calm, that man!' snapped the Matriarch. 'I will not have emotional displays in my War Room. Someone sit him down and get him a strong cup of tea. Edwin, which of our major players are still capable of leading a strike force?'

I checked. The Sarjeant-At-Arms and Mr Stab were clearing out a Nest in northern China. Callan was still in the Infirmary. And Giles Deathstalker, having personally led over thirty missions, was lying on a cot beside Callan, too exhausted to go on, though he'd never admit it. That left Harry, and Roger Morningstar. They were catching a quick break between missions, and awing the younger Droods with exaggerated tales of their exploits. I had them brought back to the War Room, and explained the situation. Harry looked very much like he wanted to spit.

'Just once I'd like things to go the way they're supposed to.'

'Are you up for this?' I said.

'Not like I have much of a choice, is it?' said Harry. 'Okay, put together a strike force, out of the best we've got that are still on their feet, and I'll lead it in.' He looked drawn and tired, but his back was straight and his eyes were sharp. He dug Roger in the ribs with his elbow. 'Who would have thought it, eh? Family pariah Harry Drood, stepping up to save the day. Would you have bet on that, Grandmother?'

Martha looked at him steadily. 'Of course. You're James's son.'

Harry deliberately turned his back on her, and grinned at Roger. 'How about it, love? You up for one last mission, to save the world?'

'I'm not sure my mother's side of the family would approve, but what the hell . . . Why not? Can't let you do this on your own. You never did learn to watch your back properly.'

I wasn't so sure Roger's going was a good idea. Basically, he looked like shit. With so much of his magic exhausted on earlier raids, a lot of his glamour was gone, and he looked . . . more of a man.

Harry made a point of looking down his nose at me. 'Well, Eddie, aren't you coming along on this little jaunt? You know how you love to snatch victory from the jaws of defeat at the very last minute.'

'I'm needed here,' I said calmly. 'Someone's got to feed you the necessary information, and point you in the right direction. But, if it should go horribly wrong, I'm your backup.'

'And me,' said Molly, digging me sharply in the ribs with her elbow.

'Of course,' I said, 'if you feel you can't do it without me . . .'

'We can handle it,' Harry said immediately.

'Damn right, lover,' said Roger Morningstar.

The Merlin Glass locked on to Truman's new base of operations easily enough; the almost complete tower was dominating the ether. But for some reason, the Glass couldn't seem to show us a view of the base's interior. Just a field, overlooking Stonehenge, with the ancient stones looming tall and dramatic against the lowering evening sky. Harry pressed in close beside me, scowling.

'The Stones look to be almost half a mile away; is that really the closest you can get us?'

'This isn't a Nest, as such,' I said. 'Not a ghoulville. It's an underground base surrounded by layer upon layer of the best scientific and magical protections money can buy. We wouldn't even know it was there if the tower wasn't poking out of it, so to speak. You'll have to sneak up on them. Unless you've changed your mind about going . . .'

'Of course I haven't! It's just . . . I don't like this. It feels like a trap.'

'I wouldn't be surprised,' I said. 'But what kind of trap could Manifest Destiny put together that could hold Harry Drood, Roger Morningstar and two hundred good men and women in golden armour?'

Harry smiled slightly. 'You really suck at the inspirational thing, you know that?' He looked at Roger. 'Let's go, bro.'

'Oh please,' said Roger. 'You know I don't do that macho stuff.'

Harry and Roger led their strike force through the Merlin Glass, and I immediately closed the gateway behind them. Truman was a sneaky bastard, and I wouldn't put anything past him, including deliberately revealing his tower's presence as a way of tricking us into opening a gateway he could then take advantage of. But it seemed quiet enough. Molly took my arm and hugged it tightly to her side as we watched

Harry hiss orders to his strike force to spread out across the open grassy field so as not to make a single target. Their golden armour gleamed dully in the sparse evening light. As far as the display screens could tell, they were alone in the field. Everything was still and quiet. And then Roger's head snapped up, and he pointed off into the gloom. And all around the scattered strike force, dark figures appeared from every direction at once, moving at impossible speeds.

The figures were human, but moving supernaturally quickly, impossibly fast, streaking across the open field at a pace even armoured Droods couldn't have matched. The Droods turned to face them, lifting their weapons, but they almost seemed to be moving in slow motion compared to their attackers. As the figures closed in, their every movement was so fast as to make them a blur on the display screens. Even their faces were unclear. They were just shapes flashing through the evening gloom.

They swarmed over the Droods, attacking and falling back almost before the Droods could react. The attackers didn't seem to possess any weapons, they beat repeatedly at the golden armour with their bare hands. When that didn't work, glowing knives appeared in their hands and they struck again. And this time Droods went down as glowing blades sliced through their armour to the men and women beneath. The strike force fell, one by one, unable to match their attackers' speed even for a moment. Harry called his people back to make a defensive circle, but by the time he'd finished speaking half of them were already dead.

There was a clamour of raised voices in the War Room as everyone tried to come up with an explanation or a theory at once. Communications yelled at Intelligence, who yelled at Information, who yelled at Records . . . and that was where the answer finally came from. Droods know everything; but sometimes it takes us a while to find it. Turned out there had been a report about the possibility of these people, from a file Callan found in Truman's old deserted underground base. The Accelerated Men. Surgically altered, technologically enhanced and drugged to the eyeballs, they were fanatics, burning up a lifetime's energy to feed their unnatural speed. Dying to be fast. But then, Manifest Destiny has never been short of fanatics.

Giles Deathstalker arrived in the War Room, looking half dead but still determined, and had to be almost physically prevented from going in to help. I decided that. No point in throwing away more lives till we had some idea of what we were facing. Giles watched the display screens with avid interest. I almost expected him to take notes. It seemed he'd finally found something he hadn't seen before, something he thought he could take back to his future time.

On the field overlooking Stonehenge, Harry's remaining people had retreated to form a tight ring around Harry and Roger. Standing shoulder to shoulder, they were better able to defend themselves, and pushing their armour's speed to its limit meant they could take out the occasional Accelerated Man with a vicious sword thrust. When these human lightning bolts crashed to the ground, dead at last, they looked like old men, their faces blasted by a terrible strain. The Droods fought on, losing a man or woman here or there, the defensive circle slowly shrinking . . . Until suddenly the Accelerated Men began to stumble and fall and collapse on the ground. At first I thought Roger had finally got some of his magic working, but it soon became clear that the Accelerated Men had used up all their lives. They ran themselves to death.

Harry and Roger and the dozen or so remaining Droods looked slowly about them. Piled up around lay dozens of old men with time-ravaged faces. They could never have been intended to last long. They were a means to an end, to forcing the Droods into one easy target. A terrible blast of light slammed aside the darkness, a light so strong and fierce it had presence and impact. The Droods started to scream. Roger clung onto Harry, shouting Words of Power that were almost washed away by the terrible light. And then the light snapped off. Evening returned, but the Droods were gone. Only Harry and Roger were left, clinging to each other. Harry was holding Roger up. The hellspawn was almost out on his feet, exhausted of strength and magic.

Only two men left, to save the world.

The War Room went mad again. It took a bit longer to get the answers this time, but it was no less disturbing when the Armourer finally supplied it. He admitted he was guessing, but it rang true. Truman had set up his new base under Stonehenge in order to seize control of the Soul of Albion. That impossibly powerful scrap of starstuff that fell out of the sky millennia ago. Truman had taken it for his own, and used Loathly One technology to turn it into a weapon: a Soul Gun. He'd found a way to release its energy in short bursts, and anything bathed in the angry light of the Soul was banished, blasted out of this reality.

The Droods we'd lost wouldn't be coming back.

Harry and Roger were calling desperately for help. It slowly went quiet in the War Room as everyone looked to the Matriarch, and then to me, for orders. Martha stood very still, wringing her hands and staring at the display screens. I thought hard. And while I was thinking, the Soul Gun fired again.

Roger must have sensed it coming, because he straightened up abruptly and pushed Harry behind him. The terrible light flared up, destroying the night, a illumination so overpowering it was beyond colour; something you experienced with your mind and soul rather than your eyes. But Roger stood up to the light and faced it down, standing between the light and the man he loved, defying the Soul Gun with every last thing he had in him. The Soul Gun blazed; and Roger met its awful power with unflinching will.

Survival couldn't have done it, or fear or anger; but this was love. And in the end the Soul Gun faded first.

The light snapped off, and Roger fell to the ground like a dead man. Harry put his arms around the unresponsive body, and rocked him back and forth, crooning like a child. In the War Room, everyone looked at me. I took a deep breath.

'Giles, Molly, you're with me. Martha, locate Mr Stab and the Sarjeant-At-Arms and get them here. And someone find me Subway Sue. We're going into Truman's bunker to take out the tower – and for that we need the Damnation Way.'

CHAPTER FIFTEEN

Journey's end in enemies meeting

And it was going so well . . . relatively speaking. Now it looked like our previous successes had been for nothing, and I was going to have to pull off one of my last-minute, odds-defying, race-against-time and save-the-bloody-day miracles. I don't think people appreciate how much those things take out of me.

On the big main display screen, Harry Drood was helping a dazed and shaken Roger Morningstar to his feet. Roger had just saved Harry's life at the risk of his own, and it was hard to tell which of them looked the most surprised or shocked. They leaned on each other tiredly, and spoke for a while, but we couldn't hear what they were saying. The communications people worked frantically to try and restore sound, urged on by the Matriarch's unwavering glare, but without success. Apparently when the Soul Gun went off it supersaturated the ether with other-dimensional energies. We were lucky we were still getting a picture. Though the communications officer had enough sense to imply that rather than state it openly to the Matriarch. On the display screen, Roger and Harry headed uncertainly across the grassy field towards Stonehenge, presumably in search of an entrance to Truman's underground bunker.

The two of them against Truman and his armies. I suppose people can always surprise you; especially if one of them is a half-demon.

I did try to call them back, tell them reinforcements were on their way, but they couldn't hear me. I even tried contacting them through Strange, but he couldn't help either.

'It's the tower,' he said, sounding strangely subdued. 'It's complete, Eddie, and almost ready to activate. It's alive and aware, though not in any way you would recognise, and I can hear it thinking. It knows I'm watching. It comes from a stranger place than I do, an even higher dimension. The sheer power locked up in this thing is frightening. The Invaders, the Many-Angled Ones, the Hungry Gods are coming . . . and I'm scared, Eddie.'

'You could leave,' I said. 'Get out of our world, withdraw to your own dimension.'

'And leave you and your family defenceless? No. That's not the kind of other-dimensional presence I am. I like this world, and you people, and your weird way of doing things. You're fun. The Hungry Gods would eat you up and never know what it was they were destroying. They're vicious, evil and basically quite stupid gods, when you get down to it. I won't desert you and your family, Eddie. Some things deserve to be fought, just on general principles.'

'Thank you, Ethel,' I said.

'Ah, hell,' said Strange. 'What are friends for?'

And that was when Subway Sue scurried into the War Room. She'd made an effort to clean herself up, including a new set of clothes that had clearly been intended for a rather larger person, but she still looked like she'd come to steal something, and stress and strain had put twenty years into her furtive face. To her credit, she was also trying hard not to look too smug at being proved right and necessary after all.

'Got the feeling you were looking for me,' she said, 'so here I am. Would I be right in assuming that your plans have gone tits up, and using the Damnation Way has become the only viable option?'

'Got it in one,' said Molly.

'Damn,' said Subway Sue. 'Then we really are in deep shit.'

Molly took Sue over to one side, to bring her up to date on what had been happening, and just how deep in it we really were, and I took the moment to think about exactly who I was going to take with us. Molly, of course, for a whole bunch of reasons. Not the Armourer; Uncle Jack would be needed here, if we screwed this up. Giles Deathstalker, because he was the most impressive fighting man I'd ever met. And Mr Stab, because he was . . . what he was, and because he was so bloody hard to kill. I would have liked Callan, but he was still out of it. So the final member of this little death or glory team would have to be the Sarjeant-At-Arms. Partly because I wanted someone with me I could trust to follow orders, and partly because I needed someone I could depend on to fight to the last drop of his blood for the family. Someone . . . expendable.

I never used to think things like that, before I became head of the family.

I looked over at Molly and Subway Sue, chatting and giggling together like the old girlfriends they were, and it was a nice touch of normality in a severely strained world. It gave my heart a bit of a lift, to see that such small happinesses were possible. But I still wasn't too sure what to make of Sue's Damnation Way. The name really didn't inspire confidence. But, if it could drop us off inside Truman's bunker, one forceful pre-emptive strike could take out the tower and put an end to this. No more Nests, no more towers, no more Loathly Ones.

Except for the one remaining inside Molly. Eating into her body, her mind, her soul. What good to save the world, if I couldn't save the woman I loved? With Molly gone, all I would have left would be the family, and a lifetime's cold duties and responsibilities. There had to be a way to save her. There had to be. Because I didn't want to live in a world without Molly.

She looked round, saw me looking at her, and smiled brightly. I smiled back. She hugged Sue quickly, and came to join me. She hugged me and I held her close. I didn't want ever to let her go, but I did. I couldn't have her suspecting what I'd been thinking.

'You looked like you needed a hug,' Molly said briskly. 'Hell, practically everyone here does. But I'm not that sort of girl. These days. I've been talking to Sue; she says she can summon up an entrance point to the Damnation Way any time you're ready, but . . . she's exhausted, Eddie. I mean, really out on her feet. It's only guts and determination that's holding her up. I don't know where she went, or who she had to deal with, to obtain the secrets of the Damnation Way, but she paid a high price.'

'Then we need to get this moving as soon as possible,' I said. 'Molly, I need Subway Sue to go with us. Is she up to that?'

'She says she is.' Molly scowled, and shrugged. 'I can't tell her no. And you wouldn't, would you, Eddie?'

'We need her,' I said steadily. 'The world needs her.'

'Funny,' said Molly. 'It never needed her before.' She looked at me thoughtfully. 'And what about me? Do you need me with you on this? Can you trust me so close to a tower, given my . . . condition?'

I smiled at her. 'I'll always need you, Molly. Do you really think I'd go anywhere without you?'

'You always were a big softy, Eddie Drood.' And she kissed me hard, right there in front of everyone. Some clapped, a few cheered. Molly finally let go of me and smiled sweetly around.

Luckily Mr Stab arrived at that point, strolling casually into the War Room like an unexploded bomb, with the Sarjeant-At-Arms marching right beside him. The Sarjeant had a gun in one hand and his gaze fixed firmly on Mr Stab; who politely pretended not to notice. After his many exertions in the field, the Sarjeant was battered and bruised, and somewhat bulkily bandaged here and there, but his back was straight and his head erect. For him, weakness would always be something that happened to other people. And to be fair, he still looked like he could take on a whole army single-handed and send the survivors running home crying for their mothers. Mr Stab, it should be said, looked exactly as he always had. Calm, cold and completely unruffled. Not a spot of blood on him, or the slightest tear in his Victorian evening wear. Even his top hat gleamed with a smug and civilised air.

I felt like throwing something at it, on general principles.

Instead, I beckoned them both over and explained the situation to them. Mr Stab frowned slightly at mention of the Damnation Way, as though the name rang a bell with him, but he had nothing to say. The Sarjeant-At-Arms all but crashed to attention before me, his eyes brightening at the prospect of further mayhem.

'Anything for the family!' he said. 'And I have to say, the family's been so much more fun since you got back, boy.'

He may be a psychopath, I thought. *But he's our psychopath.*

'This new mission,' said Mr Stab. Will I get to kill more people?'

'Almost certainly,' I said.

'Good. And is there a chance that I might be killed?'

'Almost certainly.'

'Even better,' said Mr Stab. 'Count me in.'

'*Incoming!*'

The shout cut across the War Room chatter, and everyone looked round sharply to see where it was coming from. One of the communication staff was standing over his work station and pointing at it with a trembling finger. The communications officer was quickly at his side, slamming him into his seat and scowling over the man's shoulder at the information flashing across his screen. The other communications staff were frantically checking their computers, crystal balls and scrying pools, and chattering excitedly to each other. A wailing alarm suddenly went off, and the Matriarch immediately ordered it shut down.

'Can't hear myself think,' she said sharply. 'Ah, that's better. Now, what's happening? Talk to me, people! What exactly is it that's "incoming"?'

'Is The Hall under threat?' I said.

'Looks like it,' said the communications officer. It was Howard Drood, efficient as always, come over from Operations to head the War Room during the attacks on the Nests. 'Something is trying to force its way into our reality, right here, pushing past The Hall's defensive shields. Which I would have said was impossible, except for the fact that something is doing it.'

'Could it be Truman, or the Invaders?' I said. 'Launching a pre-emptive strike against us?'

'Yes. No. Maybe. I don't know! The screens can't make head nor tail of what's happening.' Howard's habitual scowl deepened as he studied the monitor screens. 'I've never seen readings like these . . . Whatever this is, it's coming at us like a bat out of hell. It's already punched through the outer defences, and it's heading straight for us.'

I flashed back to the old attacks on The Hall, when the Heart was still in residence. We never did find out for sure who was behind them. Had they chosen this moment to attack us again, while we were at our weakest and most vulnerable?

'Ethel,' I said. 'Talk to me. Do you know who or what this is?'

'No, Eddie.' His voice in my head was surprisingly tentative. 'It's coming from a direction I don't recognise. From outside everything I understand as reality. It's not very large, but it does seem to be very determined. And no, Eddie, I can't keep it out.'

Giles Deathstalker had his long sword unsheathed and was looking around for an enemy. Not to be outdone, the Sarjeant called up a gun in each hand.

'Put those away!' the Matriarch snapped immediately. 'You can't have weapons in the War Room! You might damage the equipment.'

Giles sheathed his sword, and bowed. The Sarjeant-At-Arms

made his guns disappear again and folded his arms tightly with a definite, *Look at me I'm not sulking even though I have cause* expression on his face. The Matriarch sighed audibly.

'Don't just stand there, Sarjeant! Armour up! Everyone, armour up!'

She had a point. We all subvocalised the activating Words, and the War Room was full of gleaming golden figures. It felt good to be back in the gold again, to feel strong and fast and sharp. Sometimes putting on the armour is like snapping fully awake from a long doze. Everyone not preoccupied at a work station peered suspiciously about them, ready for action, golden blades and other weapons extruding silently from golden fists. There was a rising tension in the War Room, a strong feeling of something coming, pushing inexorably closer. We could feel it pressing in on us from all sides at once. Molly stood close beside me, her arms lifted in the stance of summoning, ready to throw seriously nasty magics at anything even remotely threatening. Mr Stab appeared . . . politely interested. And the Armourer, not surprisingly, had pulled a really powerful-looking weapon out of nowhere and was swivelling it back and forth in search of a target while everyone else hurried to get out of his way.

Heaven help anyone who dares to face the Droods on their own territory.

A rising babble of voices filled the War Room as the various technicians struggled to understand what was happening. Whatever was coming slammed through layer after layer of protections, and the tension in the air was almost physically painful. Martha Drood, in armour for the first time I could remember, moved from station to station, peering over shoulders and dispensing a cautionary word or a bracing murmur as required. If she was reduced to rallying the troops, we really were in trouble. A rising tone rang out on the air, sharp and distinct, as though approaching from somewhere inconceivably far away.

'It's here!' Howard shouted. 'It's materialising!'

'Where?' said Martha. 'Where exactly in The Hall?'

'*Here!*' screamed Howard. 'Right here in the bloody War Room!'

The rising note peaked, a shuddering vibration that reverberated inside our heads, despite the shielding armour. We clapped useless hands over our ears and staggered back and forth, and then flinched back as the world itself split apart in the very centre of the War Room . . . and Janissary Jane came through. She threw herself through the gap, her combat fatigues blackened and scorched and actually on fire in places. Explosions and brilliant lights and raised angry voices spilled out of a split in the air, and then it was cut off as the split slammed together again. The tension was gone in a moment, and we armoured down a little sheepishly as Janissary Jane stood shaking and breathless before us. She was weeping violently, and looked like she'd fought her way through Hell itself to get to us. She raised a bruised face, sniffed back tears, and glared at me triumphantly; and then she sat down suddenly on the floor, as though the last of the strength had gone out of her legs.

'All right!' I yelled, glaring about me. 'Everyone calm down! The emergency is over. I know who this is. Concentrate your attention on reinstating our defences, and making sure no one followed her from . . . wherever the hell that was.' I moved forward and knelt down beside Janissary Jane. She was shuddering violently and breathing hard. Her eyes weren't tracking properly. 'Jane?' I said. 'It's me, Eddie. Are you all right?'

She did look pretty bad, up close. Her army fatigues had been burned away in places, and were soaked with blood from a dozen nasty looking wounds. Parts of her battle armour were half melted. Her face kept going slack, as pain and stress and exhaustion caught up with her. When the last of the adrenalin coursing through her ran out, she was going to crash, and hard. I needed to get answers out of her now, while I still could. I grabbed her by the shoulders, made her look at me and said her name again, and her head jerked up as though I'd pulled her out of a deep sleep.

'Eddie. I made it back. Damn—'

'I saw the note you left pinned to your door with a knife,' I said, trying for a light touch. 'So did you find us some really big guns?'

'The biggest,' said Janissary Jane, trying for a smile and not quite bringing it off. 'Remember, Eddie, I told you about the last demon war I fought in? The one where some damned fools accidentally opened a Hellgate, and an army of demons came flooding out?'

'Yes,' I said, my heart suddenly sinking. I really didn't like where this was going. 'In the end, things got so bad you had to use a superweapon to destroy the whole universe, so the demons couldn't use it as a base to invade other universes. I remember. I still have nightmares.'

'This is it,' said Janissary Jane. 'The super-weapon. The last resort. The Deplorable End.'

She held it out to me on the palm of a surprisingly steady hand. The weapon didn't actually look like much, but then the really nasty ones often don't. The Deplorable End was a flat silver box, dull and lifeless, with a red button on top. It barely filled Jane's palm, but there was still something about it. The more I looked at it, the more uneasy I felt, as though a large and dangerous animal had just entered the room. I studied the box carefully, and had enough sense not to try and touch it. The Armourer had come forward and was peering over my shoulder at it, breathing hard in his excitement.

'Now that is impressive,' he said. 'You don't often see craft and workmanship like that, these days. How many spatial dimensions has it got? I keep losing count. And the energy signatures are off the scale . . . You have got to let me get that down to the Armoury and take it apart.'

'No, Uncle Jack,' I said firmly.

'Oh, come on! I've got this really cool hyper-hammer I've being dying to try out.'

'No, Uncle Jack! Have you stopped taking your medication again? Jane, what is that, exactly? What does it do?'

'Simple to operate,' she said, her voice dull and lifeless. Her eyes were drooping shut again as the last of her strength went out of her. 'Press the button, and . . . Boom.'

'No more tower?' I said hopefully.

'No more anything,' said Jane, blinking owlishly. 'No more universe. And no, you don't get a timer. The Deplorable End is a one-time-only deal. What I've got here is the original device, the prototype. We used a somewhat improved version to put an end to the demon war. What I've brought you is, therefore, technically speaking, untested. But it should work. No reason I know of why it shouldn't.' She slowly lowered her hand, as though the awful thing squatting on her palm was getting heavier. 'I stole this from the Multiversal Mercenaries' Black Museum. I had to kill a lot of people to get this to you, Eddie. Some of them were friends, once. But now I have closed the book and burned my boats . . . I can never go back. So don't you ever give me cause to regret this, Drood.'

'How does it work?' I said, because you have to say something.

'Like you'd understand, even if I could explain it,' said Janissary Jane, with some of the old force in her voice. 'I don't need to know how weapons work; I'm a mercenary, not a mechanic. But I'm told it's a largely conceptual weapon. What we've got here is a hyperspatial key, activating the real weapon, which is hidden away in some other dimensional fold waiting to be unleashed. When pressed, the button on the box gives the weapon the target coordinates and . . . Boom! There you have it. Or rather, there you suddenly don't. One less universe to trouble the gaze of God. The Deplorable End, for everyone and everything.'

'But, basically, it's an untested prototype,' I said carefully. 'So there is a small but nonetheless definite chance that it might not, actually, work? As such?'

'It's a last resort,' Janissary Jane said tiredly. 'When you've tried absolutely everything, and the Hungry Gods are coming through to eat all there is that lives, then the Deplorable End is your last chance for revenge. A way to take the bastards down with you, and to make sure no other universes will have to face the horrors we did.'

Her eyes fluttered closed as exhaustion finally took her. I gingerly took the gleaming metal box from her hand and had her taken away to the Infirmary to get some rest. By the time she woke up, hopefully it would all be over: one way or another. Though if things went really bad, it might be a mercy if she never woke up.

I held the end of the world on my palm. It hardly weighed a thing. The Armourer peered closely at it, but didn't attempt to touch it.

'I wonder who made it?' he said, almost wistfully.

'Armourer!' said the Matriarch, and the sharp authority in her voice snapped his head round immediately. He moved quickly over to join her and she fixed him with a cold implacable stare. 'Armourer, I hereby authorise you to open the Armageddon Codex. We have need of the forbidden weapons. Bring out Sunwrack, the Time Hammer, the Juggernaut Jumpsuit and Winter's Sorrow, and ready them for use.'

'No!' I said immediately, and my voice cracked so sharply across the Matriarch's that everyone in the War Room stopped what they were doing to look at both of us. I went over to join the Armourer and the Matriarch, carefully not hurrying. I stared directly into Martha's cold eyes, not flinching one little bit. 'Not yet, Grandmother. We can't use any of the forbidden weapons against the Invaders until they're actually in our reality; and a clash of such powerful forces would almost certainly tear our world apart. With no guarantee the weapons would destroy the Hungry Gods anyway. We save the Armageddon Codex for when all our plans have failed. And I'm not out of plans yet.'

'The Deplorable End would destroy the whole universe, not just this world,' said the Matriarch, not giving an inch.

'Trust me,' I said. 'I have no intention of blowing up the universe. I've got a much better idea. If I should fail in my mission, then it's up to you. But for now, trust me, Grandmother.'

'Well,' said the Matriarch, after a moment. 'Just this once, Edwin.'

She actually managed a small smile for me, and I smiled back. And then, as if things weren't already complicated enough, the ghost of Jacob Drood and the living Jay Drood decided it was time they made their appearance. All the time I was talking with the Matriarch I had the feeling someone was watching me. I finally looked round, and my gaze fell on the Merlin Glass, currently showing a reflection of the War Room. But there was something wrong with the image in the mirror, and when I strode over to study it, I realised there were too many people in it. In the mirror's reflection, Jacob and Jay were standing behind me, grinning at me over my shoulder. I looked behind me, but there was no one there. I looked back at the mirror, and there they were. It gave me the shivers. Especially when the two of them shouldered past my reflected image, strode forward and stepped out of the mirror into the War Room. I had to back-pedal fast to get out of their way. People jumped and yelled and even screamed, and Jacob and Jay grinned and sniggered and elbowed each other as though they'd pulled off a particularly clever and childish trick. I had to take a deep breath to get my heartbeat back to something like normal.

Jacob was now wearing an old-fashioned bottle-green engine driver's uniform, complete with peaked cap, with the front of his silver-buttoned jacket hanging open to reveal a T shirt bearing the legend 'Engineers Get You There Quicker'. He looked very sharp and focused, with hardly any blue-grey trails of ectoplasm following him when he moved. Jay was in the full finery of his original period, and looked almost as excited as his future ghostly self, but there was something in his eyes . . . I folded my arms across my chest and gave them both my best hard stare.

'Nice trick,' I said coldly. 'I'll bear it in mind if we ever need to give someone a coronary. I didn't know you could do that, Jacob.'

'You'd be surprised at what you can do when you're dead, boy,' Jacob said cheerfully. 'It's really very liberating.'

Jay glanced severely at his future self. 'I'm boasting again and I do wish I wouldn't. We have a plan to save the day, Eddie.'

'Of course,' I said. 'Doesn't everyone? Does your plan by any chance involve blowing up the whole damned universe?'

'Well, no,' said Jay. 'Not as such.'

'I like it already,' I said.

'Oh, you tell him, Jacob,' said Jay. 'You know you're dying to, and you'll only butt in and interrupt if I try. I apparently become very grumpy after my death.'

'Try hanging around this family for centuries,' Jacob growled. 'They could make a Pope swear and throw things. Listen, Eddie. We have a way to stop the Invaders in their tracks. We're going to use the Time Train.'

'You've only just started describing your plan, and already I hate it,' I said. 'Going back in Time to undo Present events never works. Never never never. It always ends up causing more problems than it solves.'

'Do calm down, Eddie,' said Jay. 'Your face has gone a very funny colour, and it really can't be good for you.'

'We are not going back in Time to stop the Invaders before they start their plans against us,' Jacob said patiently. 'I know enough about Time travel to know that wouldn't work. I watch television. No, we've got a much better idea. We're going to use the Time Train to sneak up on the Invaders' home dimension, and attack them from the one direction they won't be expecting: the Past!'

'Run that by me again,' I said. 'I think I fell off at the corner.'

'It's really very simple,' said Jay.

'No, it isn't,' I said. 'No explanation that begins that way ever is.'

'Look,' said Jacob, prodding me firmly in the chest with a surprisingly solid finger, 'the Invaders come from a higher dimension than ours, right? That means to them, Time is just another direction to move in. We can use the Time Train to access their dimension and attack their homeworld from the Past! They'll never see us coming!'

'They're bound to have hidden their homeworld,' said Jay, 'inside some pocket universe or dimensional fold, confident no lesser beings from some lower dimension could ever find it. But Jacob is dead, while I'm still alive; and together we can see things no one else can.'

'Only we could hope to survive the stresses of a Time journey like this,' said Jacob. 'Because we're the same person in two different states of existence. It has to be us, Eddie. Tony's already reworked the engine so it will soak up Time energies as it travels. So that when we finally get to the Invaders' homeworld we can drive the Train into it at full speed and release all the Time energies at once, blowing the whole nasty place apart like a firecracker in a rotten apple!'

'End of homeworld, end of Invaders!' said Jay.

'An interesting plan,' I had to admit. 'Even if my mind does seem to slide off the edges when I try to grasp it. But are you sure you can find the Hungry Gods' homeworld?'

'You can't hide things from the dead,' said Jacob. He looked at Molly, and then at me, and didn't say anything.

'You have to let us try,' said Jay. 'This . . . is how I die. Jacob finally remembered. I don't mind, really. It's a good death. Spitting in the face of the enemy, saving the innocent, for the family. A Drood's death.'

'And this is what I've waited for, all this time,' said Jacob. 'This is my end, at last. None of you here could hope to do this. Only me, and me. Jay dies striking down our enemies, and somehow ends up here, in the Past, as the family ghost, waiting to do it again. And I . . . finally get to go on, to whatever's next. I'm quite looking forward to it. I've grown awfully thin, down the centuries, and I'm really very tired.'

'Go for it,' I said. 'The Time Train is all yours.'

'You still have to keep the Invaders occupied, distracted, so they won't think to look for us coming,' said Jay.

'I reckon we can do that,' I said.

Martha surprised me then by stepping forward to face Jacob. 'Go with God, Jacob,' she said. 'I shall miss you.'

He grinned crookedly. 'Then you should aim better. Goodbye, great-great-great-great-granddaughter.' He looked around the War Room. 'You are all my children, my descendants, and I have always been so very proud of you.'

He and Jay turned as one and strode back into the reflection in the Merlin Glass. For a moment they moved eerily among our watching reflections, and then the image in the Glass changed, to show them walking through the old hangar at the back of The Hall. They climbed up into the gleaming black cab of the Time Train, and waved goodbye to Tony, who waved back with tears in his eyes, knowing he'd never see his beloved Ivor again. Jacob manipulated the controls with professional skill while Jay shovelled crystallised tachyons into the boiler with fierce nervous energy. He was going to his death, and he knew it; and knowing he was coming back as Jacob probably didn't help.

Ivor lurched suddenly forward. The Time pressure peaked and Jacob put the hammer down. The Time Train accelerated, disappearing at speed in a direction no human eye could follow; and they were gone.

I waited for a moment, looking around me, but nothing changed. So I got on with my own plan. What else could I do?

Molly and Subway Sue took my small group off to a relatively quiet corner of the War Room so they could explain the Damnation Way to us. There was a certain amount of disagreement between them over details, the two of them almost coming to blows over certain obscure references and sources until I separated them, but they seemed firm enough on the main outline. They started at the beginning, which turned out not to be the Damnation Way itself.

'You see,' said Subway Sue, 'in order to understand that, you have to understand the Rainbow Run.'

'The Rainbow Run is an expression, or manifestation, of the old Wild Magic,' said Molly. 'A race against time and destiny, to save the day. It's not given to many to attempt it, and even fewer survive to see it through successfully to the end. I don't know anyone who's even tried, since Arthurian times. But it is said that anyone who can run the hidden way, follow the Rainbow to its End, will find their heart's desire. If they're strong enough, in heart and soul and will.'

'It's not how fast you run,' said Subway Sue. 'It's how badly you need it. How much you're prepared to endure . . . to run down the Rainbow is not given to everyone. And there are those who say that what you find at the Rainbow's End isn't necessarily what you want, but what you need.'

'The Rainbow Run is an ancient ritual,' said Molly. 'Older than history.'

'Older than the family?' I said.

'Older than Humanity, probably,' said Molly. 'It's . . . an archetype, a primal thing, spanning realities. A thing of dreams and glories, grail quests and honour satisfied. One last chance to defy the Dark, and snatch victory for the Light. Or so they say.'

'Who created it?' I said.

'Who knows?' said Subway Sue. 'This is the old Wild Magic we're talking about. Some things just are. Because they're needed.'

'So why can't we use the Rainbow Run instead of the Damnation Way?' I said.

Molly and Subway Sue looked at each other. 'Because we don't know how to find it,' Molly said quietly. 'We're not . . . good enough, pure enough.'

'The Damnation Way is the underside, the dark reflection of the Rainbow Run,' said Subway Sue. 'The other face of some unimaginable coin.'

'Look,' said Molly, 'forget the spiritual crap and keep it simple. The Many-Angled Ones, the Hungry Gods, come from a higher dimension, right? Well, if there are higher dimensions than ours, then it stands to reason that there must also be lesser, lower dimensions. The broken universes, where natural laws never really got their act together. The Damnation Way can take us through one such world. And you don't run there, you walk. For as long as it takes. This isn't about speed, it's about stamina.'

I could feel myself scowling. No one else was saying anything. They were all looking at me. 'We really don't have a lot of time,' I said. 'Truman's tower is pretty much complete, and probably activating even as we speak. The Hungry Gods could come through any time now.'

And you have no other means of getting into Truman's Base,' said Molly. 'His defences will keep out anything, except the Damnation Way.'

'Time means something different, in the lower universes,' said Subway Sue. 'Theoretically, we should emerge inside Truman's base at exactly the same moment as we leave here.'

I could feel my scowl deepening. 'Yeah, that worked out really well with the Time Train—'

'That was science, this is magic,' Molly said quickly. 'The Damnation Way follows ancient laws, written into the bedrock of reality itself.'

'Oh . . . what the hell,' I said. I had to stop scowling because it was making my head hurt. 'We have to get to the tower, and I don't see any other way.' I looked at the others: Mr Stab and the Sarjeant-At-Arms and Giles Deathstalker. 'Given the . . . uncertain nature of what we're about to do, I don't feel right about ordering you to join me. I wouldn't be going if I didn't think I had to. So this is strictly volunteers only. Anyone wants to say no, or even hell no, I quite understand.' I looked from face to face, but they all stared calmly back: Giles ready for action, the Sarjeant for a fight and Mr Stab . . . looked like he always looked.

'Let's go,' I said. 'Time to save the world. Again.'

To enter the Damnation Way, it turned out, you have to go down. All the way down. Molly and Subway Sue worked old magic together, swaying and chanting in tongues inside a chalked circle. The Armourer watched closely, fascinated. Giles Deathstalker watched with a curled lip, as though he didn't really expect anything to happen. I wasn't sure what to expect, but even so I was startled when a standard, very ordinary elevator rose calmly up out of the floor in front of Sue and Molly. The thing pinged importantly to announce its arrival, and then the doors slid open, revealing a standard elevator interior. I walked around the door a few times. From the front, a waiting elevator. From the back, it wasn't there. Giles walked around it a few times too, muttering about subspace engineering and pocket dimensions. Whatever kept him happy.

Martha glared at the thing that had appeared inside her nice, normal War Room. 'Why didn't it set off any of our alarms?'

'Because it's not really here, as such,' said Molly. 'I mean, it's a magical construct that looks like an elevator because that's a concept our limited minds can cope with.'

'Your senses aren't equipped to recognise things like this,' said Subway Sue. 'So they show you the nearest equivalent.'

'Right!' said Molly. 'This is really old magic, remember. Wild magic, from when we all lived in the forest.'

'I still don't see why it has to look like an elevator,' I said, just a bit sulkily, feeling way out of my depth.

'Group mind consensus,' Molly said briskly. 'Be grateful. It could have come as an escalator. Hate those things.'

I sighed, deeply and meaningfully, and stepped cautiously inside the elevator. The steel floor was firm under my feet, and the mirrored walls showed I was scowling again. I tried hard not to, in case it upset the troops. They followed me in, with various amounts of confidence, and when we were all in we filled the damn thing from wall to wall, with hardly any room to move, unless one of us breathed in to make a bit of space. Molly made a point of pressing her breasts against my chest, for which I was quietly grateful. The doors closed unhurriedly and without any instruction or warning, the elevator started down.

We seemed to descend for a long, long time. I could feel the movement, sense it in my bones and in my water, even though the elevator made no sound and had no controls or indicators. It grew slowly hotter, until we were sweating profusely and trying unsuccessfully to back away from each other. And then the heat vanished, gone in a moment, and the temperature in the confined space plummeted, growing colder and colder, until our breath steamed on the air and we huddled together to share our body warmth. And then that was gone too, and I felt neither hot nor cold, as though we had left such things behind us.

Then, the sounds. From outside the steel walls came noises, from far away at first, then drawing inexorably closer. Roars of rage, howls and screams, and something very like laughter, but not quite. Basic, primal emotions given voice, without the burden or restraint of conscious thought. The horrid empty voices we hear in childhood nightmares, from things we know would hurt us, if they could only find us . . . The voices sank into words, and that was worse; as though plague or fate or evil had learned to talk. They circled the descending elevator, coming at us from this side and that, rushing in and falling back, threatening and pleading, mocking and begging, trying to persuade us to open the elevator doors and let them in. I can't remember exactly what they said, and I'm glad.

Some of us tried putting our hands over our ears, to keep the voices out; but it didn't work. We weren't hearing them with our ears.

We left the voices behind, their cheated screams receding into the distance, and after that there was only silence, and the descent, and the feeling of something really bad drawing slowly closer. At the end, there was no sensation of stopping. The elevator doors slid open, without cause or warning, and the standard colourless light spilled out on to a terrible caliginous plain. None of us moved. It didn't feel safe. What we could see of the world outside was dark and dismal, the only light a deep dull purple, like a bruise. I moved reluctantly forward, stepping out of the elevator, and one by one the others followed. A terrible, grinding oppression fell across me the moment I left the comfortingly normal light of the elevator, as though I was suddenly carrying all the troubles of the world on my shoulders. There was no sound anywhere, as such, but something like an unending roll of thunder growled in the air, like a long bass note you could only hear with your soul, like a threatened storm you somehow knew had been on its way for ever.

We all stood together, keeping close for the comfort of living company in the face of this dead or dying world. We didn't belong in a place like this, and we knew it. And then the elevator doors slid shut, cutting off the bright healthy light, and we spun round in time to see the elevator disappearing down into the cracked stone ground, leaving us alone in the awful place it had brought us to. A purple-stained plain that seemed to stretch away for ever in whatever direction I looked.

It felt like the end of the world. A darkling plain under an endless night. Above, a blood-red moon hung low on the sky where one by one the stars were going out. Already there were great dark gaps in the unfamiliar constellations. The endless plain was bare stone, marked here and there with huge craters and deep crevices. Like the bottom of the ocean after the seas have boiled away. There was a crevice nearby, a long jagged line with crumbling edges. I moved over to it and stared down into the gap. It seemed to fall away for ever. I made some kind of sound, and Molly was quickly there to take my arm and pull me back from the edge. As though the sound of my voice had triggered something, strange twisting vegetation, rough creepers with huge dark leaves covered with pulsing red veins, curled slowly up out of the crevice. Molly and I backed away, and the twitching plants tried to follow us, but already they were rotting and falling apart. Alive and dying at the same time, as though they hadn't developed enough to hold a form properly.

Other cracks and crevices held crimson magma, seething sluggishly, but even though they weren't that deep, the magma's heat didn't rise to the surface, as though the heat lacked the strength to travel that far. The air itself was thin, and disturbingly lacking in any smell. I clapped my hands sharply, and there was no echo. I was pretty sure the sound wouldn't travel far either. We all stuck close together, because we were the only living things in this running-down world.

'This is the place where quests fail,' Subway Sue said quietly. 'Where love is always unrequited, promises are broken, and only bad dreams come true.'

'Then how the hell are we supposed to succeed in our mission?' said the Sarjeant-At-Arms. He sounded like he wanted to be angry, but it was too much of an effort.

'We brought something of our own universe with us,' said Molly. 'Enough to give us a fighting chance. But the longer we stay here, the sooner that insulation will wear away. We really need to get moving.'

'This is the broken world,' said Subway Sue, almost hypnotised. 'The shoddy lands, the abandoned territory—'

'All right,' I said. 'You're starting to get on my nerves now, Sue. This is a bad place. Got it. Now get over it, and tell me where the hell we're supposed to head for.'

She looked at me with big, unfocused eyes. 'Say the name, Eddie Drood. Say the name of where you want to get to.'

'Just do it, Eddie,' Molly murmured in my ear. 'She's more in tune with this place than I am. She understands the hidden ways; they talk to her.'

'We need to get inside Truman's base under Stonehenge,' I announced, speaking clearly and distinctly into the silence and feeling a bit silly. My words didn't echo. They seemed to fall flat and lifeless on the still air.

'There!' said Subway Sue, pointing to one side with a sharp finger. 'There is our destination.'

Far off in the distance, a beam of light stabbed up into the dying sky like a beacon. It was bright and clear and glorious, very definitely not a natural part of this world. It shone like hope, like a promise . . . like a way out.

'This is a dying world,' Giles Deathstalker said unexpectedly. 'Where entropy is King.'

'Don't you start,' I said firmly.

I have no idea how long we walked under that bloody moon and the disappearing stars, across that sere and blasted plain. The night never ended, landmarks were few and far between, and we soon discovered none of our watches worked. But it felt like forever. I did my best to set a steady pace, leading from the front, circling around the deep craters and jumping across the cracks and crevices. The ground was hard-packed and unyielding under my feet, but strangely there was hardly any impact, no matter how hard I stamped. We made no sound as we walked, and our few conversations seemed to trail away to nothing until, set against such an overwhelming silence even the impulse to talk faded. So we trudged on, across the endless plain, while the grinding silence wore away at our thoughts and emotions and plans. Until only slow, dogged determination kept me moving, a simple refusal to be beaten by this awful place.

At some point, we passed a long row of overpoweringly huge stone structures, that might have been buildings. Tall as skyscrapers, fashioned from some faintly shimmering unfamiliar stone, they towered over us like brooding giants, strange disturbing shapes with deep-set caverns up the sides like so many dark watchful eyes. The lower reaches were covered with long curling displays of unreadable glyphs. Threats, or warnings, or perhaps just, *Do not forget us. We lived here and built these things, despite the nature of our world.* And yet somehow these solid signs of life gave no comfort; there was in the end a feeling of cold malice about them, as though whatever ugly things had lived in these ugly shapes would have resented our presence, our purpose, our life. We kept walking, and eventually we left the stone structures behind us.

'Is this what Hell is like?' I said to Molly at some point.

'No,' she said. 'Hell is more alive than this.'

As though encouraged by the sound of voices, Mr Stab abruptly announced, 'Something is watching us.'

I stopped, and the others stopped with me. We looked around. Just cracks and crevices and craters.

'Are you sure?' said Molly, frowning.

'No, he's right,' said the Sarjeant-At-Arms. The more we talked, the less of an effort it was. 'I've been feeling watching eyes on us for ages. Haven't seen anything, though.'

'We are definitely being observed,' said Mr Stab. His voice was entirely calm and easy, as though proposing tea on the lawn.

'Yes,' said Subway Sue. 'There's something here with us. I can feel it . . . I told you something had come to live here, and prey on travellers. That's why people stopped using the Damnation Way.'

'Maybe you should have changed the name,' I said. 'Advertising is everything these days.'

'Not now, Eddie,' said Molly.

Giles Deathstalker drew his long sword and turned slowly round in a full circle. 'They're here. Close. Close and deadly.'

'But who the hell would want to live in a place like this?' said Molly.

We moved to form a circle, shoulder to shoulder, facing outwards. I felt suddenly more awake and alert, as though shaking off a long doze. I glared out across the endless plain, the dull and sullen purple stone, but nothing moved anywhere. Whatever was here had to be pretty powerful, and decidedly dangerous. From what Subway Sue had said, some fairly major players had used this route, and never showed up at the other end. I was looking for something big and impressive and obviously deadly; I should have known better.

This was a dying world, after all. And what do dead and dying bodies attract? Scavengers, parasites, carrion eaters.

They came up out of the cracks and craters, crawling and creeping, on two legs and four, swarming across the dead ground towards us. They were all around us, running and leaping, wave after wave of them, seething like maggots in an open wound. I didn't know if they originated here or came from somewhere else, but the nature of this place had got to them. They looked like they were aspiring to be human, but falling short. They were rough, unfinished, the details of their bodies blurred or corrupted or missing. They didn't even have faces; just phosphorescent rotting eyes and sharp-toothed circular mouths, like lampreys.

They surged forward from every side, and there seemed no end to their numbers. I subvocalised my activating Words, but nothing happened. I tried them again, but my armour didn't respond. I looked at the Sarjeant-At-Arms, and the shock in his face told me all I needed to know. He made grasping motions with his hands, trying to summon the guns that came to him by right, and nothing happened. Molly raised her arms in the stance of summoning, and then looked at me blankly as nothing happened.

'It's this place,' said Subway Sue. 'Complicated magics can't work here. Or complicated sciences. The disintegrating laws of reality can't support them. That's why so many major players never made it out. We're helpless. Defenceless.'

'Speak for yourself,' said Giles Deathstalker. He swept his sword back and forth before him. 'A strong right arm, a good blade and a forthright heart always works.'

'Indeed,' said Mr Stab, his long blade suddenly in his hand.

Molly reached down into the tops of her boots and pulled out two slender silver blades. 'Arthames,' she said crisply. 'Witch daggers. I mostly use them for ceremonial work, but they're no less sharp and nasty for that.'

She handed one to me. It felt surprisingly heavy for such a delicate looking thing. The Sarjeant-At-Arms pulled a long blade with jagged edges out of his sleeve.

'Albanian punch dagger,' he said. 'Always a good idea to have a little surprise in reserve. For when you absolutely have to kill every living thing that annoys you.'

'Knives won't work,' said Subway Sue hollowly. 'Swords won't work. There are too many of them. We're going to die here. Like everybody else.'

'I think this place is getting to you,' said Molly. 'Stay behind me and you'll be fine.'

'Numbers are never any guarantee of success,' said Giles. 'Any trained soldier knows that. Stand your ground, make every blow count, and remember your training. It'll be all right. A trained soldier with a blade is a match for any number of unarmed rabble.'

We stood shoulder to shoulder, our weapons held out before us. Subway Sue sat down suddenly inside the circle, and covered her face with her hands. The scavengers were running towards us, bounding across the broken ground, driving forward from every side at once. Wave upon wave, in numbers too great to count. If there'd been anywhere to run, I'd have run. But the bright pillar of light seemed as far away as ever, and we were surrounded. So all that was left was to stand and fight, and, if need be, die well.

Hopefully, someone else would find a way to get to the tower in time, and stop it. I wished . . . well. There were so many things I wished I'd done, or said. So many things I meant to do – but I suppose that's always true, no matter when you die. I glanced at Molly, and we shared one last sweet, savage smile. And then the scavengers hit us.

They reached Giles first, and he cut them down with effortless ease. His long blade swept back and forth as though it was weightless, the incredibly keen edge slicing through flesh and bone alike. Dark blood spurted and the scavengers fell, but they never made a sound. Giles laughed happily, doing what he did best and glorying in it. Mr Stab reached out casually with his blade, cutting throats, piercing bellies, stabbing eyes with graceful skill. He smiled too, but there was no human emotion in his eyes, only a dark desperate need forever unsatisfied. The Sarjeant-At-Arms stamped and thrust with brutal efficiency, killing everything that came within reach. He was frowning, as though engaged in necessary, distasteful work.

Molly and I fought side by side, hacking and stabbing at the horribly unfinished creatures that kept looming up before us. The scavengers had no sense of tactics, or even self-preservation. They came at us with clawed hands brittle as dead twigs, their rotting eyes glowing, dark saliva dripping from their circular mouths. There was nothing in them but the need to kill and feed. To drag us down and tear us apart, and never know or care who it was they were destroying.

The dead piled up around us, the flesh already decaying, the dark blood eagerly soaked up by the parched stone ground. My whole body ached from the strain of wielding the silver blade without pause or rest, of hacking and cutting through flesh like mud, that seemed to suck and catch at the blade. I was bruised and cut, my clothes torn, sweat and blood running down my face. I could hear Molly breathing harshly beside me, and Giles singing some obscure battle song to my other side. There was something almost inhuman about his cheerful refusal to be stopped or even slowed by the impossible numbers set before him. He killed and killed, and was always ready for more, like a starving man at a feast. It crossed my mind, then, that in some ways Giles Deathstalker was even scarier than Mr Stab.

And then suddenly, as though some unheard cry had been given, the scavengers retreated. One moment they were attacking with all their silent fury, and the next they were scrabbling away across the dried-up plain, falling back like a retreating tide. Giles flicked drops of black blood off his long blade and leaned on it. He looked around him, smiling at the piled-up bodies littered around us, and then nodded briefly, as though contemplating a good day's work. Molly and I leaned on each other, breathing hard.

'They'll be back,' Subway Sue said from behind us. I turned and glared at her.

'We have to get out of here. There must be a way. Find it!'

'Yes,' Sue said slowly. 'I have been communing with this place. It speaks to me. One of us must make a stand here, so the others can get to the light.'

'What?' said Molly. 'Where did that come from?'

Subway Sue looked at her tiredly. 'I know the ways of hidden paths. I can see the rules here, written into the dying world. If we all stay, we all die. One of us must make a stand, sacrifice themselves for the sake of the others. So they can go.'

'We should draw lots,' said Giles.

'No,' Sue said immediately. 'It has to be a willing sacrifice. A positive act, set against the entropy of this place. It's not how far you walk, here. You could walk all the days of your life and never reach the light. But you can draw it to you by a noble act. So which of us is ready to die, so the others can live?'

'There has to be another way,' said Molly. 'We don't abandon our own people. Tell them, Eddie!'

'I'll stay,' I said.

'What?' Molly looked at me numbly.

'I'll stay,' I said. 'This was my mission, my idea. My responsibility.'

'No, it isn't!' Molly glared round at the others. 'Tell him!'

'You can't stay, Edwin,' said the Sarjeant-At-Arms calmly. 'The family needs you to take down Truman and destroy the tower. You're the man, these days. So I'll stay. I said anything for the family and the world, and I meant it. You're all going to be needed, where you're going. You're special. I'm not.'

'Sarjeant,' I said, but he cut me off.

'Eddie, I want this. I want what I do to matter, for once. To be the hero, not just the one who trains them and sends them out. I always dreamed of a last stand like this, defying impossible odds for a noble cause. To save the family, and the world. So get them out of here, Eddie. Take down Truman and the tower. Make the family proud.'

He walked off without waiting for an answer, heading straight for the nearest group of scavengers. They watched him coming from their craters and crevices, and stirred uneasily. I gathered up the others and we left him behind as we headed for the shining pillar of light, already speeding towards us. I heard the scavengers scrabbling out of their hiding places behind us, but I didn't look back. The pillar of light swept through the surrounding scavengers, summoned by the price of a willing sacrifice. It flared up before us, promising hope and life and a way out. But not for the Sarjeant-At-Arms. Molly and Subway Sue plunged forward into the brilliant light and disappeared, followed by Giles and Mr Stab. And only I paused to look back, and see the Sarjeant standing firm against a living tide of flailing, clawing scavengers. He cut savagely about him, throwing bodies to every side with the force of his blows. He stood firm right up to the moment when they swarmed all over him and dragged him down, and he disappeared from sight. He didn't cry out. And only then did I step into the light.

And that was how Cyril Drood died, fighting his enemies to the end, dying as a Drood should. For the family. And the whole, damned, uncaring world.

When the light died away, I was back in my own world. It was night, but the moon was bright and full, and the sky was packed with stars that might last for millennia yet. My wounds were healed, and I felt strong again. The air was bracingly cool, rich with scents, a pleasure to breath. I stamped my feet on the dewy grass, delighting in its solid presence beneath me. The whole night felt alive, and so did I.

I glanced around, and realised for the first time that the others were gathered around a body lying on the ground. I hurried over to them. Molly was kneeling on the grass beside Subway Sue, who was dead. No mark on her; the scavengers didn't get her. But dead, just the same. Molly looked up at me.

'Sue didn't make it,' she said dully. 'Too much strain, too much magic; she never was strong.'

'I'm sorry,' I said.

'Not your fault,' said Molly. 'She volunteered.' She rose awkwardly to her feet. 'We'll come back for you, Sue. Later. We have work to do.'

'She'll be fine here,' I said, because you have to say something.

'Sue was my friend,' Molly said sharply. 'She wasn't always like this. You never saw her in her prime, rich and glamorous and a name to be reckoned with.'

'I know,' I said.

'She was my friend,' Molly repeated. 'She only got involved in this because I asked her to.'

'Yes,' I said. 'Lot of that going around.'

'The Sarjeant was a good man,' said Giles Deathstalker. 'He knew his duty, and he stood his ground.'

'Of course,' I said. 'He was a Drood.'

I looked around again. We were in a great grassy field looking out over Stonehenge, about half a mile away. There was no sign of Harry or Roger, or any of Truman's Accelerated Men.

'We have arrived only a moment after we departed,' said Giles.

'How can you tell?' said Molly. 'Even I can't read the night sky that accurately.'

'I can tell because the clock implanted in my head just started working again,' said Giles.

'Smart arse,' said Molly. She paused. 'I wonder how Jacob and Jay are getting on?'

'I doubt we'll ever know,' I said. 'It was one hell of a long shot. Either way, we can't depend on them to save the day; we're here, so it's up to us.'

'There's an entrance to an underground bunker not far away,' Mr Stab announced suddenly. He pointed confidently out into the gloom. He realised we were all staring at him, and smiled briefly. 'I have many abilities,' he said calmly. 'I just don't choose to display them unnecessarily. Shall we go?'

'By all means,' I said. 'Lead the way.'

He nodded and strode off across the open field, and we followed. I was quite happy to have him lead. With the Sarjeant gone, I didn't want Mr Stab behind me. He might be a part of this mission, but I was never going to trust him. Not after Penny. He stopped abruptly, staring down at a part of the field that appeared no different from any other. And then he stamped twice, hard, and a large section of grass lifted slowly upwards as he stepped back, revealing a dark tunnel leading down. Mr Stab started forward, but I stopped him and took back the lead, while giving Molly a significant look. If this really was a way into Truman's bunker, I didn't want Mr Stab up front making decisions for the rest of us. Molly could keep an eye on him.

Electric lights came on as we entered the tunnel, triggered by some hidden sensor. The walls were curving beaten steel, gleaming dully. Truman had a thing about steel. Personally, I figured he'd seen too many James Bond movies. But then, so had I. We walked down the corridor, which gave way to another, equally stark and bare and unadorned. Our feet clattered loudly on the grilled floor, and I half expected armed guards to appear at any moment, but no one came to investigate. No alarms, no raised voices . . . nothing. The whole place was unnaturally quiet. Molly pushed in beside me, glaring about her, so close I could feel the tension in her too.

'This isn't right,' she said quietly. 'Truman's last base was crawling with people. Where is everyone?'

'Good question,' I said. 'Bear in mind, this isn't just a Manifest Destiny base, it's also a Loathly Ones' Nest.'

She had to know what I was thinking. There was a Loathly One inside her, growing and developing. Who knew what it might do, now it was among its own kind at last?

I hoped we'd come across some armed guards soon. I really felt like taking out my frustrations on a whole bunch of poor helpless armed guards.

But as we rounded the last steel corner, and glimpsed at last the first open space of the bunker, a huge metal slab slammed down from the ceiling, shutting off the corridor and blocking our way with two tons of solid steel. It hit the floor with a hell of a bang, so loud I actually winced, but still no alarms sounded and still there was no clamour of raised voices demanding to know what was going on.

Where had everyone gone? What was Truman doing down here?

I subvocalised my activating Words, and then punched the air with joy as the golden armour flowed smoothly over me. It was good to have it back. Good to feel fast and strong and fully alive again. I hit the steel slab, putting all my armoured strength into it. My golden fist sank a good three inches into the steel, but that was it. I had to jerk my hand back out, an inch at a time. I crouched down and slammed both hands into the bottom edge of the slab, forcing my fingers deep into the metal, and then strained to lift the massive slab. It shook and groaned but hardly raised an inch off the floor. I just didn't have the leverage. My fingers slipped slowly through the solid steel like thick mud, unable to find a purchase. I pulled my hands out and stepped back to glare at the slab, baffled and frustrated.

'I do have an energy gun,' Giles Deathstalker said diffidently.

'No,' I said immediately. 'There's no telling what kind of defences or booby traps Truman might have set up here. Let's not make things worse than they already are.'

Molly sniffed, and elbowed me aside. 'Men,' she said scathingly. 'If you can't hit it or shoot it, you're lost for an alternative.'

She stabbed an imperious finger at the steel slab, said two very old and potent Words of Power, and the slab actually shook all over before reluctantly rising back up into its slot in the ceiling. Molly smiled condescendingly at me and Giles, no doubt ready to say something extremely cutting, and that was when the machine guns opened up. Giles grabbed Molly and threw her to the floor, covering her body with his own, ignoring her startled curses. I moved quickly to block the way, shielding everyone with my armoured form. Bullets sprayed the corridor, but my armour absorbed everything that hit it. I didn't even feel the impact. I strode slowly forward into the hail of bullets, and almost immediately realised there weren't any guards. Just two automated machine guns, set to cover the end of the corridor with suppressing fire, swivelling slowly back and forth on their gimbals. It looked like they were almost out of bullets, but I was in the mood to hit something, so I ripped them both off their supports and crumpled them in my golden hands. They made satisfying squealing noises, and I threw them aside. A blessed silence fell across the corridor, apart from Molly cursing Giles Deathstalker as he tried to help her to her feet.

'I can protect myself, thank you very much,' she snarled. 'I do not need to be slammed into the floor by an over-anxious, over-muscled drama queen!'

'Fine by me,' said Giles. 'I'll leave you to die next time.'

'I should,' I said. 'It's less trouble in the long run.'

'I'm fine, by the way,' said Mr Stab.

'Never doubted it,' I said, not looking round.

We made our way slowly and cautiously through the guts of Truman's underground base. Everything was a mess: furniture overturned, papers scattered, doors left open to secure areas. There were no people. Just empty rooms and abandoned corridors. Half the lights weren't working and strange shadows loomed up everywhere. As we got deeper in, we found work stations where computers and other technology had been ripped apart and gutted. Great rents began appearing in the steel walls, long and jagged as though made by claws, with wiring and cables hanging out like entrails from open wounds. And the only sounds we heard in the whole base were the ones we brought with us.

Finally, as we neared the centre of operations, we started finding bodies; piled up in careless heaps, as though they'd been dropped there and dumped out of the way. There were signs of struggle now, to show they hadn't gone quietly to their deaths. Bullets holes in the walls, scorch marks from grenades, the remains of improvised barricades. They'd put up a fight, only to end up like their computers, torn apart, gutted, harvested. Broken open for their parts. Whole organs were missing, and hands, and eyes. Blood and discarded offal lay all around, still steaming and stinking on the cool, still air.

Mr Stab checked the bodies for details. No one else wanted to get close enough.

'They did this to complete their tower,' I said, because someone had to put it into words. 'Technology and . . . organic components, to finish the job. Because they were in a hurry. Because they knew we were coming.'

'Don't you dare blame yourself,' Molly said immediately. 'None of this is your fault. Manifest Destiny brought this on themselves, by allying with the Loathly Ones. Come on. Let's find Truman.'

'How do you know he's still alive?' said Giles.

'Because rats like him always find a hole to hide in,' said Molly.

It didn't take long to track him down. We followed the signs on the walls to his private office, and sure enough there were more dead men piled up outside the locked and no doubt barricaded door. A green light showed above the door, indicating that the leader was IN. And a single security camera swivelled back and forth, looking us over with its little red light. I pounded on the door with my fist.

'You know who this is, Truman. Surprisingly enough, I'm not here to kill you. In fact, I'm probably your best chance of getting out of this mess alive. Open up, so we can talk about the Loathly Ones.'

'Go away!' screamed a voice from inside, shrill and cracked. 'You can't fool me! You're not people! Not any more!'

'This is Edwin Drood, Truman. Now let me in, or I'll rip the door clean off its hinges.'

There was a long pause, followed by something that might have been a chuckle. 'A Drood has come to save me. That it should come to this—'

There was the sound of furniture being dragged away from the door, and then after a bit the door unlocked itself. I pushed it open, and we filed into Truman's office. Once it might have been luxurious, even impressive, but now it looked like a bolt-hole. The place was a mess, and it stank of sweat and fear. Truman was sitting stiffly behind his desk, half a dozen guns set out before him, though he had the sense to keep his hands well away from them. He held his head erect, no doubt braced by implants, to support what he'd done to himself, to his head and his brain. Truman believed in the gains to be made from extensive trepanation, or the making of holes in the skull to allow the brain to expand. So he'd drilled a dozen holes in his skull and then inserted long steel rods deep into his brain. The steel spikes protruded from his head, radiating in a wide circle connected by a steel hoop like a metal halo. This was supposed to make him smarter than the average human but I couldn't say I'd ever seen any evidence of it. Truman looked pale and drawn, with eyes like a hunted animal. He managed a shaky smile for me and Molly.

'Just when I think things couldn't possibly get any worse, you two turn up.'

'Tell us what happened,' Molly said flatly. 'And then we'll decide whether your miserable arse is worth saving. What have you done here, Truman?'

'I never wanted to ally Manifest Destiny with the Loathly Ones,' he said, looking at his hands so he wouldn't have to look at us. 'They are everything I hate and despise. But after you destroyed my old organisation, I had to go underground; and my advisors insisted that we needed powerful support if we were to protect ourselves while we rebuilt. And they came to me, the Loathly Ones, and said all the right things, and promised me the world and everything in it if I would let them build one of their damned towers here. I knew the risks, can't say I didn't, but I was so sure I could control them, use them, and then destroy the tower before they could do anything with it . . . I was a fool. They infected my people one by one, starting with my advisors, so I only heard what they wanted me to hear. The first I knew something was wrong was when the infected drones suddenly attacked the rest of my people, right here in my own base.' He smiled suddenly, an odd crooked smile. 'They even infected me. Oh yes. One of my oldest friends did it, putting their filthy presence inside me. But I killed him, and then I killed it. Killed it dead. My augmented brain was more than a match for the small weak thing they put in my head. I ate it, and savoured its dying screams in my mind.'

He actually laughed out loud then, enjoying the memory, and only sobered as he took in the expressions on our faces. 'Of course, by then it was too late. My people had been taken over or butchered, my base had been torn apart to provide the final material for their stinking tower. But I shall still have the last laugh! Oh yes! I have a secret weapon, specially prepared for the day they might rise up against me. The Soul Gun . . . Only I have the access codes. No one else can get to it, or fire it. Let them activate their tower! I shall activate my Soul Gun, drain the power out of the Soul of Albion and use it to banish the Loathly Ones from this world for ever!'

He glared round at us triumphantly, but Molly and I were already shaking our heads.

'Won't work,' I said. 'You never did take the trouble to work out what the Soul of Albion really is, did you? It's not a thing, an object you can use. The Soul fell to earth from a higher dimension, like the Drood Heart. It might even be a splinter that broke off from the

Heart during its descent. Strictly speaking, the Soul is a baby crystal intelligence, only centuries old, too young to have developed a full personality. It protects England, because this is what it thinks of as home. You try and drain its power, suck the life out of it, and it'll destroy you and your base and go back to sleep again.'

'And even if you could make it work,' said Molly. 'Do you really think one baby crystal could hope to hold back the Invaders, the Many-Angled Ones, the Hungry Gods? You do know that's what the tower is designed to bring here?'

'No,' said Truman. 'No, no . . . You're trying to frighten me . . .'

'Trust me,' I said. 'We're already scared enough. We have to destroy the tower before the Invaders come through. Where is it?'

An alarm went off, deafeningly loud in the small office. Truman stabbed at the controls on his desk top and a monitor screen blared into life on the wall – showing Harry Drood and Roger Morningstar moving cautiously through the underground base. They'd finally got here. I had to smile. Harry would so hate coming second.

'Damn,' said Molly. 'In all the excitement, I'd forgotten about them.'

'I haven't forgotten about the Droods they brought with them,' I said. I fixed Truman with a cold stare. 'Your Accelerated Men, and your damned Soul Gun, killed hundreds of my family.'

He smiled spitefully at me. 'I only wish it could have been more. You brought me to this, brought me so low I had to ally myself with alien scum! Everything that's happened here is your fault, Drood!'

'Oh, shut up, you wimp,' said Molly, and the sheer distaste in her voice stopped him like a slap in the face. She moved round beside the desk, found the general address, and called Harry and Roger by name. They looked up, startled, and Molly grinned as she gave them directions to join us in Truman's office.

'Excuse me,' Giles Deathstalker said quietly, 'but what is that thing on his head?'

'Cutting-edge technology,' I said solemnly.

Giles raised an eyebrow. 'In my day, we find it more useful to put the technology inside the head. Mind you, we also find it useful to shoot over-ambitious idiots like this on sight.'

Harry and Roger finally found their way to Truman's office, and barged in without knocking. Harry glared at me.

'Might have known you'd find a way to be here for the end and grab the glory for yourself.'

'That's right,' I said. 'Because I'm so like you, Harry.'

'Boys, boys,' said Molly. 'Put them away or I'll cut them off. We are on something of a deadline here . . . Truman's going to take us to the tower.'

'You do know he's infected?' said Roger.

'I used to be,' Truman said haughtily. 'I destroyed it with my augmented brain.'

'Actually, no,' said Roger, gazing thoughtfully at Truman. 'With my amazing demon X-ray vision, I can See it's still in there. Hell, I can practically smell it, it's so advanced. It let you think you'd destroyed it, so it could grow and influence you undetected. Sorry. There's never any cure, once you're infected.'

'Never?' said Molly.

'No chance,' said Roger.

Truman started to say something, and then stopped. He looked distracted, as though listening to some inner voice. And then he looked at us, looking at him, and his face firmed.

'Kill me,' he said. 'I will die a human being, and myself; not some damned alien thing. Kill me!'

'Glad to,' said Roger Morningstar.

He leaned over the desk, grabbed the steel halo connecting Truman's implanted spikes, and ripped it away. Truman screamed piteously, in pain and shock. Roger grabbed the spikes, and pulled them out one by one. They came out in sudden jerks, inch by inch, under his demonic strength, accompanied by gouting blood and bits of brain, and the sound of cracking, splintering bone. Truman was screaming constantly by now, an almost animal-like sound, his arms flailing helplessly, but none of us moved forward to stop Roger. I wanted to look away, but I made myself watch it, as punishment. By the time it was over, Truman was slumped forward over his desk, his head torn apart, twitching slowly as the last of his life went out of him. Roger studied the last spike closely, as though it might hold secrets, then shrugged and tossed it aside.

Harry stared at him, open-mouthed. 'There was no need for it to be that brutal!'

'Oh, no need,' said Roger. 'But it was fun.' He smiled at me. 'You can't tell us you never dreamed of doing that, Eddie.'

'No,' I said. 'I never dreamed of doing anything like that, hellspawn.'

'Oh well,' said Roger. 'No point crying over spilled brains.'

'I could kill the hellspawn for you, if you like,' said Mr Stab.

He might have been discussing the weather. Roger started to say something, looked at Mr Stab, and thought better of it.

'Thanks for the thought,' I said. 'But no.'

'We have to get to the tower,' said Molly, her voice cold and focused. 'It's not far. I can feel its presence, with my magics.'

'Then lead the way,' I said.

We followed Molly through the maze of steel corridors and down into the deepest part of the underground bunker until we were in a great steel-walled chamber directly under the standing stones of Stonehenge. And there it was, sunk deep into a pit hollowed out of the bare earth, tall and complex and unnaturally shaped: the last tower of the Loathly Ones. There wasn't room to build it high, so they'd sunk it deep. We could only see the top twenty feet or so, a jagged structure of alien technology combined with flesh and blood. Metal and crystal seamlessly fused with living parts. We circled slowly around the exposed top of the tower, our feet sinking into the wet earth. This close, there was no doubt the thing was alive, in its own awful way. It was alive and it was aware. It knew we were there . . . and it didn't care. It was complete and it was activated. We'd arrived too late.

Already a gateway was forming, an opening to another place. I couldn't see or hear it, but I could feel it on some deeper, primal level, like a vast eye watching me, like a wound in the world, like a door into Hell. Like a bitter, cold wind blowing at me from a direction I couldn't name, chilling me down to the soul. Slowly I became aware of sounds too. I don't think I was hearing them with my ears. Voices: howling, screaming, laughing, coupled with the sound of tearing flesh and great siege engines slamming together for ever. The sounds of Hell on earth.

Molly grabbed me by the arm and shook me fiercely, and I came to myself again. Harry and Roger and Giles and even Mr Stab were still staring wide-eyed and entranced at the forming gateway, as strange energies swirled and coalesced around the tower.

'We've got to do something!' said Molly. 'The gateway's opening! They're coming!'

'I guess Jacob and Jay never got through after all,' I said numbly.

'Eddie—!'

'I know,' I said. 'I know.' I looked at her. 'How do you feel, Molly?'

'I'm still me,' she said, meeting my gaze squarely. 'But I don't know for how much longer.'

'Then let's do it,' I said. I reached into my jacket pocket and brought out Janissary Jane's weapon of last resort, the Deplorable End. It still didn't look like much.

'Do we have the right to destroy our whole universe, just to wipe out the Hungry Gods?' said Molly.

'Hell, no,' said Roger, unexpectedly. He'd torn his attention away from the tower, and was now looking at the thing squatting on my palm. 'Is that what I think it is? Eddie, you can't use it. Not while there's still a chance, any chance.'

I had to smile. 'A demon who believes in hope. Now I've seen everything.'

'I believe in him,' said Roger, looking at Harry. 'I have to hope that we can find a way to be together. Not even a half-demon is automatically damned for all time. You have to save the world, Eddie, so we can have a place to grow old in.'

'If the Hungry Gods come through, they'll destroy this world and everything in it,' said Molly. 'And then move on, from world to world, until there isn't a living thing left anywhere. That's what they do. Cosmic locusts.'

'I have no intention of destroying this universe, or this world,' I said. 'I never did. I think . . . I'll wait till the gateway has opened enough, and then I'll go through it into their universe, their world; and blow it to shit before they can come through.'

'You're not going in there alone,' Molly said immediately. 'You'll need my magics to survive in their world long enough to press the button. I won't let you die alone.'

'Molly . . .'

'What reason have I got to live without you?' said Molly. 'What reason have I got to live, as I am?'

'And you're going to need me,' said Giles Deathstalker. He had

Harry and Mr Stab by the arms, pulling them away from the tower. They were both shaking their heads, coming to themselves again. Giles looked at me calmly. 'You'll need me to help you survive and operate in an alien environment. You're not used to that. I am.'

'Fine by me,' said Harry, blinking his eyes hard, careful not to look directly at the tower. 'Roger and I and Mr Stab will stay here, and . . . guard the situation.'

'Quite right,' said Mr Stab. 'I know my limitations.' He nodded briefly to me. 'You, of course, are a Drood and therefore have no limitations. Everyone knows that.'

I looked at Giles.

He shrugged easily. 'I am a warrior. Fighting is what I do. And besides, this is about family as well as saving Humanity. You took me in, made me feel like one of you. I never knew that before. Never really had a family before. You taught me the worth of duty and honour and responsibility. You have shown me what it really is to be a man. To be a Drood, and a Deathstalker. So I will fight, and if need be die, for what you gave me. Anything, for the family.'

Roger glared at the tower. 'It knows we're planning something. It's just put out some kind of call, or alarm . . . summoning something.'

We looked round sharply as from back inside the bunker we heard movement. The sound of bodies rising up, and slow dragging feet . . . and I knew what it had to be. All the dead bodies in Truman's base, raised up by the tower's power and summoned to defend it in its time of need. The dead, called to strike down the living. I grinned at Harry.

'Looks like you're going to have to guard the situation, after all. Hold your ground, keep those things back for as long as you can. In case the three of us can find a way to come home. You never know.'

'I'll hold this ground till you return, or Hell freezes over,' said Harry. 'I may be a bit of a bastard, but I'm still a Drood. As long as there's a fragment of hope left, I'll wait here for you to return.'

The gateway opened around the tower, unfolding and unfolding like some monstrous alien flower. And I could sense something behind and beyond it. Something becoming more real by the moment. I walked forward into the cascading energies, with Molly Metcalf on one side and Giles Deathstalker on the other, and the world fell away behind us.

CHAPTER SIXTEEN
High tension

The new place hit me like a hammer, driving me to my knees. Just the weight of the world was so much more than I could stand. It was like being inside a ghoulville, only much more and far worse. The sky blazed with a fierce light, blindingly bright, as though the whole sky was a sun. The air was packed with a hundred scents, so rich and foul and intense they fought to fill my head. Sounds everywhere, sharp and cutting, deep and disturbing, shuddering through my flesh and reverberating in my bones; as though someone was scraping their nails down my soul. I hugged myself tightly, to keep from flying apart. I looked down, to save myself from the incandescent sky, and the ground beneath me heaved and squirmed, covered with over-complicated shapes that might have been vegetation or insects or something else entirely. There was so much detail my eyes watered, trying to cope with it all. Everything in this new world beat with life, as if even the ground and the stones were alive and aware, everything pulsating with an appalling aggressive vitality. There was movement all around me, swift and sharp, as though nothing here ever rested, even for a moment.

Welcome to the higher dimension. Welcome to the greater world. Welcome to the home of the Hungry Gods. It was all I could do not to puke.

I felt as much as saw Molly fall to her knees beside me, shaking and shuddering from the shock of the transition. I grabbed blindly for her, and she grabbed me, and we clung tightly together for comfort, overpowered by a reality and a world we were never equipped to deal with. In this higher dimension, everything was too big, too real, too insanely complicated. We'd have been lost if it hadn't been for Giles Deathstalker. As he'd said, his experience of surviving alien worlds gave him enough of an edge to help him cope. He crouched beside us, speaking calmly and soothingly, his voice coming clearly to us as the only sane and normal thing in this new existence.

'It's only another place,' he said. 'The details change, but that's all. You can cope. You can adapt. Because you're human, and that's what humans do. We roll with the punch, and we come back fighting. If you can't cope with what you're seeing, let your mind translate it into something you *can* cope with. You're stronger than you think, Eddie, Molly. No matter how weird things get here, remember: it's only another place.'

His voice, his calm sanity, was a lifeline I could cling to, something I could use to ground myself. Slowly, I built a shell of defiance around me, refusing to be beaten down by the sheer loudness of the place, and bit by bit I got control of my senses. Until finally I was able to get to my feet again, and Molly with me. We were both breathing hard, and clinging to each other for mutual support, but we were back in the game. It might be a very small thing to be human, in this largest of worlds, but even the smallest insect can pack a deadly sting. A deplorable sting.

'As long as the gateway remains open, and we stick close to it, we bring some of our world here with us,' said Molly. 'Like on the Damnation Way. It insulates us from the full force of the experience.'

'Well thank the good God for that,' I said. 'I really don't think I could cope with the full-on experience. It's like everything here has been cranked up to eleven.'

'It is a bit of a strain,' said Giles. 'And I've been around.'

'We need to do what we came here to do, while we still can,' I said. 'Molly, I think . . . Molly?'

'Oh, shit,' said Molly.

I forced myself to raise my eyes from the ground, and looked where she was looking. I heard Giles gasp as he saw them too. They were all around us. The Invaders, the Many-Angled Ones, the Hungry Gods. Huge and vast, living things big as mountains. They existed in more than three physical dimensions at once, so that my mind interpreted their appearance as a series of overlapping images, always subtly shifting, never quite the same twice. Their aspect strobed in my head, as much an impression as an image. There were circles of them, rank upon rank, impossible numbers, stretching as far away into the distance as I could bear to look. Waiting.

They rose into the sky, all of them moving slowly but inexorably forward. Towards the gateway, still pulsating and unfolding behind us. Looking up at them gave me vertigo, as though I might suddenly be plucked off my feet and sent hurtling into the unbearable sky. I couldn't tell what the living mountains were made of; only that it was vile and awful, like sentient cancers, with implications my mind didn't dare consider. They had no obvious limbs, or sense organs, but I knew they knew we were there. Small as we were in comparison, they saw us, and knew us, and hated us.

There was so much more to them than my limited human mind could cope with, more than I was capable of comprehending. I knew that. I made myself concentrate on what my eyes were showing me. They were vast and they were ancient and they were monsters. Their nature blazed forth from them, unhidden by any trace of self-deception. They knew what they were, what they had made of themselves, and they gloried in it. They were evil, evil as an almost pure concept, hating everything that wasn't them. Because the only thing they wouldn't or couldn't feed on was each other. They ate life, and not only for sustenance: for the sheer joy of destroying it. Anti-gods, concerned only with consuming creation.

'How do we fight . . . that?' I said.

'You don't,' said Molly.

I looked quickly round at her, disturbed at something in her voice, and saw something else looking back at me through Molly's eyes. She looked . . . different, her whole face suffused with a new personality. She even held herself differently, as though new things were forming inside her, changing her shape and her balance. Giles swore softly beside me and reached for his sword. I gestured urgently for him to stop, and then gave the new Molly my full attention. I knew what had happened. The Loathly Ones were only ever extensions of the Hungry Gods, and this close to the real thing the drone inside Molly had awakened and taken control.

'That's right,' said Molly. It didn't sound like her at all. She smiled in a way Molly never would have, her gaze full of hate and spite. 'I'm in the driving seat now. Molly's having a little nap while I talk to you. I've done this before, you know, when I killed Subway Sue.

Oh yes, that was me. So simple and easy, and no one even noticed. Didn't it strike you as a bit suspicious, her dying so suddenly? For no good reason? No? Well, you mustn't blame yourself, Eddie. You've had a lot on your mind.'

She stretched slowly, luxuriously, in a not entirely human way. 'It's good to be out in the open instead of trapped inside such a small and limited thing, watching the world from behind her eyes and making my plans. I'm not strong enough to take over yet, to subsume her mind and soul in mine. I'm more . . . potential, than actual. But you should never have brought me here, Eddie. You never should have brought me home.'

'How long have you been switching her off and taking over?' I said. My mouth was dry, but I fought to keep my voice steady.

'Not long. It hasn't been easy, corrupting Molly from within, protected as she is by her magics, and the terms of the various unpleasant bargains she made in return for power. You wouldn't believe some of the things she's done, and some of the things she had to promise, so she could become the wild witch of the woods. I think you suspected me, didn't you Eddie, but you never asked because you didn't want to know. Still, no need to worry about that now. I will become her, and she will be just another drone serving the Masters for as long as she lasts.'

'Why kill Subway Sue?' I said. 'She was your friend.'

'Not my friend, Eddie. Dear Sue had to go because she might eventually have realised you could use the Damnation Way to access the higher realms. And we don't like visitors. We really don't.'

'Why kill Sebastian?' I said.

'That wasn't me, sweetie,' said the thing inside Molly. 'Why would I kill one of us? Now, hand over the weapon. The box. The Deplorable End. Your quest is over, your mission a failure, your war at an end.'

'I can't do that,' I said. 'Molly wouldn't want me to.'

A silver blade appeared in Molly's hand, and she put the edge to her own throat. It was the arthame, its supernaturally sharp edge already cutting the skin so that blood coursed down her neck. Molly smiled, her eyes full of a vicious glee. 'Do as you're told, little human, or I'll cut my throat. And after she's dead, I'll take the box from you anyway.'

'You're really ready to die?' said Giles.

'I can't die. I am part of a greater thing. You wouldn't understand. I exist only to serve a function. Give me the box, Eddie, and you can have her back. For a while.'

'She'd rather die,' I said, 'than become you. She'd die happily, if it meant she could take you and your masters with her.' I slowly raised my right hand, to show her the flat silver box with its red button. 'If I press this button, this whole place goes away, for ever. A second big bang, to end a universe. No more here, no more you, no more Hungry Gods. Molly would see her death as a triumph, to bring that about.'

'Are you sure?' said the thing, in a voice so like the real Molly it cut me to the heart.

'Yes,' I said. 'I'm pretty sure she came here expecting to die. And I think perhaps I did too. We never really thought we'd find our way back again. And at least this way, we could go out together.'

'And when were you planning on telling me this?' said Giles.

'You can get away,' I said. 'Gateway's still there, still open. You've done all that could be asked of you: held Molly and me together long enough so that we can do what's necessary.'

'No,' said Giles. 'There's a better way. Give me the Deplorable End.'

'What?' I said.

'I'll do it,' said Giles.

'Excuse me,' said the drone inside Molly. 'But I am still holding a very sharp knife to my throat.'

'Take Molly back through the gateway,' said Giles. 'I'll do the business with the button, blow up the Hungry Gods, bring down the curtain. With them destroyed, the Loathly Ones should perish too, including the one inside your Molly. You can have a life together, Eddie. My gift to you.' He smiled briefly. 'For showing me things I never would have believed possible. For taking me into your family. And because . . . I have never had, never known, what you and Molly have and know.'

'I thought you said something about woman trouble, back in your time?' I said.

'Oh, there were always women,' said Giles Deathstalker. 'Comes with the territory, when you're Warrior Prime. But never anyone special. Never anyone who mattered. So take your Molly and go. I can do this. In fact, I have to do it. Someone has to shut the gateway from this side, to make sure the universe-destroying energies don't blow back through the opening into your world. I've got some energy grenades that should do the trick; disrupt the energy matrix and collapse the hole.'

'I didn't bring you back all these thousands of years just so you could die,' I said.

'Maybe you did,' said Giles. 'Who knows? Time plays strange tricks on all of us.'

'I have a dagger at my throat!' yelled Molly.

Giles's arm snapped out and he snatched the dagger out of her hand. 'No, you haven't. Now behave yourself.'

Molly glared at him, and then at me, her eyes darkening dangerously. 'You 'really think you can threaten Gods with a mechanism? With your little box full of clockwork?'

'Only one way to find out,' said Giles. 'Give me the box, Eddie.'

'It won't work,' said Molly. 'We won't let it work. Nothing happens here that we do not allow.'

And then we looked up, startled, as a new sound entered the higher dimension, a triumphant howl like a great steam whistle dopplering down from some unimaginable distance. The sky split apart and the Time Train came thundering across the brilliant sky, hammering over the very tops of the mountainous Hungry Gods. A big black beast of an old-fashioned steam train, its engine roaring, strange energies sparking and cascading around it, marking its trail across the sky with a rainbow of discarded tachyons.

Jay and Jacob Drood, the living and dead man, had made it through.

The Hungry Gods cried out, a terrible unbearable sound full of rage and malice and spite, outraged that something from a lower world should dare force its way into their hidden home. Ivor blew his steam whistle defiantly, a sharp, clear sound. The Time Train was falling now, descending at a controlled speed . . . and then it stopped, hanging there, as time itself slammed to a halt. Nothing moved anywhere, everything was quiet, and suddenly the ghost of Jacob Drood was standing in front of me, smiling his old crafty smile.

He reached out sharply and prodded Molly on the forehead with his forefinger. She swayed suddenly, and shook her head.

'What?' she said. 'What happened? Eddie, why are you looking at me like that? And Jacob, what are you doing here?'

'Saving the day!' Jacob said grandly. 'I just hit your reset button. Don't know how long it'll last, so pay attention. I have things to tell you.'

'What are you doing here?' I said. 'I mean, why aren't you in the Time Train?'

'I am,' said Jacob. 'I'm up there and I'm down here. It's amazing what you can learn to do when you're dead. Being in two places at the same time is child's play when you don't have a material body to worry about. Well, I do now, but Jay's in charge of that.' His ancient face grew serious as he glanced up at Ivor the Time Train, hanging suspended in the awful sky above the living mountains. 'Listen. Time will start up again any moment. Ivor can't hold this for long, not against the combined will of the Hungry Gods, even with the extra power he's accumulated during his long trip. Oh, the places we've been, Eddie, and the things we've seen . . . It's a much bigger universe than any of us ever expected. Now, when Time starts up again I'll be back aboard Ivor, and then Jay and I will steer him down to a probably apocalyptic impact right in the midst of the Hungry Gods. And all the temporal energies he's holding will be discharged in one almighty explosion. Not enough of a bang to destroy the Hungry Gods, but quite enough to set off the Deplorable End, no matter how hard the Invaders try to suppress it. So you can't be here, Eddie.'

'But if the gateway's left open—' said Giles.

'We can spare enough energy to close it, just before the crash,' said Jacob. 'Ivor's a remarkably sophisticated machine, once you learn to speak his language. He's capable of far more than was ever asked of him. He doesn't want to die, but he's a Drood, and he understands duty. He's very pragmatic, for a steam engine. And, of course, I have to be here. Both of me. I've arranged things with Ivor, so that he will use some of the Time energies to ensure that my death works out the way it should. On impact, Jay will die but his spirit will be sent back in Time to become the family ghost. And I . . . will be set free at last. To go on . . . and make trouble there, too. I'm quite looking forward to it.'

'Does it have to be this way?' I said. 'Aren't there any other options?'

'We're lucky to have this one, Eddie,' Jacob said kindly. 'The Hungry Gods will be destroyed, the world will be saved. We don't really have a right to expect any more.' He looked at Giles. 'There's even enough spare temporal energy to send you home, boy. All the way to the future. Stand by the box, and trust me. Close your eyes, if it helps.' He turned back to me. 'Goodbye, Eddie. You always were a good friend. And the son I never had. Don't stop giving the family hell, just because I'm not around to prompt you.'

'Goodbye, Jacob,' I said. 'I wish—'

'I know,' he said.

He disappeared, and Ivor's defiant steam whistle sounded again, striking right through the awful raised clamour of the Hungry Gods. The Time Train was plummeting through the incandescent sky, trailing tachyon steam as it headed remorselessly for the living mountains. Giles held out his hand for the Deplorable End, and I gave him the box. He hefted it once, and smiled briefly.

'Goodbye, Eddie. Goodbye, Molly. I've enjoyed my time with you. It's been . . . interesting.'

'Goodbye, Giles,' I said. 'And wherever you go, and wherever you end up, remember you're still family.'

I took Molly by the arm and headed for the gateway. It snapped shut before me, gone in a moment. And Molly jerked her arm out of my hand. She laughed exultantly, her face and her body no longer her own again.

'You'll never get out of here! We have shut down the gateway. You're trapped here with us! Jacob will never destroy this world as long as you're here!'

'Of course he will,' I said. 'He's a Drood.'

'Yes,' said Giles. 'Nothing matters but family, honour and duty. I understand that now.'

The Time Train was dropping fast, hammering towards the surface, accelerating all the while. Wild energies exploded around the steam engine, as the living mountains struggled to slow or stop it. But wherever Ivor had been, he'd become so strong that even the Hungry Gods couldn't touch him. He howled down out of the sky, and I swear I saw Jacob and Jay leaning out of the black cab laughing and cheering like schoolboys.

There had to be a way out of this. There had to be a way. We couldn't have come this far to die now. I pushed Molly into Giles's arms, and he held her securely while she fought him and snarled curses and threats. I searched my pockets with both hands, looking for something, anything, that could help. I was never short of gadgets, the Armourer saw to that. But nothing I had on me could help me here. I should have asked Uncle Jack for something special before I left, but he was always saying I never used what he gave me anyway . . .

I stopped, and looked at my wrist. And there was the teleport bracelet he'd given me that I'd never got around to trying because I was always too busy. Only a short-range jump, but if it could tap into the remaining energies of the gateway . . . I grabbed Molly out of Giles's arms, shouted him a quick goodbye and threw both Molly and I into the place where the gateway had been, while yelling the Words that activated the bracelet. A very small space unfolded between us, and swallowed us up. Molly stiffened in my arms, her voice abruptly shut off. I glanced back at Giles. He was waving goodbye, the steel box in his hand.

Behind him, I saw Ivor the Time Train come crashing down into the midst of the living mountains, his steam whistle blowing defiantly to the last. There was a concerted scream from the Hungry Gods, and then a great light and a greater sound, and a wave of energy blew me back through the gateway, with Molly in my arms.

EPILOGUE

Arriving back in our own world was like coming home again after long years away. Everything felt so right, so normal and so welcoming. Truman's underground base slammed into place around us, and Molly and I hit the ground hard, rolling along in a flail of limbs; leaves blown on the wind of an other-dimensional storm. We skidded to a halt right at the edge of the great pit Truman had dug to hide his tower, and for a time we just lay there together, battered and bruised and breathing hard. Molly was herself again, and she clung to me like she'd never let me go. We were home again, back where we belonged, and I felt so good I would have laughed out loud if I'd only had the energy.

Molly and I slowly got to our feet, helping each other, and only looked round vaguely at the sound of approaching footsteps. Harry Drood and Roger Morningstar were running up the corridor. They both looked happy to see us, which was a first. They crashed to a halt before us, and Harry grabbed my hand and shook it hard in both of his.

'You're back! Finally! Where the hell have you been?' said Harry, still pumping my hand. 'We've been waiting here for you for ages!'

'We were beginning to wonder if you'd ever show up,' said Roger.

'Oh hell,' I said. 'Not another time lapse. I should have expected it, if Ivor was involved . . . All right, how long have we been away this time?'

'Almost twelve hours!' said Harry.

'We were becoming quite concerned,' said Roger. 'Well, I say we, but . . .'

'Twelve hours?' I said. 'That's not bad, for Ivor. Twelve hours I can live with. Harry, I'd quite like that hand back now, please. Thank you. I take it from that sloppy grin on your face that we succeeded. What's been happening while we were away?'

'Every Loathly One in the world is dead,' said Harry. 'All gone, from every Nest in every country. It was clear you must have succeeded in your mission, and we were safe now from the Hungry Gods, so we set up a detail here to wait for your return. I volunteered to take first shot. The Matriarch said someone would be waiting here for you to come back, no matter how long it took.'

'For ever, if necessary,' said Roger. 'The Matriarch was most firm on the matter. Sentimental old thing.'

'Grandmother always did have a taste for the big gesture,' I said. I looked at the tower in its pit. The thing was obviously dead. It was slowly melting, its steel and technology and living parts all slipping and sliding away, rotting and falling apart. Slumping slowly back into the pit Truman had dug for it; and I couldn't think of a better place to bury it.

'I feel like hell,' Molly said abruptly. She shook her head, as though to clean out the cobwebs, and then winced. 'Damn! It feels like someone took a dump in my head . . . Did I hear you right? We killed the Hungry Gods? I can't seem to remember much about what happened on the other side . . .'

'Probably just the stress of dimensional travel,' I said quickly. 'Bound to play hell with the memory.'

'At least you aren't infected any more,' said Roger. 'The Loathly One that was growing inside you is completely gone.'

We all looked at him. 'Molly was infected?' said Harry.

'How long have you known?' I said.

'Almost from the beginning,' said Roger. 'You can't hide something like that from my superior half-demon senses.'

'Then why didn't you say anything?' said Molly.

'None of my business,' Roger said easily. 'Your magics were doing a perfectly good job of suppressing it, and it was clear Eddie knew about it . . . Besides; I was interested to see what would happen.'

'And just when were you planning on tell me?' said Harry. 'No one ever tells me anything . . .'

'So I'm just me again?' said Molly. She grinned suddenly. 'Any more of this and I'll start believing in happy endings.'

'Where's Giles?' said Roger. 'Didn't he make it?'

'Giles has gone home,' I said. 'I hope. Where is Mr Stab?'

'Here,' said the calm cold voice of the immortal serial killer. He appeared from behind the decaying tower and nodded briefly to Molly and me. 'I've been studying the tower as it dies. Most fascinating. I've cut out a few particularly interesting bits for souvenirs. The odd eyeball, and so on. I hope no one objects.'

'You've been doing that for twelve hours?' said Molly.

'Just filling in time,' said Mr Stab. 'I knew you'd be back. And I wanted to say goodbye before I left. I won't be going back to The Hall. There's nothing there for me now, with Penny dead, and I'm sure most of the family will bear a grudge. Present company included.'

'I trusted you!' said Molly. 'I vouched for you!'

'You really should have known better,' said Mr Stab. 'The damned, above all, must be true to their nature. If I thought anyone could actually kill me, I might go back with you, but as it is . . . I will go back into the world again, and walk up and down in it, and do terrible things . . . because I must. Until finally I do something so awful you'll have to find a way to destroy me. Goodbye, everyone. Until we meet again . . .'

He bowed briefly, turned, and walked away. We let him go. What else could we do?

'At least Manifest Destiny is finished now,' said Harry, after a while. 'Truman's dead, along with all his people here, and the base is destroyed. One less evil in the world to worry about.'

'Don't be naïve, Harry,' Molly said tiredly. 'Manifest Destiny is an idea, a philosophy. It'll always be around, in some form or another. There'll always be small, bitter people ready to follow some charismatic leader who promises them peace and happiness through justified violence and the killing of scapegoats.'

'But that's a matter for another day,' I said firmly. 'Come on, let's go home.'

The Merlin Glass appeared abruptly before us, opening out onto the War Room. We filed through, and everyone there burst into applause, cheering my name and Molly's. The Armourer was waiting to greet us.

'Knew you'd be back,' he said gruffly. 'Never doubted it. What was the higher dimension like? What did the Hungry Gods look like? Did you bring me back any interesting souvenirs?'

'Hello, Uncle Jack,' I said. 'Good to be back.'

There had to be a great celebration, of course. The family has always been big on ceremonies and celebrations. So after Molly and I had gone straight to bed and slept the clock round, word was sent that we were expected in the Ballroom. We dressed up in our best, and went along, to find pretty much the whole damned family gathered together in one place, dancing and drinking and feasting, in jubilant celebration that the world wasn't going to end after all. They looked like they'd been at it for some time, too. The noise was deafening. Strange – ethel – had manifested his rosy glow up by the high ceiling, and was broadcasting dance music out of nowhere. People were dancing wildly, drinking freely, and chattering loudly together as they devoured the wide array of food laid out on buffet tables lining all four walls.

And then everything stopped as we entered, and everyone turned to cheer us, clapping their hands and stamping their feet, and basically going out of their minds just at the sight of us. The sheer volume and sentiment was so overwhelming I practically blushed. I nodded stiffly, smiled, and waved tentatively. Molly smiled sweetly and basked in it all. Molly had never been bashful in her entire life.

We made our way into the Ballroom, and everyone went straight back to dancing and drinking and eating. We've always been a very pragmatic family. The Matriarch had wanted Molly and me to be the guests of honour, with speeches and presentations and the like, but I put my foot down. This was a celebration by the family, of the family. We all did our part. We all did our duty.

Molly and I wandered along a buffet table, trying a little of this and a little of that. Most of the food on display was the usual party nibbles, family style. Molly loved the pâté-stuffed baby mice on cocktail sticks, and I was quite taken with the baby octopus stuffed with caviar. Then there was lemming mouse, devilled brains in a brimstone sauce, and any amount of roast swan. We don't like the lake to get over-crowded. Her Majesty the Queen had given us special dispensation to eat swan. Like we cared.

I was still bone tired, despite many hours of deep and dreamless sleep, and even Molly lacked some of her usual sparkle. So we just strolled around, saying hi to people and shaking hands, and allowing ourselves to be clapped on the shoulder, which actually gets quite painful after a while, and just generally let everyone tell us how marvellous we were. Familiar faces popped up here and there. The Librarians William and Rafe nodded briefly to us in passing, intent on devouring everything on the buffet tables that didn't actually get up from its plate and run away. Harry and Roger sailed past, dancing together to the strains of a Strauss waltz, and very dashing they looked too. Young Freddie Drood was dancing with the Matriarch, the pair of them sailing smoothly and gracefully across the floor; and just for a moment I caught a glimpse of the magnificent woman Martha must have been in her prime.

Callan came limping over to join us, with a large drink in one hand and an even larger drumstick in the other. 'Hi there! Welcome back! What the hell did you think you were doing, going off to save the world without me? I woke up in a hospital bed and had to fight my way out with a steel bedpan and a walking stick. Only to find you were already gone! I always miss out on the good stuff . . .'

'Maybe next time,' Molly said kindly. 'Did you see Janissary Jane in the Infirmary?'

'Oh sure. She's recovering. Slowly. Tough old bird.' Callan took a deep breath, and looked suddenly subdued. 'Lot of others didn't make it. The funerals alone will take weeks to get through. The family will be a long time getting over this.'

'All the more need for good people to step forward and take up the strain,' I said. 'I've already talked to the Matriarch about making you a full field agent.'

Callan grinned. 'About time. I'll show you all how it's done.'

And off he went to inflict his personality on someone else.

The Armourer wandered over, holding one of his special long-stemmed glasses, that he swore was specially designed to never spill a drop, no matter what you did with it. Judging by the wine stains all down the front of his lab coat, the mark fifteen was no more successful than any of the previous models. The Armourer smiled vaguely at Molly and me, and then remembered why he'd come over to us, and launched into a briefing update. He never was much of a one for small talk.

'We knew the Hungry Gods were dead the moment it must have

happened, because every drone in every Nest and all over the world died or disappeared at the exact same instant. They even vanished from inside the possessed souls we were holding in the isolation tanks. All trace of infection gone; just like that. Most of the poor bastards are still suffering from internal changes, and even some brain damage, but there's a lot the medical people can do. If not . . . well, the family will care for them till the day they die, if need be . . . The important thing is, there's not a single Loathly One left in the whole wide world! Hell of an achievement, the pair of you!'

'Thank you, Uncle Jack,' I said. 'You know, we wouldn't have made it out if it wasn't for you. Your teleport bracelet came in handy after all.'

'I knew it!' he said happily. 'I'm glad you finally got around to testing it for me. I was almost sure it would work.'

He wandered off again, before I could hit him. *Almost sure?* Molly shuddered suddenly beside me.

'I don't remember much about how it felt to be infected. To have that thing inside me, eating away at my mind, and my soul. Probably just as well.'

'Yes,' I said. I hadn't told her about the drone taking control of her body, and using it to kill her old friend Subway Sue. What good would it do? Sometimes love is in the things we don't tell each other.

'Did they ever find out who killed Sebastian?' she said suddenly.

'Apparently not,' I said. 'Odds are he was killed by the original traitor, the Drood who first brought the Loathly Ones through into our world. Presumably Sebastian knew something, or the traitor thought he did . . .'

'And you're not worried the bastard is still here?'

I had to smile. 'If I could believe there was only one traitor left in this family, I'd be a happy man. Sooner or later, he or she will give themselves away. Traitors always do. But that is business for another day.'

The Matriarch came over to join us, stiff-backed and regal as always, and everyone else hurried to get out of her way.

'Well done,' she said, brisk as ever. 'One crisis averted, so many more to go.'

'Business as usual, for the family,' I said.

'Quite.' She considered me thoughtfully. 'If you're willing, I'm quite prepared to continue running the day to day business of the family, while leaving you to set policy and make operational decisions. You would still be in charge . . . but there's a lot I could do for the family.'

'Of course there is,' I said. 'I can use your experience. But I don't plan to run things for ever. I have no wish to be Patriarch. The sooner I can set up some kind of democratic system in the family, to choose our leaders, the sooner I can get back to being a field agent; where I belong.'

The Matriarch shrugged. 'The family has tried pretty much every way there is of running things, at one time or another, but we always come back to a Matriarch. Because that's what works. But, you've earned the right to your little experiment with democracy.'

'Thank you, Grandmother,' I said drily. 'You do realise I'll have people watching you like a hawk all the time, just in case?'

'Of course,' she said. 'I'd expect nothing less.' She paused, looking out over the great throng of dancing couples filling the Ballroom floor. 'I do miss Cyril. He was always such a good dancer, as a boy.'

'Him?' I said. 'The Sarjeant-At-Arms? The man was a thug and a bully!'

'That was just his job,' said the Matriarch. 'Cyril was always so much more than that. He was such a promising student . . . Tell me he died well, Edwin.'

'Yes,' I said. 'He died well. He stood his ground against overwhelming odds, so that the rest of us could get away. He was a credit to the family.'

'Of course,' said the Matriarch. 'I'd expect nothing less. We'll have to appoint a new Sarjeant-At-Arms, as soon as possible. He represents discipline, and dedication to the family.' She looked at me sternly. 'But what in the good God's name were you thinking of, Edwin, in bringing a half-elf into The Hall? Now the Fae Court have their very own golden torc! You have to get it back, Edwin!'

'It's right at the top of my list of things to do,' I said.

'Good,' said the Matriarch. She allowed herself a small smile. 'You have done well, grandson. You've achieved what you set out to do, re-establishing the Droods as a power in the world, by stamping out the Loathly Ones once and for all; and saved the whole world at the same time. You have redeemed the family's honour, and proved our worth in the eyes of those who matter. Keep it up.'

And off she went, to circulate among the family, and make sure no one was having too much fun.

Harry and Roger came by, talking quietly but animatedly together. Molly and I trailed quietly along behind, shamelessly eavesdropping.

'What do you mean, you were sent to seduce me?' said Harry.

'Just what I said,' Roger said patiently. 'I was set in place in that Parisian night club specially to bump into you, and ensnare you with my charms. The idea was that if we became a couple, I'd get you to bring me here to meet the family, and then Hell would have its own agent and informer, right at the heart of the Droods. The sheer amount of information I could have passed on, down the years . . . Hell always takes the long view.'

'But you risked your life to save mine, warding off the Soul Gun!' said Harry.

'Yes . . .' said Roger. 'Well, it would appear even hellspawn can have their off days . . . Relax, sweetie. I'm only telling you this now to prove how much I trust you. Things have changed between us. A fake relationship has become the real thing, much to my surprise. Who knew a half demon could be capable of love?'

'Yes,' said Harry. 'Who knew?'

They walked on, arm in arm, and Molly and I let them go.

'I think I'm insulted,' said Molly. 'He and I were a couple for months, and he never fell in love with me.'

'He was never worthy of you,' I said.

'Well of course,' said Molly. 'That goes without saying.'

We looked out over the assembled family, filling the huge Ballroom from wall to wall, full of good cheer and celebration.

'At least it's all over now,' said Molly.

'You know better than that,' I said. 'It's never over. That's why the Droods are so necessary. Men are mortal, but demons are for ever.'

'Let's get out of here,' said Molly. 'Go back to bed.'

'Feeling tired?' I said.

'No,' said Molly, grinning.

'All right,' I said. 'I think they can manage here without us. Let's go. I've got something to show you.'

'Well I should hope so,' said Molly.

Back in my room at the top of The Hall, I had my surprise already installed. The Merlin Glass, standing upright and fixed firmly in place, at the back of the room. I said the Words, and our reflection disappeared, replaced by a gateway into the wild wood that was Molly's home. She gasped, and clapped her hands delightedly, and hugged me hard.

'A permanent doorway,' I said. 'A direct link between my room and your beloved wood, so you can come and go as you please, and never be more than a door away from me. The best of both worlds. If this is what you want . . .'

'Oh I want,' said Molly, pushing me onto the bed. 'I want.'

Shaman Bond will return
in
FROM HELL WITH LOVE